DEATH KNOCK

DEATH KNOCK

Frederic Lindsay

Hodder & Stoughton

First published in Great Britain in 2000
by Hodder and Stoughton
A division of Hodder Headline

10 9 8 7 6 5 4 3 2 I

British Library Cataloguing in Publication Data
Lindsay, Frederic, 1933–
Death Knock
I. Title
823.9'14 [F}

ISBN 0 340 76570 4

Typeset by Hewer Text Ltd, Edinburgh
Printed and bound in Great Britain by
Mackays of Chatham plc, Chatham, Kent

Hodder and Stoughton
A division of Hodder Headline
338 Euston Road
London NWI 3BH

For Fiona

CAT IN THE DARK

In the strip of marled tile at the top of the side column on the mantelshelf, I make out a face with a pointed white beard and wide moustaches, a brow, a suggestion of white hair, nose, deep-set eyes: the effect noble and judgemental. I've seen that face before

As he moved to make the next word, the interruption came. He stared at the phone where it rang against the wall, and reflected on this idea of making a word. Made with a pen, a pencil, tapping it out on the keys of a computer, a typewriter, chiselling on a rock, didn't matter, an abstraction meaning nothing till laid beside other abstractions, made in the mind, what mind? not his, not made in his, in some communal mind in the past, chosen then by him, selected by him, live long enough and it was hardly even a choice, take a card the conjuror said, they had ways of forcing a card on you, the brain plodded round its track, like a donkey tied to a pole, hooves pounding a trench in dry earth, take a card time said.

If it was his wife ringing, she would assume he was in bed and had fallen asleep waiting for her call. He had already seen her that evening in her room at the hospital; fat white pillows, television, his flowers; the phone by her bed. There was no need for him to phone her, her to phone him, she was due home tomorrow. All the same, he had no doubt that the call came from her. It sounded like her. If you were married long enough, you could tell when your wife called, conjugal telepathy.

The phone stopped.

Make a word.

The room was quiet, lined with books, a place to occupy alone, a place he liked to be. He sat still, not really thinking, not what he would dignify as thought, a little persistent, half-formed idea running under an almost blankness like a thread of water trailing through dust. Even after he'd shut down the computer, he sat on for a time unseeing in front of the blank screen.

When finally he started to his feet, it was as abrupt as wakening out of a bad dream; and still, an hour later, having crossed the city, the long room in which he found himself, and the people crowding it, felt as insubstantial to him as a box of shadows.

'I enjoy conversation,' he said to the fat man who had tried to begin one, 'given intelligent company.'

'You don't think I'm intelligent?' the fat man said. Raising his voice over the noise, he smiled as if responding to a joke. 'You don't know anything about me.' He thought for a moment. 'Give you a for example. I like good food and wine.'

'I can see that.'

'You could tell, could you? What else? Want to guess? And thinking. About things worth thinking about. Arguments. About things worth arguing about.'

Though certainly not a coward, he had no addiction to danger. That being so, why come from home, out of his quiet study, to risk reputation and even health? Why did he do it? Over the fat man's shoulder, he could see this time's answer, hands clasped around a glass, red hair falling in waves the colour of flames. Glancing aside from her conversation, high cheekbones, full mouth, the woman took a lazy-eyed, lingering moment's notice of him and turned away. For a woman she was tall; he had a weakness for tall women. It was the second time he'd seen her. The first had been in the restaurant upstairs, late in the evening. She'd sat with another woman at a table near him, and he hadn't been able to take his eyes off her. Long legs, tight buttocks. He could picture their movement; he'd followed the two women from the casino as they walked laughing along George Street. Followed them to the door of a pub and then inside, although, after a glance round, he'd left again.

'Fucking,' the fat man said.

'What?'

In one city or another, he'd searched for women, under streetlamps, ranged like targets at a funfair. Sometimes, not often enough, he'd driven away and been glad in the morning. Not most times, though. Against his better judgement. And, afterwards, always, playing it over in his head, been left disappointed. One time last year, he'd been too slow and the girl went into a bar, so that he'd had to get out of the car, like the shedding of armour, out in the open, vulnerable. He'd walked past the bar entrance first, counting his steps. At ten, turned and gone back. He'd been thinking, *what if I go in and someone recognises me? Nonsense!* he'd decided. *So far from home?* He'd been smiling at the idea as he pushed open the door and went in. That had happened in a German city, and ended badly.

This time was different. There was no reason to think this woman was for sale. And yet another difference. This wasn't a strange city, it was his city, which made it more stupid and raised the stakes.

'Doesn't matter.' The fat man shook his head. 'Forget it.'

'Forget what?'

Instead of answering, the fat man swivelled slowly, a ponderous movement, freighted with flesh, seeking out perhaps the cause of being ignored. Did the twitch of his lips as he turned back mean that he'd found it? Maybe he'd followed the line of sight, or found her like a heat-seeking missile, the best thing in the room.

'I was telling you,' the fat man said, 'not that it matters, how this woman I used to fuck would whisper to me – imagine that's your cock in a transvestite's mouth. When I was inside her, you know?'

'And a dildo up your arse?'

'That's cheap psychology. I'm not homosexual, in or out of the closet.' The fat man looked offended. 'What's so funny?' Now, suddenly, he was aggrieved.

'The collocation.'

The colonocation.

'Eh?'

'Adjective and noun – cheap and psychology. They don't go together.'

'I don't know what you're talking about.'

Now there's a surprise, he thought. He became elaborately, visibly patient, a mode in which he had some practice. 'Put it this way. The more cheaply you buy your advice, the dearer it may be to take it.'

'I don't know what the *fuck* you're talking about.'

Surprise, again. There was a temptation to go on. Scum, would that be a word you'd understand? Look round this long room hazed with blue cigar smoke, what else would you call them, drunk, greedy or even slightly mad, my obese friend, and don't you fit right in? More bother than it was worth; he started to move away. Even so, he tasted the word in his mouth, struggling to get itself said. The fat man caught him by the arm. Unpleasant to jump at the unexpectedness of that; unpleasant to feel his heart beating in his chest. He leaned into the man's bulk, and looking up into the tiny eyes encased in flesh shaped the word with his lips.

Scum.

Fat could be hard or soft. This belly he was pressing against felt hard, and the fingers that clutched him were big, a big hand, sausage-fingered. As he glanced down, though, the fingers unclenched, releasing him.

Without waiting for any other response, he moved off, as if going out of the room, but at the last moment veering towards the gaming tables. His course brought him to a stop behind the redheaded woman's chair. She glanced up at him, eyes wide and incurious, blank like mockery.

'Why am I not surprised?' she asked. Her voice was husky, a little rough; hearing it, a charge of excitement went through him.

He bent close and asked, 'Can I offer you a drink?' and before she could answer, added, 'Somewhere quieter, I mean.'

Something about the way she stood up, a little swaying moment, made him wonder, and then in the car he caught the sweet heaviness of her breath. She'd had a lot to drink.

'Are you all right to drive?'

'It saves having to guide you.'

He didn't know where he was being taken; he was being driven too fast; the driver had drunk too much. Par for the course, for the kind of course he set himself on nights like this. He put his hand on her leg. When he slid it up, she lifted it off her thigh.

'Are you well hung?'

'What?'

'I'll bet you are,' she said. 'Isn't it often the way?'

'Call me Adler,' he said.

'I thought your name was Jack?'

'It is.'

'Jack Adler?'

No, Sprat, stupid bitch, with a liking for lean. 'Mr Adler had a complex,' he told her.

'Tell me about it.'

'You wouldn't understand.'

'Go play your mouth organ,' she said, husky-voiced like a smoker, and laughed.

He sat back and watched the purple lamps space out. Night outside darkened the windows. They had left the city.

Later he would reconstruct, as if his life depended on it, from the clock in his head, glimpses of road signs, an instinct for direction, the route they'd taken. The last clue was a stretch of wall, grey stone with a coping, that went on and on as estate walls do. The car had been slowing along its length and, he wasn't surprised when where it ended, they turned in through an open gate. Bending his head, he saw trees flicking by on either side.

'Is this where you live?' he asked.

As they got out, he saw they had made their way past a half-circle of cars parked tight around a forecourt and had squeezed into a space between the last car and a stone parapet. Above them a dark bulk replaced the stars with a rising scatter of lit windows. He could hear from somewhere inside a muffled steady insistence of music. Following her up to the front door, his foot slid on a sheen of moss on a worn stone step.

As he recovered, she said, 'This will be different from any night you ever had.'

Inside, though, the heavy door opening easily so that he had no sense of her needing a key, there was a perfectly ordinary, if very large, wood-panelled hall, with a wide stair and a fire blazing in an open hearth. Somewhere a clock chimed, he counted the strokes, midnight. In that moment of inattention, the woman had disappeared. He went softly along inspecting the doors on the right-hand wall, then peered down the corridor at the back. Listening, he heard the same music, but faintly as if somehow more distant. Drifting back, he came to rest before the hearth. As he unbuttoned his coat to the warmth, he saw the blaze was gas licking tongues of flame around ceramic logs. A noise made him raise his head.

A figure was passing across the landing at the head of the stairs. The noise he'd heard was the tapping of heels on a wooden floor. High heels. A woman in a flesh-coloured dress. Where her head should have been there was the mask and high feathered skull of a bird. Only a glimpse and she was gone.

Behind him there was the sound of a throat being cleared, a brief dry sound, polite, peremptory. A man was standing by the nearest door, watching him.

'I'm sorry,' he heard himself say.

Why did he say that? Being in a strange house was no reason. If he'd found other words, everything might have gone differently. He apologised because of who he was; because of the man's calmness, the stillness of his authority.

'John Bellany,' the man said. A tall, wide-shouldered man, big-boned but slim, in black casual gear so that the pale, strong-featured face stood out like the blade of an axe. Above it, hair so black it shone; a single streak of white running back from the brow.

'What?'

'I took it you were admiring the painting. It's an early Bellany.'

High on the other wall, colour like slashes of blood, heraldic beak poised above a naked head.

'We're proud of our collection,' the man said. 'Rae, Howson—'

'No Vettrianos?'

The man watched him in silence. There was no tension in him, his hands hung by his sides, he might have been alone lost in thought. At last, he turned and went out through the door. Almost at once, it opened again and the redheaded woman appeared. She spread her hands. 'Fuck it,' she said.

'What was that about?' He crossed the hall after her and followed her outside. A full moon lit the sky. Along the drive treetops unravelled like badly tied parcels of blackness. 'Who was that?'

'Who?'

'The man with the white hair.' He ran a finger up from his brow.

'Our host. Only he's decided not to be,' she said. 'Isn't it a gorgeous night?'

He reached from the step above and put a hand round the back of her neck. Her lips under his were warm and firm. He pressed between them with his tongue and slid it into her mouth. When he'd had enough, he moved to take it out and she caught it between her teeth. He didn't resist and she bit it, a soft pressure, and let go.

'Where now?' he wondered.

'Don't worry about that.'

She had to manoeuvre back and forward to get out.

'You've pulled in too tight,' he told her. 'With all this space to park in.'

With the taste of her in his mouth, the instinct of the bully rose in him.

She hauled the wheel round. As she started to clear the space, he put his hand on her leg and rubbed along the inside of her thigh.

'Fuck!' she said.

Misjudging, she'd struck the edge of a bumper. The car jerked forward. Metal squealed. He went to open the door.

'Do you know whose car you've made me hit?' She pointed across him. The edge of her hand touched his chest.

'Should I care?'

'Shut the door,' she said. He hesitated. 'Hurry!'

She swung the car out into the drive.

As they passed the house, a man was standing outside the open front door.

At the top of the broad flight of steps, the figure seemed to lean forward, one hand resting on the balustrade. The stillness made an unpleasant impression as if he stood on watch. Caught like that, though, glimpsed for a moment, in silhouette against the light, it could have been anyone stepped outside to smoke or take a breath of fresher air.

'Where are you going now?' he asked. At the end of the drive, she'd turned right instead of left towards the main road.

'My way. Trust me.'

'I don't think so,' he said.

'Do you have a choice?'

Before he could answer, he was jerked forward as she hit the brakes. The narrow road had shrunk to a bridge only wide enough for one vehicle. On the other side, they passed a building with the look of a farm house. It was in darkness except for a light in one downstairs window. They might have been on a Highland road, fifty miles from anywhere. The headlights on main beam cored out the night in long sweeps ahead of them. At last he said, 'Your way. Are you offering to take me home? Oddly enough, that hadn't occurred to me.'

'Would you rather we went to your place?'

'No.'

'If we did, you wouldn't need to get a taxi home.'

'I said, no.'

'You look like somebody who would have to get to work in the morning. Do you have to get to work in the morning?'

'If we go back into Edinburgh,' he said, 'I know a good hotel.'

'I'm sure you do. Is your wife waiting for you at home?'

'A discreet hotel.'

'Have you ever eaten breakfast there?'

'What does that mean?'

'If you don't want breakfast,' she said, 'I know a place. There's a house belonging to a friend of mine.'

'She won't be there? It is she, not he?'

'Oh, you married men,' she said. 'Nervous as cats. What are you afraid of?' And when he didn't answer (take your pick, from ambush to blackmail) added on a note of mockery, 'No, she won't be there. Or anyone else either. Just you and me.'

Soon he recognised that they were coming back into the city. They ran along London Road and came out into Leith Walk. From there he watched familiar markers go by, until they came to the junction with Lothian Road. The route they began to follow was one he knew well. As they came through Marchmont into Morningside Road, the dark pavements gleaming after a shower of rain were almost deserted. The street they finally turned into curved up a hill between substantial detached houses. Without looking at his watch, he knew it was somewhere between midnight and one; not late at all. When she stopped the car and they got out, he couldn't hear any sound of traffic. Somewhere a holiday had been called and no one had told him.

'I'll tell you something funny,' he said. His voice sounded loud in the quiet street. 'The first time I saw you, you were with a woman. I followed the two of you to a gay pub. I thought you were a lesbian.'

He followed her up a path. Storm doors were folded back. He listened to the scratch and knock of metal as she searched with the key to get it into the lock. A plane of darkness, a glint of reflected light from the street, he heard more than saw the door open. After a moment, stupid to hesitate, he'd come this far, some animal reaction made him want to avoid the black cave, he followed her inside.

In under two hours, he was home again, back where he'd started, a million miles from where he'd started. He wandered about the house, washed his hands, stood under a shower, looked at his face in the mirror. It didn't look any different. In his study, he stood for a long time at the window. The sky lightened behind the hill and he realised it was almost morning.

I've seen that face before (On the screen, he read the paragraph to where it stopped. The phone had rung interrupting him at that point, and after a while he'd got up and gone out. He began to type:) *as a cloud shape that held for minutes one summer afternoon when I was a child. A face by Michelangelo, omniscient and omnipotent, but not necessarily kind. It is so familiar, familiar from a lifetime ago, and here it is again. I'm haunted by a patriarch.*

Reading the completed paragraph, there was no way of telling where the interruption had come, or how between one word and the next a violent death had broken the sentence apart.

BOOK ONE

Cold Steel

CHAPTER ONE

L urid in red against chipped and faded brick on the wall of a disused
industrial unit, a cry from the heart. FUCK THE PIGS. DS Shields stared
gloomily through the window on the passenger side, turned and saw he was
being watched.

'Funny way to spell Pope,' he said.

Meldrum grunted.

'Joke.'

'Right.'

'Don't know why I bother.'

The bitterness might well be genuine, but a big soft grin kept the words
company. A big just-kidding grin. That was Bobbie Shields. Meldrum had
given up wondering why the stout sergeant didn't put in for a transfer, find
somebody who might see the joke. Certainly, not because a transfer might
look bad on his record; Shields made no secret that his only ambition was to
get to the pension and get out. Maybe for a man just putting his time in,
going for a change would be more bother than it was worth. They shared
some hours of most days. They shared a car. Meldrum drove, he always
drove, which irritated Shields. He, too, didn't like being the passenger. They
had that in common.

Out in the country, on the wrong side of the city, like the joke about the
man who asked how to get to Dublin, when the call came about the dead
woman they wouldn't have chosen to start from where they were.

Ten minutes later, they were cutting in through Niddrie, travelling at speed.
If you were given an invitation to a murder, the etiquette was to get there fast.

'See that!' Shields exclaimed.

Meldrum got a glimpse of what was going on in the side street, braked and tyre-squealed through the corner.

'Oh, Jesus Christ!' Shields said, fumbling to get his seat belt fastened. He'd a bad habit of leaving it off because he found it uncomfortable. His tone meant, what are you doing? It meant, this is nothing to do with us. Most of all, it meant, I've done my share of that shit, thank you very much.

From the top of the road, it had the appearance of a riot, not a big one, but a lot of stones were flying from a crowd aged twelve and upwards. One of the firemen was lying on the ground. The water from the hydrant plumed white into the air and frayed out in the wind. Coming down the hill fast in the unmarked car, Meldrum saw the nearest figures swing round, among them a blond head picked out above the crowd with his arm drawn back, posed like an athlete with a javelin. The stone bounced up off the bonnet and banged the glass. As the windscreen starred in front of Meldrum's eyes, he hit the brake and was out of the car before it had stopped rolling. The speed and ferocity of his charge split the crowd and carried him out again, gripping the stone thrower, a boy of about eighteen, bent in a wristlock. Shields must have reckoned the surprise would hold until the prisoner was shoved into the back of the car, but as he scrambled out the stones started to fly. Meldrum staggered and swung round to face the assault. As he edged backwards, he grabbed a handful of the boy's hair, vivid blond, bad move in a mob, and pulled him upright. For a man well over six feet, it wasn't a perfect shield, but a thud and moan of pain suggested it was working.

He pulled the boy after him into the back seat. Shields slammed the door shut behind them and himself dived into the front, huddling across the passenger's seat to get behind the wheel. He pulled across the road. Stones banged the roof, rattled along the side, one smacked the glass by the boy's head. The boy cowered against Meldrum, who shoved him off and shouted, 'Cover them!' In response, Shields spun the wheel and stamped on the brake, putting the car close beside the two firemen crouched over the man on the ground. No sooner had they stopped, though, than the crowd on the other side of the road was in flight, first one or two, then by contagion all of them at once running as if for their lives, the sirens scattering them like oil off a hotplate.

If Meldrum or Shields had been looking for thanks, he would have been disappointed. They stood as spectators to a shouting match between the fire crew and the uniforms who had tumbled out of the cars. 'Too fucking late.' 'You can't get an escort unless you tell us.' 'Should have known it was a false alarm.' '*We* knew — but that fucking idiot wouldn't listen.' 'Never again. Burn the fucking place down for me.' 'Best thing for it.' As they walked the boy Meldrum had caught to a police car, one of the fire crew, fright turned to anger, blocked their way cursing. 'Take it easy. We're police,' Meldrum told him. 'Fuck that! My mate could be dead lying there. Don't grin at me, you wee bastard!' He aimed a punch at the boy, a good punch, unsignalled, like a man who'd done some boxing. Meldrum's forearm block spun him off his feet. In shock, on his knees staring up, he mouthed, 'Jesus, I'm sorry.' The interest of the watching policemen turned to half-concealed amusement as they recognised Meldrum. The older one put his hand on the boy's head, guided him into the car. Turning, he asked, 'You'll be doing the write-up, sir?' The look on the younger one's face would have been called dumb insolence in the army. Or again, living dangerously. The arrival of an ambulance, broken note dying as it pulled in, saved him. At the best of times, Meldrum didn't have a great sense of humour, and the pain shooting from his ear up the side of his head meant this wasn't the best of times.

It was the ambulance man who noticed the blood. 'You should get that seen to,' he'd said. 'You don't know what the damage is.' Meldrum refolded the pad of gauze for the third or fourth time and held it to his head, resting his elbow on the ledge of the car window. There was a lump behind his ear, but the blood was coming from a ragged wound across the lobe, torn by something like the edge of a half brick.

'Stopped yet?' Shields asked. 'Should have stopped by this time.'

'Just making sure.'

'Right enough.' He couldn't help sounding cheerful. Driving made a nice change for him. 'Don't want them thinking it's you been murdered.'

CHAPTER TWO

They came into Morningside Road, traffic as usual coagulating at every set of lights. Half an hour ago the sun had been shining down on the riot round the fire engine. Now clouds had blown across, turning the air grey. A thin rain drizzled on shoppers crowding the pavements.

'Through the Cross and it's second or third right,' Meldrum said. The bleeding had stopped, but his head ached and shards of coloured light tumbled slowly on the edge of his vision. When he yawned, he felt sick.

The house in Greenbank was at the end of a substantial terrace: grey stone, tall narrow windows facing north, with old trees at the front overshadowing grass patched with moss. A constable stood at the gate, and parked nearby Meldrum recognised the Morgan kit car belonging to Bob Ross, the medical examiner.

'The body's been identified, sir. By a neighbour, a Mr Warren. He was the one who called us.'

'Where is he?'

'That's his house.' Did I ask you where he lived? Wrong answer; answer to a different question. The eager constable pointed helpfully. 'Over there, sir.'

Fuck it, Meldrum thought. Talking to idiots was no cure for a headache.

The front door lay open inside the porch, and Meldrum had that familiar feeling of a place turned, at least for the moment, into public property, not a home any more but a crime scene. As they went upstairs, he paused and bent for a closer look at a disc of dried mud tucked into the corner of a step. Looking up, he saw Cowan scowling over the bannister at him.

'Don't bother,' he said. '*That* belongs to the next-door neighbour.'

'It happens.' Meldrum didn't bother to ask how the forensic scientist knew.

Cowan was good, and it was a piece of luck to have him involved this early. Most times pressure of work meant forensics had to depend on SOC officers to gather evidence. 'What brings you out into the real world?'

'Walls closing in.'

'I know the feeling.'

'Lab walls.'

'Oh, *that* feeling.' From the door, the bedroom seemed crowded. It was a large room and there were only three men in it, but even at first glance it was a very feminine room, pink walls, curtains, big swathes of cloth swooping down to the bed, call it overdone, call it traditional, not just a woman's room, a very feminine bedroom. Overalled and gloved, three men crowded it.

'Where's Bob Ross?' Meldrum asked them. 'I saw his car outside.'

'Here a minute ago.'

'Just went out.'

'Gone for a piss, likely. Lavatory on the landing.'

The Three Stooges.

'He'd bloody better not be.' Cowan rose to the bait.

The three grinned. One said, 'Find a ball hair in there, you'll know where to check first.'

Where was the body? The downie piled up along the edge of the bed just might have concealed one, but that it would still be uncovered made no sense. Maybe it was all a mistake. Maybe Bob Ross had found nothing dead here and gone home, and all the bustling around now was only about confirming that. The Scene of No Crime Officers. That would be nice. Nice if they could all find something else to do, go home to the kids, take a walk in the park, go to the pictures, when was the last time he'd been in a cinema? Take the afternoon off, that would be nice, sit in the dark and watch a movie, eat an ice-cream, boy meets girl.

But, of course, there was a body. He'd have to watch it, a brick bounced off the skull let in some stupid ideas. As he came farther in, it was there on the floor beside the bed. He saw the hair first, a great fan of it spread up from the skull, vivid and red as a pool of fresh blood. The body lay on its side in the indignity of violent death, high-heeled shoes still on the feet though the skirt was off and the buttocks were bare.

'Next-door neighbour, you said.' He turned to Cowan and almost bumped into Shields staring down at the body with an expression that said, nice arse. 'What made him come up here?'

'Thought there had been a burglary. Looked around downstairs. Then came up and—' He waved a hand at the body. 'Must have been a shock.'

A voice asked, 'What war have you been in?'

'Where have you been?' Cowan demanded.

'I can see you lost,' Bob Ross said, coming in from the doorway. A stocky man with a drinker's nose and a fund of golfing stories, he had to crane up to inspect the side of Meldrum's head. 'That looks nasty. You should take a minute and let me clean and stitch it.'

'I'm fine.'

'How does your head feel? Eyes all right? No double vision?'

'It'll clear.'

'If it doesn't, see your doctor.' He nodded towards the window. 'Got a glimpse of the garden and couldn't resist going to the other room for a better view. It's been someone's pride and joy — once upon a time — badly neglected recently.'

To Meldrum's irritation, Bobbie Shields went to the window. One of the SOCs joined him.

'What made him think there'd been a burglary?'

'The neighbour? He saw the door lying open when he went out for a paper. It was still like that when he came back. He decided something might be wrong.'

'Is there a husband?'

'How do you mean?' Cowan asked.

'Damn it,' Meldrum said. 'I don't even know her name. Married? Separated? Divorced?'

'Whose name?'

Meldrum stared at him and jerked a thumb in the direction of the corpse.

Ross gave a sudden exclamation. 'Good God!' he said. 'I see.' He crouched down beside the bed and took a handful of the red hair. As he pulled it came free of the scalp.

Shields had swung round from the window. He was staring at the middle of the body where it lay facing him.

'Fuck!' he said. 'It's a man.'

From the expression on his face, the arse didn't seem so nice, not any more.

CHAPTER THREE

'I'd bin that shirt,' Ross said. 'You'll never get the blood out of the collar.'
'Speaking of blood,' Meldrum said.

Crouched down on the other side of the body, he could see the entry wound just behind the left ear. Shredded fibres from the red wig lay on the corpse's shoulder. The dead man's own hair was black, but shot through with grey. This close Meldrum could see a dark shadow along the jaw and upper lip; however close the shave, hair grew again, even for a time after death. A little fat under the chin, lines at the eyes, very fine lines, in life he could have been into his forties. Rubbed, smeared and starting to cake, powder and paint made it hard to tell.

'Whatever bleeding there was would have been internal. I've an idea what happened,' Ross tapped the skull lightly, 'but we'll know for sure later.'

'Did we get the weapon?'

'In the bag,' Cowan said. Literally, he meant, holding it up by one corner. The knife appeared to be made of brass with a wrought handle and a narrow blade, about seven or eight inches long.

'Now where did that come from? It's not the kind of thing you'd carry around.'

'Paper knife?' Cowan wondered. 'Or is that old-fashioned?'

'Paper knife in here?'

'Maybe he read his letters in bed.'

'Maybe.'

'See the stain on the sheet there,' Cowan pointed, 'that's where it was lying. It either fell out or was pulled out.'

Meldrum thought about that. 'He could have been in the bed and struggled out after he got hit. Shock would do that.'

'Or trying to escape. Assuming the murderer was in the bed with him.'

'Any semen?'

'Haven't found any on the bed.'

'I'll check for it inside,' Ross said.

'No sign of semen so far,' Cowan said, 'his or anybody else's – or any other kind of emission.'

Looking around at the make-up and creams on the dressing table, the pink drapes and curtains, Meldrum said, 'If this is his bedroom,' and somehow he'd assumed it was, perhaps because a front door left open suggested whoever had taken flight wasn't the owner of the house, 'and he brought somebody back, what the hell would a man make of it, walking into this?'

'Right man would love it,' Cowan said.

Meldrum grunted and crouched down beside Ross who was taking another look at the head wound.

'But with him being a cross-dresser, isn't it just as likely he'd be with a woman, eh?' Ross wondered. Looking up, he caught a grin between two of the SOC officers and added, 'Not that I'd know. You're the experts,' which didn't improve matters.

'Same difference,' Cowan said. 'Right woman would love it.'

'Get on top?' the SOC photographer suggested.

The one dusting for prints wondered, 'Before or after she killed him?'

Meldrum blew his breath out in disdain.

'You're old-fashioned, like me.' Ross nodded cheerfully across the body.

'Thank Christ,' Meldrum said. Getting to his feet, he scowled round the room, 'Did he live alone? Let's talk to this neighbour who claims he found him.'

Outside, the constable at the gate was still eager to be of service. For the second time, unasked, he indicated the house across the road, 'That's where Mr Warren lives, sir. We took the call, and I spoke to him when we got here.'

'When was that?'

'More than an hour ago.'

'Right.' To Shields he said, 'Let's go talk to him.'

But as they started off, the constable said, 'You want to talk to him?'

Meldrum swung round so abruptly Shields had to sidestep. 'What did you say?'

The constable swallowed. 'He's not there.' He pointed the way they'd come. 'After he spoke to me, he went home to tell his wife what had happened. She'd be wondering he said, since he'd just gone out to get a paper. But he came back about quarter of an hour ago. I told him to wait downstairs.'

As overstuffed as the sofa he was sitting on, Ivor Warren, purple-cheeked, at a guess nearer eighty than seventy, was ready to complain. 'Are you the officer in charge? I am surprised it took you such a time to get here. It was my impression you'd pull out all the stops. Speaking as a layman, that is, an ordinary citizen. A concerned citizen. We don't have so many murders, do we? Even if the world's going mad, this is Edinburgh not Chicago.'

Watching the petulant quiver of jowls as the fruity voice rolled on, Meldrum was reminded of why he was late by a stab of pain behind the eyes. Naturally, it didn't for a moment occur to him to mention the mini-riot round the fire engines. Never explain, never apologise.

'What made you decide to come in here?' he asked.

Stopped in mid-flow, Warren gaped. 'Don't follow you. I told your people, the front door was open.' By his tone, he wasn't used to being interrupted and it wasn't an experience he relished.

'That was your only reason for coming in? Why would you take notice of that particularly?'

'I was going to get a paper. Don't believe in having it delivered. God gave us legs to use them. First thing I noticed was that the garden gate was open. The gate was kept shut, it shouldn't have been open. Then I saw the front door was open as well.'

'The hedge at the front is overgrown. It's not easy to see up the path.'

'Not hard either. Not from our gate – we're directly opposite. I'm the observant type. I was a naval officer. I cut my usual walk short, and had another look when I came back. And saw it was still open, front door that is.'

'And that was enough to make you suspicious?'

'Make anyone wonder what was going on, I'd've thought. You know this is a Neighbourhood Watch area?'

'No, I didn't notice that.'

'There you are then.'

'So you felt you should come across and make sure everything was all right?'

'I've told you so.'

'So then what happened?'

'I stood at the front door and called. Got no answer. Looked in the front rooms, walked through to the kitchen. Had a look out into the garden. Then went upstairs.'

'You didn't hesitate about doing that?'

'I had my stick. I'm not a young man, but, worst comes to the worst, I could still give an account of myself.'

'No. I mean, did you know your way round the house?'

'Downstairs a few times, never upstairs, if that's what you're implying.'

The tone was brusque enough, but Warren accompanied it with what seemed to be an involuntary smirk. The effect was unpleasant.

'Would you describe yourself as a close friend?'

'No, I would not. Because I went in to make sure all was well? Least I could do, woman living on her own. Well, good as, eh? No man in the house.'

'What woman?'

It was Warren's turn to frown. 'How do you mean?'

'What woman living on her own?'

'Well, not *living* – not any more – is that what you mean? You're cutting it fine, too fine for my taste, if you want to take me up in that way.'

Meldrum felt a strong desire to shut his eyes and lie down on the floor. He opened them to see Warren staring at him. A glance to the side showed that Shields, too, was watching him. In the DS's case, this was done without moving the head, a surveillance conducted from the corner of the eye. Minimum effort, maximum deniability. He resisted the temptation to shut his eyes again.

Time to take a grip. 'I understand you identified the body, Mr Warren. Would you confirm that identification for me, please?'

There, that was easy enough.

'Toni Ashton, of course. Lying in her bedroom, who else would it be? No mistaking that hair.' The old man's voice quavered. 'Sorry, just hitting me. What an awful business this is. Most beautiful woman I ever saw.'

Meldrum gave in. He shut his eyes. Just for a moment.

CHAPTER FOUR

There was a simple pleasure in making them vanish. Drop your lids and they were gone. You could still hear them, of course. Unless you stuffed your fingers in your ears. Which didn't always work. You'd have to put your fingers in your ears and chant to yourself – lalalalalala – white noise. That would do it, gone good riddance not there. Look a bit odd though and the chanting would draw attention. Even the eyes shut bit would if it went on too long.

Even in a church.

Meldrum opened his eyes.

Or a registry office.

His ex-wife Carole was at the front with the others. Instead of a wedding dress, she was wearing a green trouser suit. It must have been expensive, but studying her back view, it struck him she'd put on a lot of weight. That might be unfair, of course. It was months since he'd visited her, and it was anyway perfectly possible he was unduly influenced by the memory of the last time he'd seen her getting married. She'd been a lot younger then, and he'd been the one standing beside her. Half a lifetime ago. He wondered if the man she'd now chosen to marry might be younger than her. From the little he'd seen of him, there wasn't any reason to think so, but all the same he wouldn't be surprised, not a bit surprised. From here near the back of the room he couldn't examine the groom's face; black hair, though, and plenty of it. Too much of it in fact, think he'd get a haircut for his wedding, maybe over the collar was the fashion in education. Bastard. No, for her sake, don't let him be a bastard. He was called Phil. Having met him only once, Meldrum had difficulty remembering his second name, which might under the circumstances be a textbook example of elementary psychology since he'd been told it often enough.

In the years since their divorce, it had never occurred to him that Carole would get married again.

He told himself firmly that at least he wouldn't be going to the reception, no chance, not the slightest intention. Any more, come to that, than he'd really meant to accept the invitation to the ceremony. So why was he here? Very civilised of them to invite him, very civilised of him to be here. So here he was. Unobtrusive, near the back, but here, being civilised. Except who was he kidding? Not himself. He was a policeman, not a lawyer or a doctor or a fucking director of education, he didn't have to be civilised. As it happened, fucking director of education was the groom's job. Phil's job.

If you had to go to a reception, the Roxburghe Hotel was a fine place for it. The decor was attractive, the room large and airy, the food good and promptly served. The cake cutting had gone well, plenty of photographs. Later there would be dancing. Earlier outside the registry office he'd even let Sandy, his son-in-law, take one with him in it, Baby Sandy in his arms, daughter Betty smiling beside him. To be fair to Sandy, you could see he hadn't been comfortable with the idea. It was Betty who'd set it up. Say cheese. Jesus. Did his daughter imagine he'd be lost without a souvenir of her mother's wedding day? Now he was at a table with Sandy and Betty, Baby Sandy in a high chair, two couples whose names he hadn't bothered to catch, and a husband and wife who'd been neighbours years ago, more Carole's friends than ever his, he'd been too busy working to get to know them. All the same, he had been grateful to get to the refuge of the meal.

'It was nice of you to come,' Carole had said. He'd shaken hands, not kissed her on the cheek.

'Civilised,' he'd said, and she'd frowned then smiled, before he'd moved to Phil the Director next in line, shaken hands and gone on into the reception area where the cake had been mounted four tiers high on its silver stand.

Carole had always been good at reading his thoughts, but then they'd lived together a long time. Got on well together, too, for the most part. Never stopped liking one another even after the divorce. No bad sex or arguments. Just too much police work that left them too little time together and eroded the marriage until you woke up one morning to be told it was over. After they separated, he'd fallen into the habit of dropping in to talk to her, sometimes about a case he was involved in, something he'd never have dreamed of doing during their marriage. Wouldn't be able to do that now. Not that it mattered, since he'd broken the habit months ago after Betty had said to him, let it go,

Dad, you won't make her happy, don't make her unhappy, she's confused. Not any more she wasn't. Obviously.

'What?'

'You're very quiet,' Betty repeated. She spoke quietly under the hum of voices, leaning towards him across the space made by the high chair pulled into the table.

'I'm enjoying,' he looked down at the plate, 'this. I was wondering what the Church would make of your mother being married in a registry office. Did they kick up hell?'

'Hell?' Betty said. 'Has that not been abolished?'

'Not for you Catholics. Not last I heard.'

'I don't know. She hasn't said anything. You haven't been to see us for ages.'

'Heavy spell at work. You know how it is.'

She nodded without any trace of satire. She knew how it was, how it had been. 'I read about that man you found dead last year, the one who killed the little boy, that must have been awful. You should have come and talked to me. Everybody needs somebody to talk to.'

Concentrating, he picked around among the stuff on the plate. He put the loaded forkful in his mouth and chewed. It didn't taste of anything much.

When she spoke again, she surprised him. She stroked the baby's cheek and said, 'People say Baby Sandy's like you.'

'Let's hope not.' When she didn't respond, he added, 'I mean, for his sake,' awkwardly trying to make a joke of it, then realising too late under her glance that it sounded too much like self-pity.

It was a relief when, before the coffee, before the speeches, he furtively switched on his mobile and it began to chirp. He listened and turned away from the table to acknowledge the message. He had been given a reason not to have to sit through the speeches. He'd been playing truant and had a murder investigation to go to. It seemed the red-haired woman Toni Ashton had turned up.

As he stood up to leave, Betty caught him by the sleeve. He bent down to her.

'Do you have to go?'

'No choice.'

After all, here it was again, the old demand of work, an excuse she had heard him make since she was old enough to understand, which all the same didn't stop it from being true. Quietly, she asked, 'You are pleased for her? You wouldn't want Mum to be lonely.'

'No,' he said as softly. 'I wouldn't want her to be lonely.'

Driving back to the Ashton house, he recalled how hard it had been the day before to convince the neighbour Ivor Warren that his first identification of the victim had been mistaken.

'I was sure it was Toni,' he'd said, a line of white suddenly running down the purple cheeks, when at last they'd persuaded him upstairs again to look at the body. 'I didn't look too closely, not when she wasn't covered. She wasn't decent—'

'You mean "he" wasn't,' Shields had interrupted him.

'Yes, but then I *thought* it was Toni Ashton. As I say, it was just the whole impression. The image, you could say. There was no question of my going closer, because – not a chance of going closer because —'

'The arse was bare,' Shields had said. Whatever the sergeant's faults, there were times when he could cut to the essence of a situation.

Whether or not in other circumstances that would have produced some kind of explosion, then Warren had simply nodded. 'It was the hair more than anything. Toni has this mass of red hair. You'll understand when you see her. Where is she?'

'We're looking for her. Can you think of anyone she might be with?'

'Visiting, you mean? I wouldn't know who her friends are. Apart from neighbours like myself. I haven't seen her for days.' He paused as a thought struck him. 'You have searched? Christ, she could be lying injured somewhere. You know there's a cellar?'

CHAPTER FIVE

Toni Ashton hadn't been in the cellar, lying strangled or with her throat cut. She hadn't been hiding there either, or anywhere else in the house for that matter; which had to have been another possibility until they could be sure she hadn't been the one who'd used the knife. That the knife was the cause of Brian Ashton's death, despite the trivial appearance of the entry wound, had been established by the autopsy report. The long narrow blade had penetrated under the floor of the skull, through the jugular vein causing minor air embolism, through the neck muscles between the arches of the first and second cervical vertebrae (dividing vertebral artery and vein), to reach with the tip of the blade the very centre of the brain stem. A typical stab wound, in fact, nothing much to look at from the outside, but causing fatal damage as it penetrated.

It was the first time Meldrum had ever been asked to describe the cause of death in detail to a victim's wife. He found it alarming, but then Toni Ashton was an alarming woman. In the first place, alarmingly beautiful. It had been someone else who'd opened the door, some friend, a little woman, dark and brown with a sharp, intelligent face, who'd shown Shields and him into the living room and then, tactfully or because it had been discussed, disappeared to the back of the house. The women must have been drinking together for there were glasses on a table between the two easy chairs and an opened bottle of wine. Smoking, too, for the air smelled of it. As Toni Ashton glanced round, her profile turning into the light from the windows, he'd recorded all that, the stuff about the glasses and the smoke tainting the air, recorded it consciously as a way of disguising his response to her. It hadn't, though; not even the smoking, which he'd tried to concentrate on because he disliked the smell. She must have spent her life since adolescence getting the tribute of that response from men. What was strange to him was that even in this situation he could see her glance flick from him to Shields, seeking it.

On a cinema screen, in a magazine, beauty was often a kind of deception, the oldest special effect of them all. Here in this ordinary room was the real thing those shadows mimicked. Close up it was overwhelming, and the complication of being there to talk about her husband's death didn't make it easier. Bad taste to use the trick when someone bothered you of picturing them naked; which, anyway, this time would have been a bad idea, a very bad idea. Her eyes were the unimprovable exact shade of green, her cheekbones, her mouth, that densely white skin, the hair. Maybe it was the hair more than anything, the richness of the colour, you wanted to touch it, feel the weight of it, the energy of life running in it. It was a red mane, coming below her shoulders, and whether that length was in fashion or out, on her it should have had a preservation order, like a listed bulding or a national treasure. You couldn't take a national treasure out of the country, though, and Toni Ashton and her friend were just back from America. They'd gone out three weeks before and flown back from Los Angeles.

'Neither Naomi or I could understand a word he was saying. As we arrived, he popped out his gate like a jack-in-the-box. Almost ran in front of the car, waving his arms. Then when we got out, he just stood gaping at us. He was an extraordinary colour, even more than usual, like he was going to have a stroke.'

'This was Mr Warren?' Shields had said. His face, too, Meldrum noted was an interesting colour. It looked as if the fat sergeant was trying to hold in his beer gut.

'Hmm. He took for ever mumbling and stuttering before he came out with it. But by then I'd seen the constable at the door.'

'It must have been a shock,' Meldrum said.

'Hmm. I always knew there was something odd about Brian. Have you seen my bedroom? Silly, of course you must have. He designed that. The whole ghastly tart's boudoir, the walls, the drapes, that awful pink, hellish for me, of course, with my colouring. I know what you're thinking. Why didn't I change it once he'd taken himself off? Everyone asked, even Naomi didn't understand. Change it for God's sake, she said.'

'You know how he was dressed when he died?'

'First thing Ivor Warren told us. It seemed to upset him as much as the murder.'

'Was that something your husband had done before?'

'Put on women's clothes? Not while we were together. He was a bastard, but not that kind of bastard.'

'Or at least not so that you knew.'

She shook her head. 'He put on those clothes to look like me. Ivor Warren thought it was me. It was to degrade me, that's why he did it. And now he's dead. I can't get my head round that. They say you don't believe it, if you're not there when someone dies. Like in a war, you know, when the next of kin would get the telegram.'

It evolved from there under her insistence, the offering of the details of the fatal wound like some salve for grieving, as Meldrum beguiled himself into the role of brother officer bringing an account of heroism in the trenches to the widow.

'How long did it take him to die?' she asked, spoiling the effect.

'How long?'

'Can't they tell things like that?'

'It wasn't immediately,' he said, too honest to lie.

'I wonder if he knew. How serious it was.'

'He might have lost consciousness at once from shock.'

'Hmm.'

Something ambivalent in the mood of that little hummed note disconcerted Meldrum. There was a silence and then he reached for the familiar ground of questions aimed at establishing a victim's background, character and state of mind.

'You were living apart? How long had you been separated?'

'One year and eleven months.' The speed of her answer surprised him. Seeing that, she said, 'Believe me, you know these things when it's a question of divorce.'

'You wanted a divorce.'

'He did.'

'You didn't want it?'

'Till death us do part. That's what I felt. I wasn't going to make it easy for him.'

'But after two years, you couldn't stop him.'

Another silence.

'Have you been divorced?' she asked. 'Is that how you know about things like that?'

'It's my job,' he said.

'Like knowing about knife wounds.' Reflecting, she touched her fingers to her hair, laying them above the place where she'd been told her husband had been stabbed. 'Does your wife mind you having to know things like that?'

There wasn't an answer to that, or not one he cared to make. He waited, then asked, 'Did your husband ever break into the house before?'

'God, no!'

'Since the separation, how often have you seen him?'

'Hardly at all – two or three times, with the lawyers, when it had to be done.'

'Did you get phone calls? Or letters?'

'From Brian?'

'Yes.'

'I can't think of any. What kind of phone calls?'

'Did he ever threaten you?'

'He wasn't violent.' She didn't make it sound like a compliment.

'Would you say, then, that you parted by agreement?'

'No. I wouldn't put it that way.'

'How would you put it?'

'I told him if he didn't get out, I'd kill him.'

Kill him. She'd spat it out as if she'd hated him. Enough to kill him? But she had an alibi. The policeman's mind made that connection automatically. At once, then, remembered from two or three years back a girl whose father had disappeared. She'd claimed to have flown up from London on the Saturday, but they'd proved she'd come one day earlier.

'For what reason?'

'There wasn't another woman. He was just – the more you got to know him – his first marriage broke up, too.' She had this disconcerting way of coming to an answer at a tangent. 'It was a lot of different things.' She frowned. 'Christ, I've just thought – the house was burgled a year ago. Stuff was taken, but not a lot, not good stuff. The worst of it was the vandalism.'

She paused for so long, Meldrum prodded, 'You were telling me why you wanted your husband to leave?'

'Oh God, how disgusting, if it was Brian.'

'What?'

'The break-in. I came home to find a pile of excrement on the bedroom floor. The police decided it was probably children. They took fingerprints, but they weren't really trying.'

In his colleagues' defence, there was no forensic science of taking finger-prints when it came to tracing shite. Meldrum nodded sympathetically. 'What makes you think that might have been your husband?'

'Not at the time, it never occurred to me at the time. A window was broken, and the police said that's how the children had got in. But he could have come in with a key and broken the window afterwards. I've never had the locks changed, never thought I needed to, not even after the break-in. Were any windows broken this time?'

'No. There were no signs of forced entry.'

'There you are then! He came in with a key! Both times!'

'It's possible, I suppose,' Meldrum said sceptically.

'If he would take some prostitute into my bed, you think he wouldn't shit on the floor? You think shitting on the floor is worse? If she hadn't killed him, God knows what he'd have done to the place. He was capable of anything.'

'But you said he wasn't violent.'

'Not physically, not with me. Mentally, though! You've seen the bedroom! Do you know why I didn't change it when he left? I kept it to remind myself how much I despised him.' She smiled unexpectedly. 'I suppose I could change it now.'

Pink everywhere in that extravagant room. Wakening in it like opening your eyes inside an ear of pink flesh. To wake to it every morning, that was a lot of reminding she'd allowed herself. How much energy would that gather, female energy, like the storing of a battery?

Outside Shields revealed an uncommon meeting of minds.

'Give that one a broomstick and she'd ride to hell. I wonder if her and that friend were really away in the States.'

'The alibi'll hold,' Meldrum said, starting the car.

'You can't be sure of that. Not till we get it checked.'

'Think about it,' Meldrum said drily. 'You think if we show her photograph people aren't going to remember if they'd seen her? She must know people don't forget her. Known since she was about twelve, I guess.'

There was a moody silence, which held until they got to Brian Ashton's flat.

'All the same, pair of fucking lezzies,' Shields said as the car was reversed into the kerb.

He had his own way of arming himself against beauty.

CHAPTER SIX

Brian Ashton had bought a flat in the New Town when he left the family home. When they pressed the buzzer beside the name under his, there was a clanking noise and the door unlocked. Inside there was a hall with a terrazzo floor and a wide carpeted stair winding around an open well.

As they climbed, Shields asked, 'How you feeling now?'

Meldrum had phoned in and lied about being sick. Unprofessional move for a bank clerk; for a senior detective on the second day of a murder enquiry, it was beyond stupidity. To follow that up by going out to a public event was certifiable. How many people had seen him at Carole's wedding? Sixty, seventy, eighty? At least that many, of whom a fair number must have known him personally or at least heard of him, he'd been in the newspapers often enough; or at the very least glanced over with curiosity when he was pointed out as the ex-husband. The ex-husband who'd come to the wedding. Fuck civilised. That lacked self-respect. And now he'd have to sweat it out until he was sure nothing got back to Chief Constable Baird about where he'd been instead of in bed with a belly ache.

'Fine,' he said.

'Not often you're sick.' On to the first landing. Start up the next flight. 'Thought I'd try you on the mobile anyway. Just in case.' Second landing. 'Just as well I did, eh? Seen the wife and now this neighbour guy.' Third landing, second door. 'You're looking fine now, but—'

The door was opened by a lean man in baggy shorts. Tanned narrow face with a long jaw, plenty of black hair, very white teeth.

'Are you the police?' He looked at Meldrum. 'Was it you I spoke to on the phone?'

What was the smile? Placatory? Anxious? Or just automatic? If he was nervous, why not? Police knocking on the door had that effect on a lot of men, most of them more or less honest. A first impression put him in his thirties, a second added another ten years. On a chair in the lobby behind him, Meldrum could see a sports bag with the handles of tennis rackets poking out.

Meldrum introduced himself. 'And this is DS Shields.'

'Alex Hodge. But you know that.' Alex: not Alec; the ending soft not hard. To Meldrum that always sounded like a girl's name. Or some kind of plural, as if there would be another Alec along in a minute.

'It was me you spoke to.' Shields, being himself, made being spoken to sound like an imposition.

'I was told you'd been knocking at doors,' Hodge said to Shields. 'I'm sorry I was out.'

'So you rang us,' Meldrum said. 'Was there any particular reason?'

'Sorry, you won't want to talk out here. I should have asked — won't you come in?'

A big room, very light, the windows open at the bottom so that sounds came in of traffic passing in the street. He had to lift magazines off the couch to let them sit down, Meldrum right at the edge, weight forward, ready to get up. From the moment the door opened, it had felt like a waste of time, and he hadn't any more time to waste that day.

'Reason?' Hodge asked. He'd taken a chair to one side so that Meldrum had to turn his head to look at him.

'For feeling you had to phone.'

'Sorry, particular reason, yes.' Leaning forward to indicate he was speaking to Shields, he said, 'I assumed you'd be working today, even though it's a Saturday.'

'You made it sound urgent,' Shields said.

'Well, I'll be away the rest of the week. Catching a plane before eight tomorrow morning, in fact. And so I thought, if you did want to see me, today would be best. Sorry if I didn't make myself clear when I called you.'

It struck Meldrum this was a man who did a lot of apologising. At his back, Meldrum heard a dry grunt from Shields. Just clearing his throat, the way you have to sometimes. Nothing to do with the fact Meldrum hadn't been there that morning when the phone call came.

'How well did you know Mr Ashton?' he asked.

Hodge grimaced, screwing his eyes shut. 'Poor Brian!' he said. 'I still can't believe it.' Like that, with the clenched muscles digging tracks in his skin, he looked older again. As Meldrum studied him, his eyes popped open. 'Not very well,' he said.

'Sorry?' Christ, Meldrum thought, he's got me doing it.

'I didn't know him well. Next-door neighbours.' He frowned. 'In a kind of way. He's on the fourth floor. God, sorry, was on the fourth. Flat above here. Sometimes I could hear him walking around. Wooden floors, you know. Not that it bothered me. It wasn't any sort of problem. Just sometimes, late in the evening usually, if I was sitting up late, reading or going over papers. Not even then most times. Just occasionally, walking back and forward — there are people who do that. Pace around when they're upset.'

'What made you think he was upset?'

'Or thinking. Thinking on your feet, I do think that's sometimes true. Literally, that is.'

'You said "upset".'

'Yes,' Hodge said. 'I knew his marriage had broken down, if that's what you're wondering. I assure you he didn't make any secret of it. Quite the reverse. He'd tell you about his wife at the drop of a hat. He was really bitter. That's why I was astonished he was killed at home. I mean, in the house he'd shared with her. Was he trying for some kind of reconciliation? And then things went wrong?'

'It's too early yet, sir, to say what happened.'

'Was his wife there . . . when it happened?'

'As I say, early days.'

'It just seemed the likeliest . . . When I heard, that's what I thought at once. From what I read of these things, a close relative can be the obvious suspect, that's often the case, isn't it?'

Evidently, his reading hadn't brought Hodge across the notion that the police were in the information getting-not-giving business. Meldrum eased himself round so that he could go on staring at him in silence without getting a crick in his neck. Through a rattle of blinks, Hodge stared back.

'How long has Mr Ashton been living upstairs?' Meldrum asked at last.

'It must be a year. He came last summer. But you've talked to the neighbours, surely they told you that?' For the moment, he seemed out of the apologising habit.

'Just a year,' Meldrum said, and paused as if he was thinking about that. 'Do you know all your neighbours to talk to, Mr Hodge?'

'Yes. Some more, of course, others less. But yes.'

When his daughter Betty was getting married, Meldrum finally, years after the separation, had got round to selling the bungalow. Not a usual arrangement, the man staying on in the family home when the marriage broke up, but then Carole was an unusual woman. I'm the one who walked out not you, she'd said. When he put the house on the market, it turned out to be worth a surprising amount more than they'd paid for it all those years before. He'd split the profit with Carole, and given her money for Betty, knowing his daughter would take money more comfortably from her mother than from him. With what was left, he'd bought a flat off Leith Walk. But he hadn't talked to any of his new neighbours, not in the nearly two years he'd been there.

'Nodding if you pass on the stair, saying hello. Is that what you mean?' he asked.

'More than that.' And when Meldrum kept a sceptical silence, Hodge explained, 'We had to repair the roof. You know what that involves — discussing what to do, going over estimates, settling a dispute with the builder. The McConnells on the first floor used to host our meetings. Wouldn't hear of anyone else doing it. And people brought wine. That's when we all got to know one another.'

'When would this be?'

'It must be . . .' He calculated, raised his brows in surprise. 'Astonishing! It must be all of fifteen years ago. It doesn't seem half so long, not until you work it out. But it's been a very stable group. I suppose that's surprising too, all of us still here fifteen years later. Except the Stewarts, of course, they were the ones who sold to Brian.' As an idea struck him, he nodded, almost twinkled. 'Ah, I see. You're going to say that doesn't account for knowing Brian. But it does! Like a village, that's what the Stewarts used to call us. And Brian is — was such a nice man, he fitted in to what was already there. The McConnells had him in for coffee the day after he moved in. Doesn't sound a bit like Edinburgh, does it? But, of course, Sam and Marie are from the West.'

In local parlance, this meant nothing more exotic than the west coast of Scotland, more particularly in reference to people from Glasgow, by repute a more open breed than those native to the opposite coast. Moved by the same sense of having started too late in the day, Meldrum had had enough of the village people for the moment.

'Even so, would you say you got to know Mr Ashton better than the other neighbours did?'

'I couldn't really be sure, but I shouldn't think so. He had dinner at the McConnells' more than once, I know. As I say, he was very outgoing.'

'And he talked about his wife?'

'I don't want to be libellous—' Hodge said, leaning forward. BUT hung in the air.

'Don't worry about it. Anything that might help, you're supposed to tell us.'

'She couldn't stop having affairs. One man after another, according to Brian, more than just being promiscuous. Nymphomaniac was the word Brian used – old-fashioned perhaps, considering the way they all behave now. But I suppose if you were the husband, you'd be pretty old-fashioned about it. I certainly would. He told me there had been one man too many, and that had been the last straw. He walked out on her.' Hodge sat back in his chair. 'But I expect you already know all that.'

'Did he say who this man was? The one who made him walk out.'

'No.'

'Well, did you get the impression he thought this man was more serious than the others?'

'I just assumed he'd lost patience. Last straw, that's what he said.'

'Did he say anything to suggest to you that he believed the relationship with this man was still going on?'

Hodge shook his head. 'But he didn't go into details at all, to be fair. Too much of a gentleman. Or is that word old-fashioned too?'

First glance put him in his thirties, second glance in his forties, listen to him talk you'd think he was ninety, Meldrum thought.

In the pause, Shields said, 'Did you ask him why he left instead of throwing her out?'

'Why would I?' Hodge sounded offended. Since the question wasn't unreasonable, Meldrum could only put it down to the Shields effect, brusque and unvarnished.

'Well,' Shields said, 'she was the one doing the sleeping around, according to him.'

Meldrum decided to call a halt. As he got up, he said, 'If you think of anything else, we'd be grateful if you got in touch, Mr Hodge.'

'Poor Brian,' Hodge said as he showed them out. 'I still can hardly believe it. It just doesn't seem like him.'

They tramped up the remaining flight in silence. Shields hadn't gone into the flat in the morning, knowing that Meldrum would want to be there when they took their first look at it. Now he used the keys that had been found on the body to open Ashton's door.

'Well,' he said, stepping aside and following Meldrum into the flat, 'there you go, eh? Ashton's wife was telling porkies.'

'Maybe.'

'How maybe?'

Meldrum walked through one high-ceilinged room full of light after another, three of them, sparsely furnished though what there was looked expensive. Dining table and eight chairs, easy chairs in leather, the television, a computer in the smallest room, the desk it was on, a music centre in the living room, stuff like that, all had the appearance of being newly acquired. There were some prints, three paintings, one of them very large, jars, carvings, all of which could have come from the family home he'd left, but again might have been been bought for the flat; and another desk plus two chairs in the hall old enough in appearance to be antiques, with a sheen on the wood and a craftsmanship the ex-carpenter in Meldrum admired; that again could have come with him from the house or been recently bought. Meldrum had no idea what it might all be worth; enough, though, if money was a motive. Plenty there, at least, together with the value of the flat, for the lawyers to argue over. Under Scots law, whether or not Ashton had left a will, the wife would be entitled to a share of his estate.

'Lying bitch didn't say he'd walked out on her, did she?' Having trailed Meldrum through the flat, Shields spoke from the door of the bedroom. 'And she didn't tell us she was screwing around.'

After seeing the room in which Ashton had been found dead the previous day, the bedroom in the flat came as an interesting contrast. It was long but narrow, which gave it a more cramped feeling than the other rooms. There were two doors on the left-hand wall, one lying open to an en suite bathroom put in, Meldrum guessed, as part of a modernising improvement. In the process, a slice had been carved off the room, which accounted for the effect of narrowness. The bed was made and had a dark blue cover drawn across it. There was one small mirror on the wall above a long chest of drawers with nothing on top apart from a pair of hairbrushes pushed together, a white crumpled handkerchief and a pile of coins that might have been change emptied out of a pocket. A room to give a masculine impression, almost spartan. Hard to believe the man who had slept here was the same one who'd designed for himself and his wife an extravagant womb of pink enclosing draperies.

If he had designed it, of course; for that too they had only Toni Ashton's word.

'She could be telling the truth,' Meldrum said.

'You think Hodge was telling lies?' Shields's tone made no secret of how absurd that seemed, but no sooner was the dismissal out of his mouth than he saw the point. 'Oh, right . . . He's just repeating what Ashton told him. You think Ashton was having him on?'

Meldrum slid open the drawers one by one. Most of them were empty. The top one had two or three sets of keys and a wallet. As he riffled through it, he said, 'He could have been.' There was the usual plastic tucked into the slots and half a dozen twenty-pound notes folded in the back.

'Yeah, you can see he wouldn't want to admit his wife booted him out. All the same, same thing for her, when you think about it. If he was telling the truth to Hodge, you can see why she'd tell a few lies to us, she wouldn't want us to know what she was like. I mean if she was a nympho. If she was a nympho, he'd have a reason for leaving.' He grinned suddenly, 'Bloody good reason for staying as well.' When Meldrum didn't respond, he frowned seriously and said, 'Her story is she threw him out, right? Well, she never said why. Not properly. You didn't ask her.'

'Nothing here,' Meldrum said. 'I'll go through the desk. You check round for anywhere else worth a look.'

Before they did either, though, he remembered the second door. Behind it he found a walk-in wardrobe. He snapped on the light and looked round. The space on the left was taken up by a high shelf with below it ironed shirts on hangers and a dozen or so pairs of shoes lined under them on the floor. At the end of the shirts, there were three shelves with sweaters and jerseys in piles, and below them a set of three narrow drawers that slid out in turn to reveal brown socks, black socks, sports socks. A wooden bar with coat hooks was on the back wall, a vest hung from one of them, from another a rack laden with ties. The whole length of the right-hand side, divided by a wooden partition with a long bar fixed on either side, was taken up with hangers of suits and jackets and trousers.

It was less a matter of being thorough than idle impulse which made him sweep back half a dozen of the hangers and look behind them.

He stood for a while, then went out and told Shields, who was turning over CDs beside the music centre, 'Never mind those. Go and take a look in the wardrobe in there.'

In the space behind the suits hung a row of women's clothes, dresses, skirts, blouses.

Shields put his hand in and slid some of the dresses aside as if searching for another layer of secrets. He peered in at the blank wall, then slid the dresses back into place. 'There you are,' he said. 'That's why his wife threw him out.'

'Looks all new gear to me,' Meldrum said. 'Maybe he bought it when he came here.'

'What I'm saying! So before that he had to use the wife's stuff. Imagine if she came in and found the poor bugger all dressed up in front of the mirror. Unreal, eh? You'd have a right red face. Not that I'd ever—' Then added with the air of a man changing the subject, 'Bet there's underwear in a drawer somewhere.'

CHAPTER SEVEN

As Henry Stanley soaped his hands, he inspected his tongue in the mirror and found it gratifyingly clean and healthy-looking. It was long and thick and very red as if packed with blood. Good enough to eat, he thought, and put it away again as there was a sound of flushing water and the door of the nearest cubicle opened.

The former occupant of the cubicle came and stood beside him. As he turned on the tap and went through the ritual of hand-washing, they looked at one another in the mirror. Eye to eye, they were the same height, an unusual experience for Stanley, who at just over five feet had to look up at most men.

'Thank you for your generous words,' Lord Crombie said.

Stanley's cheeks felt stiff as he forced reluctant muscles into a smile. 'No question of generosity. Your career speaks for itself.'

Crombie contemplated this as with precise little shakes he scattered the last drops of water from his fingertips. He pulled out a paper towel. 'All the same,' he said, 'you expressed it very well.'

Stanley restored the smile which had faded. It wasn't done without effort, but he was a believer in the importance of will-power.

'I envy you,' he said. 'You have had a ringside seat at more than one big *cause célèbre*.'

When Crombie instead of answering raised an eyebrow and slightly narrowed his eyes, Stanley had a moment of self-doubt. Immediate and vertiginous, it made him wonder if he'd used *cause célèbre* correctly, of course he had, or if putting 'big' in front of it might be a solecism, or even if there had been something wrong with his pronunciation, but how could that be? Unless, horrid possibility, when he spoke the foreign phrase some lingering trace of his original Birmingham accent, eradicated long ago in ordinary speech, somehow undetected by him crept up to the surface. Just for that moment, it didn't matter that it wasn't his nature to suffer from self-doubt. If you stepped over a cliff you fell, passing ledges bushes trees absurd ideas in falling. That was nature too, a law, like gravity.

'I wouldn't,' Crombie said, pulling out and unfolding another paper towel, 'call it being in a ringside seat. A judge is *in* the ring. In fact, he is the ringmaster.'

'Cracking the whip.'

' 'I wouldn't,' Crombie began for a second time, just as unsmilingly, 'put it like that.' He threw the towel in the bin. 'Nasty thing!' Stanley took a beat to recognise he was referring to the towel. 'Not so nasty as a hand-drier, but nasty enough. I should think they might do you better than that.'

This conversation bothered Stanley at intervals for the rest of the day, and was still prickling like a heat rash when, having encountered Meldrum that evening, he should have had more immediate things on his mind.

It had been an evening for encounters. In a bar he'd rarely been into off the upper end of the High Street, he met Mary Preston and, almost as soon as she'd said hello, the door opened and Cormack and Paterson came in arguing about which of them had lost a bet. Cormack gave in first and bought the drinks. He insisted on getting them in for him as well and for Mary Preston, and that was it, of course. They were still seated round a table in the corner an hour later and he was just opening his mouth to make an excuse and go, when Detective Inspector Jim Meldrum put in an appearance, looming and scowling above the heads of the crowd.

'See who's come in?' Paterson leaned over the table. 'At the door. Don't make it bloody obvious you're looking!'

'Is this where he drinks?' Cormack wondered.

'Search me,' Paterson said. 'I'm never usually in here.'

'If it is,' Mary Preston said, 'he'll not be pleased to see us.'

Body language, Stanley thought, sitting back and watching as the three detective constables bent heads and inclined closer.

'Oh God,' Cormack muttered, 'he's not coming over, is he?'

'Very funny,' Mary Preston said. 'That'll be the day.'

Her voice faded as she realised Meldrum was standing behind her.

'Dr Stanley,' he said. He put his drink on the table. 'Dr Stanley, I presume.' He dangled a chair he must have collected on the way over, and set it down carefully between Stanley and Mary Preston. 'I never thought this was a place anybody came to.'

'Won't you join us?' Stanley said.

Meldrum sat down and stared round the table. Nobody said anything. After a moment, he picked up his pint and drank slowly so that Stanley could see corded neck muscles pulsing as he swallowed. He set the drink down, and seemed to lapse into his own thoughts. The level in the glass had fallen by a third.

'Three police,' Meldrum said suddenly into the silence. 'You're in funny company, Henry.'

This wasn't strictly true. Stanley cultivated police company, and claimed to learn useful things from it. He said, 'One of them's pretty.'

'Should I curtsey?' Mary Preston asked. She sounded more offended than amused, but it might have come out more sharply than she intended, for now she took up her glass and stared into it intently.

'I'd pay to see that,' Cormack said. 'Curtsey's a lovely word. Don't you think it has a dirty sound to it? . . . Curtsey.'

'We all know you've a small vocabulary,' Paterson said.

'You should see it extended.' Cormack grinned from Mary Preston to Stanley. 'One pretty. And the other two of us are ugly buggers.'

'I'd worked that out on my own,' Meldrum said.

Conversation lapsed.

A social animal with a low tolerance for silence, Stanley told about his morning with Lord Crombie, naturally omitting what mattered to him, the encounter in the lavatory. Anger and self-doubt were his own business. 'He was giving this year's MacMillan Lecture. Filled the big lecture hall in the new building, staff and students, of course, but a lot of the general public there as well. The Faculty did a bit of mailing around, which helped, and it was advertised in the *Scotsman*. I was chairing him.'

'Little Lord Fondletheboy,' Cormack said. 'What was he talking about?'

'The influence of sentencing policy on crime.'

'Bring back hanging, eh?' Cormack said. 'If they did, he'd be stringing them up right and left.'

'The Hanging Judge,' Stanley said appreciatively. 'There was a tendency in that direction, but he couldn't quite bring himself to break cover. If he did, can you imagine the headlines?'

'Fuck headlines,' Paterson said. 'It's what most of the punters want.'

'If the bleeding hearts saw some of the things we have to look at,' Cormack agreed, 'they'd want it, too.'

'They'd think different,' Paterson said.

'You're right about what most people want,' Stanley agreed. 'And the majority in favour of capital punishment is even higher in the United States than it is here. As high as eighty per cent according to a survey in 1994. But it doesn't work, of course.'

'How?' Paterson could make a single word sound like a challenge to come outside. 'How not?'

'Simple arithmetic. Capital punishment started up again in the United States in 1977. And since then the numbers executed have gone up year after year. No sign of a deterrent effect there.'

'Something wrong with that,' Mary Preston said, then softened the blunt statement with 'Isn't there?', seeking agreement the way women do when around testosterone. 'They could be executing more of them, doesn't mean there are more murders every year.'

'Could you give us that in English?' Paterson wondered sardonically.

'I suppose you know the figures,' she said to Stanley. 'I don't know the figures. All I'm saying is that they could be executing more murderers every year, because they found it worked and the murder rate was going down.'

'I didn't think you'd be for bringing back hanging,' he said to her.

Not that he'd ever discussed it with her, just that he'd have taken it for granted not favouring capital punishment would have been another point of difference between her and Paterson and Cormack, like being pretty and smart and ambitious.

'Like Donnie said,' she nodded at Cormack, 'some of the things we see.'

'That kid down at the foreshore, last year wasn't it?' Paterson said suddenly. 'That was bad.'

'What one?' Cormack asked.

'I'd have hung the guy that did that. Done it myself. No problem.'

'Where was this again?'

'At Joppa. On the shore. You know those big concrete blocks left over from the war to stop tanks or that? He was all folded up and pushed in between two of them.'

'I wasn't there.'

'I was there. He'd a hole where his nose should have been. The rats had it off.'

'That's it,' Mary Preston said, standing up. 'I'm out of here.'

'Safe home,' Stanley said. He turned to Meldrum, 'I suppose you'll believe in capital punishment, too.'

Meldrum watched Mary Preston walking away. With part of his mind, he registered the tight jut of her backside; it had been a long time since he'd slept with a woman. 'Not any more,' he said.

Paterson poured the dregs of his whisky into his pint. He spoke slowly, as if his thoughts were coming back from somewhere far off. 'They should've stuck him in a room with some of us were there that night. Give us time to put our kicking boots on, they wouldn't have needed a rope.'

When he thought about it afterwards, Meldrum couldn't exactly recall how it was that he'd found himself going off with Henry Stanley to continue the evening. They made an unlikely pairing, the detective more inches over six feet than the dapper little man was over five. Before that night, they were acquaintances, certainly nothing like friends. Stanley had first approached the police to suggest he might be able to help with a series of assaults on schoolgirls. He was in the Sociology Department of one of the city's newer universities. Before that, he'd lectured in anthropology at Edinburgh University until he'd quarrelled with his Head of Department. The story of the quarrel had filtered down from Baird, the Chief Constable. He'd been at a dinner party where that same Head of Department had called Stanley 'My biggest mistake', and confided, 'Arrogant and impossible little man'. Policemen having suspicious minds, there were at once advocates of the notion Stanley'd come forward to help because he'd attacked the girls himself. The sceptics objected that he didn't match any of the descriptions and at least two of the girls were taller than him. 'Could have been on stilts,' had been the canteen answer to that one.

Even though the schoolgirls' investigation had run into the sand and was attracting fierce press criticism, Meldrum, though not directly involved, had dismissed as contemptuously as any of them the idea that Stanley might actually have something useful to offer. He'd shared, too, the general amusement and irritation when the late Detective Chief Superintendent Billy Ord, for his own reasons, had accepted the offer.

From the first, though, the tabloids found Henry Stanley made good copy and gave plenty of space to the predictions he took care to share with them about the attacker's age, occupation, family background, probable area of residence. When the man was finally caught, as so often it was by chance in the middle of an attack. All the same, the fit between the culprit and the predictions was remarkable. Stanley had made his point. Since then a lot of water had gone under the bridge, and he'd become for the Edinburgh force the nearest thing they had to the fashionable notion of a profiler.

'I had the feeling you'd had about enough of those two,' Stanley said, bringing back a tray with two whiskies, one each, and a pint of Belhaven for Meldrum. 'A little of them goes a long way. Anyway, it was getting too noisy. It's quieter in here. I hate having to shout. Don't you hate having to shout when you're trying to have a conversation?'

Meldrum looked round. Easy chairs and low tables. Very comfortable, it wouldn't be hard to fall asleep. It might be the lounge of an hotel. It looked more like that than anything else. Two beefy shirtsleeved men with the air of residents sat heads together at a table near the door, while sitting by himself a white-haired man alternated sips from a glass of what might have been gin with crisps taken in turn from one of three bags lined up in front of him. Meldrum wondered if the crisps were different flavours. It wouldn't make sense if they were all the same flavour. Unless the guy wanted three packets and couldn't be bothered getting up and down for a new one every time. He'd no memory of coming in here. Was it an hotel lounge? He couldn't ask Stanley; sign of weakness. I'll see when we go outside, he thought.

'You were there that night, too, weren't you?' Stanley asked. 'At Joppa. When they found poor little Sam Chaney's body.'

'In my time, I've seen a lot of bodies.'

Meldrum sipped his whisky and listened to what he'd just said. He didn't like the sound of it. 'In my time', fuck it, what kind of way was that to talk? What was it, a boast, self-pity? Either way, too loud, not his style, too loud altogether. One excuse: it wasn't every day a man went to his ex-wife's wedding. Another: he'd been drinking on an empty stomach since he'd left Shields after they'd run the toothcomb through Brian Ashton's flat.

'Keith Chaney's son. The dead boy they found at Joppa that Paterson was talking about.'

'So?' Meldrum blinked and yawned. But then he said, 'Keith Chaney? The boy's father? How come you remember his name?'

'Because I've written the case up. I wanted to tell you it's just been published in the *Journal of Forensic Psychology*. A happy coincidence seeing you tonight.' He nodded at the whisky. 'I asked for the rarest malt they had. By way of celebration. I think what I have to say about the mentality of a killer and child abuser will make a stir. I'd like to send you a copy. Shall I?'

'If you do, I won't read it.' *Celebration*, he thought with disgust.

'My biggest regret is that I never met the man. That first time when you told me about him the hair went up on the back of my neck. Even before we knew he was the killer, I told you how strange a type he was. And after it was over, of course, I spoke to everyone I possibly could. But it's not the same.'

'He wasn't interesting.'

'How can you say that?'

'None of them are interesting,' Meldrum said.

'Murderers?'

'None of the lot of them. They're crap human beings.'

Stanley gave a little bark of laughter at this, but at the same time his brows drew together in a frown.

'We don't have to like them,' he said. 'It's not about liking them. It's about understanding them.'

'You wouldn't want to have a drink with any of them.'

'Not with Leopold and Loeb? Well, more Leopold, of course.' Stanley was showing his annoyance. 'Or Herbert Mills, who smiled at the judge when he was sentenced to hang? He was only nineteen. Or Ted Bundy? Or Peter Kurten?' He paused, perhaps casting around for one that Meldrum would be sure to recognise. 'Or what about Brady? I mean, *Ian* Brady.'

'None of them. Or Hitler. That's *Adolf* Hitler.'

'You can't learn about disease from dissecting the healthy. But if you go deeply enough into disease, you learn what makes for health also. My first degree was in psychology,' Stanley said, 'and I've spent a lifetime studying human nature. It is vital that experts are given access to these people. If society is too punitive to be interested in cure, then at least out of self-protection it ought to care about prevention. My God, sometimes it's hard to believe we're on the threshold of a new millennium. In Russia, even now, they don't set a date for an execution. No one is told when it's going to be done. A bullet in the back of the head in secret, and the relatives aren't even allowed to claim the body. Or take what happens in Japan . . .'

But Meldrum was asking himself: how could he have been so stupid, what kind of masochist was he, why had he gone to Carole's wedding? The morning seemed a lifetime distant. Maybe he'd gone because he had to see her married with his own eyes. Like in the war when the next of kin got the telegram; you don't believe in a death unless you're there. Who had said that? The dead man's wife, Toni Ashton, red hair thick as a rope you could wrap around your hand.

'— deserved to die, because of what he did to Sam Chaney, didn't you think that?'

'Not me,' Meldrum said. His heart pounded in his ears.

Stanley stared at him in surprise. 'I was only saying at bottom you'd be like the rest of them. It's what policemen really believe.'

'I went to the house to arrest him for murder.' He could carry his drink; he could walk straight; he didn't slur his words. The lie he'd lived with for a year came automatically to his tongue. 'When I got there, he was dead.'

'That's the point I'm making,' Stanley said. 'What a waste!'

'You'd have preferred he went to prison.'

'Yes. Where we could have tried to understand what makes a man behave like that.'

'Prove he was mad, you mean.' If he had drunk too much, he didn't show it. He never showed it. 'Put him in Carstairs with all the other mental cases. Study him for ten years, and say he's cured.' He'd have been all right if he hadn't looked back when he was leaving the wedding reception. 'Let him out, because he won't be a danger to anyone.' At the top table beside her new husband, Carole had been watching him go. Their eyes had met and it had been as if the crowded room had emptied, leaving the two of them alone. 'And then when he fucks some kid up the arse and kills him, take him back into Carstairs and study him some more.'

He shouldn't have looked back.

'If that's the price that had to be paid,' Stanley said, 'yes.'

A year ago his daughter Betty had told him, every time you go to visit mother and sit and talk with her as if nothing was changed between you, she's upset for days. That had amazed him. What would have happened if he'd ignored Betty and gone on visiting Carole, sitting at the other side of the fire from her, talking about his work the way he'd never managed when they were married? What would have happened if after Betty said, leave her alone, he'd gone the other way and asked Carole to marry him again?

'What?'

'I'll put it as plainly as you like,' Stanley said. 'We are creatures of reason or we're nothing. Whatever the price of knowledge, we have to pay it.'

What would have happened? Been told, no, and made a fool of himself. Been told, yes, and thought, what the hell have I done? A fool anyway even to think about it now. Over and done.

'Price? We're not talking about money. Do you know what that bastard *did* to the boy? This isn't about money.'

Gentle Jesus meek and mild if I should die before I wake my soul to take my soul to take. Night after night for weeks after finding Sam Chaney he'd prayed the prayer he'd learned as a child prayed as an unbeliever a talisman against the dark so that he could sleep.

'It's not about *what* he did,' Stanley said. 'Of course, I know about the what, I've read the forensics as well as everything else. It's about why. The absolute primacy of the need to know why, that's the credo I've lived my life by. I don't apologise for it.'

'Credo,' Meldrum said. He considered the word. 'Tell you something.' With a forefinger, he beckoned Stanley to lean closer. 'The door was lying open and I found him in the front room. He was listening to music. And I'd just come from the beach where we'd found Sam Chaney.'

'Do you remember which piece of music?' Stanley wondered. 'That would be very . . . But you said he was dead when you got there! You've always—'

'Lied,' Meldrum said. 'You want the truth? I'll tell you the truth.'

When he'd finished, they sat looking at one another in silence.

Credo. Something to live by. Carole had told him one time about a priest who'd recounted a story about an Irish archbishop to a group of children. Primary Two, for heaven's sake, Carole had said, they had no idea what he was talking about. This Irish archbishop had been vehemently opposed to the belief in papal infallibility, but then, at the very instant it was declared as Church doctrine, he had leaped to his feet and cried out, credo! credo! That means I believe! she'd explained. Good career move, Meldrum had said.

Law. Justice. Those were words too. Like credo. Like vocation. Not job, vocation. He was a policeman by vocation. Take that away and he had nothing.

'So now two of us know,' Meldrum said.

CAT IN A TREE

patriarch.

Strange, like any word when you looked at it on its own. Say it over and it lost meaning. *patriarch patriarch patriarch.* What did it mean? He thought of his own father.

'I think not,' he said aloud. 'I don't think so.'

He had slept badly since the murder. Broken nights, not because of guilt, but some mix of other feelings. He would lie and try to identify them, fear of punishment must be one and for another an excitement indistinguishable from pleasure, and more than anything a sense of himself as fluid, capable now of anything. He had become an unknown quantity, unknown even to himself. He puzzled over that lack of guilt. Did it mean he was a worse man than he had imagined himself to be? Killing another human being wasn't something he'd envisaged himself, that imagined self made up of accidents and fragments, ever doing. He knew that in this he was unusual, since reading and observation suggested that imagining the death of a rival in love or a thug in the street was a common fantasy. He ran through in his mind images of small boys play-fighting, karate chops and mimed kicks, the firing of guns, and even sword play of the light sabre star-warring kind, clumsier than Flynn or Fairbanks, elegance being out of fashion. Games like that weren't games he'd ever played as a child. Yet he'd killed. Killed his man. He groaned aloud and his wife turned towards him, sighed and sank more deeply into sleep. The red numbers on the clock face glittered half one.

He'd followed her up a path. Storm doors were folded back. He'd listened to the scratch and knock of metal as she'd searched with the key to get it into the lock. A plane of darkness, a glint of reflected light from the street, he'd heard more than seen the door open. After a moment, stupid to hesitate, he'd come this far, some animal reaction made him want to avoid the black cave, he had followed her into the hall and up a flight of stairs. 'Why don't you put on the light?' A dim shape moving ahead of him, she'd laughed without answering. It was even darker on the landing and he'd stood unmoving, one foot still on the last step of the stair, listening as he leaned forward. Suddenly, there was a patch of lighter darkness. A door had been opened. He stepped up on to the landing. At the same time, air rushed from his open mouth; he'd been holding his breath. The light went on through the doorway and he saw the woman standing with her back to him beside a bed swathed in great swoops of curtain. She had found her way across the room in the dark to put on the bedside lamp. He said, 'Your friend likes pink.' The thin lightness of his voice surprised him. 'This *is* a friend's house, isn't it?' Twisting round to unzip her skirt, the woman didn't answer. 'Or is this your own place after all?' She let the skirt slide down her body to the floor. As she stepped out of it, he asked, 'Tell me you don't have a husband hiding somewhere.' He heard this strange thin voice, as if from lungs emptied of all but a spoonful of air, and knew something was wrong, almost knew what it was, the breadth of white shoulders, the shape of the back, as she turned, thumbs hooked into her pants. 'Clever you,' she said, and pulled them down, white pants edged with lace, 'here he is.'

He sat bolt upright in bed. As soon as he heard the scream from the street, he knew what it was. Scrambling out from under the downie, he padded across on bare feet to the window. He pulled the curtain open a cautious couple of inches, no more than would give an angle to peep through without being seen.

Behind him, his wife's voice murmured from the bed, 'What is it? What's that awful noise?' She sounded still more than half asleep.

In the pool of light under the lamp at the gate, a tall thin youth in a black T-shirt was dancing on one leg and squealing in pain.

'Like a stuck pig,' he said. 'Not that I've ever heard a pig being stuck.' He spoke without looking round. 'I read, though, that it sounds human.' He smiled down at the spectacle under the lamp. 'Squealing like a stuck human.'

In the morning when he went out to see, glancing around to make sure he was unobserved, a finger run along the metal of the basket base found an indentation. On a succession of Saturday nights, the bottom had been kicked out of the waste basket that was fixed to the lamp by the gate. Each time he reported it, the council, who took good care of the expensive districts, would replace the basket, only to have the base kicked out of it again the next Saturday. The police took note of what was happening, but were never there when it was done since the drunk, homeward bound, seemed to strike at any time between about eleven and two in the morning. The litter that fell through the basket and lay on the pavement, the senselessness of causing that kind of damage, the cost of it to the community, the whole thing caused him disproportionate irritation. His wife told him not to upset himself, but he had an obsessional streak and caught himself thinking about it even at work. It began to feel as if he was the target of some malicious vendetta.

When the previous Saturday it had happened yet again, he had thought hard and taken the decision not to report it. All week he had collected the scatter of rubbish from the pavement and out of the gutter and carried it in a pail round the house to the bin. Keeping the place tidy, he told his wife, and ignored her protests that it was undignified.

Feeling the dent in the metal rim, he thought, that took a full-blooded kick, it's a wonder the little bastard didn't cut his foot off at the ankle; and paced off light of heart through morning mist thinning with the first heat of the day to collect the Sunday papers. On a fine morning like this, he liked to make a walk of it, briskly all the way down to Kay's shop in Morningside Road.

It was on his way back with the fat wad of papers tucked under his arm that he knew something wasn't right. He wasn't a petrolhead. With one part of his mind, he could still savour the word, since, though suddenly uneasy, he didn't yet know how serious a turn things were about to take. Petrolhead: a car fanatic. Car addict. A new formation, compare acidhead. He loved the ramifications of words. German made new words all the time by that kind of compounding of elements. He wasn't a petrolhead. He didn't pay much attention to cars as they went by . . .

But there it was again, a large red car, with a glimpse of the driver, almost certainly a man, at the wheel. He was sure it had already passed him twice on his way down to the shops, once on one side of the road and then again going the other way. Chances were he wouldn't have remarked it – even on a Sunday morning, there were plenty of cars around – except that he was almost certain it was this same car which had been parked opposite when he came out of his gate. Normally, he wouldn't have noticed, but this morning he'd paused to examine the broken waste-paper basket on the lamp-post.

He broke stride as the car approached on the other side of the road, then turned and followed it with his gaze all the way down the hill until it was held up by the lights at Morningside Cross. As they changed to green, it went left round the corner out of sight.

When he got home and saw it parked in the same place, facing the wrong way on the road opposite his gate, his heart sank. Who was it who'd written, live long enough and all the clichés, 'long in the tooth' and all the rest of them, turn true? He felt his heart sink like a stone in a bog. It was so quiet in the hot still morning that as he came nearer he heard the hum of the glass being slid down. A hand flopped out of the open window and beckoned to him. As he crossed the road, the passenger door swung open to admit him.

Lying awake during the night, he had wondered if he was a worse man than he had ever believed himself to be. Now, he took pleasure in finding he was a more reckless one.

'You know me.' It was a statement not a question.

'You're mistaken,' he said.

'That's why you got into the car.'

The grossly enormous man behind the wheel smelled of an oniony sweat. His shirtsleeves were rolled up over massive forearms, and the shirt was dark with moisture over the breasts and from the armpit to the waist.

'I can see why you might think that. But it was you who called me over. I wondered why. Now I see you've mistaken me for someone else.'

'I was at Crombie's lecture. You were introducing him, and you stumbled over a word. You'd seen me.'

'At Lord Crombie's lecture?'

'You saw me.'

'No,' and that was the truth. Introducing Crombie, he'd looked around to gather attention, but only really seen two or three faces randomly picked out as as sympathetic. As for when Crombie was actually droning on, for the most part he'd stared at his hands folded in his lap, careful occasionally to look up in appreciation, smile, just a little, not wanting to claim any attention that belonged to the speaker, look thoughtful. And while taking questions as chairman after the talk, he'd paid attention only to raised hands. It wasn't his way to stare into an audience.

'It would be easier if we were straight with one another,' the fat man said.

'I take your word you were there. I didn't see you. And what difference would it have made to me if I had, since I've no idea who you are?' This was also true.

To twist round, the fat man had to lever one great ham forward and force his whole bulk to turn. With the effort, sweat billowed from him and a sickening smell of grease and fried onion crammed the interior. Close up, the soaked breasts were as large as a woman's.

'I'm the one that knows what you've done,' he gasped. Above the furious red slab of face the pink scalp shone between damp spikes of mouse-brown hair.

'And what would that be?' Jeering the question: it seemed this man he was becoming reacted with anger not fright when challenged.

'If it comes to it,' the fat man said, 'I won't be the only one. Don't fool yourself. It won't be my word against yours. You were watched. All the time, in a place like that people are watching you. Don't you know that? And then you and Brian went off together.' He sighed and subsided back sprawling against the door. 'You know what I'm talking about. I wasn't sure before. Now I'm sure.'

If he had given himself away, that was understandable. It wasn't a matter of self-control. Unprepared for the word 'Brian', he had been taken by surprise. He couldn't blame himself for that. Watched? He saw himself standing in front of the fire in the hall of the house on the estate. No one there. Then the girl on the landing with the head of a bird. The man with the streak of white in his hair who'd talked about paintings. What had she — *he*, the dead man, called him? Our host.

'Did he send you?'

His lips felt numb as if he'd taken a shot at the dentist's. He was in shock. 'Nobody sent me.'

He had to think, faster than he ever had, think for his life.

'Suppose I believe you, suppose you were watching, hidden somewhere. Suppose others were too? Whatever was going on, it was bad.'

The fat man frowned and wheezed, and asked at last, 'Hiding?'

'Out there in the middle of the country. Safe behind those high estate walls. What was it? Sex? Drugs? Something worse? And then we blundered in and I was a stranger. He couldn't let me stay.'

'Ashton couldn't let you stay?'

'The one with,' he brushed a hand back from his forehead, 'the streak of white hair. Don't play games with me.'

The fat man stared back in silence, mouth lying open. Looking at him, his shock hardened into something edged and savage. At a sudden thought, he snatched the door open and got out. He swung it shut with a bang, then waited. The car dipped and rose as the fat man struggled free.

'If you have anything else to say to me, you can say it out here.'

Without waiting to see if his instructions were followed, he walked away, but could only move slowly as in a nightmare, so that soon he heard the fat man's breath whistling just behind him.

'Look!' the voice gasped. The fat man had unbuttoned his shirt and now pulled at the vest until it rode up over his belly. 'No recorders. Not on me, not in the car. Is that what was bothering you? I can recognise a bad conscience.'

He forced himself to step up the pace. Listening to the wheezing chuckle choke off into a fight for breath gave him a sense of being in control. He took courage. 'You were at a party, call it that. And you claim you saw me. Doing what that was so terrible? Leaving with someone called Brian?'

'Ashton.' Getting the name out, bubbles popped at the corners of his lips. 'Didn't recognise him, not dressed like that. But was something. Soon as read how he'd been found, knew. Seen him with you.'

'You didn't recognise him. But then you read something in the papers and suddenly you're sure it was him. As for me, you couldn't recognise me — you don't know me, I don't know you. I think this is all your imagination!'

For a moment, he felt invulnerable.

But the fat man caught him by the elbow and stopped him in full stride, like an anchor. Glancing down, he saw the big fingers folded right round his arm. With that grip memory flooded back. He knew where the fat man had seen him. Not in the estate house. In the casino. The fat man who'd wanted an argument. And grabbed him by the arm.

'*Of course*, I recognised you that night.' Giving the arm a playful shake, 'You don't want to be recognised, you shouldn't get your face in the papers.'

He let himself be pulled into movement, walking back towards the car, resisting would only have emphasised their difference in physical strength. He wondered if a neighbour might be watching from a window. Turning to urge: come and see! there's something odd going on.

'I can't prove you killed Ashton,' the fat man said. Moving slowly, he breathed more easily. 'But I saw you going off with him. I don't think you want me telling that to the police.'

Holding his nerve to his own admiration, he said, 'If you've read about me, you'll know I'm not without friends in the police.'

With a sigh of relief, the fat man rested his weight against the car. 'The police don't have to come into it. And you can forget about anybody else seeing you. You're right about that. You just have me. And I've got nothing to lose. I'm in trouble.'

'What kind of trouble?'

'Wrong question. Not what. Ask me how much trouble.'

'How much?'

'A quarter of a million.'

He laughed at the absurdity of it. 'If you're trying to blackmail me, you're wasting your time. I don't have that kind of money.'

'No, but your wife has. You think I haven't gone into all this carefully?' The same playful shake of the arm, and then it was released. The fat man made his way round and opened the driver's door. 'This is a shock. You need time to work out how you're going to raise the money. Take a few days. I'll be in touch, and you can tell me then.'

As the car drove off, he took a step in pursuit, gesturing with his hand. It didn't stop.

The fat man had driven off with his Sunday papers on the passenger seat.

BOOK TWO

Masks

CHAPTER EIGHT

Even if in the end, because of Toni Ashton, Sunday turned out to be a washout as far as Meldrum was concerned, there would still be plenty going on. In every investigation, most activity went by the book. Following familiar routine, neighbours round the house in which Brian Ashton had met his death were being interviewed. The reports would be sifted for anything worth a second interview; filed and collated into the computer. In theory, then, as the record grew every piece of data should be available for cross-checking, and if there were any significant connections they should be found. In practice, it didn't work entirely like that; in the past often because of deficient or badly handled software, now mostly because of the human factor. Garbage in, garbage out: not every doorstep interview was well conducted by tired constables at the end of a long shift. Murders that were solved had a tendency to be solved early. In the first five minutes, say, the guilty party found weeping beside the body, a husband, a wife, the son of an abusive father. That kind of collision of wasted lives was good for the clear-up statistics. Failing that, it was important to do as much, as well, as early, as possible.

What Meldrum had most wanted that Sunday, however, was to put to Toni Ashton the account of their marriage break-up her husband had given his neighbour Alex Hodge. If she stuck to her version, then he needed the details of what had made her demand a separation. If, on the other hand, she admitted the husband's story was true, then he needed to know about the men in her life, and most particularly about the lover Ashton had called 'the last straw'. Who was he? Was the affair still going on? Had there ever been a confrontation between him and Brian Ashton? If he existed, questions lined up to be asked. Breaking the rules, he found himself imagining her answers as well, all of the possibilities played out as dialogues between him and the beautiful redhead, including one in which she confessed to conspiracy and murder.

When he went with Shields early on the Sunday morning to the Greenbank house, however, the bell brought no answer. Meldrum stepped back to look up and saw all the curtains upstairs were drawn. As he glanced down, two men came round the house from the back. The taller of the two had a bag over his shoulder and was carrying a camera. He broke step at sight of the detectives, while his older companion seemed entirely undisconcerted.

'Well met, Inspector,' the older one, pork-pie hat and face to match, cried cheerfully. 'Any developments?'

'What were you doing round there?'

'Trying to check if Mrs Ashton really wasn't at home. She hasn't been answering her phone.'

'She doesn't want to talk to the papers,' Shields said, 'take the hint, Stevie.'

'You could be right.' He peered up at the curtained windows. 'Think she's keeking out at us? If you tried, she might open the door.'

'If you bugger off, she might,' Meldrum said. 'Don't push your luck.'

'Couldn't stay, even if you wanted me to. We've an OD junkie's heartbroken Mammy waiting for us in the Pilton.'

'Another death knock,' the photographer said morosely. 'I hate those jobs.'

'Hello,' Shields said. 'Here's a man in a hurry.'

All four of them watched as Ivor Warren crossed the road, the old man waving a hand as if to command their attention. Pushing open the gate, he called, 'She's not here! Went off this morning.' He padded up, shook his flushed jowls at Meldrum, and said accusingly, 'I should have thought you'd have known that.'

Purely by chance, as he put it, he'd happened to be looking out of his window when the two women left about eight that morning. 'The little dark one carried out a couple of cases and put them into the boot of the car. Then Mrs Ashton came out. Two of them got into the car, Mrs Ashton driving, and off they went. I take it you wanted to see Mrs Ashton?'

'Just a minute,' Meldrum said. But already the reporter was heading down the path followed by the photographer. Twenty years of covering the crime beat for the local evening paper had taught Stevie Stephens when to beat a tactical retreat. Dourly, Meldrum watched the two men cross the road and wait for Warren at his gate.

'As I say, she's gone. Cases and all. Off on holiday again, would you think?

Even if you'd known, dare say you couldn't have stopped her, could you? Free country and all that.'

'This is a murder investigation.'

'I agree, extraordinary thing, what could she be thinking of? Did say to myself, hello! wonder if the ladies should be doing that. But never occurred to me to give you a ring, since I assumed you'd know about it. Information's the key to victory is what I was taught. But that was the navy, not the police, eh? We'd a war to fight.'

He described the car, rhyming off the colour, the make and year, even the registration number. Either he was very observant, or took an unusual interest in his beautiful neighbour. It would be useful, if things developed in that direction, to know if he'd taken note of her visitors and what opinion he'd formed of her lifestyle.

Meldrum decided that before too long, the old man would find himself tested on how much time he'd spent at that window of his. As a believer in the value of information, presumably he wouldn't mind.

CHAPTER NINE

As they left the Colinton house, Meldrum's top priority was finding Toni Ashton, and he had an idea where he might find her. If, naturally enough, she'd wanted out of the murder house, staying with her friend would have been the easiest way. A phone call to the Incident Room checked that Naomi Morgan had given the constable who'd interviewed her briefly on the Friday her home address, which turned out to be a flat in Marchmont, no more than a twenty-minute drive away.

Coming into the curve of the terrace, Meldrum was too busy thinking ahead to notice where they were. The shock of recognition came when he got out of the car. The close where Naomi Morgan lived was to the left of a ground floor flat in which every detail of a long ago murder was still vivid to him. To a young detective constable, Arthur Hull's death had been a big case. Years later Meldrum had risked his career trying to prove the innocence of the man who'd been given life for the killing. Now as he followed Shields across the pavement into the close, he was thinking, small world, small city. Given the size of Edinburgh, you were bound to come across places again, sooner or later, the places the same, maybe the reasons too. And climbing the stairs, he had the notion which had occurred to him before that everyone who lived in a city held a different map of it in mind. It just happened his was a stranger one than most, marked as it was with stains of blood.

Three doors to a landing, they checked every nameplate. As they climbed to the third floor, a woman passed them going down. Under a large brass knocker, the first door had a plate MORGAN. As Meldrum raised his hand, a voice from below said, 'I wouldn't bother.'

The woman who'd passed them had come half-way back up the flight of steps.

'What?'

She came up a few more steps. 'Is it something official?'

'We're police officers.'

'I knew it was something like that. She's not there.'

Shields grunted and began to bang on the knocker.

Meldrum asked, 'How can you be sure of that?'

'Because I've just tried.'

Shields stopped knocking. As she came up the last of the steps, the woman was fumbling in her handbag to produce a key. Her very black hair had a home-dyed look, and the cheap cloth coat was too heavy for the warm weather. 'Look for yourself if you want. You can do that, can't you, if it's official?'

Meldrum shook his head. It was tempting. In the Pilton he might have risked it; but not in a district where flats went for over a hundred thousand.

'Who are you anyway?' Shields asked. The aggressive note suggested he'd picked up on the hair and the cheap coat.

'Mrs Lynch. I come in to clean once a week.'

'On a Sunday?' Shields asked on a note of disbelief.

'I thought I might catch her. She left money because she was on holiday, but it didn't cover this week. That's why I expected her back when I came on Friday afternoon. She wasn't here, though. Is something wrong? Is she in some kind of trouble?'

'No,' Meldrum said. 'What makes you think she might be?'

Before she could answer, Shields asked, 'Did you just knock or did you go in? You must have a key.'

'Only for a Friday! That's the day I come, Friday, so she has it nice for the weekend. I wouldn't let myself in any other time.'

'Not even if she owed you money?'

'Only a week! I wouldn't go in any other time. Just because I had the key wouldn't be a reason. She trusts me. It wouldn't be right.' She hesitated. 'But you could. Just to make sure she hadn't fallen or anything?'

'Tell you what,' Meldrum said. 'If you're concerned, you go in and see for yourself. It'll be all right, since we're here.'

'My mother had a fall. She was calling for help, and the neighbours didn't hear a thing. She lay in the kitchen all night. She was ninety at the time.' With the key in the lock, she asked, 'Are you not coming in?'

'You carry on,' Meldrum said.

She disappeared inside. After a moment, Shields grinned. 'That her shouting? I think that was a shout.'

Unsmiling, Meldrum said, 'If you say so.'

Shields exchanged the grin for a scowl and followed him in.

A quick impression gave a count of five doors, all of them lying open. The first one in the longer passage took them into a living room. The general impression was severe: dark blue leather couch, a long glass table with four thin metal chairs set round it, two big paintings in dark wood frames on the wall facing the windows, one a sea harbour, the other a range of hills Meldrum almost recognised, in Sutherland maybe, a harsh landscape bare of trees. No newspapers or magazines lying around.

Mrs Lynch appeared in the doorway.

'We thought we heard you shout,' Shields said.

'She's not here. I had a look in the kitchen and bathroom and took a peep in her bedroom.'

'Is it all as tidy as this?' Meldrum asked.

'I take the hoover over it. You won't find any dust. Oh, but she's tidy right enough. She always was, but even more than she used to be. I've wondered sometimes the last few months how often she's here at all.'

'If you were getting your money, she must have been here.'

'She works, so I didn't often see her anyway. What happened usually, she'd leave an envelope with my money. See there, against that clock, she'd lean the envelope against the clock. She never missed — like she left the money for the three weeks in the envelope with the note to say she was going on holiday. That's why, her being due back on the Friday, when it wasn't there, I couldn't believe it. I was that sure it must be there, I got down and looked under the chairs, thinking it had maybe somehow got blown off the mantelshelf.'

'So what makes you think she wasn't living here?'

'I just didn't see any sign of it. Right enough, she was always tidy — but that doesn't mean there wasn't a plate and a cup after her breakfast or some clothes lying about or a pair of dirty shoes at the door. But not the last few months. And another thing,' she hesitated, 'her bed wasn't being slept in.'

'Did you normally make it?'

'No, she always did that herself. But,' another hesitation, 'I started checking. Same sheets, never a wrinkle. That bed wasn't being slept in.'

'But your money was always here?'

'She could put the envelope on the mantelpiece any day. Any day she was passing the door. How would I know how long it had been there? I'm only here once a week.'

'I just don't see it,' Meldrum said. 'Why would she pay you to clean the place, if she wasn't living here?'

'Maybe she wanted people to think she was still living here. Her family, like. They're always very involved with their families, aren't they? And the money wouldn't bother her. They're never short of money, are they?'

Meldrum caught Shields glancing over at him with a smug little grin. Was it that obvious he'd lost the thread of what the bloody woman was talking about?

'How often have you met a poor Jew?' Mrs Lynch asked.

CHAPTER TEN

Motives for murder: hate, fear, greed; or sex, which could involve all or any of the other three. Meldrum wakened before seven on the Monday morning and lay watching the pattern of the blowing curtain against sunlight on the ceiling. He listened to the gathering noise of the traffic pouring up and down Leith Walk. An ambulance siren wailed and faded. In a murder investigation, keep the options open was a good rule of thumb. Every time, the temptation was very strong to get fixated on one line of enquiry. From superiors, from the press sometimes, always from pride, there was so much pressure to come up with an arrest. Like everyone, he'd read of cases where that kind of tunnel vision had led to a miscarriage of justice. Professionally, he'd seen them close to home, and made himself unpopular, once almost at the cost of his career, by standing out against the easy option. He was aware of the dangers, of course, he was; but all the same, hands behind head watching the play of sunlight, he was telling himself that in the real world, admit it, crimes were solved by focusing scarce resources. Every detective if he was any good had a hunter's instinct, and he knew Toni Ashton had murdered her husband. He could feel it in his bones. He could taste it.

All the same, she was a widow, the victim's wife, with an alibi, even if it was one yet to be properly tested. Any search for her would have to be limited, and would be hampered by lack of publicity. She might turn up within a few days. It was even possible she might phone to tell them where she was. If the two women had taken refuge from press photographers and phone calls, what could be more natural? Check friends and relatives, he thought, hers and Naomi Morgan's.

In any case, instinct aside, for sure they didn't know nearly enough about

Brian Ashton yet. Start with the basics. Same as in ordinary everyday life: two men meet socially, at a wedding, a party, whatever, it's not long before each finds out what the other does. One of the things that defined a man was what he did for a living. That held true even when the living had been abruptly ended.

According to the wife, Ashton had been the owner of a restaurant. 'It started well,' Toni Ashton had said. 'For what that's worth. With Brian, his things go downhill, but they start well. Like his marriages. All I can tell you is it was fashionable just after he opened it about five years ago. I've no idea how it's doing now.'

There was no way of telling in the middle of the morning, after they'd been admitted to Templars and had the door relocked behind them, how well the restaurant might be doing. A girl with a bandage on her thumb drifted around setting tables, and a radio blaring out of sight from somewhere in the rear suggested activity in the kitchen. Presumably there would be an office back there, too, but for some reason, maybe a dislike of disc jockeys at full volume, the man who'd let them in led the way over to a table set for four by the window. All the time they talked, he stared at some point between the two policemen as if intent on the traffic of the street.

'I've known Brian all his life,' he said. 'He was younger, of course, and even a few years make a difference when you're a child. But that gap narrows as you get older. Does it ever quite vanish?' He stared past them into the street. 'Do you have any brothers, Inspector?'

'No.'

'Nor I. Observation suggests you get that tension between brothers. The younger one envying the fact that the older had mother to himself for a time.'

Guessing, Meldrum put him in his early fifties, but wouldn't have argued if told he was ten years older. Though his hair was white, there was a full head of it, beautifully cut with a deep wave which might even have been natural. He was plump and lightly tanned with the kind of skin which didn't take lines. His name was George Snoddy, and on the phone he'd identified himself as 'Brian's partner'. Everything about him, from the hair through the double line of hand-stitching on the lapels of his suit jacket to the narrow black shoes, looked expensive. After all, then, the restaurant must be turning a nice profit; always assuming his income depended on it.

'Were the two of you related?' Shields asked.

'My grandmother and Brian's were cousins. What would that make us?

Second cousins? I've no idea. More importantly, his parents and mine were great friends, so we saw a good deal of each other. Actually, our mothers were the real friends. My father and his, not so much. But it's the mothers that count in these matters, don't you think? And living near one another, that had to help. Propinquity, its role is underestimated in human *affairs* – in every sense of the word.' He laughed as if he'd said something amusing, flicking the briefest of glances at Meldrum as if to check whether he'd caught the joke. Whatever he saw sobered him. Shaking his head, he said, 'I feel lost. I can't take it in. I simply cannot take it in. He was a vital spirit with so much still to do.'

'You know what he did?' Shields asked.

'What do you mean?'

'Dressing up in women's clothes, for one thing.'

Sometimes, not least when he wasn't sure what there might be to find, Meldrum would listen for as long as a witness was willing to talk. His sergeant wasn't so patient.

'That is an outrageous suggestion!'

Meldrum said, 'I can understand his friends being upset. But you must know that's how he was found.'

Snoddy glanced round. The girl with the bandaged thumb was at the far end of the room. All the same, he lowered his voice. 'You can confirm that?'

Before Meldrum could speak, Shields said, 'It was in all the papers.'

Meldrum said, 'I take it you'd no idea?'

'Not in all the years I've known him.'

'Was there anyone else who might have known?'

'I don't think he'd confide in anyone before me. I really don't.'

'Well, if you do remember anything, I'd be grateful if you'd get in touch.'

'I'm sure I won't.'

'Give yourself a chance to think it over. He might have mentioned something like that in passing. Did he ever talk about anyone you knew – maybe just as a joke? Or about a bar? Or a club? Anything like that? Knowing him as well as you did and for so long, there's a chance he might have let something slip.'

'Let what slip? About being a transvestite? What would it matter?'

'You called it outrageous,' Shields said. 'It mattered to you.'

'Yes, I was shocked. You would be too if it was a friend of yours. I was shocked because it was humiliating and pathetic. But what *mattered* was his

death. That he'd died in that horrible way. And even if Brian dressed as a
woman every night of his life, it wouldn't be a crime, would it?'

'Is that what he did?' Shields asked.

'What?'

'Dress up as a woman every night?'

'Christ, no! I told you so. All I'm saying is, what would it matter?'

'We have to take account of it,' Meldrum said, 'in looking for his killer. He
wasn't fully dressed when he was found. He was in the bedroom and —'

Snoddy held up a hand. It was large, but white and uncalloused. 'He wasn't a
homosexual.' He tapped the table with the carefully manicured nail of a
forefinger for emphasis. 'Put that idea right out of your head. I *couldn't* be
mistaken about that. For one thing, he was obsessed with his wife.'

'Did he talk about her to you?'

'All the time. And not just to me. He went on and on about her having an
affair. That's why he left her.'

'Did he tell you who the man was?'

'No, he didn't.'

Meldrum looked at him sympathetically. 'You were close friends. Yet he
seems to have kept a lot from you. He talked to you all the time about his wife
having an affair. And never mentioned the man's name?'

'Because he didn't know it. I'm not even sure how he discovered what was
going on. He talked round it, but he found the details too painful to go into.
Once he said something that made me think he'd found a message on the
answerphone at home. Whatever aroused his suspicions, she admitted it.
Apparently, when he challenged her with a man's name, she started laughing.'

'Laughing?'

'As if it was enormously funny, that's what he told me.'

'Did he ever talk about his wife having other affairs?'

'Of course not.' Snoddy looked surprised. 'Other affairs? Whatever gave you
that idea? I find that astonishing. Who has it been mentioned by? The wrong
kind of neighbour? You shouldn't – I was going to say you shouldn't pay any
attention to gossip, but that's silly, I understand you have to. All the same, I
dare say your experience will have told you how much it's usually worth.'

Whether or not she'd had lovers, impossible to believe she hadn't had plenty
of offers, Meldrum thought.

'In your opinion, then, this hadn't happened before?'

'I very much doubt it. I'll tell you what I am certain of – if there have been other men, Brian didn't know about them. Like I say, he was besotted with her. Even when he stumbled on this, it's my impression he'd have accepted a lie and been only too glad to believe it. But she didn't give him the option.'

There was no point in pressing him further.

'That's very helpful, sir.'

Snoddy looked at his watch. 'We'll be opening soon.'

Involuntarily, Meldrum glanced round into the street. Nothing to account for the interest Snoddy took in what was going on outside. Parked cars and pedestrians. Maybe he was estimating numbers for lunch.

'Just another couple of things. It won't take long. I understand Mr Ashton and yourself were partners in this restaurant, isn't that right?'

'Yes.'

'Would you say everything was going well?'

'Why?'

'If Mr Ashton had any business worries or if he was in financial difficulties, it might be relevant.'

'You don't think he committed suicide?'

Meldrum shook his head. 'This is a murder investigation, sir.'

'So what could —'

'That's why I'd hope you'd want to help us. So as far as you know he had no financial worries?'

But Snoddy had thought of something else. 'Why don't you ask her?'

'Who? Mrs Ashton?'

'About other men. See what she says.'

'We'll be talking to Mrs Ashton, of course.'

'Does that mean you've asked her already? You must have. If there were other affairs, she didn't say Brian knew about them, did she? I'd find that very hard to believe.'

Meldrum weighed the options, then said, 'When we get a chance to speak to Mrs Ashton, I'm sure she'll clear matters up.'

'Well, why don't you? Where is she . . . ?' And when Meldrum met his gaze without saying anything, 'My God, she hasn't run off? Has she? She has! Did she kill him?'

'We have no reason to think so.'

'It would explain Brian being dressed in that grotesque way.' Buffed nails gleaming, Snoddy scrubbed his forehead in excitement. 'Suppose he went there, and she didn't see the joke. That woman could be frightening when she was angry.'

'Joke?'

'Oh, stupid, of course. But when you have an obsession! He felt very bitter towards her.'

'Had he done anything like that before?'

'Dressed as a woman? Haven't we been over that? I told you, no.'

'I meant, played what you called a joke. Had he done anything malicious towards her before?'

'I shouldn't think so.'

'Mrs Ashton said her house had been broken into during the winter. Whoever did it defecated in the bedroom.'

'What an offensive suggestion,' Snoddy said. 'That would be totally, utterly, unspeakably out of character.'

'Out of character?' A brief explosion of words, the first Shields had spoken for a while. It was as if at some unnoticed moment he'd withdrawn, big hands slack on the bulging meat of his thighs, heavy frame slumped forward. Meldrum had fallen into the bad habit of accepting how little he contributed. At some point, he'd got it into his head that being given Shields was part of being disvalued by his superiors. Too proud or indifferent to complain, he'd let the months working together turn into one year and then almost two. Now, however, Shields gave a grunt and suddenly shifted his chair, half lifting himself to edge it nearer Meldrum. The abrupt move stopped exactly where it enabled him to intercept Snoddy's gaze into the street. 'Out of character? But it's in character for him to dress up as a woman and break into a house?'

'For those of us who knew him,' Snoddy said, 'some things are possible, others are not.'

In the car Meldrum ran through the interview. It occurred to him if Snoddy was Toni Ashton's 'last straw' lover that would account for his being so upset by the suggestion there might have been earlier affairs. He gave himself a moment to enjoy it as an intriguing notion, then put it aside as too fanciful. The probability was Snoddy'd been upset by the idea of Brian Ashton not telling him. And if Toni had been – what had Alex Hodge called it? a nympho – why would Ashton spill something like that to a new neighbour like Hodge? Why would he do that after keeping it to himself, for years presumably, without ever confiding in his business partner and childhood friend George Snoddy? That he might have kept it bottled up inside himself, even for years, was natural enough. You didn't necessarily want to share even with an old friend – especially not with an old friend? – that your wife was whoring around. But then, when he'd finally walked out, suppose it all got to be too much for him, he had to talk to somebody and the new neighbours including Alex Hodge were there. That would make sense too.

It would be useful to talk this kind of stuff over with someone while it was fresh, but with Shields he'd got out of the habit.

While he was thinking this, Shields said suddenly, 'Tell you something for nothing. I wouldn't take Netta to that place for a meal.'

'Why not?'

As far as Meldrum could remember, Shields had never mentioned taking his wife any place at all for a meal.

'I know, what you don't see you don't worry about. All the same, I don't fancy eating round that guy.'

'Snoddy isn't the cook.'

'I don't eat in poof places.'

'You think Snoddy's queer?'

Shields looked at him in disbelief. 'Bloody obvious, isn't it?'

At least they'd discussed the interview.

As they drove on in silence, Meldrum was recalling the moment when Shields had moved his chair, or rather the odd way in which Snoddy had reacted. Instead of avoiding the sergeant's stare by glancing down or shifting in his seat, he'd managed somehow to give the impression of looking past or even through Shields, *unfocusing* his gaze as if refusing to acknowledge what he didn't want to see.

CHAPTER ELEVEN

On a murder enquiry every day was a long day, but this one hadn't been helped by a summons late in the afternoon from Chief Constable Baird. Meldrum had finished a conference with detectives working Brian Ashton's murder, and had been hoping to clear an hour to ready the paperwork on a fatal stabbing in Wester Hailes for the Procurator Fiscal. Back up from the canteen with coffee, crisps and a packet of sandwiches, turkey on mayonnaise with folds of tired lettuce, he'd just prised off the lid on the coffee and raised it to his lips when the phone rang. He put it down untasted and headed for the stairs. 'There you are,' Baird said. His tone held the faintest shade of accusation, as if Meldrum might have been loitering on the way. As he registered this, Meldrum had an image of a wisp of steam rising from a plastic container. He'd forgotten to put the lid back on the coffee. 'You know one another, don't you?'

As the man seated opposite Baird turned and stood up, Meldrum recognised Henry Stanley.

'I'm here to ask an enormous favour,' Stanley said, smiling and holding out his hand.

'I'm pretty busy.'

'Sit down,' Baird said, then modified it at once to 'Why don't you sit down?' accompanying the request this time with his man manager's smile, cold as a gunsight.

'I promise,' Stanley said, 'not to get in the way.'

Meldrum looked to Baird in search of an explanation.

'Dr Stanley's is an unusual request,' the Chief Constable said, 'and not one we'd consider from anyone else.'

Stanley looked modest.

'Request?' Meldrum loaded the word with the instinctive distrust of a man in a hierarchy who's seen a lot of burdens filter down from above disguised as bright ideas.

'As you know, Dr Stanley's been of help to us on a number of enquiries. I think you've worked with him?'

'Worked with? I wouldn't put it like that.'

'Exactly,' Stanley said, nodding his approval, 'the point I've been making. I wouldn't describe it as "working with" either. In all of these enquiries I've been invited to join, the investigation has been under way, on several occasions for a long period of time, before I became involved. Sometimes, to be honest, it's been more or less running down. Once I was asked to give an opinion on a murder committed in the late Seventies.'

'Helen Bradbury,' Meldrum said.

'I'm flattered.'

'But that wasn't for us,' Meldrum said. 'That was a newspaper stunt.'

Baird frowned, but before he could say anything Stanley was off again. 'The nature of the beast. But their reasons weren't my reasons, though I wasn't under any illusions why they'd approached me. I can assure you that any publication this time will be confined to the appropriate academic and professional journals.'

Baird cleared his throat. 'What Dr Stanley has asked us to consider is the possibility he might be involved with a case from beginning to end.'

'Closely involved,' Stanley said. 'I'd like to sit in on witness interviews and case conferences. What I'm envisaging would be that I'd be more or less at the elbow of the senior investigating officer during the course of the enquiry.'

'I've discussed this,' Baird said, 'and the consensus is that there's no reason in principle why we should refuse.' He didn't say who the discussion had been with; at a guess, not just the Police Committee, but whoever else he needed to commit to make sure his back was covered if the project went sour. Baird was a political animal. 'More importantly,' he went on, 'to the best of our knowledge, this kind of access hasn't been offered before. In his written proposal, Henry – Dr Stanley – made a persuasive case that the lessons and implications should be of very general interest, here and abroad.'

That's it, Meldrum realised, the magic words: here and abroad, publicity and attention. It was going to happen. You couldn't argue with the magic words.

'I'd be glad to let you have a copy,' Stanley said, 'of my proposal.'

Go and fuck yourself would have been the response in an ideal world. Since it wasn't an ideal world, Meldrum contented himself with nodding.

'I'm very pleased,' Baird said. Having got what he wanted, he was smiling again with a shade more warmth. 'Now it's settled, I don't mind telling you, as far as Henry was concerned, you were the only name on his wish list. If you hadn't been willing to co-operate, the project would have fallen through.'

Now he tells me, Meldrum thought. But he couldn't help a touch of gratification all the same, even though he knew perfectly well what Baird was doing. To work, flattery didn't have to be the subtlest tool in the box of tricks.

'Remember a murder in the Borders couple of years since? Hawthorne the Australian would have been serving a life sentence if you hadn't traced the pawn ticket for his camera. That made me a fan,' Stanley said. 'At the back of my mind, you know, I honestly believe that's when the idea of a project like this began to take shape. But it did involve waiting for the right case. In retrospect, as I explained to the Chief Constable, I regret not making an approach to see if it would have been possible with the murders of the Bower brothers. And Sam Chaney.'

'But you were able to write about them,' Meldrum said. Without following me around, he meant.

'You've read the article?'

'Not yet.'

'I sent him a copy of the *Journal* article,' Stanley explained to Baird, 'the one I enclosed with the proposal.'

'I found it interesting,' Baird said. 'You should read it.'

'I don't have a lot of time for reading,' Meldrum said, 'not right now.'

In the middle of a murder investigation.

Baird gave him the faint smile of a man clever enough to pack enough work for two men into any given day.

'You don't have to tell me you're busy because of the Brian Ashton murder,' Stanley said. 'You've probably guessed that's the one.'

'One what?' Meldrum genuinely had no idea what he meant.

'I think it's worth going for. I'd like to use the Ashton investigation for the project.'

'But it's — you won't be in at the beginning.' He appealed to Baird. 'I thought the idea was to be in at the beginning.'

'Or near enough,' Baird said.

'Right at the beginning wouldn't be practical,' Stanley said. 'I've always been clear on that. And whatever case one chose has to be a gamble. After all, the ultimate aim for me is to attempt to understand what makes someone kill another human being. There's no way of telling in advance that an investigation will end in success. And even if the murderer is caught, the man or woman may have more or less, perhaps very little, to offer in the way of seeking that wider understanding. From that point of view, in all honesty, the choice has to be more a matter of instinct than science.'

'Ashton's murder could be a domestic,' Meldrum said. 'The wife's gone off. That wouldn't be what you're interested in, would it? I mean, that wouldn't be anything like the Bowers and Sam Chaney.'

'My instinct is for the Ashton case. I'd appreciate the chance to test it.'

While Meldrum was thinking about that, Baird repeated with a frown, 'Gone off? What do you mean the wife's gone off? Gone off where?'

'We don't know. A neighbour saw her and a friend – a woman friend – put luggage in the boot of a car in the drive outside the house and drive off.'

'Why would she do that?'

'Maybe she couldn't bear to stay in the house. With him being murdered there. And the press was trying to doorstep her, and they'd be phoning all the time.'

'You're looking for her, of course.'

'I was hoping she'd get in touch.'

'But she hasn't?'

'Not yet.'

'Apart from her going off, is there anything to support the idea Ashton's wife might have been involved in his death?'

'We've witnesses who claim Ashton broke up the marriage because he discovered the wife had a lover.'

'How reliable?'

'Ashton's partner for one, they ran a restaurant together. They seem to have been pretty close, distant relations, they'd known one another a long time. And a neighbour of Ashton's in the flat he bought after leaving the family home. According to the neighbour, there was more than one lover. He claims Ashton described his wife as being promiscuous.'

'Interesting. What about the partner – what's his name?'

'George Snoddy.'

'Did he confirm that? About her being promiscuous?'

Meldrum shook his head. 'Ashton had told him about her having a lover. Snoddy's convinced that was a first.'

'If he was close to Ashton, that's probably the truth then.'

'Could be. But according to the neighbour – his name's Hodge – Ashton had told other neighbours the same story about his wife being promiscuous. If we believe what Ashton told Hodge, some new lover she'd taken was the last straw for him – and that's why he'd walked out on her.'

Stanley, who had been listening intently, after a glance at Baird seeking permission to make his contribution, asked, 'What was the wife's response?'

'She was gone before we could ask her.'

'It would seem you'd reasonable cause to make a fuss about finding her,' Stanley said. 'Will you go public about looking for her?'

'Too soon for that. Anyway, she has an alibi. When Ashton was killed, she was on a plane back from holidaying in America. We've checked flight crew and staff at the airport.'

Stanley, who'd been leaning forward in his chair, sat back.

'There isn't any doubt?' Baird asked.

'She's a remarkable-looking woman. People remember her.'

Baird was frowning again. 'So why suggest it might be a domestic? If the wife has an alibi?'

'Ah,' Stanley said, 'I see.' He put his fingertips together, a lecturer's mannerism. 'You're thinking of conspiracy. It's a possibility, of course. So it's a case of find the missing lover, eh?'

'It's one line of enquiry.' Meldrum hesitated. 'Most of police work is routine, you know. I mean, I don't suppose you want to go through all of that? It's not very exciting.'

'Don't worry about me,' Stanley said. His eyes were sparkling. 'I won't be bored, not for an instant. Not with this case. I'd be grateful if you'd let me go with my instinct.'

'What about your own work, Dr Stanley?' Baird asked abruptly.

It struck Meldrum that the Chief Constable, a clever man himself, hadn't much enjoyed Stanley's quick-wittedness over the conspiracy option.

'The pressures being what they are these days, I'll still have some commitments unfortunately. But the university has been sympathetic. I won't be able to be with you all the time, but as much as I can.'

'Right,' Baird said. He stood up. 'It's settled then. You two can arrange the details together.'

CHAPTER TWELVE

'You'll have had your tea?' Sam McConnell said. 'You've heard that one?'
Indeed Meldrum had. He offered the tribute of a vague smile. Perhaps
he would get used to it, it seemed as though he would have to, but for the moment,
not much more than an hour after they'd left Baird's office together, he felt as if he
was imposing Stanley on the McConnells. Shields and himself interviewing
witnesses was what the job was about. Add Stanley on, and he felt as if the three of
them were invading these people's home. It put him off his stroke.

'But in Glasgow, it's, have you had your tea? I love Edinburgh people, been
here twenty years, but that's the difference. *You'll have had your tea*, they ask you
here, eh? Well, Marie and I love company. We're from Glasgow,' McConnell
said, 'and our motto's, come in, our door's always open. So, of course, we had
Brian in for a drink not long after he came here. And a meal later. And after
that, he was in and out all the time.'

As he said this, he grinned and waved his hand, taking in his wife, the room
and no doubt the entire flat, in the same inclusive gesture. They were two
floors below the flat in which Brian Ashton had lived. The room was done in
dramatic reds and blacks; the furniture either skeletal tubes or plump chairs
piled with overstuffed cushions; an outsize mirror reflected on the opposite
wall a pair of silver masks for laughter and sorrow. In her mid-thirties perhaps,
and if so probably ten years younger than her husband, the wife had an
abundance of honey-blonde hair, a round soft face and a little-girl manner. She
also had very long legs encased in leather pants. With each creak of the leather
as she eased herself against her husband where they sat side by side on the
couch, Shields's eyes flickered to her and away again.

'Poor Brian!' she said.

McConnell wiped away the grin. 'We've lived here for fifteen years,' he said. 'Plenty of times, we've thought of moving. Particularly recently. The way things have gone, we can well afford to.' Husband and wife ran a hairdressing salon that had become fashionable. 'But as I say, we get to know people, that's our style. We don't have neighbours, we have friends. And, honestly, I liked Brian as much as anyone we've had through that door. He was hurting, mind. He couldn't stop talking about his wife.' He shook his head. 'The stories he told about her. Men are an illness with her, that's what he said. But he – I don't know how to explain this – you know how marriage losers can be so wrapped up in themselves they get on your nerves? Go on and on about how hard done by they've been, fight all the marriage wars over for you, battlefield by battlefield? Piss you off in fact. He wasn't like that. He was so angry, it sounds a funny thing to say, he was good company. He wasn't a bore.' The grin sneaked back at the corners of his mouth. 'He told terrible jokes.'

'Sam,' the wife said, 'don't!'

'I think that's what he was after going to her house that night. Playing some kind of a joke. I mean, you should have heard his jokes.' He glanced down at his wife. 'But I know you're not here to listen to jokes.'

As Meldrum went to speak, he paused, noticing Henry Stanley had leaned forward in his chair. Since he'd been introduced, Stanley had sat well back, even slumping down a little as if to underline his role as that of a mere observer.

'Tell us one of his jokes,' Stanley said. 'You knew Brian. That's something we can't do. It's important we try to understand what he was like.'

'Well, if it would help.' McConnell looked at Meldrum, who neither objected nor agreed. 'God, which one? It's funny, somebody asks you for a joke and – eh, right. Right! A question, okay? How many nymphomaniacs does it take to screw in a light-bulb?' A glance around was met by Meldrum's impassivity, Shields's reluctant grin and a whole series of little nods of encouragement from Stanley. 'Just the one! But the blood gets everywhere.'

'Nobody's laughing,' his wife said.

'You laughed when he told it.'

Marie McConnell shrugged. 'Maybe I did.' She looked more irritated than embarrassed. 'But it's not funny.'

'Context,' Stanley said. 'If he'd been telling you his marriage problems, that must have created a certain tension. Any professional comedian will tell you tension can release itself in laughter.'

'Could be,' McConnell said. 'And chances are he would've been talking about his wife. After all, he talked about her all the time.'

'About them breaking up, yes. Did he say why it happened?' Meldrum asked.

'It's obvious, isn't it?'

'According to his wife, she asked him to leave.'

Husband and wife matched glances of incredulity.

'I don't think so,' he said. 'No way.'

'Not unless Brian was the biggest liar ever,' she said.

'And the best actor.' He shook his head, repeated more emphatically, 'No way! Threw *him* out! Did she say why?'

Ignoring the question, Meldrum asked, 'So from what he told you, he left her, not the other way round.'

'Definitely!'

'Did he say why he waited?'

'How do you mean?'

'I was wondering why he didn't leave before. If what he said about her was true, there had been a lot of men – and he knew about them.'

Sam McConnell nodded. 'Good point. I asked him that. He said the last guy was one too many. You know how you can go along with stuff for a long time and then one day you snap? That made sense to me.'

'Did he put a name to this last lover?'

'No.' He glanced down at his wife as if for confirmation.

'If he didn't to you, he wouldn't to me, would he?' she said.

'You suggested maybe he broke into his wife's house to play a joke,' Meldrum said. 'Were you serious? You do know he was dressed as a woman – and that he had someone else with him? Do you really think he could have done that for a joke?'

'He could have! If you'd met him, you'd know what I mean. Sure he could've done that. He was very Edinburgh, very respectable, public schoolboy, he went to Fettes, all that stuff, but I could tell the wiring was loose. Come to think of it, that's what I liked about him. The business suit had a crazy man inside.'

'All the same,' Meldrum said, 'it's the joke idea that bothers me. A man leaves his wife. He tells you he's known about her lovers for a long time, and then he – your word – snaps. He's obsessed by her – talks about her constantly. If I was told he'd broken into her house, I wouldn't think it was for a joke.'

'I don't think he would hurt her. He didn't say anything that made me think he would hurt her.'

'He *was* angry,' Marie McConnell said.

'Anyway, he's the one who got hurt, so what difference—' McConnell broke off. The glance he gave Meldrum was unexpectedly shrewd. 'Wait a minute, I see what you're getting at. She wakes up in the middle of the night. He's there at the side of the bed. It wouldn't matter why he'd broken in. Christ, she'd be terrified.'

Meldrum said, 'According to Mrs Ashton, it wasn't the first time the house had been broken into. It had happened before, a few months ago. Nothing was stolen, and the police at the time assumed it was kids.' He hadn't corrected McConnell on the impossibility of Toni Ashton having been in the house that night. Carefully, he avoided catching Stanley's eye. 'Now she thinks it might have been her husband.'

'Why?'

'Somebody defecated in the bedroom.'

'That's disgusting,' Marie McConnell exclaimed, breaking the small silence.

'All the same, it's the kind of thing he might have done,' McConnell said. He grinned at Meldrum. 'I said he could make you laugh. I didn't say he was nice.'

Leather creaked as his wife eased away from him. 'There was one thing,' she said. 'About why Brian left her. Those other men she had didn't worry him. I don't know, maybe he even got a kick out of it. But this last one was different. It was serious.'

'In what way?' Meldrum asked.

'She was in love with this one.'

'Where did you get that shit from?' McConnell demanded.

'He said it.'

'I don't remember that.'

'You weren't there.'

McConnell grunted. 'Can't argue with that,' he said to Meldrum. 'All you need is love, eh? Does that mean she killed him?'

'We've no reason to think so.'

Why did I say that, put it that way, Meldrum asked himself, as McConnell's complicit response made it clear the man thought he'd just been told yes, she did, but we haven't proved it yet. Again, why couldn't he have said, no, we've checked, she was on a plane from America when her husband was killed?

A policeman's habit of secrecy.

Or something less acceptable. His unreasoning conviction that somehow or other she was involved.

CHAPTER THIRTEEN

In the car driving away from the McConnells' flat, Stanley went on a talking jag, chattering about what he made of the couple and what they'd said. It took some time for him to run down, mostly from lack of response. Working with Shields, Meldrum was out of the habit of talking things over. As for the sergeant, he preserved a frowning silence until he was about to get out of the car. With the door held open, he volunteered, 'I'll bet she's getting a cuffing right now. See McConnell's face when she said to him, you weren't there? She'd been screwing Ashton. Ask me, she's another bloody nympho.'

Watching him cross the yard to his own car, Stanley said, 'Your sergeant doesn't say much, but when he does he gets to the point.'

Meldrum grunted. 'You want a run home?'

'I can get a taxi. I came in a taxi.'

Meldrum put the car in gear, following Shields's Fiesta out into the street. 'No problem.'

'I'll bring my own car tomorrow. I wasn't sure of the routine.'

'You'd better clear it that you can park here.'

'Mmm.' After a moment's silence, he said, 'Is he always like that? What's wrong with him?'

'Who?'

'Your sergeant.'

'Maybe it's you being there. Bobbie likes everything to go by the book. Changes makes him uncomfortable.'

'So he's *not* always like that?'

'Bobbie Shields,' Meldrum said, 'is a star in the Lodge. He plays in a band. He can be the life and soul of the party. So they tell me.'

'Well, he certainly enjoyed Mrs McConnell's little act. He couldn't take his eyes off those legs.'

'Enjoys isn't the right word. He's not as easy-going as he looks.'

Stanley laughed. 'Anyway, the husband appreciated his attentions. I'm not sure Shields got it right about the husband being jealous of her. It was my impression McConnell likes his wife to be looked at.'

Meldrum was taken aback when Stanley asked him if he'd like to come in for a drink. Though Stanley had a reputation for being gregarious, Meldrum couldn't recall anybody claiming to have seen inside his house. It was getting dark. The rain had come on and he watched the wipers swipe the drops left and right. He surprised himself by accepting.

As Stanley put the key in the lock, he reached over with his left hand and rang the bell. 'Habit,' he said. 'My wife doesn't like surprises.'

Meldrum took the bell to be a signal warning her he'd brought someone home, but as they went into the front room the woman was obviously startled to see him. She got up in a flurry of belt tightening and hair patting, a plain stout woman, in her dressing gown as if ready for bed. She looked as if she could be ten, perhaps even fifteen, years older than her husband.

'Detective Inspector Jim Meldrum. My wife Eileen. I was telling Jim, I ring the bell because you don't like surprises.'

'No,' she said to Meldrum, holding out her hand, 'he rings because he doesn't.'

As he bent down to her, Meldrum caught the unmistakable heavy sweetness of wine on her breath. There was no sign of bottle or glass on the table beside her chair by the fire. Perhaps, he thought, that's what the warning bell's about.

'Would you excuse me for a minute,' Stanley said.

'Would you like something to eat?' the wife wondered to Meldrum. 'Or to drink?'

'It's late,' Stanley said. 'We'll look after ourselves.'

Left with her visitor, she glanced at the chairs by the fire, but didn't say anything about sitting down.

'I don't know what he means,' she said. 'I'm perfectly capable of getting you something. Are you hungry?'

'No. Fine, I'm fine.' They contemplated one another during an awkward pause. 'I'm sorry to be landing on you like this. Unexpectedly at this time of night.'

'Henry doesn't often bring people home.'

There wasn't anything to say to that.

'You're very tall,' she said.

Or to that either.

'How tall are you?'

'Six foot four.'

'That's tall.'

'Not as tall as it used to be,' he said, and smiled at the way he'd put it. She smiled back. She had a good smile that made her look younger. 'I mean, it seems to me that a lot of the young men now are tall. More than there used to be. That's my impression.'

She nodded slowly, thinking about it perhaps, not that he could see much to think about. Gradually, though, her face lost expression until she seemed to be no longer conscious of his presence.

The fire was low in the grate, though despite what had been said it wasn't all that late. A lamp by her chair made a single island of light. The room was large, and dark wooden furniture bulking out of the gloom gave the impression less of having been chosen than unfashionably inherited.

At the sound of a door closing somewhere in the hall, she blinked and focused again on him.

'I'm fond of company,' she said.

Stanley spoke from the doorway. 'Come through. I've lit the fire in the study.'

'You don't have to,' Eileen Stanley said. 'Not for me.'

'Shop talk, dear.'

'Stay here then. I'm ready to go to bed.'

'I've lit the fire.'

'I could fetch you something to drink.'

'I've put a tray through. *And* biscuits.'

As he went to follow Stanley out, Meldrum half turned. He'd spread his hands in a vaguely apologetic gesture, but she was already going back to the chair under the circle of lamplight.

In the study, a room at the back of the house, Stanley had drawn the curtains. A gas fire full on, flames licking up out of the fake coals, had begun to warm the air. He waved Meldrum into a comfortable leather chair beside a music centre, discs in racks filling half the bookcase beside it, and carried another chair round from behind his desk.

'A nightcap?' The computer monitor glowed behind a bottle of Glenmorangie, two tumblers and a water jug arranged on a tray on the desk. No sign, though, of a plate of biscuits, Meldrum realised, and felt a sharp stab of hunger. 'That about right?' It was a very large whisky, cut with just the amount of water Meldrum took. As he handed over the tumbler, Stanley laid a coaster on the lid of the music centre.

'Slainte!'

Meldrum lifted his glass in response to the toast. 'Cheers!' he said.

By contrast with the one they'd just left, in this room white plastic or pine wood isolated under the bright intensity of an overhead light looked as if it might have been bought the day before.

Stanley stretched out his legs comfortably, short legs, black shoes with a high polish. He'd very small feet. 'You think Ashton's wife killed him, don't you?'

'I told you about the alibi.'

'Had him killed then? McConnell thought that's what you were after. And alibi or no alibi, I wouldn't say he was wrong.'

Meldrum sipped his whisky. It struck him how tidy the room was. He wondered how much work Stanley did in here. He would have an office at the university, he supposed. There weren't any papers on the desk, and the monitor was facing the wrong way, out into the room. Maybe he'd shifted it to make room for the tray.

'I'll tell you something,' he said. He felt the whisky warm in his chest and began to relax. 'Remember when Baird called me in and you told me you wanted to cover this murder? Remember I talked about Ashton's neighbour?'

'Hodge, wasn't it?' Stanley said.

'I'm impressed. Alex Hodge.'

'I'll take the first chance I get to read up properly on the case notes.'

'Ashton didn't just call his wife promiscuous. If you believe Hodge, he described her as a raving nymphomaniac.'

'Collocations,' Stanley said. 'Why are nymphomaniacs always raving? Surely, it should be ravening. We must ask your sergeant.'

'Sorry to ask,' Meldrum said, 'but any chance of a biscuit? Otherwise I won't be safe to drive.'

Stanley stared blankly, blinking, as if considering the request. 'Of course. It's all been so interesting. I haven't had anything either, not since lunchtime.'

Left alone, Meldrum finished his whisky. When he looked at his watch, he'd been on his own for almost quarter of an hour. Another five minutes passed.

His head jerked up out of a doze. Yawning, he got up and poured himself another whisky; so much for sober driving. Removing the bottle had given him a clear view of the monitor screen. His curiosity was automatic.

hair, nose, deep set eyes: the effect noble and judgemental. I've seen that face before as a cloud shape that held for minutes one summer afternoon when I was a child. A face by Michelangelo, omniscient and omnipotent, but not necessarily kind. It is so familiar, familiar from a lifetime ago, and here it is again. I'm haunted by a patriarch.

'Just a nonsense,' Stanley said from the doorway, 'to please myself.'

'I never thought you were the religious type.'

'I'm not. If you put that chair over, I'll put the tray between us.'

'You shouldn't have gone to so much trouble.'

On the tray as well as a plate of sweet biscuits there was another piled high with sandwiches.

'I wasn't pretending,' Stanley said as they settled down, 'when I said I admired your work. What I've been privileged to share in a small way, and the cases I've read about and researched. You're absolutely honest, which is commoner than the cynics care to believe. But you have rarer qualities as well. All in all, I think you're arguably the best detective I've met personally. What's the joke?'

Stanley sounded irked, and at that, despite himself, Meldrum felt his smile widen. 'Do you have to be intelligent to be a good detective?'

Stanley looked wary, like a fox sniffing round a trap. 'I should think so. Why?'

'You told me once I was a good listener, but I wasn't clever.'

'Did I say that? When did I say that? I don't think I ever said that.'

'You're a good listener, but you're not clever. That's what you said.'

'Whatever my faults, I'm not discourteous. I'll cite it being uncharacteristic as evidence it wasn't said by me.'

'Take my word for it.'

'When was this?'

'Last year.'

'At a guess, during the Iain Bower affair? I must have said it as some kind of joke, and it got under your skin. I forget it as soon as I've said it, but you remember. That's human nature, Jim. But believe me, in this city, in my opinion, you're the pick of the bunch. I used to be puzzled why you haven't got further.' On the last word, he rose and collected the bottle and water jug from the desk. 'Same again? Please! I don't like drinking on my own.'

As his glass was refilled, Meldrum said, 'To be fair, you did say it was possible I might be cleverer than I pretended.'

At the desk, Stanley topped up his drink.

'Had I had too much to drink, by any chance?' he wondered.

'You were drunk. You said you'd have to commit a murder to find out.'

'That was tempting fate.' He switched off the monitor, the computer screen went dark. 'Stupid of me.' When he turned, glass in hand, he was smiling. 'The things we say when we're drunk shouldn't be held against us in the morning.'

CHAPTER FOURTEEN

'N ot a word. He asked me if you were always like that. The strong silent
type.'

'That's not true.' Shields frowned out of the window at the passing street. 'I
said something.'

'Not a word,' Meldrum repeated, 'from we went into the McConnells last
night until we came out again.'

There was a brooding silence as they came through Tollcross into
Marchmont Road.

'What did you say to him?'

'When?'

'When he asked, was I always like that?'

'Oh.' Meldrum braked to catch the green at the pedestrian crossing just
before the King's Theatre. 'I told him you weren't as easy-going as you looked.'

'What does *that* mean?' Shields blurted in exasperation.

'No idea,' Meldrum said. 'But it probably meant something to him.'

'Why?'

'With him being a psychologist.'

The silence this time lasted until they reached the clock at Morningside.
'I hate a fucking wind up,' Shields said.

They were on their way to talk to some of Toni Ashton's neighbours. The
preliminary interviews had been filed and sifted. Now Meldrum wanted to put
faces to some of the things that had been said.

It was just after eleven when they walked up the path of a couple entered on
the list as David and Amy Finlay. They lived half a dozen streets away from the
murder house, farther than anyone else who'd been spoken to, but their names

had come up twice in interviews as close friends of the Ashtons. Warned of the visit by a phone call from Shields, they were both at home.

'We saw a lot of them before they split up,' David Finlay said. 'After was different. Always is, isn't it? Kind of awful bloody shame you can't help feeling didn't need to happen. He was good company. So was she. They both were.'

As he talked on, Meldrum recognised him as a type. Heavy-featured, about fifty, Finlay was an ex-pupil of a fee-paying school, possibly the city's least prestigious, but good enough to have got him slotted into a career in the Bank of Scotland. Members of the same club, Brian Ashton and he had played a lot of golf together. Though the two couples visited, dined out on occasion and had even holidayed together, most memorably, it seemed, on a canal holiday in France, the game seemed to have been the two men's main point of contact. 'Amy,' he said, nodding at his wife, a little bird of a woman perched on very high heels, 'enjoyed a foursome, but Toni wasn't keen. She played a few times, but it was always as if she was doing us a favour. Of course, she had Brian on a string. Irritated me, to be honest.'

As a type, he irritated Meldrum, which should be irrelevant to conducting an interview, but played its part when the interviewer had a dull pain behind his eyes from drinking too much whisky the night before.

'How would you describe the relations between Mr Ashton and his wife?'

'I've just told you. She had him on a string.'

' 'I know you did, sir. What I was wondering was, could you explain what you mean by that?'

'What's to explain?' He bunched thick fingers and danced an invisible puppet. 'Like that.'

'She was the boss.' Shields said these words with the unmistakable air of a man making a contribution.

Ignoring him, Meldrum asked, 'Did they ever quarrel?'

'Why do you ask that?'

'You seem to have known them better than most people we've spoken to.'

'What difference does it make if they quarrelled or not? Anyway, they didn't.'

'Did she kill him?' Amy Finlay asked. The unexpected question, already put by Ashton's neighbour Sam McConnell, chirped this time like a bird from a hedge, disconcerted Meldrum.

'Don't be a fool,' the husband told her. 'She wasn't even there. Isn't that right?'

Meldrum nodded. 'Mrs Ashton was on her way back from holiday.'

'But their marriage did break up,' Amy Finlay said. 'So it's *silly* to say they never quarrelled.'

A boy who looked about eighteen had wandered in, and stopped abruptly on seeing the two detectives.

Husband and wife looked at one another. David Finlay said, 'This is my son Terry. Terry's playing to a handicap of three at the moment.'

After a moment's hesitation, the boy took a seat on the couch beside Amy Finlay.

'Brilliant,' Shields said. 'I wouldn't mind seeing my son do that. You must put in a lot of practice.'

'You have to,' said the proud father before the boy could respond. 'But the talent has to be there.'

'My boy's only four.'

'Never too early to make a start. First time I saw Terry swing a club, I said to myself, he'll do. He couldn't have been all that much more than four at the time.'

Meldrum's headache had just got worse.

'You were going to tell me about Mr Ashton,' he said quietly. 'Would you describe him as being jealous?'

'Hadn't any cause to be.'

Amy Finlay blew out her breath in disbelief.

'Terry,' Finlay said, 'did you not say you'd work to hand in? You'd be as well getting on with it. You don't want another night sitting up till all hours.' The son stood up. Slim, a graceful mover, a good-looking boy. As he went to the door, his father said, 'Knows he'll get nowhere unless he puts his back into it. I was just the same.'

His silence maintained, the boy left.

Meldrum waited. When no one volunteered to speak, he said, 'We've heard differing stories about why the marriage split up.'

'Different in what way?' Finlay asked warily.

'You knew them well. Is it true Mr Ashton walked out because his wife was having an affair?'

'I'm not sure.'

'Oh, David!' his wife said impatiently. 'Of course he did!'

'It's not so simple! Look. After the break-up, Brian and I played a few rounds, met a couple of times for a drink, but it wasn't the same. He raved on about what a bitch Toni was, and when I didn't say yes-sir-yes-sir-three-bags-full, he didn't want to know.'

As he paused, Shields asked, 'Did he say who the man was?'

'All I can tell you is, he'd got this idea into his head and that's why he left her. Whether it was true or not, I've no idea.'

Meldrum felt the slackening of attention that came with disappointment.

'When he was abusing his wife to you,' he asked, 'did you get the impression there had been other affairs?'

'I'm sure there weren't,' Finlay said firmly. 'I think he got this idea into his head and blurted it out like a damned fool. Big mistake. Toni wasn't the type to put up with nonsense from him. Or anyone else come to that.'

'Oh, David,' Amy Finlay shook her head at her husband, 'you can't see past what a fine golfer he was. And, all right, Brian was wonderful company when he was in the mood. I liked him too. He made me laugh. But she was afraid of him.'

Finlay looked as startled as the others at this storm of birdsong.

'First I've heard of it.'

'That doesn't mean it isn't true.'

'Woman's intuition?' Finlay asked.

'More than,' she said. 'Johnnie Mitchell — that's my dentist, Inspector — he was at school with Brian. He told me he was a better player, but Brian got picked every time for the team — because he was a vicious bastard.'

'She's talking about rugby!' Finlay said, with a smile for Meldrum and almost a wink. Clearly, he was deeply offended and exasperated.

'If she did have an affair,' his wife said, 'she'd have been a fool not to be terrified of him.'

CHAPTER FIFTEEN

'Easy enough to pick him up,' Meldrum said. 'It's on our way.'
Placating Shields didn't come naturally to him, but the first of the pint
had settled his stomach and he was inclined to the easy life while he ate his
cheese rolls.

'Targets and mission statements,' Shields grumbled. 'Record this, video that.
Know what'll happen next? Charter up in the interview room, just in case the
swine don't know their rights. Here's my fucking mission statement: Roll on
the pension! And trying to do a murder enquiry with that wee cunt Knife
Stanley looking over your shoulder. The job's going to buggery.' Shields lifted
his empty glass. 'You want another?'

'No. And if I was you, I wouldn't either. You can get us a couple of
coffees.'

'Give me a break! Just because that wee shite's going to be with us—'

'Makes no difference whether you like him there or not. Stanley's going to
sit in whenever he wants. That's it. Period. And that's it from the top.'

So much for the quiet life. Chewing on a powdery wad of roll, Meldrum
sighed as he watched Shields shove through to the bar. He toyed with the idea
of telling him how lousy an idea it would be to let the 'Knife' nickname slip to
Stanley, but decided to let it go.

Shields came back with a coffee and a half pint.

'Don't worry, I think I'll be able to manage this,' he said, settling himself in
front of the half pint, 'seeing as I'm not driving.'

Meldrum studied the saucer in which a slopped moat of his coffee
surrounded the cup. 'And talking of wind ups,' he said, 'when I mentioned
what Stanley said about you sitting in the back of the car like a dummy, it was

for a reason. I'm used to you – but it could be nasty if he puts it around that you're a passenger. And I'm not talking about driving either.'

Fortunately, Stanley was punctually in advance of them. A bay in the visitors' car park had been marked 'reserved' for his use, and as Meldrum turned in he was getting out of his car.

'Waiting long?'

'Half an hour, but it wasn't a problem.'

'That's police work for you.' Shields's voice came from the back seat.

'I'd papers to look at so the time wasn't wasted.'

'Don't get anything to eat half the time,' Shields said.

Meldrum caught a side glance of curiosity from Stanley. He'd the unwelcome thought that Stanley's monograph or book or whatever the hell he was planning might run to an appendix on working relationships, featuring himself and Shields as the Odd Couple.

'I'd rather have been with you than lecturing this morning,' Stanley said.

'Is that you free for the day?'

'Free as a bird. For just as long as it takes.' Over his shoulder he said, 'I don't eat a great deal.' Turning round again, half smiling, he asked, 'Which one first?'

'Sorry?'

'You're talking to the neighbours, wasn't that what you said?'

'Change of plan. We got a response to the Ashton photo.'

'Did I know about that?'

'You'd be amazed how much gets done when you're not here,' Shields offered, not quite talking to himself.

Meldrum said, 'They've been showing Ashton's photographs round the pubs and clubs. Asking particularly about the night he was killed.'

'Would anyone recognise him?' Stanley objected. 'After all, he was dressed as a woman that night!'

'The teams were showing two photographs. We got one of them from his flat, him in ordinary gear. The one as a woman was taken after he was dead. They put the wig back on. Fixed his make-up.'

'Of course, you can do that,' Stanley said. 'Stupid of me.'

'Pretty sexy photo, matter of fact,' Shields chipped in. 'Wee Sharkey told me when he showed it around, guys who weren't in the know really fancied her. Should've seen their faces when I told them, he said, hell of a funny.'

Oh God, Meldrum groaned to himself. What about respect for the dead? How much ammunition do you want to hand this man?

When Stanley, however, murmured only, 'That kind of photograph, I've been told the eyes give it away, even though they're taped open,' it seemed he was intrigued not offended.

'It was still good enough,' Meldrum said, 'for someone to recognise it this morning. Apparently, this guy claims he saw her – *him*, that is.'

'When?'

'The night he was killed,' Meldrum said with a touch of impatience. 'About eight o'clock.'

'Dressed as a woman?'

'Pretty as a fucking picture,' Shields said.

'So now we jog his memory. Ask if he remembers Ashton being with somebody.'

'Where was—' Stanley cleared his throat. 'Sorry. Where was this?'

'In a bar called The Flying Fox. You ever hear of it?'

'Passed it,' Stanley said. 'And gone on by, knowing its reputation. It'll be interesting to see inside.'

CHAPTER SIXTEEN

Early days, Meldrum had still been in uniform, encountering vice among the rest of the routine stuff, when he'd first come across Billie Hunter. Two decades later Hunter was still managing The Flying Fox, which in and out of fashion over the years survived as the city's best-known gay bar.

It was, it seemed, in one of its periods of maximum popularity. The place had been crowded to capacity the night Hunter had noticed the redheaded woman.

'I clocked the bitch. At a table over against the wall. As far away from me as she could get.'

There was nothing camp about his manner or in the hoarse, growling voice. Leaning over the paper-littered desk in his cramped office, not much more than a glorified cupboard at the end of a corridor that began with the toilets, Hunter, with his bald scarred head, broken nose and meaty hands, looked like a middle-weight wrestler who'd won a few lost a few. He liked young men and inflicting violence, but neither Meldrum nor anyone else had ever got him inside a courtroom.

'We're talking about Brian Ashton,' Meldrum said. His back ached after the late night, but he'd waved Stanley into the only seat, a stool in front of the desk. Crowding the space, Shields, too, was on his feet, leaning his back against the door as if guarding the exit. 'Cut out the bitch crap.'

'I thought of her that way then, don't tell me it should be poor bitch, dead or alive leave it at bitch.'

'Did you know it was a man?' Stanley asked.

'You joking?'

'I didn't think it was so obvious,' Stanley said; he smiled, 'having seen the picture.'

'Shoulders he had on him? Picture doesn't catch that. You'd have had to be an idiot not to know.'

'Ye-es,' Stanley said. 'You'll be experienced in these matters. It's all new to me.'

Intervening across Hunter's scowl, Meldrum asked, 'Was anybody with him?'

'No.'

'Are you sure?'

'Like I said, we'd got busy. Real busy, the place was packed to the door.' He shook his head. 'Couldn't believe my eyes. Considering I'd already warned them off.'

Them?

'Warned who off?'

'The bitch.' A finger poked the photograph he'd laid on the desk. 'Ashton. And the other one, the blonde. Two of them came in, don't ask me how often, too often, put it that way.'

'Both of them dressed as women?'

'One blonde, one redhead. Ashton was the redhead, the other one was blonde.'

'And the blonde, was she there as well that night?'

'Definitely not. This time it was just the redhead. The time before when I saw her, the blonde was there as well. But that was weeks ago. Been at this game long as I have, you can tell something's not kosher. First time I spotted them, I told them they were barred. Two or three weeks passed, there they were again.'

Again Stanley intervened. 'I don't understand what you mean, it wasn't kosher. Because they were dressed as women? I'd have thought that would be acceptable in a place like this.'

'Place like what?' Hunter asked. 'What the fuck you mean?'

'Cut it out,' Meldrum said.

Behaving as if he hadn't heard, Hunter turned elaborately patient as he explained to Stanley, 'They were tourists. And I throw tourists out because they mean trouble.'

He paused for so long, staring at the desk, that Meldrum prompted him. 'So?'

'I don't know why I didn't throw them out that second time. Just when I saw them, I was shouted to answer the phone. Long call. I forgot about them. And we were busy, we're always busy on a Saturday night. Then couple of days later I heard, you always hear, know what I mean?'

'Jungle drums,' Meldrum suggested, and heard Shields snort.

'People get a kicking all the time. But this fellow McCluskie had taken an awful hammering. Whoever did it took their time. And he wasn't a young man. He nearly died. By the time they found him on the Sunday morning, he'd been lying out all night. Soon as I heard, I remembered him sitting at a table with those two.'

'Ashton and his friend.'

'Right.'

'You saying they did it?'

'Stone dead certain, not a doubt in the world. When I warned the pair of them off, I could smell the violence on him.' He nodded. 'Ashton. Wish the cunt had tried to have a go.'

'You should have reported it,' Shields said.

'And did. You can check. Two of your lot came in, went through the routine, couldn't have cared less. Like a mug, I even phoned to find out what was happening. "We'll keep you in touch." Never heard another word.' He addressed himself to Stanley. 'It's not what you'd call top priority. A queer gets bashed, people think he had it coming.'

'I don't think that's entirely fair,' Stanley said. As he leaned forward, the stool swayed. It was one of the tall ones from the bar and his little feet rested on the rung. He caught his balance imperturbably, not losing a beat, a born lecturer. 'This is a violent culture and crimes of violence generally aren't given the attention they should. Apart from murder, of course. Since the days of the town guard, law enforcement has been fundamentally about the protection of property.'

Good to have friends, Meldrum thought, leaping to your defence.

'Homophobic wee bastard, aren't you?' Hunter said.

CHAPTER SEVENTEEN

On a murder enquiry time passed slowly with every hour packed at first, but then came a day that slipped imperceptibly into the next and that went on till there came a morning when you woke up with the idea this one's going to end in failure. The strange thing was how, like women herded together synchronising menstruation, that day would find the persuasion of failure mysteriously in the air, unspoken, shared by everyone. The enquiry wasn't a week old when Meldrum opened his eyes on that feeling.

There was still no word from Toni Ashton. It was as if she and her friend Naomi had vanished off the face of the earth, a phrase he'd heard too often from relatives of the missing. Sometimes the cliché had come true literally, off the face of the earth into a grave, in a cellar or dug in woods. Meldrum had an uncle who'd vanished off the face of the earth during the war, died it was supposed, until someone spotted a little item thirty years later about him being killed in a car accident in Calgary. He'd rated an obituary because one year in the Fifties he'd won the world piping championship in Canada, where he must have jumped ship and settled, lived and been buried. Brian Ashton's body had just been released for burial. As far as he could find out, the partner in the restaurant — what was his name, Snoddy? — had been left to make the arrangements, there didn't seem to be anyone else. Chances were, even if the wife hadn't gone off, she wouldn't have wanted to attend the funeral. How much money had Ashton left when he died? They were still going through the usual rigmarole with the lawyer to get the contents of the will. It would be interesting to know if he'd named his wife as a beneficiary; but even if he'd tried to write her out, she'd still be entitled to half the estate, Scots law being strong on family values. Maybe she'd contact the lawyer to find out how much

was in the kitty. Maybe they'd find her that way. So far the search for the
women had been too low key. How long would he have to wait before he could
go public to trace them? They could have driven to Manchester and got a plane
to London. They could have driven to London and caught a plane for
anywhere. Thinking about Toni Ashton, Meldrum lay staring at the ceiling,
until he found himself with an erection and rolled out of bed.

As for the idea of failing, it was too early for that, ridiculously too early.
When he went into work, there was no sign of it from anyone else and for him
the feeling faded as the day began.

In mid-morning, he surprised himself by being pleased to see Stanley
hovering in the car park waiting for them. He was called Knife by detectives
not just for the accident of his surname but for his far-fetched analogies and
elaborate speculations. They were overworked men who liked to get to the
point quickly, while Stanley in interdisciplinary mode was apt to favour the
scenic route. If Meldrum had been asked beforehand, he'd have expected
prolonged exposure to the little man's chatter to get on his nerves. For the first
time, however, it occurred to him that a man like him living on his own with
Shields for a sidekick might have too much silence altogether in his life.

If Stanley had seemed subdued the day before at The Flying Fox, this
morning he was in good spirits. Meldrum half listened to the flow of talk. 'And
as for crime and punishment, the ever interesting topic. What about the South
Africans in the days of apartheid? They had their own refinement on capital
punishment. For his last meal, the condemned man could have a chicken. If he
was white, that is. If he was black, he got half a chicken.'

What if you didn't like chicken? Meldrum smiled at the thought, then
glancing at the mirror caught a glimpse of Bobbie Shields glum in the back seat.

'. . . reading a *Journal* piece on serial killers. An American psychiatrist
discussing multiple causation. Usual stuff – bad childhood plus brain damage,
combinations like that, the hereditary factor too, of course. But what startled
him was the *extent* to which men who'd committed terrible crimes had been
abused as children. One man's body was covered in burns, his mother used to
correct him by throwing pans of boiling water over him. Another had wounds
in wrists and ankles. His mother would punish him by taking out her pistol and
shooting him in the wrist or an ankle.'

'Sounds like bollocks to me.' Shields's voice sounded disapprovingly from
the back.

'Don't say it! Hang them, eh? Isn't that what you're going to say? I hear that all the time. And, of course, if people *do* things they have to *pay* for them. Otherwise civilisation would be impossible. Man is expelled from Eden, no question. But that doesn't prevent us from trying to understand.'

Bee in his bonnet, heard him going on about this before, Meldrum thought, but didn't bother to intervene. Perhaps that's what he'd been missing. Someone talking non-stop who didn't need a response: that was a peaceful situation, though to work it was one that required an egomaniac. Would that be the talker? Or the listener?

'It's more complicated than simple good and evil. It isn't simple. It's far from simple. It's so far from simple, I honestly believe if you could analyse all the elements the motive for every murder would be different. Almost the same in many cases, same enough to be put into categories, well, they have to be, we can work with categories. But if you could know enough about them, still you'd find shades of difference – and who knows, maybe the clues we need to predict the future murderer in the child will lie in those shades. So you see, I don't think this psychiatrist can be dismissed as what you'd call a bleeding heart.'

After a pause, as if to make sure he'd finished, Shields said, 'I was only going to say that stuff about getting shot in the ankles sounded to me like bollocks. Smash up the bones, he'd be in a wheelchair not running around murdering folk.'

They were on their way to Glasgow to talk to Naomi Morgan's sister, which was enough in itself to lift Meldrum's spirits. As if to match the lightening of his mood, the sun came out from behind the clouds as he left the by-pass to join the M8. Squinting in the mirror, he imagined Bobbie Shields cartoon-style with a raincloud above his head, and the smile came again. He relaxed the grip of his hands on the wheel. He hadn't made allowance for how much he'd been stressed by Toni Ashton's disappearance. She was involved, he was sure of it. Find her, find the answer. Nothing to take to Baird to back up that hunch; days going by; meanwhile, a feeling of marking time. His hands were clenched again and he made them slacken on the wheel. To be involved directly in the search for her released some of the tension of his frustration.

It took less than an hour to get to their destination.

Gold against dark green, the name *ELAINE* ran in slanted lettering above the shopfront. The other two paused beside him as he looked up at it. They'd assume he was checking the address. In fact, he was taking in with the usual slight sense of shock the sense of difference. Two cities less than fifty miles apart, but to him Glasgow felt utterly different from Edinburgh, the new buildings brasher, the old more run down, the streets full of a darker energy with pavements crowded or suddenly, in mid-morning, eerily empty. Impatient, Shields was already heading for the entrance. Meldrum followed, with Stanley bringing up the rear. From the gowns in the window, it was a dress shop. It was the right place, not a doubt of it. They'd been told the sister owned a dress shop, though her name was Stephanie not Elaine. Maybe along with the goodwill she'd bought the name from a previous owner.

As he came into the shop, he saw a woman with her back to him moving dresses from the middle of a long shallow double curve of racks. Tall, slim, redheaded, for a startled instant he thought that he had found Toni Ashton. At once, from the harder, more ordinary shade of that tight cap of hair, even before she turned, he realised his mistake.

She looked at the three of them. 'You want to see Mrs Laurie.' She made it a statement not a question.

'Detective Inspector Meldrum. Yes. She's expecting us.'

'Through this way. Mrs Laurie is in the stockroom.' Over her shoulder, she offered a surprisingly broad smile, more of a grin, and said, 'I guessed you weren't in for a frock.'

In a long crowded room like a corridor, Mrs Laurie acknowledged their arrival, admitted Naomi was her younger sister, but didn't volunteer to stop what she was doing. Questions and answers were punctuated by her signing for a delivery and supervising its unpacking by a melancholy boy about sixteen whose hands looked raw and outsized among the fabrics. 'He's more of a hindrance than a help,' she kept saying.

No, she hadn't heard from Naomi. No, she had no idea where she might be. Yes, Naomi had worked in the shop, but she'd never taken a real interest. Their parents were dead. There were no brothers or sisters. Some cousins, but Naomi had never been close to her family. As for friends, she'd no idea. If she'd been asked whether her sister had a friend, she'd have mentioned Mrs Ashton, but they already knew about her.

At the end of an irritating encounter, Meldrum waited for her to ask questions of her own, but even when she sent the boy off to do something else she showed no curiosity about the murder. For Mrs Laurie, unlike her sister, the buying and selling of frocks was evidently a real interest.

The break came with the redheaded woman, who emerged from the shop as they were getting into the car.

'Today I take lunch out of the shop,' she said. 'It's quiet, and she owes me a half day. If you want to talk to me, it'll need to be while I eat. I only have an hour.'

Settled across the table from Meldrum in the Italian restaurant at the top of Pitt Street, she gave that broad disconcerting grin and said, 'What do you mean, why should you want to talk to me? That's the kind of question does wonders for a girl's confidence.'

'Nothing personal.' He'd to raise his voice slightly. The place was crowded and noisy. Meldrum glanced beyond her to where Shields and an irate-looking Stanley were having to share a table for four.

'Exactly.' Her name was Ella Crossan. She laughed. 'What did you make of her?'

'Mrs Laurie?'

'She isn't married, never has been. It's a business convenience, she thinks it makes the customers more comfortable with her. Laurie! Fine old Scots name, fine old Estonian family. But I suppose you could tell. You can tell, can't you?'

Meldrum hadn't. He seldom did, not having a mind that worked that way.

If he'd been in any doubt about what she meant, it would have been cleared as she laughed again and went on, 'I asked her the other day, do you know the difference between a Jewish woman and a Catholic woman? Then I told her, I'm a Catholic. I get the fake jewellery and the real orgasms.'

'You must get on well with her.'

'You don't have much of a sense of humour, you know that?' And without waiting for an answer, 'I know I should move on, I've never been so long in one job. But I don't, so I get pissed off. If she fired me, she'd be doing me a favour. Being her, though, she just laughs, God knows what at, she's got *no* sense of humour. And she's got no flair. It's me brings people back. With her it's all money, you know the way.'

Conversation had to wait while they were served by a waitress who was casual and friendly, and made sensible noises about the food. She was different from anyone he'd encountered in an Italian restaurant in Edinburgh, which probably had more to do with her being a Glaswegian than which part of Italy her grandparents came from.

'I'll tell you why,' Ella Crossan said as they began to eat. 'Why you should talk to me. Wee Naomi worked in the shop for six months. I liked her, she didn't have much time for the big sister. And like me she wanted to leave, but kept putting it off. She wanted to pack it in the day she started!'

'Did she talk to you about how she felt?'

'Not in the shop. But she stayed with me for a couple of weeks while she was looking for a flat. This was just after she'd come back.'

'Back? Where'd she been?'

'London. She didn't talk about it, but I got the impression something had happened before she went down there. Anyway, she was home again. And big sister gave her a job. But she wasn't happy. She really didn't want to be here. I could understand her being restless when she was just back. But even when she got her own flat, she felt the same. Nice place over in Hyndland, she had me there once for a meal. I was pleased to go, as I say I liked her, but it was just the once, a kind of thank you for putting her up, I hate when people think that way. Like I say, happy or not, it began to feel the two of us would be selling frocks there till we were due the pension. Maybe if she hadn't gone, I would have. Bad luck on me.'

'So what happened?'

'Mrs Ashton.' She looked at her watch. 'Christ, is that the time?' She pushed away her plate. 'I'll have to get back.'

'You've hardly eaten.'

'It's how I diet. If you weren't here, I'd be blethering to somebody else.'

As she got up, Meldrum caught her by the arm and pushed her down into her seat. As he did, two thoughts occurred to him. One was they must look like a couple who had just quarrelled. The other, a police thought, he'd just committed a technical assault.

'Take a minute,' he said. 'How do you mean, Mrs Ashton happened?'

When she'd gone, Stanley, watching from a table nearby, leaped up as if afraid someone might beat him to her place. He lifted her plate aside and set down his own with his glass of wine. Like Meldrum, he'd half his meal still uneaten.

'Well?' he asked.

'Can I tell you in the car? Otherwise I'll have to go over it again for Shields.'

'Will he care?'

'He should.'

Stanley forked in a mouthful of penne and thought about it.

Still chewing, he said, 'Duty, you mean. That's the big thing in your life.'

Bollocks, Meldrum wanted to say; or, you're the psychiatrist. He'd heard people who could meet a compliment, if that's what it was, with a joke, turning it off and accepting it at the same time. But it had to be the right joke, or you'd embarrass yourself thinking about it later. He chewed stolidly and said nothing.

'You remind me of William Cowper,' Stanley said.

'You've got me there.'

'Poet, round the time of Robert Burns. As Burns knew, most of the people who believed in predestination managed to have a revelation they were holding a winner's ticket in the lottery. After all, if you didn't you'd to live with the terror of endless suffering. But many of the best couldn't so easily make themselves comfortable. Cowper couldn't persuade himself he was saved by Grace. He came to believe that he was among those predestined for eternal damnation. That was the way he thought, he couldn't help himself, he had that kind of nature. I see you as being like that, Jim.'

'Which part of Scotland did he come from?'

'He was English.'

'You surprise me. What happened to him?'

'He went mad.'

There should have been some easy flippant answer to that; but again Meldrum wasn't glib enough to find one. In the pause, the idea of the poet's madness impressed itself on him. It settled into his memory. He saw that Bobbie Shields was talking to the women who were sharing his table. As he watched, Shields said something and the two women were laughing with him, one turning to the other, both of them leaning forward. It was strange how in the middle of the buzz of eating, a conversation could give the impression of being intimate and enclosed. Shields had made a hit.

'Don't be embarrassed,' Stanley said, 'but I've always thought of you as a good man, if that word isn't entirely out of fashion. I know, for example, that you fought hard to get a murder conviction overturned a few years ago. I tracked down the rumours about that as far as I could. I learned enough to know it damaged your career. And then you astonished me by telling me what happened the night you went to arrest Sam Chaney's killer.'

Meldrum froze for an instant. It came as a shock to hear this casual reference in a public place to the night when he'd brokes faith with every rule by which he lived his life as a policeman. He couldn't find anything to say.

Stanley held up his hand, the smeared fork projecting from his fist. 'Sorry. All I mean is, a man's nature isn't set in stone. Not mine any more than yours.' His cheeks had flushed with the intensity of his desire to make himself understood. 'Things happen, we surprise ourselves. A man's nature is a plastic substance, one that shifts and alters. Mine, yours, all of us. Do you see that? Think of the analogy that over seven years every cell in the body will be renewed.'

This time, however, the answer came to Meldrum at once.

'No, I don't believe that,' he said. 'It's my experience people don't change much at all.'

CHAPTER EIGHTEEN

As they were about to go, at the end of their first interview with him, in the doorway looking from the shadowy empty morning restaurant into the busy street, George Snoddy had wiped two large white hands down his cheeks and said, 'I'd like to come with you when you go to see him.'

Meldrum had just asked for the name of the lawyer Brian Ashton and he had used when they bought the restaurant. Having given a name and addresss, Snoddy had indicated he was more or less sure this must be the lawyer who would have handled Brian Ashton's other legal affairs, including his will, assuming he'd made one.

'Arthur Macleavy's grandfather was Brian's grandfather's lawyer,' he'd said. 'And mine. An old family firm, it was natural for us to use them. If you are going to see him about Brian's affairs, I'd like to be there. Would that be unacceptable?'

Normally, the answer would have been yes, totally unacceptable. Apart from the police instinct for keeping the left hand in ignorance of what the right was up to, this lawyer Macleavy would be well within his rights to object to Snoddy's presence on the grounds of client confidentiality. Meldrum, though, had been curious as to why Snoddy should have wanted to be there when they talked to the lawyer. Doubting he'd be given any helpful answer if he asked, he'd decided that he'd give Snoddy the time of any appointment and let Macleavy and him take it from there.

As he finished explaining this to Henry Stanley, it occurred to Meldrum that Shields, listening from the back seat, might be asking himself why none of the calculations behind the decision had been shared with him at the time.

Simple answer; he hadn't asked. All the same, not for the first time, Meldrum felt a pang of bad conscience.

'What do you think, Bobbie?' he asked, raising his voice. 'Think Snoddy will be there waiting for us?'

Shields mumbled something he couldn't hear. 'What?'

Much louder, so that it sounded perhaps unintentionally aggressive, Shields said, 'What for? I don't get it.'

'I'd like to know what reason he had for asking to be there,' Meldrum explained again. 'Anyway, either way, it can't do any harm.'

'Don't see why he'd bother.'

'Maybe he won't.'

When they went into the office of Carter, Macleavy and Smillie in Hanover Street, the receptionist shook her head. Arthur Macleavy wasn't there. 'Did you change the appointment? Maybe that's what's done it. He's always in the Bridges office on a Friday.'

It was busy and they had to wait in a line of cars to cross each intersection until they rounded the statue, ran down to cross Princes Street and go up by the Mound, queuing at one light after another, until they turned on to the South Bridge.

'Might even have been the same bloody woman,' Shields was complaining. 'The one I spoke to on the phone sounded like that – and she said Hanover Street. *Definitely.*'

'Just check the numbers,' Meldrum said, keeping a grip on his temper.

'There it is! You've passed it.'

Meldrum stood on the brake and jammed the car backwards into a gap behind a van.

As they got out, Shields said again, 'Bloody woman.'

'Perhaps,' Stanley said, 'you should sue her for wasting police time.'

At least he's enjoying himself, Meldrum thought.

They walked past the office and had to retrace their steps. No stone balustrades or elegant hall this time; the Bridges office was marked by a shopfront, and inside most of a cramped reception space was taken up by a counter. The brown carpet had seen better days, the walls needed a fresh coat of paint; even the receptionist, a stout woman in her late fifties, seemed dispirited. When Meldrum explained who he was, she said, 'He thought you weren't coming, so he's seeing someone at the moment.' It was said pleasantly enough, but in a practised tone which suggested she spent a lot of her time offering excuses. She spoke briefly into the phone. 'He'll be with you as quickly as he can manage.'

Ten minutes passed, Stanley had gone to the lavatory, when a door to the left of the back wall opened. The woman who came out was offering profuse thanks over her shoulder to someone out of sight, but as she turned the smile was already fading into a settled expectation of disappointment.

'Just go in,' the receptionist said. 'That's easiest.'

Easiest? Meldrum saw who it was easier for as he went into the room. The man levering himself out of the chair behind the desk was gross. He wasn't wearing a jacket, and great patches of perspiration stained under the arms and across the chest.

'Don't bother getting up,' Meldrum said.

At that the man gave up the effort and sank back.

'You'll be Inspector Meldrum?'

'Yes. And Detective Sergeant Shields. And I've brought along—'

But before he could explain that Stanley was with them and why, and ask if it would be all right if he could sit in once he appeared, the fat man broke in, 'Fine, fine. Sit down, please.'

As Meldrum took the nearest seat to the desk, he caught the smell of sweat, a sickening mixture of grease and fried onion. Close up, the soaked breasts were as large as a woman's.

'I can't tell you how shocked I was by Brian's death. His grandfather and father were clients of the firm – in those days it was just Carter and Macleavy, of course. Smillie came along more recently, very recently. And the Carters are gone – brain tumour killed the son and then the father went less than two years afterwards. Cancer and a broken heart's bad enough, but murder!' Macleavy blew out his cheeks in a long sigh. 'Anything I can do to help, ask away.'

'You told my sergeant that Mr Ashton had left a will.'

'That's right. Oh, by the way, there's no problem about Mr Snoddy coming in. He's a beneficiary.'

'He's been in touch with you then?'

'I told him when he called me. That he was in the will, that is. Of course, I didn't give the details.'

Meldrum looked at his watch. 'He must have decided against coming.'

'Eh?' Macleavy looked puzzled. 'Did you not say he was here?'

At that moment there was a light firm knock, immediately followed by the sound of the door being opened. In the same moment, Meldrum was transfixed by what was happening to the man on the other side of the desk. Macleavy's eyes were bulging. The furious red slab of face under the damp spikes of mouse-brown hair had gone grey. His mouth gaped as he whistled for air. It seemed the lawyer was having a stroke.

Shields was the one who moved. No lightweight himself, he stepped round the desk with a suprising economy of movement and with neat deft movements slid the knot down the tie to let him tug the fat man's collar open. Two things then impinged together on Meldrum. The first was the rattle of a collar button as it spun across the desk. The second was Henry Stanley's voice asking, 'Is he all right?'

Wide-eyed, he was by the door, which he hadn't closed. It was obvious to Meldrum that walking in on the confusion had startled him badly.

'Damn!' Shields said. Macleavy had taken a grip on his hand and he was tugging to release it.

'Sorry.' Macleavy opened his fist. 'Sorry.'

'Do you want to call a doctor?' Meldrum asked.

'Come in.' Macleavy gestured to Stanley. To Shields, he said, 'You can sit down. Really, I'm all right.'

As the two men took seats, Meldrum said, 'I'm not sure we should go on.'

'It looks dramatic, but it's nothing.' Macleavy fumbled at his collar and, finding the button gone, pushed the tie knot up to hold it shut. Although he had sweat on his forehead, his colour had come back to normal. 'An indigestion spasm.' Glancing from one man to the other, he managed a smile.

Realising he hadn't introduced him, Meldrum volunteered, 'Dr Henry Stanley. Dr Stanley is doing research. He's helped us in the past, but if you'd prefer him not to be here he can wait outside.'

'Research?'

'Into the criminal mind,' Stanley said.

'A lawyer comes across that. Even in an old family practice where it's mostly conveyancing and estate work. I don't mind if you stay.'

'Thank you.'

'I'd like to see Brian Ashton's murderer caught. It's a pity they've abolished hanging.' He pulled out a handkerchief the size of a dinner napkin and wiped his face.

'I'm not a medical doctor,' Stanley said. 'All the same, you should be careful.'

'I'm a lot stronger than I look.'

'Well, if you're sure,' Meldrum said, 'you could tell us who benefits by Mr Ashton's will. You've already mentioned Mr Snoddy.'

'He's been left a substantial bequest.'

Meldrum nodded. 'Is anyone else named in the will?'

'Small bequests. To his old school. To a Heart Foundation – his father died of a heart attack. Nothing of significance.'

'In that case,' Meldrum said, 'it sounds as if everything else has been willed to Mr Snoddy.'

Macleavy thought about it. 'If it weren't for the wife's claim, the whole estate would have gone to him.'

'How much are we talking about? For the wife?'

'It would be impossible at the moment to give an exact sum.'

'The house alone must be worth a lot. It's big, good district, the way prices in the city are going.'

'Mr Ashton's wife had already been given the house.'

Now why would he do that, Meldrum asked himself. We're told he's walked out on her because of a lover. We're told he bad-mouths her to everyone as a nymphomaniac. Now I'm told he's given her the house.

More than ever, he wanted to find Toni Ashton.

Turning all that over, he found when he got into the car that he was looking forward to hearing what Henry made of it. Stanley, though, was unusually quiet.

Into the silence, Shields made his contribution from the back seat.

'Christ, fat bugger wasn't kidding about being strong,' he said. 'While I was opening his collar, he took a grip of my hand. I've never felt anything like it. Like being in a mincer.'

CAT ON THE PROWL

I'm haunted by a patriarch. Frame that face in a wig and it belongs to a judge. A hanging judge. An anachronism, yet I see in those eyes the knowledge I am not one of those made to survive the humiliations and brutality of a prison. Sentenced to death then. And so the Hanging Judge still.

Naturally enough, crime and punishment were on his mind. No matter how he turned it round, there seemed no way out of his problems unless someone else died. He put his head in his hands and stared at the screen. The curtains were drawn and the only light was the lamp on the desk. It gathered bottle and glass under its white circle like an old-fashioned advertisement for the good life. But a man whose survival depended on a clear head shouldn't be drinking. It was true, despite his size, he'd always been able to carry his liquor. Like most things, he had a theory about that. The secret was to eat well and piss frequently. On the other hand, the body couldn't replace brain cells. Every day, cohorts of them died. As people lived longer, their brains accumulated enough loss for the damage to show. Kill cells with alcohol as well, the odds got worse.

One in the morning. The window curtains were velvet; there wasn't a sound from the street. The length of a stair, two shut doors, it must be imagination that he could still hear the sound of a television in his wife's bedroom. He poured himself another glass and drank.

Foolish to worry about brain cells, until you knew whether growing old was going to be an option.

There was an AB, an AC and an AG as well us two Arthurs listed under Macleavy in the phonebook. Too many to tell the right one. After midnight, anyway too late. Best phone the Bridges office of Carter, Macleavy and Smillie in the morning. Early. Soon as it opened. Take the initiative. Even as he decided this, he slid the phonebook back into the circle of light and ran a finger down the five addresses: Dunbar, too far for a fat man to travel; Pilton, wrong district; Bruntsfield, flats. Musselburgh then, or Murrayfield. Suppose Macleavy had inherited his house from his father; family of lawyers; make Murrayfield the favourite. Carefully, checking each digit, he dialled the number.

Why should Macleavy sleep?

When it rang, he held the phone away from him and stared at in disbelief. Insistent, unmistakable, the engaged tone shrilled on and on. He put the phone down. It rang at once.

He picked the handset up gingerly and listened to the silence. Heard a sigh. A wheeze of breath taken.

'Well?' he asked at last, and heard the same heavy sighing.

'You're up late,' the voice said.

'You, too.'

And after all it wasn't impossible that Macleavy might be sitting in a room much like this one. It was possible that for him too, glass in hand, midnight had come and gone. Alone with his thoughts in a house of many rooms. Was it possible there in that private place that he too might be hearing, or imagining he heard, the sound of a radio in an upstairs bedroom? He knew nothing about him.

'Are you married?' he asked.

There was a grunt, as if of surprise. 'There's no one in the world you can threaten me with,' Macleavy said.

'Of course, you had a bad surprise, when I walked into your office.' He listened to the labouring breath. 'It seemed you were going to have a heart attack.'

'Unfortunately for you, no.'

'All the same, at least now I know who's trying to blackmail me.'

'That doesn't change the situation. I still have nothing to lose.'

'The sum you mentioned . . .'

'Yes?'

'It's too much.'

'For your reputation? Your freedom? So you don't get buggered in a prison lavatory? It's coming cheap.'

'If I had it, do you think I wouldn't pay? My wife has the money, and she won't give me it. That's the whole truth.'

'I don't believe you.'

All right, half truth. And despite everything smiled to himself. Guess which half, he thought.

'I don't believe you've asked her.'

'In my wife's family they don't give that kind of money away. If I ask her, she'll want to know why.'

'Tell her.'

'If I tell her, she'll go to the police.'

'If you want my professional advice, wives often don't. Standing by their man they call it. Like in the song.'

'She'll go to her father for advice. He'll tell her to go to the police. And if she didn't, he would.'

'I told you I've nothing to lose. Not one damned thing!' He broke off, began to cough, seemed unable to stop.

'You're not having another attack, are you? I recognise the symptoms. My wife has a bad heart.'

'Damn you, I don't!'

'Her doctor's told me she could go at any time. He doesn't expect her to make old bones.'

'What are you getting at?'

'I could kill my wife. You'd have to wait for your money, but it would come.'

There was a long wheezing silence. At last Macleavy said, 'I can't wait.'

'How long would it take, before I could give it to you? You're the lawyer, you tell me.'

'You're sure you inherit?'

'I get everything after she's dead.'

'I'd need proof of that.'

'I could do that.'

'Wait! You're going too fast. Listen, listen to me . . . Are you still there?'

'You say you can't wait. All right, tell me when you need the money. How much time do we have?'

'I don't believe you'd harm your wife.'

'I can't see any other way you'll get your money.'

'Not that way.'

'You're right about me not wanting to harm her. I don't want to harm anyone. You were the one who spelled it out – disgrace, going to prison.'

'We're talking about a human being.'

'One of God's creatures. Are you religious?'

For a second time, Macleavy lost control. 'Know you *won't* harm her. Doesn't *matter* what I want.' Great choked breaths made it hard to understand the words. '*I'll* go to the police. Tomorrow. I told you, nothing to lose.'

'I can kill her. According to you, I've taken a life already. The difference this time, you'll be an accomplice before the fact.' He hesitated, then pushed on. 'Equally guilty. So I'd be safer every way.'

But at this, there was a pause at the other end, then the sound of a deeply drawn breath. 'You have a nerve, say that for you. The cheek of the devil. I see what you're doing. Am I supposed to argue with you? Am I supposed to say, please, don't kill your wife? Forget the money, is that what I'm supposed to tell you?'

'Is that what you're saying?'

'*I can't forget the money.*'

No, he thought. Of course not. Reputation, freedom, they must be at stake for him too. And he'd die in prison even faster than I would.

Faintly then in the silence, it seemed as if he could hear music again being played overhead, somewhere in the house.

BOOK THREE

Walls

CHAPTER NINETEEN

'I'll tell you the absolute truth, Inspector, why I didn't come to the reading of Brian's will. Even though I said I would, promised you even. I suppose you could say, gave my word. The simple truth is, I've always hated unpleasantness.'

Meldrum was puzzled. George Snoddy had been in his office for quarter of an hour and had still to explain why he'd asked to be there. Sitting back in the hard chair on the other side of the desk, the late Brian Ashton's partner looked as elegant and abstracted as he had staring out of the window of his restaurant at the passing life of the street. Now, one leg thrown over the other, foot in the expensive black shoe tapping on air, his gaze kept drifting to the window, though the only view it gave was on to a brick wall.

'Naturally you were upset by Mr Ashton's death,' Meldrum ventured.

'I still think I'll wake up one morning and find it's been a bad dream.' He ran a hand back through the deep swoop of white hair without leaving a single one out of place. Meldrum wondered if a trick like that had to be practised in front of the mirror, then decided probably not. Maybe if you went to a top-name hairdresser, it had less to do with barbering scissors than dog-training class. As he watched, Snoddy did it again, the same combing gesture all the way from front to back. Down, Rover!

'There's no reason, though, for you to feel you should apologise to me. After all, it was your idea that you should come along to the lawyer's when we were asking him about Mr Ashton's will. I mean, whether you did that or not was entirely up to you. Not us. Not me.' For God's sake, he told himself, stop, enough! The man had a bad effect on him.

'I'm afraid you're missing the point,' George Snoddy said. He spoke firmly enough, but again his eyes slid to the window. Lunch numbers maybe of interest, people passing in the street possibly, brick wall certainly not. He just refuses to see what he'd rather not see, Meldrum thought, that's what it is. Snoddy wasn't fooling about not liking unpleasantness. Maybe that's why talking to him felt like wandering in the kind of mist that clears and thickens in patches. 'It was Arthur Macleavy I was reluctant to meet.'

'You didn't want to meet Arthur Macleavy?'

Before he could ask why, Snoddy said, 'It was embarrassing.'

Meldrum waited, watching the elegantly shod foot bob up and down. Snoddy caught his eye then glanced beyond him to the window. It seemed as if he felt that he'd explained sufficiently.

'Meeting him would be embarrassing?' A belated edge of impatience entered Meldrum's tone. 'Why would that be?'

'When you came to see me at Templars, I gave you the impression the restaurant was in profit. Wouldn't that be so?'

'I had the impression it was doing well.'

'I find it isn't in profit.'

Meldrum coped with the protracted silence better this time. Suddenly he had a notion his time wasn't going to be wasted after all. Quietly, he coaxed, 'Not in profit?'

'Quite the reverse. Rather badly so. When I spoke to you before, I had no idea. Everything came to Brian, you see.' His gaze unfocused. 'Papers, bills, correspondence, Brian dealt with that side of things. I . . .' Meldrum waited. With a sigh, he resumed, 'I dealt with the public. And with the look of the restaurant, the concept, the kind of food we served. Even now I have to say all of that was, is, a triumph. If I told you the establishments in Paris and London Templars has been compared to. And by people who matter . . . You'd recognise some of the names.'

Otherwise, as a mere policeman, you'd have no idea what I was talking about! Or so Meldrum read the expression that flickered across Snoddy's face as his gaze refocused on him.

'Ashton did the books,' Meldrum summarised brusquely, 'and now he's dead, you've discovered the business is in trouble.'

'Oh, worse than that. If I did nothing, it would cease to exist. But I have no intention of letting that happen.'

'Let me get this straight. My interest is in Brian Ashton. What was his financial position? When we spoke to the lawyer, Macleavy described what you'd get from Ashton's will as a substantial bequest. And that was *after* Ashton's wife had been given her share of the estate.'

'Well, he doesn't know. That's why it's embarrassing.'

'You'll have to explain that.'

'Well, I'd already been to him twice. Three times actually. And he'd advised me — twice actually — that I shouldn't.'

'Sorry?'

Like an echo, Shields's voice chimed, 'Sorry,' as he put his head round the door and saw Snoddy being interviewed.

Meldrum frowned and nodded him in.

After a glance round at Shields who was settling himself into a chair opposite the filing cabinets, Snoddy turned again as Meldrum asked, 'Could you explain, please? You'd been to Macleavy?'

Perhaps it was the sense of a larger audience, but at last the mist cleared and Snoddy emerged into clarity. 'When Brian came to me with the idea of Templars, I imagined the kind of place we could make and fell in love with it. Believe me, from that moment I was the one who was absolutely enthusiastic. Brian showed me the advertisement: just on the market, it had been some kind of ghastly hamburger and chips operation, but the site was perfect. New Town, on a corner, ground floor. It was a chance in a thousand. The thing was, we had to move fast. I went to Arthur Macleavy and told him I had to have money from the Trust Fund.'

'Trust Fund?'

'Didn't I say? I'm the last beneficiary of a Trust set up by an uncle of my grandfather's just before he died aged eighty. Money came from tea in Ceylon. Opium in China, too, perhaps, if you can believe family rumour. I have to say Macleavy was difficult. He asked me quite insistently if it was a wise investment. In the end I'd to tell him to do what he was told. It was very unpleasant.'

'What's his position with this Trust Fund?'

'The firm were lawyers for the Trust from the beginning back in 1924. Capital was invested very shrewdly by old Peter Carter, then by his son. When the son and young Tommy died — tragic business — Arthur Macleavy took over.'

'Did Brian Ashton put money into the restaurant as well?'

Snoddy put a fist to his lips, resting his head, glancing up as he shook his head. 'What he could. Before you ask, not half, not anything like half. He'd lost rather a lot of money, you see, in a previous venture. Well, we both did.'

'So you'd been in business together before?'

'Import-export with Eastern Europe. Brian spotted the opportunity, but we didn't allow for the morals of some of the people involved. We got in early, and if things had worked out we'd have done well. As Brian put it, we gambled and we lost.'

'But you didn't hesitate when Mr Ashton approached you with the restaurant idea?'

'Hesitate?'

'You didn't have any doubts. You'd already lost money in this previous venture — also suggested by him.'

'Not Brian's fault. Blame me too, if it's a matter of blame, which I don't accept. As I say, we were early into Eastern Europe, and early to learn the dangers. Since then a lot of others, banks, big companies, have had their fingers burned by the ex-comrades. You don't learn business ethics from reading Karl Marx. That's what I told Arthur Macleavy.'

'This would be when he was advising you not to put money into the restaurant?'

'Yes. And he went over the same ground again six months ago. I told him harking back to the European thing was totally inappropriate. I told him the money wasn't at risk at all. It wasn't for some new idea, it was to expand the business we had, because the restaurant had been such a tremendous success. That's what I told him.' Snoddy, who had been looking in the direction of the window, now closed his eyes altogether. 'As soon as I discovered the real state of affairs, I wrote to Macleavy to tell him why I needed more money from the Fund. A very great deal more. But I'm not looking forward to facing him.'

'I don't want to pry into your private affairs,' Meldrum said, 'but, as you can understand, Brian Ashton's state of mind is relevant to an investigation of his murder. It seems in the period leading up to his death he was concealing a very bad financial situation from you.'

'Conceal, oh, yes, he concealed, debts, borrowings, a second mortgage on the property. Six months ago I lifted sixty thousand from the Fund — to expand, would you believe! That's gone, God knows where. To save Templars, I'll have to put in, not sure yet, half a million anyway. But I'll do it. And I've been thinking hard and I made up my mind this morning I'll do it alone. I don't want a penny from Toni Ashton. There may not be any money for her, but at least I'll make sure she will get the house.'

There's chivalry for you, Meldrum thought.

He said, 'She's already got it. Ashton gave it to her when they broke up.'

'Ah,' Snoddy said. 'Ah. Oh, dear.' Pulling himself together, he went on, 'I was the partner. I should have been keeping an eye on things. Not her fault. The responsibility is mine.' His voice quavered with distress, but again as he put a hand through his hair it fell back precisely into place. 'What I find so hard, you speak of his state of mind. That's what I find so hard. He was just the Brian he's always been. There was the bother with his wife, of course, but basically he was just the same confident, ebullient Brian. If I were to tell you the truth, without him I feel absolutely lost.'

CHAPTER TWENTY

This time Stanley had insisted on taking the back seat, and it was from there, having caught up on recent events, that he asked, 'Half a million?'

'That's what Snoddy was estimating it would take to keep his business from bankruptcy.' Meldrum raised his voice, hoping Stanley would do the same. The light, hasty voice was harder to follow from the back than Shields's had been. 'So if we're thinking about Ashton's state of mind, now we know a failed marriage wasn't all that had gone wrong in his life. He wasn't just broke, he owed something like quarter of a million – assuming he and Snoddy were responsible for half each of the debt . . . And probably he'd have had criminal charges to face as well.'

'Why criminal charges?'

'Ashton had taken a second mortgage on the property. Snoddy claims he knew nothing about it, but as a partner any agreement would have needed his signature.'

'You think Ashton forged Snoddy's signature?'

'If he did, it would be something else for him to worry about.'

In the passenger seat, Shields unexpectedly chuckled, patting big hands on his knees. 'So he put on a frock.' Twisting round, he asked Stanley, 'Is that not what you call stress management?'

'Among certain African tribes, why yes, it would be.'

'Is that why there's a lot of black queers?'

'Is there? I've no idea. According to the research I've seen, the release into ritual behaviour means there's practically no mental illness in those tribes.'

'That right?' Shields asked, sounding interested despite himself. 'We talking about the men or the women? Bet the women aren't too happy.' Getting no answer, he settled back and commented sourly, 'Anyway, maybe Ashton thought the money wasn't a big deal. Cost you that for a shitty house on one of these new estates.'

Stanley said, 'What are you saying, two hundred and fifty thousand pounds is no big deal to you?'

He'd leaned right forward, his face between the seats, the sharpness of his tone taking them by surprise.

Shields reacted with a flash of anger. 'I didn't say it wasn't a big deal for me. But I'm just a policeman. Not a crook or a fucking businessman.'

'We're in agreement.' Stanley leaned back. From behind them he said, 'I couldn't find two hundred and fifty thousand pounds either,' his voice so soft Meldrum had to strain to hear him.

They drove in silence for a while until Shields said, 'Nearly home.'

Meldrum explained, 'Bobbie lives in Musselburgh.'

'One of the estates up the back,' Shields said, and added, 'Four in a block. Cost me a hell of a lot less than two fifty grand.'

After a bit, out on the open road beyond the port town, Meldrum raised his voice and said, 'You've never seen Snoddy.'

'Snoddy? Why?'

'Sorry. Just something I was thinking.'

'Would it make a difference if I did?' Stanley asked.

'I'd like to know what you made of him. I've talked to him twice, and it's just occurred to me chances are he'd have signed anything Ashton put in front of him.'

'Without reading it?'

'That's my guess. So it's possible Ashton could have slipped the agreement for this second mortgage into a pile of documents and handed them to him for signing. I could imagine Snoddy scribbling his signature on one thing after another while he was telling Ashton about a new menu, taking it all on trust.'

'I'll bear it in mind if I get a chance to talk to him.'

After a pause, catching some smouldering vibration from the passenger seat, Meldrum said, 'You saw Snoddy, Bobbie. You think he could have signed without reading what Ashton put in front of him?'

'If he did, he'd be a bloody fool.'

'Goes without saying.'

'I've a niece training to be a lawyer,' Shields said. 'She told me, your signature is the most valuable thing you own. Only nineteen, but she's a warmer.'

'In fact, if Snoddy *had* found out what was going on while Ashton was alive,' Meldrum said, 'I'm nearly sure he wouldn't have gone to the police.'

'So what would he've done?'

'Just what he says he'll do now. He'd've gone to that Trust Fund of his and taken out whatever was needed to fix it.'

Shields said, 'You think they were a couple of poofters?'

'Not necessarily.'

'Just good friends, eh?' And Shields managed another chuckle, this time not sounding really amused.

Stanley had leaned forward again, listening intently. He said, 'A man who's never had to worry about money from the day he was born might behave that way. If you start with empty hands, you either solve the world or go under. That's a hard lesson someone like Snoddy might not learn until it's too late. The bother with being born with a silver spoon in your mouth is you can choke on it.'

In the end, though, way things turned out, Meldrum thought as they crossed the flat East Lothian plain, it was Brian Ashton who choked first.

Another twenty minutes took them to the junction he was looking for, and he turned the car towards the Forth.

'Are we going in the right direction?' Stanley asked. 'I thought you said the other side of Haddington.'

'You're thinking of Gifford,' Shields said. 'How long have you lived in Edinburgh?'

'I must have misheard,' Stanley said.

'I'm not exactly sure where this place is myself.' Meldrum the peacemaker. 'We're looking for an estate wall, isn't that right, Bobbie? Grey stone, follow it along to the gate.'

'I'm surprised,' Stanley said, 'this man's willing to be interviewed where he works.'

'He doesn't know we're coming. Bobbie phoned and got instructions from some secretary how to get there.'

'Heard the word police, she got verbal diarrhoea,' Shields said, turning to grin at Meldrum, who concentrated on the road. 'They've had bother with trespassers apparently. Not my fault she got the impression that's what I was phoning about. Couldn't get a word in edgeways.'

They passed the ruins of a castle in a field. The water ahead of them reflected the blue summer sky. Over in Fife, on the other side of the Forth, there was a wink of light like a signal. Sun catching a car window, Meldrum thought, something like that. He remembered reading somewhere that in the desert the human eye could see a match being lit sixty miles away. They turned their backs on the water as the road looped inland again.

'This it?' Shields asked.

Grey estate wall. It went on for a surprising time. He had been slowing along its length and where it ended he braked gently and turned in through an open gate. Trees lined the drive on either side. Behind them stock fences wired off parkland with sheep and a scatter of lazy moving cattle.

'If you have to work somewhere,' Shields said, 'this would do, eh?' As he spoke, the drive widened and they came out in front of a house. The first impression was that it was enormous. 'Are we at the right place?'

As Meldrum steered from the drive into a forecourt and parked, he was asking himself the same question. Climbing out, he looked up at the bulk of grey stone looming above them, and told Shields, 'You were the one got the directions.'

'I'm beginning to wonder who was kidding who.'

'Henry?' Meldrum bent to open the rear door. 'Coming?'

'Sorry. Yes. Of course.'

Meldrum was struck by how small Stanley seemed, standing between him and Shields. The thought took him by surprise, that kind of comparison being forestalled normally by the force of Stanley's personality. Now, however, silently examining their surroundings, he gave the impression of having withdrawn into himself. Suddenly rousing, without a word he started towards the flight of stone steps at the front of the house. Shields and Meldrum, who'd been watching him, followed.

The matt steel plate carrying the company name set at the side of the door column seemed incongruously modern. Pressing a bell under it brought a woman's voice, and Shields's answer was followed by the release of the door lock.

Inside they found themselves in a large wood-panelled hall. Meldrum hardly had time to register the width of the staircase facing them and, surprising after the bright sunshine outside, a large fire blazing in an open hearth. The woman's voice called, 'In here, please,' and again as they looked around, 'Over here, please.' A door on the right lay open and, as they crossed to it, a clock somewhere out of sight began to chime the hour.

They went into what might once have been a small morning room, but now had the appearance of a cross between an office and a reception area. By the window, comfortable chairs were set around a low table furnished with magazines. From behind a computer on a large curved desk covered with papers, the woman who had been calling lost her smile as she saw the three men.

'Sergeant Shields?'

'Good morning,' Shields said, his tone pleasant and avuncular. 'We found our way, you see.'

'Yes. You're not—'

'Yes?'

'I thought you'd be in uniform.'

'Ah, no. Not for a long time. This is Detective Inspector Meldrum. And Dr Stanley.'

'We're here to see Mr Amott,' Meldrum said.

'I don't—' Standing up, she was taller than he'd have expected. As she came round the table, he realised that was because she had very long legs. She was too thin and too elegant for his taste and he didn't go around during work hours staring at women's legs, but he'd slept alone for too long. 'I thought you were here to – you said it was about the trespassers.'

Shields shook his head. 'You must have misunderstood. That would be uniformed branch. That kind of trouble I'd report it to your nearest police station.'

'Would you tell Mr Amott we're here, please?' Meldrum said in a tone suggesting he didn't have time to waste.

'He may not be here.'

'He works here.'

She recovered enough to indulge herself in a small sneer. 'The associates are as likely to be in London – or Europe or the United States, come to that – as here. In that case, you'll have had a wasted journey.'

Meldrum smiled. 'I'm sure you're too efficient not to know where they all are. Would you tell him we're here?'

She blinked. He watched her thinking about it.

'If you'd like to wait,' she said, and went out.

They listened to her heels tapping away down the hall.

'It might have been better to check he was here before we came,' Stanley said.

Meldrum grunted what might have been agreement. Without explaining Detective Constable Mary Preston had covered that in a call before Shields, he went over to the table by the window and picked up a magazine. He was half-way down the list of contents, when a noise made him raise his head. The brief dry sound, polite, peremptory, of a man clearing his throat. A tall man with the build of an athlete, in black casual gear so that the pale face above it stood out like the blade of an axe. He had very black hair with a single streak of white running back from the brow.

'Mr Amott?' Meldrum asked.

'Hardly.' The single word was unemphatic, a statement of what should have been obvious. After a pause, he said, 'You must be Inspector Meldrum.'

'That's right.'

Meldrum's automatic showing of identification got no more than a cursory glance. Ignoring Shields, the man fixed on Stanley and asked, 'Dr Stanley?'

'I'm not a policeman,' Stanley said.

'No.' He paused. 'I thought not.' Turning his attention to Meldrum, he said, 'Val tells me you want to speak to Roddie. May I ask what it's about? I'm John Markham.'

That brushed steel plate by the door. In discreet lettering: John Markham and Partners. Went some way to explaining, Meldrum thought, how the man had come into the room and taken charge as if it were the most natural thing in the world. It was unusual for that to happen to Meldrum. He felt authority in this man, the force of an unusually strong personality.

'Mr Amott may be able to help us with our enquiries.'

'Into?'

'The murder of a man called Brian Ashton. Mr Amott was a friend of his.'

'You surprise me.'

'Why would that be?'

'Bit of an age gap. I'd be more a friend of Brian's than Roddie's ever likely to have been.'

'You were a friend of Mr Ashton's?'

'We were at school together. Our ways parted, but I kept a residual affection for him. I was pained to hear how he died.'

'We're trying to find out what happened. Whether we do, depends on the help people can give us.'

'Which takes us back to Roddie. You can use the chairs by the window. If I close this door,' suiting the action to the word, he began to draw the doors shut behind him, 'you'll not be interrupted.'

Shields asked, 'I assume that means he's going to send the guy along?'

Meldrum shrugged and picked up the magazine again. From the corner of his eye he watched Stanley pacing back and forward. He decided the little man must be upset because Markham had made it clear they'd arrived unannounced. Though Henry could provide profiles, sometimes startlingly accurate, of criminals, he was still an academic who didn't really understand what had to be done to catch one. That was the difficulty of having him so closely involved; and now he'd another angle for when he wrote up the case. The Odd Couple cutting a corner. That should be worth a footnote on police ethics.

His thoughts were interrupted by a tap of knuckles on wood, followed at once by the door being opened too energetically, swung wide as if with a flourish.

'Roddie Amott. You really want to speak to me? What's it about?'

Glancing at Stanley, Meldrum caught his look of surprise. Though well preserved, Amott was not the young man Markham's talk of an age gap had obviously led Stanley to expect. In fact, the age gap with Ashton was the other way. According to the police file Meldrum had accessed, Amott was sixty-two.

'Mr Markham has given us the use of this room. Could we sit over here, please?'

As they arranged themselves round the table by the window, Meldrum introduced the other two and explained Stanley's presence. 'If you don't wish him to, Dr Stanley won't sit in on this interview.'

With a literal brushing movement, Amott put that aside. Pink and plump, hand matched face, the one manicured, the other shaved and pampered.

'Why should I object?' With a nod of acknowledgement, he said to Stanley, 'I understand the value of research. I spend half my life preparing reports and the other half reading them.'

'What does Markham and Partners do?' Stanley asked.

That he should have asked surprised Meldrum, for in earlier interviews after being introduced Stanley had made a point, at least initially, of fading into the background.

'Fund management. Investment advice. We're a conduit,' Amott said, and gave a fat little chuckle. 'Think of it this way, we direct where the money goes.'

And again uncharacteristically Stanley took the initiative. 'A place like this. You must give remarkably good advice.'

'We haven't made many mistakes. Back in the Eighties, we burnt our fingers with Goldcrest. That cured us of investing in films. And a steelworks in the former Czechoslovakia didn't turn out well.'

And for the third time, Stanley responded before Meldrum could speak. 'A place like this,' he said, untypically repeating himself.

Amott looked smug. 'It impresses clients.'

Meldrum opened his mouth to find Stanley ahead of him again. 'It can't all be offices?'

'It's used for hospitality.'

'Is it lived in?'

'In a way.'

'Does Mr Markham live here?'

But Amott hesitated and with a glance, as if seeking an explanation of this persistence, asked Meldrum, 'What was it you wanted to see me about?'

'Didn't Mr Markham tell you I'm investigating the death of Brian Ashton?'

'Yes. I didn't know what to make of it.'

'Why is that?'

'Well, obviously, I couldn't see what it has to do with me.'

'But you did know Brian Ashton?'

'Well, yes, but that doesn't mean I can help you. I know a lot of people. He's the only one who's ever been murdered, thank God.'

'How well would you say you knew him?'

'Something between an acquaintance and a friend.'

'You had shared interests?'

'Music, more than anything. One or two events at the Festival most years, plus the occasional visit over the winter to the Queen's Hall. He had a particular passion for Mahler – the composer?'

'How did you first meet him?'

'It's a long time. Ten, fifteen years, bit more maybe. I don't know. Mutual friends.'

'You couldn't be more specific?'

'No. Why would you want me to be?'

'You're telling me you can't name these mutual friends?'

'Hold on. I've changed my mind.' Indicating Stanley, Amott hitched himself to the edge of his chair. 'Either he leaves or I do. I don't want him here.'

Stanley stood up at once. 'I'm sorry you feel like that, but of course. I'll take a walk in the grounds while I'm waiting.'

There was a silence until the door closed behind him.

'I told you it's a long time ago,' Amott said.

'Leave that for the moment then. We were talking about the interests you shared with Ashton. Did they include gambling?'

'Oh.' The fingertips of a plump hand patted his lips. 'You people never forget, do you?'

At the end of August two years before, Amott and Brian Ashton had been in the Rex Casino in George Street. There had been a discussion between Ashton and another man across a blackjack table. Later in the restaurant of the casino while the man was having supper Ashton had come over and resumed the topic. By that time, both men had consumed enough alcohol for the discussion to become heated and finally abusive. Before entering the casino, the man had parked in a lane off Hanover Street, and it was there he was found about four in the morning in a doorway not far from his car, unconscious and badly beaten.

'You're talking about something that happened years ago.'

'Two years. It was during the Festival, but maybe there wasn't anything by Mahler – the composer – on that night.'

'Don't take that tone with me!'

Meldrum raised his eyebrows as if in surprise. 'It didn't bother you that the man might have been seriously injured?'

'He wasn't.'

'It's too soon to tell. When a man's head gets stamped on, it may cause damage that won't show up at once.'

'If you've read —'

'Oh yes, I've gone through the records.'

'Then you'll know it was a fine not a custodial sentence. That tells you how trivial the incident was.'

'Do you remember the lawyer you had for the defence?'

'Not really. Vaguely, two years since. Why?'

'John Brennan would be disappointed. He takes pride in knowing everyone – and vice versa.'

'John Brennan. Yes, I remember. So?'

'The best criminal lawyer in Scotland. He can afford to pick and choose. He does pick and choose. You were lucky to get him for a trivial incident.'

Amott shrugged. 'We could pay.'

'Does Mr Markham know about it?'

'If he does, he's never mentioned it.'

'I wondered, because it wasn't in any of the papers.'

'Because it wasn't important.'

'That could be it.'

With that, Meldrum sat back. As the silence went on, Amott became increasingly restless. At last he said, 'Is that all?' Getting no response, he stood up. 'If that's all, then there's no reason for me to stay.' But he hesitated fractionally, less certain now, before moving towards the door.

'Aren't you curious?' Meldrum asked. Amott broke stride and turned. 'Why I'm asking about something that happened two years ago? That would be the natural question.'

'Right, I *don't* know why you're talking to me. And I don't like the manner in which you're talking to me. Where do you think you are?' As his voice rose, the colour in his face darkened. 'Maybe *I* should talk. How would that be? To one of your superior officers?'

'Before you do, let me tell you why I decided to check if Ashton had any record of violence. In the course of our enquiries into his death, a reliable witness told us Ashton and another man had made an attack on a homosexual, probably one of a series of similar attacks. This one apparently was a very violent assault, though no one was caught for it. But then they say attacks on homosexuals are like attacks on Asians or Chinese, don't they? The public doesn't care and so the police don't try very hard. Have you heard that? Anyway, when I learned of this assault, I sent an officer to talk to the victim. A man called James McCluskie. He worked in an insurance office. According to his employer, he was competent and well liked. His wife described him as someone who went out of his way to help people. Unfortunately, the officer couldn't interview McCluskie himself. He died suddenly about eight weeks after the assault. He'd been complaining of headaches. His head had been stamped on, too.' As if answering a question, Meldrum had laid all this out quietly, his manner matter of fact. By the end, the high colour had ebbed from Amott's face. Now Meldrum asked, 'Would you sit down again, please?'

Back in the seat he'd left, Amott cut a very different figure. His voice sounded thinner. 'If you're suggesting – that would be an outrageous suggestion. I had the bad luck to be with Ashton that night. If you've read about it, you'll know it was Ashton people remembered because of the way he lost his temper. I'd never been in the place before, he was a member – he was the one people knew – I was only at the casino because he signed me in as a guest. If I was any kind of a friend of his it was because we went to concerts together. And then he mentioned this casino, asked me if I'd like to go there. As it turned out, he was a lot keener on gambling than he was on music. He was the one who attacked the man. The police searched his house and they found . . . He'd cleaned his shoes, but the police found blood on them.'

'In the corrugations on the soles.'

'You don't need to tell me how ghastly it is. But there were mitigating circumstances. The man was horribly rude to him and—'

'And he was Chinese. And you had a lawyer who could make the telephone directory sound like the Lord's Prayer.'

Amott stared at his hands clasped tight in his lap. 'When I walked out of the courtroom, it felt like a miracle.' He looked up and met Meldrum's gaze. 'Do you think I'd ever, ever again in my life, risk that nightmare again? I haven't seen Ashton since we were in court. You can't find one person in the whole world who could say they've seen me with him since that day.'

'That presents a difficulty,' Meldrum said 'According to my witness, Ashton and this other man dressed themselves as women. You can see how that complicates an identification.'

'Look at me.' Amott got to his feet. 'Look at my face. I'm over sixty. I eat too much. Look at the shape of me.' He plucked at his shirt as if he would pull it up to expose the soft bulge of his belly, the slack body inside the well-cut suit, plucked at the loose skin of his cheek, screwed up his eyes. Obscenely, fright stripped him of vanity, as if he'd thrown himself from the long plateau the well-fed live on and become an old man. 'How could I pretend to be a woman?'

On the steps outside Meldrum took a deep breath. The air drawn down into his lungs felt good, salt and clean.

'Careful.' Shields shot out a big hand and caught him by the elbow.

Looking down, Meldrum saw the stone of the step he'd slipped on was worn and covered in a sheen of green moss.

They stood by the car, looking around, waiting for Stanley to put in an appearance.

'You can smell the money,' Shields said.

'Yes.'

'Bastards,' Shields said.

'Plenty of them about.'

'Interesting about Ashton being a gambler,' Shields said.

'Yes?' Meldrum said, taken by surprise.

'Thing is, that could explain where all the restaurant cash went. A gambler that loses his temper. That's a gambler that's a loser, eh?'

'Right.'

'Another thing, we should check that casino — what did he call it?'

'The Rex. It's not open all that long.'

'Aye, the Rex. We should check and see if Ashton was there the night he was killed. You know, in the woman's gear. We've tried the clubs and gay bars. He had to have been out somewhere dressed like that. Worth a shot, eh?'

'Yes, sure. Absolutely.'

'Did you notice, when you said to that guy about telling his boss, he wasn't bothered? What did you make of that?'

This was more than Shields volunteered in a normal month. Recovering, Meldrum began to respond. 'It could be because Markham knows. Though it's true the court case was kept out of the papers somehow or other. I almost got the impression Amott was pleased at the idea I might tell him. It was strange.'

Meldrum, now into this unexpected swing of things, paused to let Shields give his opinion. There was, however, a long silence, which Shields seemed disinclined to break. Whistling softly, he'd turned to lean with both hands on the parapet, looking at the trees that lined the hill as if trying to see through them to the sea beyond. Without looking round, he said, 'You really go at it with rich folk.'

'What?' Meldrum had been checking the time, as he wondered about walking to the end of the house on the chance he might spot Stanley.

'You give them a hard time. You know that? Maybe you don't realise.'

'Realise what?'

'All I'm saying is, there's no sense looking for trouble.'

'Fuck,' Meldrum said in disgust. 'Me landing you in the shit, is that what this is about? I wondered what'd wakened you up. Don't worry. If Amott complained, what could he say about you? You never opened your fucking mouth. As usual.'

The interval till Stanley came back passed in silence.

CAT IN A TRAP

'John Bellany,' the man said. A tall, wide-shouldered man, big-boned but slim, in black casual gear so that the pale face stood out like the blade of an axe. Above it, hair so black it shone; a single streak of white running back from the brow. He knew now that the man's name was John Markham.

'What?'

'I took it you were admiring the painting, Dr Stanley. It's Bellany from his best period.'

High on the other wall, colour like slashes of blood, heraldic beak poised above a naked head.

As he had shut the door of the reception area behind him, all he'd wanted was to get out of the house as fast as possible. But when he'd seen the hall empty in front of him, the tight discipline he had maintained till then had given way. He'd closed his eyes, his legs shook, he was afraid he would faint. Lingeringly, then, as if under compulsion, he'd gone over to the fire. Momentarily, he'd hallucinated the tapping of heels on a wooden floor and been afraid to look up from the red lick of burning gas through the fake logs for fear of seeing a naked woman with the high feathered skull of a bird pass across the landing above. As he'd forced himself to raise his head, from behind him there had come the sound of a throat being cleared, a brief dry sound, polite, peremptory. Naked flesh. The fierce head of a bird.

John Markham had been standing by the last door at the end of the hall, watching him.

'We're proud of our collection,' Markham continued. 'Rae, Howson—'

'I know.'

'Yes, of course you do.' He came forward, smiling. 'I'm grateful to you for not pretending you've had a lapse of memory. It saves time, and neither of us has time to waste.'

Deliberately misunderstanding, Stanley said, 'I don't know how long the police will be with Mr Amott. I suppose it will depend on how frank he is with them.'

He heard his voice, firm and quiet, and it pleased him. As quickly as needed, he had brought himself under control.

'Oh, I shouldn't care for him to be frank. Let's settle for persuasive.'

'You know they're here to question him about an assault?'

'As I understand it, nothing too serious. It's not as if he murdered someone,' Markham said casually, and in the same tone. 'There's something I'd like to show you upstairs.'

Stanley glanced at the closed door of the reception area. 'They'll expect to find me waiting for them.'

'Don't worry.' Markham was amused. As if, Stanley thought, he imagines I meant that as a warning – people know I'm here. Like the girl in the horror movie. 'If they're too quick and have to wait for you, tell them you went for a walk in the grounds.'

Stanley shrugged. 'Why not then?'

As they started up, he gripped the bannister at each step, pulling himself forward against his own resistance. Beside him, in the middle of the staircase's impressive width, Markham moved lightly with a kind of constrained energy as he adjusted to a slower pace. Sunlight from above flooded down on them. Looking up, Stanley had the illusion of looking down through the cupola into an unblemished bowl of blue sky.

'Do you live here?'

'I can.'

'Your business must do well.'

They turned left on the landing and came into what must once have been the picture gallery.

'It does, but it would have to do spectacularly well to justify all this.' Long windows displayed the traditional prospects of the country mansion: lawns, fields, woods, hills. 'The estate was bought for a client, who's happy to let us have office space on the ground floor. Our main client, you could say our indispensable client, the source of ninety per cent of our investment capital.' Their footsteps echoed on the uncarpeted wooden floor. 'We've bought golf courses in Scotland for him and holiday complexes in Spain. Grand country living is just another investment. At some point, he'll sell the house, grounds and all.' Patches of lighter space on the drab wall to their right testified to where pictures must once have been hung. 'But I hope that won't be for a long time to come.' As they approached the gallery's farther end, Markham stopped in front of the last window. 'I'd miss the grounds.'

Brought to a halt, however, Stanley was struck not by the view, so splendid in glimpses caught in passing, but by the unwashed, smeared glass which separated them from it.

'In the meantime, he has the whole top floor as living quarters. It's a place for parties. When he flies in from LA, he expects them to be laid on.' Dust layered grey siftings on the ledge and floor. 'Very private parties. Very discreet.'

Stanley wet a forefinger and rubbed a tiny circle clear on the glass. 'Let our servants live for us,' he said.

'What?'

'Leconte de Lisle said that. I'm reminded of it when you tell me a millionaire from California has to come here for an orgy.'

Markham smiled. 'Wherever it goes, a pig needs a trough. This particular pig is a throwback to a more innocent age. He has the soul of a Dominican friar. Lack of guilt takes the fun out of his sin. For him, that's the charm of Edinburgh. He knows it's fading here as everywhere, but he likes to believe we preserve the remnants of disapproval. We try to keep it from him that nowadays our factory girls crowd into halls to fondle the buttocks of black strippers.'

'*Factory* girls?'

'Buildings may be obsolete. The poor white trash are always with us.'

They emerged from the gallery into a narrow corridor. 'There's a stair at the end here. But it's been walled off. We'll use this.' He opened a door and instead of going in paused, blocking Stanley's view of what might be inside. There was the sound of metal moving on metal. Stepping aside, he waved Stanley to go in ahead of him. As he did and sensed Markham close at his back, he found himself in a windowless room about six feet square. In a claustrophobic instant, he felt an impulse of panic. Only when the floor pressed up against his feet did he realise they were in a lift. When it stopped, the change was so smooth as to be almost imperceptible. Markham slid back the grille.

Walls papered in heavy purple. Thick carpeting underfoot. Up here, the air was warm and still. One open door offered the impression of a room as big as a ballroom. Another room seemed to have a bar along the wall. The next: leather armchairs and wood-panelled walls like a reminiscence of a gentlemen's club. And pictures everywhere. Part, no doubt, of that collection of which Markham was so proud. But, seeing him glance from side to side, as if reading his mind, Markham said, 'I chose the paintings for downstairs. These were bought under advice for our American Saatchi.' Finally, they came to a room which Markham entered without knocking. He didn't make any attempt to be quiet. Yet going in after him, Stanley saw not only that they were in a bedroom but that a trail of discarded clothes, tie shirt pants trousers one plaid sock, led from the door to the bed. In the bed a heavy-set man with a very hairy chest lay snoring on a downie. He was naked apart from one plaid sock. Markham walked over and stood looking down at him. 'Come and see.' He spoke in a normal voice. 'Doesn't he resemble a pig? He is a pig. A very rich American pig. His name is Michael Hamas.'

'Your main client,' Stanley said in not much more than a whisper.

'My *indispensable* client.'

'Should I be here if he wakes up?'

At this Markham threw back his head and laughed. 'I shouldn't advise it. He's a violent man. As that unfortunate Chinaman, the one you were so concerned about, discovered.'

'Ah,' Stanley said, 'I thought Amott was covering up for you.'

'No, for Hamas. Clever of you all the same.' Markham looked at the floor and shook his head. 'I wonder what in the world he imagined he was searching for?'

Stanley followed Markham's gaze downwards. Hamas must have sat on the edge of the bed fumbling through his wallet for it lay on the floor amongst a spill of plastic cards with notes in at least three currencies fanned out around it.

'Happiness, do you think?' Markham stirred the mess on the floor with the toe of his shoe. 'Probably not. No, it was Hamas who was with Ashton that night at the casino. Given the vicious streak in them both, the Chinaman was lucky to survive. When Ashton was identified, Roddie Amott came forward and confessed to being the second assailant.'

'Why?'

'It's what he's there for.'

'Why would he do that?'

'Oh, think about it!' Markham said with impatience, almost contempt.

Stung, Stanley said, 'Because Hamas had to be protected. Because without him, Markham and Partners would be nothing.'

Markham nodded. 'Because I like the view from these windows.'

As he spoke, he went over to the french windows. When he opened them, Stanley felt a touch of cooler air. The man on the bed blew out his lips in a sigh, but did not stir.

'It's too bad about Brian Ashton. If I'd seen you with him that night anywhere else on earth but here, I'd have cheerfully helped to put you away for life. A short life perhaps. You don't look like a man who could cope with prison. But rest easy. I've shown you all this, so you'll understand why we have a common interest in keeping attention away from here.'

'I can do that,' Stanley said. 'I've made myself part of the investigation. Meldrum listens to me. More than he realises. Believe me, I can handle him.'

Again, he listened to himself, his voice calm and sure. Thinking of it afterwards, once again he would marvel at the man he had become.

'There is one difficulty,' Markham said. 'Arthur Macleavy is trying to blackmail me.'

Without waiting for a response, he stepped out on to the balcony. When Stanley got there, he saw him leaning on the balustrade staring out as if admiring the view. Without looking round, Markham said, 'It seems he's very badly in need of money.'

'Blackmailing you? I don't understand.'

'About Ashton bringing you here that night. About me seeing you with him. Since I haven't gone to the police, he assumes I have something to hide.'

'But how could he know?'

'I assume because you told him.' He glanced over his shoulder. At something in Stanley's expression, he nodded to himself. 'Maybe without meaning to. He seems to be unusually quick on the uptake.'

'Are you going to pay him?' Stanley fought to keep the upsurge of hope out of his voice.

'For your sake, I'd like to be able to say yes. But the answer's no.'

'Not even if it would prevent a scandal? If that happens, Hamas will walk away. You were willing to cover up for me.'

'You,' Markham said, 'don't cost anything. Macleavy is greedy. If I paid the extravagant amount he's asking, do you think he wouldn't come back for more?'

'What are you going to do?'

'Me? Not a thing. If there's a solution, you'd better find it.'

From the room behind, Stanley heard a groan. Hamas had rolled on to his side and lay facing the window. Instinctively, Stanley retreated to the balcony. As he came to the balustrade, he saw Meldrum and Shields below like toys beside a toy car. He stepped back out of sight.

'They've been there for some time,' Markham said. 'You should get back to them, before they start wondering where you've been.'

BOOK FOUR

Cold Hearts

CHAPTER TWENTY-ONE

Meldrum had been only once in the Rex Casino, part of a group taken there by John Brennan. This was during the months when he was living with the woman who had been one of Brennan's lovers and later became the lawyer's second wife. As a policeman, from the beginning he'd been scrupulous about taking no favours, since even casual hospitality could come back as a request for a favour returned. Under the circumstances, though, there hadn't seemed a choice about making Brennan an exception to his rule; but he'd accepted the invitation with a bad grace and a conscience to match. Predictably, he hadn't enjoyed himself. Even so, his memory was of lights and glitter, other people's laughter. The surprisingly faded look of the place in the morning gave him a moment of grim satisfaction.

The woman Shields and he had come to see, however, was young and cheerful. She'd only had four hours sleep and if she hadn't set two alarms when she went to bed, she'd still be out to the world. Yet as she told them this, laughing, she looked fresh as a week at a health farm. She had left Australia three years before and seen a lot of the world since, supporting her travels by working as a croupier and dealer at the card tables. More importantly, while a number of the staff knew Brian Ashton, she was the only one who had claimed to recognise the photograph of him dressed as a woman.

'I know what you're going to tell me,' she said. 'I was through it all with the two who came and showed the photos round. Yes, it's a couple of weeks ago. Yes, the place was packed that night. Yes, I've seen hundreds of people since. Am I sure it's him? Am I *sure* I'm sure? How can I be sure? No problem. I'm *bloody* sure.'

This flooded out with such a pleasant emphasis, as if asking, isn't that great?

Aren't you in luck? that Meldrum found himself grinning. 'I believe you. But time has passed. The place would be crowded, you'd be busy. If Ashton was really in here that night, then chances are this is where he met the person who killed him. That could be very important. Suppose you had to swear to it in court. We have to know what makes you so sure.'

The girl's cheerfulness dimmed. 'Don't count on me being in any court. Not because I'm backing down. I'd go to court all right, no problem. If I was here. But I might not be. One of these days I'll wake up and that'll be it, I'll be ready to go home.'

'I'll let you into a secret,' Meldrum said. 'With murderers, the longer it takes the less chance you have of catching them.'

'Right then,' she said, brightening, 'it's a race. I hope you win. If I'm here when you catch your murderer, I'll tell a jury it's not every day you see a man in a frock.'

'You knew it was a man? Was it that obvious?'

'It wasn't just about was it a man or a woman, was it? It's who it was, isn't that the point? I recognised *Brian Ashton*.'

'Under make-up? In a red wig?'

'He was at the table for an hour. Close as I am to you now. He's a member. I've seen him often before. Jesus, he made a pass at me. You know there's a nice way to do that and a nasty way? He was nasty. And I was there when he quarrelled with the Chinaman – you know about that? That was at my table. He wasn't wearing a frock that night, of course. The night you're talking about, when he was in drag, he was losing. And right from the start he wasn't happy about losing. But like the night with the Chinaman, he didn't stop. The bets got bigger. And then he went for it, biggest bet I'd seen him making ever. And when he lost he got the same look on his face I saw that night with the Chinaman. Wig and paint make no difference. He wanted to hurt somebody. He wanted to hurt somebody real bad.'

CHAPTER TWENTY-TWO

'On the whole,' Stanley said, 'I can't see things progressing until the missing wife turns up.'

They were waiting for Shields, who was collecting the latest data from the collators on interviews with patrons of the Rex Casino. Meantime, as a courtesy, Meldrum, long legs stretched out behind his desk, was taking Stanley through the things he'd missed, including that morning's briefing of the police team.

'You think Toni Ashton's involved?'

Stanley smiled. 'I'm not sure. But I've a feeling you are. There's a danger you'll be threshing around until you can get to grips with her. If you'll pardon the expression.'

'Finding her came up at the briefing. I've put somebody on to backtracking everything we've got on her. Bother is she doesn't seem to have any relatives – or friends apart from Naomi Morgan. And we've seen how Morgan's family was a dead end. It's probably time to push Baird, clear it with him that I want to go public and see if we can find them that way. Have you had any more thoughts about Amott?'

'I wish I'd been able to sit in while you were talking to him.'

'He took fright when he trumbled we were there about the assault on the Chinaman. If that's what we'd come to talk about, then the fewer people there the better as far as he was concerned. But yet, like I told you, he didn't seem bothered if Markham was told he'd been involved in a court case.'

Stanley shrugged. 'I don't see much significance in that. After all, why should he be too bothered, if he's a partner – I assume he is?'

'No idea. Associates, partners, I've no idea what that kind of set-up would involve.'

'Well, put it this way. His job may not depend on Markham.'

'Maybe . . . But Markham was pretty formidable. Didn't he strike you that way? Boss or not, what he thought of you would matter to most people. He was that kind of man. A strong man.'

'I wasn't so impressed by him as you seem to have been,' Stanley said. 'But in any case, to be honest, I can't see Amott being relevant at all. The incident itself, yes, the assault on the Chinaman tells us that Ashton was violent, vicious even. And that's confirmed by the girl from the casino's impression of him. It looks more and more as if Ashton was one of the two men involved in the attacks on homosexuals. But, as for Amott, he seems to lack hardihood both physically and mentally, not tough or a tough guy. At a guess, he had the bad luck to be with the wrong man on the wrong night, when Ashton quarrelled with the Chinaman. But if we want to find Ashton's accomplice, we'd be wasting our time looking at Amott. Apart from anything else, it's true you couldn't imagine him dressed as a woman – not an attractive one anyway.'

'Hard to imagine anyone could think Ashton was either. He was a big man.'

Ignoring the objection, Stanley hurried on. 'Ashton and AN Other play this game – get into drag – cruise gay bars – pick up queers and when they get them somewhere quiet, beat them half to death. If they'd gone on, chances were they'd have escalated to killing. Maybe after torturing their victims. But on this particular night, Ashton is on his own. Possibly they'd arranged to meet in the casino and the accomplice was late. While he's waiting, Ashton is gambling and losing and getting angrier. And this unfortunate man makes the mistake of coming on to him. The mood Ashton was in, this could well have been the night when assault escalated to murder. Only this time he's on his own and it goes wrong.'

'And it's Ashton who gets killed,' Meldrum said. 'If that's anywhere near the truth, Ashton was a dangerous bastard. Makes you wonder why he didn't try to sort out the wife's lover.'

'If he knew who he was.'

'Broke up his marriage, called it the last straw, he must have known.'

'To come back to the pick-up in the casino,' Stanley said. 'We'd be looking for a homosexual. But one who's firmly in the closet. And one who's physically strong. Even on his own without the accomplice, it would take a big man to deal with Ashton.'

'It wasn't a fist fight,' Meldrum said. 'Ashton was killed with a knife.'

'Doesn't a knife take strength? I mean, it's not like a gun.'

Meldrum thought about it, nodded. 'Probably you're right. But I'm not sure we're looking for a homosexual. This wasn't a gay bar like the other times. It was in a casino, Ashton was dressed as a woman. Maybe the killer thought he was picking up a woman.'

Stanley looked sceptical. 'Not a very attractive one. As you said, apart from anything else, he was big.'

'It depends how badly the man who saw him wanted to be deceived. A man who was obsessed enough would see what he wanted to see. Some men like big women.'

'That's very subtle.'

'No. It's talking to girls on the game.'

'Let me play the policeman then, since you're playing the psychologist. I'll stick to the simple explanation. Isn't that usually better?' He smiled as if at a sudden thought. 'Straight man or gay, either way we could forget Toni Ashton.'

Meldrum grunted. 'And either way, it would be unpremeditated. And probably in self-defence. Not an interesting murderer, in fact a bad pick for your project. Seems as if that instinct of yours has let you down, Henry.'

'Worst of all for us both,' Stanley said, 'with an unpremeditated crime, the chances of anyone, interesting or not, ever being caught for the murder are pretty low.'

'No.'

'No?'

'I'll catch him.'

There was a silence. Stanley said, 'I'm amazed Ashton was still a member of the casino. I'd have imagined they'd have banned him after the assault.'

'He was a heavy loser.'

'Still, if the Chinaman was a member, surely they'd have had to do something if he objected?'

Meldrum laughed, something he didn't often do. 'Maybe the Chinaman was a heavy winner.'

'Policemen are cynics.'

'Member or not, how did Ashton get into the casino?' Meldrum wondered. 'Dressed as a woman, he's not going to get the nod from a doorman. So how did he get in?'

'I've no idea.'

'No? You're disappointing me, Henry. Usually you'd have half a dozen ways. Something wrong?'

'Not a thing,' Stanley said. Suddenly he smiled and said, 'You're giving me a hard time, because I once said you weren't clever. *Once*, when I'd had too much to drink.'

Meldrum returned his smile. 'Right enough, I'm not so clever. But I did think of one way Ashton could have got in. As well as trying to get a check on the casino's membership, I've got Cormack and Mary Preston taking a look at the guest list for that night.'

'You think somebody might have signed him in?'

'Suppose Ashton's accomplice was there as well after all. Suppose that's how Ashton got in. If the accomplice was a member and signed him in, then we should be looking for that. A member who signed in *a woman guest*.'

'Bit risky. Both of them members, getting up to their tricks in a place where they're known.'

'Maybe Ashton was bored with the gay bars. Wanted something different. So he persuaded the other guy. Who knows?'

'It's possible,' Stanley said. 'Ashton had stolen money and almost ruined his business, he was obsessed with the loss of his wife. He was angry and unhappy and probably a little crazy. It would be a fair guess the cross-dressing and assaults were his idea. If so, chances are he'd be the dominant one of the pair. But if the accomplice was there that night in the casino, why didn't he follow Ashton and the pick-up?'

'What makes you think he didn't?' And when Stanley seemed lost for an answer, Meldrum answered his own question. 'All right, I don't think he did either. If he had, there would have been some sign of a third man in the house where Ashton was killed. Maybe the other guy was supposed to follow and got prevented somehow. Or maybe Ashton decided he wanted to do this one on his own.' He broke off. 'What is it?'

Stanley had begun to laugh, light, high, uncontrollable, almost a giggle.

'I just had a thought. If the accomplice was there, whether he was going to be involved or not, he'd almost certainly have been keeping an eye on Ashton. In that case, chances are he would see the man who picked Ashton up. So now we have another possible witness who could identify the murderer.'

'What's funny about that?'

'Nothing,' Stanley said, his shoulders shaking. 'I'm being silly.'

CHAPTER TWENTY-THREE

The call came to the switchboard in the middle of the afternoon, when Meldrum, as it happened, had crossed the Forth Road Bridge into Fife to talk to a baker, Colin Pates, whose name had been turned up by a computer search of the files. Eleven months earlier, Pates had gone to the police to complain that he'd been assaulted after an evening's drinking in a gay club. He'd been knocked about, bruised, humiliated, but not badly hurt. The kind of incident, in other words, that had a tendency to go unreported, the victim, not untypically with wife, family, respectable day job, deciding in the morning to leave the night world to the night. Not so, however, the morally outraged Pates who, as ignorant as the next layman of the symbiotic relationship between some policemen and some news desks, in due course found himself in the papers. Fortunately, in a tolerant community his sexual proclivities seemed to have aroused no animosity, and Pates's mutton pies had retained their local celebrity. He had been attacked by two men, and reading the case, though they hadn't been in drag, Meldrum's instinct had been strong enough to make him decide to go and talk to Pates himself. An hour talking to the baker, though, had pretty well decided him it was a wild goose chase. So much for instinct.

Towards the end of the afternoon, then, Meldrum arrived back with Shields by his side and a bag of pies on the back seat to find that Ivor Warren's phone call had been logged almost three hours earlier.

'Do you know what this is? No, look at it. What is it? I can't hear you. A mobile phone. So it is, so it fucking is. Plumbers have them, gasmen have them, everyone has them. So even if I'm out of the car you can get in touch. That's why I've got one. So if something important happens, you get in touch. This call comes in at three o'clock, and I hear about it at – what is it? – ten to six, I hear about it at ten to six. You think it's not important? It's important, it's *fucking important.*'

All this was said quietly. Meldrum had got out of the habit of raising his voice. If he'd been asked, his feeling would have been that he'd taken the error too quietly, that he should have made himself heard on the top floor of the building. He would have believed that he was not being emphatic enough over things that needed to be dealt with forcefully. He would even have felt, as he'd done increasingly in his lower moods recently, that he was allowing himself to be disregarded.

Yet in the car on their way through Bruntsfield, Shields blew out his breath and with a side glance said, 'You almost gave that poor bastard a heart attack. Not often you lose your temper.'

Meldrum said nothing, hiding his surprise. The truth was that he hadn't lost but gripped his temper. For more than a year, since he had connived at the suicide of a child molester, he had been afraid to lose it again.

When they pulled up outside the house, Ivor Warren was out of the opposite gate before Meldrum had time to switch off the engine.

'I recognised your car,' he bellowed in mid-approach. 'Couldn't tell you the make, but the look of it, shape, colour, size, does the trick. Like birdwatching.' Confiding as he came to rest, 'I thought you'd be here damn sight quicker than this.'

Meldrum gazed over his head at the house. The upstairs curtains were still drawn. 'I just got your call,' he said, and regretted the admission, like a disloyalty, or because it entailed the tedium of having to explain.

Warren, however, contented himself with 'Machines get fancier, people stay the same. Human error, they call it now. In the war, we called it a cock-up. Thing is, I can't tell you whether Mrs Ashton and friend are still in there.'

Shields said, 'If they are, they're not answering the phone.'

'Aren't they? I didn't try to phone. Not that I wasn't tempted when I realised the car had gone from where they'd parked it. I'd been keeping watch since I saw them arrive. And that was just a lucky accident, I happened to be sitting at the window. Couldn't believe my eyes. Looked up from my paper and the little dark one, the Morgan woman, was opening the gate to let the car into the drive. I ran downstairs and was just in time. From the corner of my garden I saw Mrs Ashton getting out of the car. Then the two of them went into the house.'

'Did they see you?' Shields asked.

'Pretty sure not. Couldn't swear to it. Be surprised if they did. Anyway, I phoned your lot and sat at the window expecting you any minute. Finally, I'd to answer a call of nature. Having to come off watch made me uneasy, though I told myself there was no reason to be. When I came back, I sat for maybe another half hour, then I just had to check. Car wasn't there. I couldn't believe my eyes. Took a chance and went over to their gate to get a proper look. Came back and had a think. Two possibilities, you see. While I was having a shit, they get in the car and go off again. *Or* they've put the car in the garage and they're still in there. Thought about phoning the house to see if anyone answered, but decided against it. Didn't want to risk frightening them off.'

'When would this be?'

'When I found the car wasn't in the drive? About half an hour ago. That's when I phoned your lot again, and was told you were on your way.'

As they went up the path, Meldrum realised that Warren was marching along behind them.

'Thanks for your help,' he said for the second time. 'We'll take it from here, sir.'

'Of course.' Warren's jowls shook an emphasis to his nod of understanding. 'You, eh, carry on then.'

Shields was laughing as he leaned on the bell. 'He'll be breaking the speed record up the stairs to his window.'

Meldrum listened to the double chime of the bell. 'Nothing doing. Check the garage.'

He watched as Shields went over to the garage and shook the doors, then tried to peer between them. Turning away in disgust, he called, 'It's too dark inside. The car *might* be there.'

Meldrum rang the bell repeatedly. Shields crunched over the gravel to join him. 'They'd need to be deaf not to hear that,' he said.

Cock-up. Human error. It took a conscious effort for Meldrum to lift his finger from the bell.

'If they were here,' Shields added.

Without answering, Meldrum started round to the back of the house. On impulse, he stopped and told Shields who was close on his heels, 'Watch the front.'

'What for?'

'Just do it.'

As he walked along the side of the house (curtains drawn on a side window, curtains everywhere, and maybe two women in a darkened room, holding still, hardly breathing, hoping *go away*, hoping against hope) Meldrum thought, watch the front! What for? What fucking for? At least he didn't ask me, you think they're going to drive out the garage? Bang through the doors, wood splintering, like an old movie. Two molls, machine-guns clattering. Christ, am I over the top? And thought, but this isn't about a sweetie shop getting robbed, this is a murder investigation, and telling himself, *Ashton was killed*, rounded the corner as a man jumped up from a crouch at the back door and fled across the garden.

A single surge of adrenaline took Meldrum in half a dozen long strides over a flowerbed and across the lawn. Astride the wall, the man was set up like a fairground target. With the savage joy of releasing frustration in physical action, a sweep of the arm smacked Meldrum's open palm on the side of the man's head and knocked him back into the garden where he sprawled on all-fours whimpering like a sick dog.

You kick a dog.

And standing above that ignominious huddle he actually drew his foot back, but told himself later he'd stopped even before he heard Shields call, 'What is it?' and recognised it wasn't a man crouched down there but a frightened boy.

CHAPTER TWENTY-FOUR

There was no time to waste on the boy.

'I know you,' Meldrum said, trying to put a name to the white, tremulous face.

'You came to see my mother and father.'

Finlay, that was the name. Son of David and Amy Finlay. Close friends of the Ashtons. The father a beefy, heavy-faced man, who'd played golf with Brian, what had he said? '. . . raved on about what a bitch Toni was and that she'd a lover'. And the little wife perched bird-like on ridiculously high heels who'd burst out, 'If she did have an affair, she'd have been terrified of him.'

'Terry,' Meldrum said. The eighteen-year-old who'd come in and sat silent while his father boasted what a fine golfer his son was. 'On your feet.'

Standing up, the boy looked better, more like he had seemed in his parents' living room, a finer-grained version of the father's blurred, heavy handsomeness.

'I wasn't doing any harm,' he said.

'So why run away?'

'Not many people could have caught me.' The boy's smile was rueful, almost self-mocking, the effect unexpectedly engaging. Under Meldrum's cold stare, it blinked out. 'Sorry.'

As Shields came up, Meldrum said, 'I told you to watch the front.'

'I heard the yell you gave. I thought someone was getting murdered.'

Meldrum had no memory of yelling. No wonder perhaps that the boy had run.

'I'm not done with you,' he told him. 'Get home and I'll talk to you later.'

The boy looked at the wall as if he would run to it even now, then, coming to his senses, went back to the path and disappeared round the house towards the front gate.

'You're letting him go?'

'I know where to find him.'

There was still no sign of life from inside the house. Meldrum walked over to the garage doors and kicked them in.

'Fuck's sake!' Shields said.

The garage was empty.

'That solves that,' Meldrum said. 'We'll try Naomi Morgan's. Maybe they've gone there.'

He was in the car and had started the engine before Shields appeared.

'Come on!'

Shields said, 'I took a minute and pulled the doors shut.' As the car jumped forward, he fumbled his seat belt into place. 'Not that it made much difference.' He glanced sideways. 'You made one hell of a mess.' And leaned back with a sigh.

As he had done before when Toni Ashton disappeared, Meldrum was heading for Naomi Morgan's flat in Marchmont. Check the obvious possibility first wasn't a bad rule.

Getting out of the car, he had an involuntary, instantly suppressed image from almost twenty years ago of the body of old Arthur Hull, murdered in the ground-floor flat of this same building, lying back in a chair with what looked at first glance like a red scarf round his neck. The throat had been cut. He'd been a new detective constable then. Strange to associate that ancient carnage with the innocence of being young. Grateful Shields couldn't see into his head to wonder at his folly, he climbed to the third floor, suppressing memories that would have made him a ghost moving amongst his own past.

Waiting an answer to his knock, for Meldrum, like a hunting dog on a double scent, the old manhunt and the new fused explosively into the need to confront Toni Ashton. When Naomi Morgan opened the door, he demanded without introduction or preamble, 'Tell Mrs Ashton I want to speak to her.'

'She's not here.'

'Don't waste my time.' She was small, like a child woman, so that her breasts seemed very large, so small she didn't come up to his shoulder, so small the temptation was simply to lift her out of his way.

'I assure you, she's not.'

'You know who I am?'

'Yes.'

'Mrs Ashton and you were seen together at her house this afternoon. You know what happens to people stupid enough to obstruct the police in a murder enquiry?'

'But she isn't here. That's the honest truth.'

'You're saying the two of you weren't at the house? You didn't leave it together?'

'Yes. But then she dropped me here. Mrs Lynch!' She turned her head calling the name. A woman carrying a tin of polish and a duster came into the hall. 'Mrs Lynch, these men are police. They're looking for Mrs Ashton.'

'Like we were before,' Meldrum said to the woman. 'We met Mrs Lynch when we were here before. She was very helpful.'

'Is that right?' Naomi Morgan said unemphatically, just an acknowledgement. The cleaning woman looked uncomfortable. 'I think you'd better come in.' She led them down the hall. 'Oh, and Mrs Lynch, you can go now.'

'But I've still the bathroom to do.'

'It'll keep for once.'

She stood aside to let the two men go into the living room. As they waited for her, they heard Mrs Lynch in the hall, 'I'll give it a real good clean next time,' and the brief, indifferent response, 'You do that.'

Shields began to whistle between his teeth, a little soft tune like a jig. It was a habit of his when something amused him. There was the sound of the outer door closing. Naomi Morgan came in purposefully. 'You'd better look. Maybe then you'll believe me. But not both of you.' She pointed at Shields. 'You stay here.'

She took Meldrum into every room in the flat, including the uncleaned bathroom, making a grim little performance of it, down to opening wardrobe doors and insisting he look inside. Even tidy people usually had a paper lying around, an unwashed cup, clothes on a chair. The cleaning woman had just finished, of course, but still the place had an odd, unlived-in feel to it.

When they came back into the front room, Shields had sat himself on the middle cushion of the blue leather couch. He wasn't whistling any more, but staring at a bare, treeless landscape of hills framed on the opposite wall. There wasn't any snow on the hills, but something about the light told it had been there the day before and was due again soon. He moved himself to one end of the couch and Meldrum took the other. They sat well back, settled heavily, men with time to spare. Naomi Morgan looked at them, then sat down herself.

There was a long moment of silence. Tired of waiting, she asked, 'Well, are you satisfied?'

'Satisfied?' Meldrum asked in disbelief.

'You've seen everywhere. She's not here.'

'So where is she?'

'I don't know. Honestly, she dropped me here and went off.'

For years, until he lost an election and went to England in search of a safe seat, there had had been a Glasgow politician who could hardly open his mouth without a 'quite honestly' or a 'to be perfectly honest'. It had never inspired Meldrum with confidence.

'Mrs Ashton and you disappeared after her husband's murder. Where did you go?'

'Nowhere in particular.'

'But you were with her?'

'Yes.'

'All the time?'

'She's my best friend. She was upset. Why wouldn't I be with her?'

'Where?'

'Toni couldn't bear to stay in the house. How could she sleep in that bedroom? We found a bed and breakfast place. On some road off the main road, I can't tell you exactly where. Somewhere on the other side of the Forth Bridge, Toni was driving, it was her I was paying attention to not where we were going. We stayed at a few other places, and then she said we had to go back, we shouldn't have gone away. So that's what we did. We went back to the house, and then she brought me here. And then I suppose she went home again.'

'She dropped you here and drove off?'

'Didn't I just say so?'

'Did she tell you she was going home?'

'I took it for granted.'

'In that case, she should be there now.'

'I suppose so.'

There was a phone on a side table. He nodded at it. 'Give her a try.'

'Now?'

'Please.'

They watched as she dialled the number and listened.

'No answer?'

'She was exhausted. Maybe she's gone to bed. Or she could be having a bath.'

As she put the phone down, Meldrum said, 'Why don't I believe that?'

'I don't understand.'

Shields stirred, the leather couch creaking under his bulk. 'We've just come from there,' he said. 'The car wasn't in the garage.'

'Maybe she went shopping.'

'So she couldn't have been all that exhausted.'

'If she isn't at home, I don't know where she is.' She looked from one to the other. They stared back in silence. Finally she said, 'That's the honest truth.'

CHAPTER TWENTY-FIVE

'Let her stew overnight. Give her time to think about whether she really wants to play silly buggers with us.'

'You know,' Shields said, 'she might be telling the truth. Maybe she doesn't know where the Ashton woman is.'

'And she doesn't remember where they've been? A bed and breakfast. And then a few other places. Oh aye, and all of them were over the Forth Bridge. Narrows it down, eh?'

On a note of apology, Shields persisted, 'Felt a wee bit sorry for her, all the same.'

'Jesus!' Meldrum said.

Shields kept a moody silence until they were past the Sheraton Hotel. 'We'll go by the Ashton house on the way to the boy's. Do you think we should check?'

'Of course we'll bloody check.'

'If she'd gone shopping, she could be there. It's possible.'

'She won't be there. And tomorrow I'm taking Naomi Morgan in. Let her sit in an interview room, maybe bring her to her senses. Sorry for her? I'm sick and tired of her. Either she talks, or one way or the other I'll see her in jail. So from here in keep your eye on the ball and off her tits.'

The flush of rage hadn't subsided from Shields's forehead and neck when Meldrum halted the car outside Stanley's house. The little man must have been watching at the window for he came hurrying down the path.

'Good of you to come here,' he said. 'who is it we're going to see?'

'A boy called Terry Finlay. We caught him earlier poking around the back of the Ashton house.'

'Who is he?'

'You weren't there when we interviewed the parents—'

'Finlay! Yes, he was a golfing acquaintance of Brian Ashton's. The notes I was sent didn't mention a son.'

'He didn't seem to matter. Probably still doesn't. I don't think this'll take long, but since you live so close—'

'I'm grateful. I wish I could be with you all the time. At the moment, I resent every minute I have to spend at university.'

'What about tomorrow? Can you make it?'

Stanley was still explaining how he hoped to clear most of the next day when they stopped at the Ashton house. Meldrum led the way up the path and getting a grip on the left-hand garage door, sagging on hinges his kick had loosened, scraped it back until they could see inside. If the empty space was to be believed, Toni Ashton hadn't come home.

David Finlay was yawning as he opened the door. The yawn lengthened into a gape. 'What do you want?'

'Didn't Terry tell you?'

'Terry?'

'I'm sorry, Mr Finlay. It would be better if we came in.'

He blocked the way for a moment, as if urged by some atavistic impulse to guard the cave, then stepped back. 'We were just going to eat.'

'We won't keep you long.' Meldrum stopped by the door of the front room, which lay a little open. From inside he could hear the racket of a studio audience, the unmistakable sound of laughter by numbers.

'In there. Yes,' Finlay said.

As Meldrum went in, followed by the others, he expected to see Amy Finlay, but the room was empty. A big armchair with footstool and a whisky glass on a sidetable was set square before the television.

'I'll put that rubbish off,' Finlay said. 'Never usually watch the box, got more to do with my time, but it's been a long day.'

Laughter quenched produced the briefest singing instant of quietness.

Meldrum said, 'You know Detective Sergeant Shields, of course. And this is Dr Henry Stanley. He's involved with this investigation in an advisory capacity, but he isn't a police officer and he won't stay if you'd prefer him not to be here.'

'Is this about Brian Ashton? I don't know what more I can tell you. Do you want to sit down?' He was flustered in the way of a man who disliked surprises. A man who needed routine, like a swimmer who performed well as long as he stuck to the shallow end. 'Did you say something about Terry?'

'He is here?'

'Upstairs in his room. We were just going to have dinner.'

'We saw Terry this afternoon. I told him I'd have to speak to him. He should have told you.'

'Saw him where?'

'He was at the back of the Ashtons' house.'

'Why?' As he spoke, Finlay shook his head signalling incredulity.

'He was at the back door of the house. When he saw me, he tried to run away. It looked as if he was trying to break in.'

'No! That doesn't . . . He'll explain.' He went out and from the hall they heard him calling his son's name, and then at once the pounding of his feet as he ran upstairs.

'Changed his mind,' Stanley said. 'Decided he wants to talk to the boy on his own first.'

'Not hard to work that out,' Shields said.

'I didn't hear the bell.' Amy Finlay stared at them from the doorway. 'It is Inspector Meldrum, isn't it? Where's David?'

'Your husband went to fetch Terry. I think he must be talking to him upstairs.'

'But,' she looked at him in bewilderment, 'doesn't he know you're here? Of course, he must have let you in. Is it something to do with Toni Ashton?'

'In a way.'

'Has she come back?'

'Not yet. You haven't seen her around?'

'No. So why are you here? Has Terry seen her?'

'What makes you think your son might have seen her?'

'I didn't say I did. Why is David upstairs with Terry?' She turned away. 'I'll go and see, shall I? I'll tell David to come down. He knows you're here, doesn't he? I'll tell him.'

And she was gone.

'Funny wee thing,' Shields said.

'She's upset about something,' Stanley agreed.

A moment passed, then another.

'How long they think we're going to wait?' Shields wondered.

At the end of another five minutes, Meldrum was asking himself the same question. But as he started for the door, he heard the man's voice and then the tramp of feet on the stairs.

The father came in first, the mother last, with the boy between them as if for protection.

'I think we've cleared up your problem,' Finlay said. 'Terry wants to apologise for wasting your time.'

Before he'd finished, the boy had begun to speak. 'I'd heard that Mrs Ashton was home again. She'd lent me this book and I wanted to give her it back. I'd had it for ages. That's why I was there. I'm sorry I ran away.' The words came in a fast monotone.

'Why did you go round to the back of the house?' Meldrum asked.

If it was intended to throw the boy off balance, it was the wrong question.

The father said, 'We always went to the back door. Old friends. Terry's been going there since he was a child.'

All right, try the obvious question.

'So why run away?'

'I don't know. You gave me a fright.' Meldrum could see the boy thinking. 'After all, there had been a murder in the house.'

No arguing with that. Meldrum had an impulse to applaud. Instead he said, 'And, of course, standing at the back door you'd just remembered that. And suddenly I come round the corner. Anybody might have run away.'

If his tone made the boy hesitate, it was for no more than an instant. With a glance at his father, he said, 'That's what happened.'

'Who told you Mrs Ashton had come back?'

'Mr Warren.'

'The neighbour across the road?'

'That's right. I was passing and he was at his gate. And he said to me, Mrs Ashton had come home.'

There didn't seem much reason to persist. A couple more questions to save face and call it a day. Three of them there because a boy had taken off from the back of a house. Overkill; foolishness almost. While Meldrum was thinking that, he heard a quiet voice ask, 'What book was it?'

And the boy was disconcerted. 'What?'

'This book you were returning to Mrs Ashton,' Stanley said. 'Did you enjoy it?'

'. . . Yes.'

'Which book was it?'

'Which one?'

Stanley held his hand up forestalling David Finlay as he opened his mouth to speak. 'Of course, it doesn't matter. But as soon as you heard Mrs Ashton might be back, you thought about this book she'd lent you. You didn't happen to have it with you, did you?'

'No.'

'So you went home and got the book. You must have been in a hurry to tell her how much you enjoyed it. That made me wonder which one it was.'

'*Catcher in the Rye*. And I *did* enjoy it. It's by J.D. Salinger. It's about somebody called Holden Caulfield. It's an American book.'

'So it is,' Stanley said. 'Written a long time ago, but it's never stopped being popular. I believe it's still set as a text in schools.'

But at this the mother, the little bird of a woman, burst out, 'Stop it! I've had enough of this!'

Staring after her as she left the room, the group of men were variously bewildered. Within moments she was back holding out what seemed to be photographs spread out like a hand of cards.

'Oh, Mum!' the boy protested.

'I'm not having them go on at you like that. Here,' she thrust the bundle at Meldrum, 'take a look at this.'

There were a dozen colour prints, a standard size, five inches perhaps. All of them were of Toni Ashton. Two of them showed her at a dressing table, Meldrum recognised it as the one in her bedroom. In the first, her reflection was caught in the mirror, frowning with concentration as she made up her eyes. In the second she was looking round, laughing into the camera. In those, it could only be seen that her shoulders were bare. In most of the others, as she moved round the room, she was wearing only a bra and pants. In one, she sat on the edge of the bed pulling on tights. There were four of her in various stages of getting clothed, and a last one of her fully dressed posing, or more exactly offering a mimicry of a model's pose, held laughing in a slant of sunlight from the window.

'I caught him with them this afternoon. Doesn't that show what she is? He had them hidden in his room.'

Stanley was holding his hand out and, without thinking, Meldrum passed the bundle to him. As he went through them, Shields bent over his shoulder to look.

'You've no right!' the boy cried.

'Stop it, Terry! It's not your fault.' If the mother was like a bird, now it was a little bundle of fury defending its nest. 'You can see it's not his fault. A woman behaving like that. What boy wouldn't have his head turned?'

'What the hell's going on?' David Finlay took the photographs as Stanley passed them to him. After a glance, he raised his head and stared at his wife. 'You bloody fool!' he said. Without a pause, turning from her, he told them, 'We knew nothing about this. Absolutely no idea. Best thing you can do is leave us to sort it out.'

To the watchers it seemed sorting it out might not be easily done, given the loathing on the boy's face as he watched the father's thick fingers automatically shuffling and reshuffling, each photograph stroked in turn.

CHAPTER TWENTY-SIX

After the Finlays, all of them had felt in need of a drink, and one turned to another in The Canny Man's so that it was nearly twelve before they called it a day, leaving Stanley, who declined a lift for the safer option of walking home.

In the morning at his desk, resting his head on a hand cupped under his chin, all that Meldrum could recall of that session was Stanley asking what kind of boy they'd say Terry Finlay was. A good golfer according to his father, Shields had told him. 'I guessed something like that,' Stanley had said. 'I could see he wasn't much of a reader.'

As he thought of this, Shields came in carrying a folder. 'That's the summary.' For a man who'd been drinking the night before, he looked surprisingly fresh.

'Put it on top there.' Sourly, Meldrum turned back to the task of reducing the accumulation of paperwork. 'What about the casino list?'

'She's coming now with it.'

'Fine.'

He didn't lift his head at the tap on the door or its being opened or Shields's murmuring something, then saying in a normal voice, 'Here she is.'

Meldrum stared frowning at the sheet of paper Mary Preston had laid on the desk; then turned it right way up so that he could read it. 'They gave you this? Just this? This is their guest list for the night?'

'There's more, sir, but I thought you'd want to see this page. I'll put the whole list into the computer for checking.'

'What the hell took so long?'

'I've been chasing the management. Then I phoned their head office in

London. They came up with the wrong night, then they'd one with half the names missing, their record-keeping's shite. I only got this out of them this morning. Name jumped out at me, soon as I looked at it. He's up on the board in the briefing room as a contact of Ashton's.'

Meldrum ran his eye down the list of names. Irritation made him miss it the first time. *Member: Alex Hodge*; and in the column beside his signature in the same hand: *Guest: Lesley Dorrit*. He passed the list to Shields.

'I ran the name past the phone directory,' Mary Preston said. 'No Lesley Dorrit listed.'

'Hodge,' Meldrum said, thinking about it. 'Ashton's downstairs neighbour.'

'Way he talked that's all they were, just neighbours,' Shields said.

'Makes you wonder,' Mary Preston said, 'what he'd do for somebody he knows.'

'Can't be sure, too soon to be sure. But it would solve the problem of how Ashton got into the place dressed as a woman. Signed in by Hodge.'

'Bingo!' Shields said. 'What's the betting Mrs Dorrit was redheaded and one hell of a big woman?'

'Let's go and ask him.'

First, however, Hodge had to be found. A phone call to his flat got the answerphone. Fortunately, the downstairs neighbour Sam McConnell, as probably the most fashionable hairdresser in the city, was easy to contact. Raising his voice above the noise of the salon in the background, he admitted he knew where Hodge worked – 'Alex is like family' – and, with an expensive head to get back to, didn't waste too much time in letting himself be persuaded to give the information.

The estate agents in which Hodge was a partner was situated on the opposite side of the New Town, and they were almost there when Meldrum remembered Stanley had been supposed to join them that morning. He swore aloud, but as Shields glanced at him in surprise didn't explain. Shields had been there the night before when the arrangement had been made. It was possible, of course, that he'd also forgotten. They'd left the building just before Stanley was due to arrive, and could easily have waited for him.

Going in, a glance at a double window with photographs of properties for sale placed the operation for Meldrum. Nothing conspicuously cheap – what was in the city at the moment? – but no country estates plus shooting rights either. Inside there were three girls busy at desks, one of whom told them that

Mr Hodge wasn't available. At his least compromising, Meldrum had not only why not but where out of her in short order.

Hodge was in Trinity showing clients a semi-detached stone property, a little run down if the garden was anything to go by. Getting out of the car, Meldrum caught a glimpse of the Forth down at Granton. Water and hills, in this city nature was a constant presence.

When he opened the door and saw them standing on the steps like nemesis, Hodge's face collapsed into itself. For a second, guilt turned him into an old man. In another, he rallied.

'Last people I expected to see! There hasn't been another murder, I hope!'

'Still the same one.'

'Sorry. I didn't mean that the way it sounded. If you want to talk to me . . .' He looked round helplessly, 'I'm with clients.'

'Tell them you've finished,' Meldrum said.

As he stepped forward, forcing Hodge back into the hall, a man and woman were coming down the stairs, their feet loud on the uncarpeted treads.

'We've had a good—' The man broke off. 'I didn't realise you'd someone else to see the house.'

'Yes,' Hodge said.

'We'll be off then.'

'Right.'

'I don't think there's anything else we need to know,' the man said.

'No.'

'From what we've seen a lot would depend on how it surveyed. A real survey, I mean, not a scamper through for a mortgage company.'

'Absolutely,' Hodge said.

The couple exchanged looks. All this agreement seemed to be upsetting them. To Meldrum, they looked very young. It must be nice, he thought involuntarily, to be that young and able to think about buying a house this size.

'We'll think about it and let you know,' the man said with an air of being vaguely offended.

'Oh yes,' the girl said, 'we'll be in touch. Definitely.' And as her partner frowned added, 'I expect.'

To Meldrum as much as Hodge, the man offered a parting shot. 'It'll need a lot of money spent on it.'

Hodge closed the door behind them. Through the glass, they could see them studying the house. The man started across the road, no doubt to stare up at the roof.

'Could we give it a minute before we leave? Do you mind? I'd rather they didn't know who you were.'

'Don't worry, I think you made a sale.' Shields grinned, and pushing past him reopened the door.

Meldrum said, 'You should have told us you were at the casino that night.'

'What's this about?'

'It's about the night Ashton got killed.'

As if in retreat from the opened door, Hodge moved further into the hall. 'I'm often in the Rex. Not that I'd call myself a gambler. Small stakes, you can get as much fun and . . . Maybe I was there. I'm a member, I don't have a regular night. I couldn't be sure.'

'We can.'

'I'm almost sure I wasn't.'

'We have a list with your signature on it. You brought a guest. Did you think we wouldn't work it out?'

Hodge sat on the stairs, folding down as if the power had left his legs. He put his head in his hands. When he spoke, his voice echoed in the emptiness.

'I've known Brian for ever. We were at school together. It was me who told him the Stewarts were selling their flat. But when he moved in he preferred to pretend we hadn't met before. We'd laugh together about the McConnells. Bloody awful little people, he called them. It was a kind of game. Brian liked to play games.'

Shields, tired of hovering, shut the door with a bang.

'We know about the games you liked to play,' Meldrum said.

CHAPTER TWENTY-SEVEN

Waiting for Hodge to answer, Meldrum let his gaze slide beyond him to Stanley. He could see that the interview room made him uncomfortable. Hands in lap, little feet in highly polished shoes neatly side by side, he was sitting bolt upright on a chair by the door. That way he was behind Hodge, which was the compromise Hodge's lawyer had settled for, before agreeing to his presence at the interview. Present but not comfortable. Stanley's knowledge of crime was extensive, Meldrum thought with amusement, but theoretical. No, not comfortable at all. Maybe it was the bareness of the room that was troubling him. The institutional green paint. The smell of fright sweat oiled into the atmosphere over the years. Or maybe, for a nonsmoker like Stanley, nothing more than a distaste for the last lingering trace of tobacco smoke.

'I wouldn't advise you to answer that question.' The lawyer spoke quietly, leaning to the side, almost caressing Hodge's ear with his lips. Same type, same age as his client. Meldrum wondered if he might be another old school chum.

'I can't see why not,' he said to Hodge, ignoring the lawyer. 'You've admitted that you signed Ashton in. That he was dressed as a woman. We know that next morning he was found murdered in his wife's bedroom. Somebody was there with him. Otherwise he wouldn't be dead. You live alone. There's no one to say where you were during the course of that night. If you could remember Ashton being with anybody in the casino, it would be in your best interests to tell me. Let's try again. Did you see Ashton talking to anybody? Did he make an approach to anyone? Did anyone approach him?'

'It's all right. I'll answer.' Hodge shook his head at the lawyer. 'I should have told Brian I'd lost my nerve. Maybe he'd have come with me when I left. But I didn't and I'll regret it for the rest of my life. I walked out without a word to him and went home.'

'How long was this after you signed him in?'

'Not more than half an hour. And before you ask, I didn't see him talking to anyone.'

'And you don't have anyone who can confirm you left the casino early?'

Hodge thought. 'I didn't want to talk to anybody that night, didn't even want to be seen. But maybe somebody saw me. Plenty of people know me.' He bit his lip. 'But why would anyone remember? There wouldn't be any reason.'

Meldrum shook his head in a parody of sympathy. 'All we have is a list of the members who'd brought guests. I've got officers going through that at the moment. Maybe from those interviews they'll come up with something, but most of the people who were there won't even be on that list. The only person we *know* was with him is you. So I'll ask you again. Did you see him with anyone?'

'Christ, that's what I was panicking about! If he picked somebody up, I didn't want to know.'

'Picked someone up? The way you'd done before?'

Again Hodge brushed aside the lawyer's objection. 'Brian had the excuse of that bitch of a wife breaking the marriage up. Made him even crazier than usual. If he wanted to get it out of his system, he should have given her a hiding. But that wasn't old Brian's style.'

'Beating up homosexuals was?'

He expected a protest at that, but the lawyer seemed to have given up on the chances of making his client be discreet.

'Pick somebody your own size. Isn't that what they tell us when we're kids?'

'And you want us to believe that the idea for all this came from Ashton.'

'Even at school Brian was the one with the ideas.'

'And you followed on. So what was different that night at the casino?'

'Because it was the bloody casino! Going there was one bright idea too many as far as I was concerned. Brian was tired of the gay bars. Too easy, he said. But he couldn't get into the Rex, not unless I signed him in. But that means although he's in drag and won't be recognised, I can't be. I'm out in the open where people know me. *Hi, Alex!* somebody said the minute I walked in. As soon as he wasn't beside me telling me what to do, I came to my senses and got out.'

'So you say.' Meldrum waited. At his side, Shields rolled a pencil end over end between his fingers. 'But no one saw you leave.' Hodge, silent, watched the pencil turn. 'Thing is, I understand what you're saying. You're there in the casino, you panic, that makes sense to me. That makes a lot of sense.' He sighed. 'It's walking out I'm not sure of. You see, if you're a follower, like you say always follow Brian, I think you panic, you go straight to him. You tell him, I can't do this, we've got to get out of here. Wait! Let me finish. Just suppose that's what happened. Then the two of you leave. Not separately. Together. And Brian comes up with another plan. Go and trash his wife's house. And you follow on, isn't that what you always did, follow on? But when you get there, up into the bedroom, something happens. Maybe he was angry with you for spoiling his evening. Maybe he wanted sex—'

'Go to hell!' Hodge was half-way up out of his seat when the lawyer caught him by the arm. 'That couldn't happen. Brian wasn't . . . Neither of us was, not ever, absolutely not.'

'All the same, suppose maybe just this one night that's the way being angry took him. And he frightened you. And then you got angry. Even the idea of it just now made you angry. And there was a knife on the table by the bed.'

'Anybody who knows me will tell you how impossible that is. I'm not a violent man.'

Meldrum gave a spontaneous, uncalculated snort of disbelief. 'Of course you are. You've admitted you were involved in the assaults on homosexuals.'

'It wasn't like that. We took the piss out of them. It was a game. One of Brian's games. No one was badly hurt.'

'Tell that to Mr McCluskie's widow.'

'Who?'

'The Flying Fox. Mid-June. There's a good chance we can tie his death to the beating you gave him. If we can, it's murder.'

'Mid-June? That wasn't us!'

'The landlord at The Fox identified Brian Ashton.'

'Then he was with someone else! I swear to God whoever was with him that night, it wasn't me.'

'If I believed you,' Meldrum said, 'I'd have to call you a very unlucky man.'

CHAPTER TWENTY-EIGHT

'Do you believe him?' Stanley asked.

They were sipping coffee in Meldrum's office, waiting for Cormack and Paterson to bring Naomi Morgan to the station for interview.

Meldrum shrugged. 'A good lawyer—'

'Not that idiot he's got,' Shields said.

'Looked like an old schoolfriend.' A flicker of acknowledgement, not quite a grin, passed between the three of them. 'A good solicitor puts the right advocate in front of a jury, he'd make mincemeat of what we've got so far.'

'That answers the question, would you get the Procurator to take him to court?' Stanley said. 'But I was asking, did you believe him?'

'Getting them into court's the way we've got to think,' Meldrum said.

'Tell you this, if you're interested,' Shields said, 'I fancy him for it.'

'Am I allowed to express an opinion?' Stanley wondered.

Could I stop you? Meldrum asked himself.

'Why not?' he said.

'I was thinking about those scientists who worry that the very act of observing affects the outcome.'

'Affect away,' Meldrum said. It seemed to him that since Stanley's first contact with the force he'd been in the business of offering assessments and opinions. Why should he hesitate now?

'Scientists? What's scientists to do with it?' Shields intervened. 'What that make us? Fucking guinea pigs?'

'Not at all,' said Stanley. 'That wasn't at all what I intended. As a matter of fact, what I wanted was to agree with you. In your own words, other things being equal, I fancy Hodge too.'

For whatever reason, this opinion disappointed Meldrum. 'Too bad for you if it does turn out that way,' he said. 'Nothing interesting about Hodge. Nothing much for you to write up.'

'A sacrifice on the altar of truth,' Stanley said, and smiled. 'If I picked the wrong case, I can live with that.'

Meldrum looked at his watch. 'What's keeping them?'

Stanley said, 'Should you bother with Naomi Morgan?'

'Bother with her?'

'If Hodge killed Ashton, and the way you described it sounds very plausible to me, then it doesn't matter where Toni Ashton's taken herself off to, does it?'

'Until Hodge puts his hand up and confesses, you can't say she isn't involved. Till then, I intend to find her.'

'And I hope you do,' Stanley said, too promptly, a shade too much edge to his voice. 'After all, I've only seen the photographs the boy Finlay took of her. She's a woman any man would want to see for himself.'

'Viagra in a frock,' Shields said.

At that, Meldrum had a spasm of what could only be unreasonable irritation. To mask it, he took a drink of coffee, bent to open a drawer, made as if to take something out, nodded to himself, closed the drawer. Pantomime time. Or what the little man might call displacement activity.

When he spoke, his tone was casual. 'About Naomi Morgan. Maybe you shouldn't be there when we interview her. I mean, maybe we shouldn't even ask her if you could be. After all, she's coming in voluntarily. I think you're right. We can't push her too hard.'

CHAPTER TWENTY-NINE

Shields put on the recorder. Meldrum gave the names, the date and time. 'Helping with your enquiries. Isn't that what you call it?' Naomi Morgan said, sitting alone on the other side of the table. Her hands were clasped in front of her, too tightly perhaps, for she moved them down into her lap out of sight. She challenged him, brown eyes intent in a sharp, intelligent face.

'We appreciate your help.'

'Well, I'm here. Can we get on with it? I don't know what more I can tell you. Toni couldn't bear to sleep in the house where her husband was killed. Quite apart from reporters pestering at the door.' Her tone gave no more weight to one cause than the other. 'I'm her friend, so I went with her. Isn't that what friends are for? We got into the car and drove. Just wanted to get away, we weren't going anywhere in particular. Like I told you before, we found a bed and breakfast. I don't remember the woman's name. I've a vague idea of the place. But I'm not much good with maps. And then we moved to another one and another and then Toni wanted to come home. But, of course, once we got back — I can only guess, but I suppose once she was in the house again it must have been just as bad for her. You can't blame her for going off again. But honestly, I've no idea where she's gone.'

She finished and looked at him expectantly. A look Meldrum had seen before. A there-you-are that's-everything-what-more-could-you-want can-I-go-home-now look. He stared back impassively. When she glanced away, he let her have time to take in the shoddy bleakness of the utilitarian space. It was a room to dampen the spirits.

'Are you worried about her?'

She blinked at him. 'No.'

'That surprises me. Her husband's been murdered. She can't bear to be in the house where it happened. She's so upset she gets into a car and drives – nowhere in particular, just to get away. But then she comes back. And right away she's so upset, you think she must have been so upset, she disappears again. Only this time she doesn't have anyone with her. I don't know why you aren't worried.'

'I didn't say I wasn't worried.'

'I thought you did.'

'Toni has money. And she's not going to do anything silly. That's all I meant.'

'Silly? You mean try to harm herself?'

'Of course not. Not because of that husband of hers. They were separated. She didn't even like him any more. If he'd got himself killed somewhere else, he'd have been good riddance.'

Meldrum leaned back and studied her thoughtfully.

'You were a good friend of Mrs Ashton's.'

'Yes.'

'A close friend. You went on holiday with her. You stayed at her house with her.'

'That holiday we went to America was our first together. Toni had only been to New England. I told her about California and she liked the sound of it.'

'Of course, that's right, you'd lived in America.' She looked at him sharply, obviously wondering how he knew, but he left it at that. 'Did you often stay with Mrs Ashton?'

'Sometimes. We were friends.'

'How long for? I mean, if you were visiting how long would you stay with her?'

'Why? What does it matter? What kind of question's that?'

'It's just that the woman who comes in to clean for you – Mrs Lynch?' he turned over a couple of the sheets in front of him, as if checking the name. 'She thought you hadn't been living in your flat for the last few months.'

'She only comes in once a week!'

'That's what I said to her. But she told me she felt the place was too tidy. Different from what it usually was. It was her impression your bed wasn't being slept in.'

'My bed? She's there to clean, she doesn't make the bed.'

'You know how people are when they get curious.'

'She won't be curious around me for much longer,' Naomi Morgan said grimly. And at once made an effort to lighten up. 'Not that it matters. It's just the idea of her poking around, you wouldn't like that, nobody would.'

'I take it then you were living away from your flat?'

'Toni was alone, rattling around in that big house. She asked me to stay with her for a bit. I was company for her.'

'So you were sharing the house with her for some months.'

'As a guest, yes.'

'How long have you known Mrs Ashton?'

'I met her after I came back to this country. I'd been in America . . . But you know that. How did you know that? Did you talk to my sister?'

'Mrs Laurie was very helpful.'

'Doesn't sound like her.'

'And we spoke to Ella Crossan. You remember Ella? You worked with her in your sister's shop. Apparently, you stayed with her too.'

She frowned. 'So I stayed with her—' But again took a breath, went on evenly, 'For a couple of weeks when I came back to Glasgow, till I got a place of my own. We got on well. Neither of us liked my sister. Or the shop much.'

'Yes, she told us that.'

'I met Toni when she came into the shop. I suppose Ella told you that as well.'

'She said Mrs Ashton came into the shop as a customer. You served her. You got to be friends.'

'You think that's odd?'

'Such good friends that you came to Edinburgh.'

'People have to meet somewhere. Or do you mean, because I was working in a shop? Isn't that snobbish?'

But it was Shields who spoke. 'I worked in a dress shop when I was young. Saturday job. Standing at the door seeing nobody took off with any of the gear. Never made any friends.'

It wasn't the first time Meldrum had noticed how disconcerting the effect of one of Shields's interventions could be. In this room a maintained silence like his could make for uneasiness. He'd caught interviewees, sometimes even their lawyers, starting to glance more and more often at Shields, as if worried by his silence into trying to guess what he might be thinking.

Naomi Morgan was snapping like a firecracker. 'You don't know what you're talking about. You don't know anything about Toni or me.'

'So tell us,' Meldrum said.

But again she controlled herself quickly. Her tone matter of fact, she explained, 'It takes a hell of a lot longer than five minutes to find the right dress. Dithering and swithering. It can take some bloody women for ever while you're thinking, buy this one, makes no difference, ugly bitch, all right, buy that one, who cares? But with Toni you knew at once it was different. She has wonderful taste. With someone like that, it takes time, but you don't mind. It's like a journey, you do it together, you're happy to do it. And by the time we'd found the right dress, I was due to go for lunch. Ella and I had this Italian restaurant we went to, and we'd just started eating when Toni came in. It was busy, and she asked if she could sit at our table. The three of us started talking. And that's how we got to be friends.'

'Mrs Ashton and you.'

'Yes.' A touch impatient. Who else, for God's sake?

'That's how Ella told me it happened,' Meldrum said. 'What she actually said was, it was amazing to watch how well you two got on. She'd never seen anything like it. When the lunch hour was over, she had to go back to the shop on her own. You didn't go back. In fact, that was it. You didn't go back to the shop at all. Not that day. Not ever.'

'Friends,' Shields said. With a glance at the tape running, he didn't make a big deal of it. Just the one word, more or less to himself, with no expression at all.

'She was the most wonderful person I'd ever met. I didn't need a long time to know that.'

Meldrum nodded. 'There's something about her. She makes a special impact on people. That's what you're saying?'

'Well, you met her. Didn't you feel that?'

'Anybody could see she's a very beautiful woman.'

'Oh, you're so *careful*.' She made it sound like an accusation.

Should I slap an erection on the table and ask you to measure it? Disturbed, Meldrum looked down as if she might read the thought in his eyes.

'I'm trying to understand,' he said. 'She certainly had an impact on Terry Finlay.'

He'd taken her off balance again. 'What?'

'The Finlays, friends of the Ashtons. Terry's their son. About eighteen. He's a good-looking boy.'

'He was a pest.'

'Always hanging about, was he? Lovesick. Isn't that what they call it?'

'A complete pest.'

'Is that what Mrs Ashton called him?' He waited for an answer, didn't get one. 'Or didn't she mind him being around? I suppose any woman might enjoy that kind of attention. Like I say, he's a good-looking boy.'

'Don't be ridiculous!'

'Then you didn't know she let him take photographs of her?'

'Photographs?'

He thought about calling them nude photographs, decided against it with the tape running. 'When she was undressed.'

'I don't believe it!'

'His mother found them in his room.'

'No, I didn't know. And I doubt if Toni knew anything about them. Maybe he took them through the window. He was capable of something like that.'

'I'm sorry if I upset you.'

'I'm not upset. Disgusted maybe. Do you get some kind of pleasure out of this? What would your bosses say if they knew you brought women in here to talk about stuff like that?'

From the corner of his eye, without wanting to he caught Shields's grin.

'This effect Mrs Ashton has on people, these are questions I have to ask.'

'I can't see why.'

'Mrs Ashton told us her marriage ended because she threw her husband out. Later, though, we learned he went around offering a very different version to anyone who would listen. According to him, she was a nymphomaniac who'd taken a string of lovers. He'd put up with this for years. But there had been one final relationship that was too much for him and that's why he'd walked out. *Not* thrown out by her. He'd walked out. As far as I can gather, he told that story to almost everyone he met — he talked about it freely, talked about it all the time. He was obsessed with this lover who'd broken up his marriage.'

'It's not true.'

'He was lying?'

'Well, you can see why he would.'

'Hurt pride?'

But as she nodded agreement, Shields said, 'Funny thing to make up, all the same. Putting up with her screwing around for years. If it's pride we're talking about.'

Into the silence, Meldrum said, 'Suppose there *was* a lover—'

'There isn't.'

'But if there was, maybe that's where she's gone. If she has, that could be why you're not worried about her.'

'There *isn't*. It couldn't possibly matter if there was, but there isn't!'

'I could think of one way it would matter,' Meldrum said. 'A woman gets involved with a man and her husband gets killed. If you're a policeman, you want to know where the lover was at the time of the murder.'

'How often do I have to tell you? Toni wasn't involved with a man.'

'You can't be sure of that.'

She closed her eyes; kept them closed as she spoke, as if she couldn't bear to look at the two men.

'Believe me, yes, I can. I am her lover.'

From that statement, there was no shaking her. She claimed they had become lovers in an hotel room on the afternoon of their first meeting. That had been more than a year after Brian and Toni Ashton had separated, but she was certain no other man had been involved in their break-up. 'She'd no secrets from me.' In the same vein, she denied the husband's stories of his wife's promiscuity. From Naomi Morgan's perspective, it seemed that Toni Ashton, however unhappy, had been a faithful wife; mostly because trance-like she'd had to wait for Princess Charming to break through the thorn hedge and waken her to her real sexual orientation. As for where Toni might be now, Naomi had no idea.

Giving up at last, Meldrum got one of the duty drivers to run her back to her flat. She had after all come in voluntarily.

Afterwards, going back up with Shields to rejoin Stanley, he thought over the interview, trying before the images faded from his memory to interpret the significance of Naomi Morgan's expression at certain moments. He was almost sure that she had been telling the truth, but for that there was no evidence, only instinct, the hunch every detective relied on and the best were most wary of. But of course the truth she was telling was only what she believed it to be. Toni Ashton could have lied to her. If she and Naomi had been lovers, all the more reason to keep certain things secret. And so, whatever Naomi believed, Toni might have been promiscuous with men. More importantly, the lover who had broken the marriage, Brian Ashton's last straw, might exist. And if he did, could he still be in touch with Toni? Could they still be lovers? Without Naomi Morgan knowing? It was possible. Even possible that the affair between the two women was useful to him, kept him out of sight. Plenty of possibilities and no way, hunch aside, of picking among them. Toni Ashton had disappeared somewhere, though, and if the lover was still around why not to him? Wherever she'd gone, he would have been prepared to believe Naomi didn't know where, except that she showed no sign of being worried.

As he was thinking how badly he needed to talk this over with someone, Shields beside him in the lift cleared his throat. For once, Meldrum turned to him expectantly.

'Just thinking. See that Saturday job I had as a kid? One of the girls in the shop made a friend, right enough. This guy that came in to get a birthday present for his wife.' He grinned. 'Got one for himself as well.'

Meldrum surprised himself by how much he was looking forward to seeing Stanley.

When, though, they got to the office it was to find Stanley perched on the edge of the desk as he talked to the man seated in front of it. The late Mr Ashton's partner in Templars restaurant looked as plumply sleek, well cared for, expensively turned out from head to toe, as ever. The fine swooping mane of white hair, too, lay as smoothly, but it should have been standing on end as he raked through it repeatedly. George Snoddy was a badly worried man. When he saw Meldrum, Snoddy got to his feet.

'I'm just going,' he said. 'Your colleague here has been explaining that there won't be anything you can do.'

Stanley hitched himself off the desk. 'Not quite a colleague,' he said.

'I'm not even sure of what I'd want you to do,' Snoddy said

'Sit down,' Meldrum said. 'Please.' He took his own seat behind the desk. 'I'm sorry you've been kept waiting. I didn't know you were here. Did you ask for me at the desk?'

Stanley, who'd beaten Shields to his usual seat, said, 'That's right. And, of course, I knew you'd be some time so—'

'Anyway. I'm here now,' Meldrum said.

There was a pause. Uncertainly, catching something of Meldrum's irritation, Snoddy looked from one to the other, not sure what was wrong. 'I'm having difficulty with the lawyer Macleavy. He's kicking up a fuss because I've decided to take over the whole debt of the business and clear it myself. I told him, it's my money. If it takes half a million to rescue the business, that's what it'll have to take. But he was so *emphatic*. The truth is I don't know how to handle him. Brian dealt with all that kind of thing.' He sighed. 'Good God, it's not as if there isn't more than enough money in the Trust.'

CAT ON MOUSE

that face before as a cloud shape

He sipped his whisky and stared at the words on the screen. Words he'd read over a hundred times since the night of Brian Ashton's death, struck each time by the finality of it, that there was no way of telling how strangely and utterly his life had been altered in the interval between one word and the next. Switch off the computer and the words were gone, not eradicated, but held in some arcane semaphore from which, however reluctantly, repeatedly he called them back into existence.

Refilled glass in hand, he went along the hall to the front room. From the door, he could only see his wife's feet under the lamp and a plump white arm where it rested on the arm of the chair. He struck down the switch and washed away her narrow island in a flood of light.

'Why do you have to sit in the dark?' he asked irritably.

But when he went to see why she wasn't answering, she was sitting with head dropped back and closed eyes. Her face turned up into the brightness lay unguarded for his inspection. Where her mouth sagged open the bottom front teeth were slightly yellow. Deep lines had scored themselves around the eyes and the dark pouched flesh under them. On the face and neck, the skin had taken on the dull, muddied texture of the chronic invalid. The cords in the neck were strained by the unnatural angle of the head, and seeing that, suddenly the pose seemed too uncomfortable for her to be only sleeping. He bent down, cheek brushing hers, listening for a breath. She sighed and, as he leaped back, opened her eyes.

When they met, he was only twenty years old. Among his university classes, on impulse he'd taken a module on poetry, Late Romantics and Early

Modernists. 'You'll get Eileen Craigie. A bit intense, but she's all right.' As a lecturer she'd seemed young. In fact, she was in her mid-thirties then, a slim, dark-haired woman with large brown eyes, typically downcast, who spoke very quickly except when reading poetry. That she read unselfconsciously well, sometimes slowing with particular poems of certain poets into a languorous, caressing attentiveness. One late autumn afternoon in a tutorial room, to illustrate one point or another she read to him:

> She too that loveth awaketh and hopes for thee;
> Her eyes already have sped the shades that flee,
> Already they watch the path thy feet shall take:
> Awake, O heart, to be loved, awake, awake!

And there at the end of the second verse she had looked up at him and gone on from memory, one more verse, another, and the last:

> Lo all things wake and tarry and look for thee:
> She looketh and saith, 'O sun, now bring him to me
> Come more adored, O adored, for his coming's sake,
> And awake my heart to be loved: awake, awake!

He'd taken the class as a kind of makeweight, he'd no great interest in poetry. Certainly, he'd no memory for it. Yet those verses, which he rather despised, he'd never forgotten. Whatever love was, had he fallen in love with her then? 'Oh, Eileen Craigie, she knows her stuff all right. And she must enjoy teaching it. She doesn't have to work. Her family's stinking rich.' He knew what people said when he married her; but whatever love was, all he had known of it was with her.

He followed the movement of her tongue as she licked her lips, and saw that they were dry and cracked. She put a hand up to shield her eyes from the light.

'Did you say something? Why is the light on?'

'You were asleep. Lying back that way, I'm surprised your head didn't fall off.'

She smiled up at him. The smile changed to a grimace of pain as she moved.

'Keep still!' He sat the glass of whisky on the mantelshelf and went beside her chair. With his fingertips he began to knead the muscles at the side of her neck. 'How does that feel?'

'Worth the pain.' She reached up and caught his hand, drawing him round to face her. 'You'd tell me if anything was wrong, Harry?'

'There's nothing wrong, Eileen.'

'You're not worrying about something?'

'Only about you.'

'But you'd tell me? You wouldn't shut me out, when I care so much for you?'

He went down on his knees and put his head in her lap. It was all the answer she needed. As she stroked his forehead, he nested in the warmth of her thighs. The comfort he obtained was real, though he knew the feeling of safety to be an illusion. When the phone rang, it took a surprising effort of will to leave her and get to his feet.

'I've been thinking over what you said.' The voice began without preamble, assuming a listener, assuming the right listener.

'Oh yes?'

'I was too hasty. If it's the only way, that's what it has to be. Do you understand what I'm saying? I've changed my mind.'

'About what?'

There was a silence. He heard the crackle and whistle of hard-taken breaths. As he waited, he smiled across at his wife. He couldn't read her expression as she watched him. He pulled a what-a-nuisance face, raising his eyebrows, drawing down the corners of his mouth.

'No,' the voice said. 'I'm not spelling it out. I don't think so. Not over the phone.'

'It'll have to be some other time then.'

'I can't wait.' The same protracted silence filled with the labouring effort after breath. 'I'm coming over.'

'Are you sure you want to do that?'

'I'll be there in half an hour. Less.'

He took his whisky from the mantelpiece and, intending to sip, tipped it all down. The spirit, eighteen years of mellowing or not, burned at the back of his throat.

'Who was that?'

'Somebody from the university.'

'I see.' She rubbed a hand across her eyes.

He waited and when she didn't go on, he said, 'You're tired, dear. You go up and I'll bring you something in bed.'

He ran up the stairs ahead of her. In the en suite bathroom (the first conversion he had insisted on after they bought this old house), he opened the cabinet and put the bottle of tablets into his pocket. When he came out, she was already undressing. He smiled at her. She turned away and began to unbutton her skirt.

He took milk from the refrigerator in the utility room and put a half cup into a pan on the middle ring of the cooker in the kitchen. While it was warming, he shook a handful of tablets out of the bottle from the upstairs bathroom. Little chunky white discs, thicker than aspirin but able to be swallowed, they wouldn't stick in the throat. He laid one beside a glass and with the back of a spoon crushed a second, holding it firmly on a plastic plate for purchase. When he'd ground it down as fine as he could manage, he slid the powder into the glass, poured in the half cup of warmed milk from the pan and stirred till he was sure the powder had dissolved.

Outside the bedroom door, he gave the glass of milk a final stir and balanced the spoon on the newel of the bannister. When he went in, she was sitting up in bed. A book was laid open on the covers in front of her, but it was face down and she seemed to be lost in thought.

'Here we are,' he said cheerfully. He handed her the tablet and the glass of milk.

She looked at the tablet on the palm of her hand.

'Come on,' he said, as if coaxing a child. Half an hour, was that what Macleavy had said? Or less. How much time was already gone?

'Where did this come from?'

'It's your tablet. Same as every night.'

'You didn't bring it from the bathroom.'

'What?' He stared at her, his mind a blank. He couldn't think what to say.

'You had it with you when you came in.'

'I must have collected it from the bathroom and taken it down with me when I went to heat the milk. Funny things we do. Then I brought it all the way back up again. Not very efficient. But at least your milk should still be warm – don't let it get cold!'

Delicately, with her lips, she nibbled up the tablet from the palm of her hand and drank some of the milk to wash it down. She made a face. 'It's bitter,' she said.

He laughed. 'You can't taste a tablet. Not unless you're chewing it.'

'The milk.'

'Can't be. I opened a fresh carton.'

'It doesn't matter.' She drank what was left in the glass.

He was at the door when her voice stopped him. She spoke softly, so that he couldn't be sure of what he heard. As he turned, she said it again. 'That phone call was from a girl, wasn't it?'

'No, it wasn't.'

'One of your students.'

'Do you want me to say I wish it had been? You're being silly, darling, and you're exhausted. You're too tired to read. Try to sleep.'

She picked up the book. Turning the page, without looking up, she said, 'You know I can't sleep unless I read. But it won't be for long.'

Running down the stairs, he thought that he should have gone over and kissed her. It would only have taken a moment, but he didn't have a moment. The clock was running.

At the kitchen table, he crushed four more of the tablets to powder. He took two coffee mugs from the cupboard and put a little milk into both; then he poured the milk from one of them, about two tablespoonfuls, into a pan and set it on the smallest electric ring to heat. He boiled a kettle, got out the big glass coffee pot and put four spoonfuls of coffee into it, hesitated and added a fifth, poured on the water just off the boil. He looked at his watch; more than thirty minutes had passed since the phone call. From a cupboard under one of the work surfaces, he took out a rectangular warmer with a slab of soapstone placed on top like a lid. He checked inside to make sure there were candles, then took it along the corridor to his study. He put the container on his desk at the back, lit the candles and replaced the soapstone cover. Half running now, he returned to the kitchen just as the milk in the pan was beginning to bubble. He poured it into a milk jug and stirred in the powdered tablets. He took the mug which still had milk in it and added just a mouthful of coffee. Putting everything on a tray, he carried it through to the study. He set the milk jug and coffee pot on the soapstone, which was already warm to the touch, and put the two mugs on the desk. In an afterthought, he fetched a clock from the front room, took out some books from the case on the far wall and set the clock into the gap.

And then he was finished, and there was nothing to do but wait. He stood drooping by the desk like a puppet with its strings cut. It was forty minutes since he'd put down the phone.

A quarter of an hour later, the front door bell rang.

In the hall as he came near, he could see the gross shadow on the glass.

'You're late!'

The accusation was stupid, he felt that as soon as he made it.

Macleavy, however, blinked at him and replied in what seemed to be all seriousness, 'It's not so easy to get away. It took me longer than I'd thought.'

What had there been to keep him? Or who? But leading the way along the hall, he couldn't easily think of Macleavy, thumping his bulk down with each cruel footfall, gasping for breath, as living with anyone. It simply hadn't occurred to him that Macleavy might, for example, have a wife; and now he suppressed the thought as one it would be better not to entertain.

He put on the overhead light as they came into the study.

In a long grey cotton raincoat hung up at the front from the mountain of his belly, Macleavy seemed to fill the room. He blinked round him. 'What's this?'

Stanley went over and put on the desk lamp. 'It's my study. Take a seat.'

As he came back to put off the overhead light, he was carrying one of the mugs. Gesturing with it so that Macleavy glanced automatically at the contents, the mouthful or two of milky coffee, he said, 'I've been having coffee. Would you like some?'

Macleavy shook his head. He asked, 'Where's your wife?'

'In bed.'

'She'll be wondering who was at the door.'

'Her bedroom is at the back of the house. Anyway she's asleep.'

'How can you be sure?'

'Well, she was when I peeped in about ten minutes ago.'

This statement produced an unexpected effect on Macleavy. With a groan of distress, he sank down on the nearest chair and put his head in his hands.

'You know why I'm here,' he said. 'I can't see any other way.'

'All I *know* is that you said something about changing your mind.'

Macleavy looked up in anger. 'Don't give me that. It was your idea. You put it into my head, and I can't get it out.'

'What idea?'

'You said if you killed your wife, you would get the money.'

'I wondered if that could be it.' Stanley lifted his seat from behind the desk and bringing it round set it down in front of Macleavy. When he sat down, their knees almost touched. Quietly, in a voice not much above a whisper, he said, 'The thing is, *I've* changed *my* mind.'

'I can't let you do that.' Macleavy spoke as softly. 'I need the money within days.'

'There you are then. Wouldn't it take time to get the money from my wife's estate? You're the lawyer. I've no idea.'

'If I get it in time, so much the better. If I can't, I can use the promise of getting it to buy my way out of trouble. I might lose my job, but I won't go to prison.' He was running with sweat, fat drops like tears coursing down his cheeks. 'I'd kill myself before I went to prison. But before I did, I'd make sure the police knew who murdered Brian Ashton.'

'How much money are we talking about?'

'Half a million.'

Stanley sat back in his chair with a gesture of disbelief. 'But you said quarter of a million before! That's what you said you wanted!'

Macleavy stared at him balefully. 'It's still worth it not to go to prison for murder.'

'You're asking me to commit a second murder to cover up the first. And what would that mean if I did? You'd know about two murders instead of one. I think you'd bleed me dry.'

'I wouldn't!'

'Promise?'

'I promise!'

But at that Stanley managed what sounded like a genuine laugh. 'I can't believe you said that. *Promise,*' he mimicked. 'You must think I'm a fool.'

'I didn't mean that, I didn't mean that. What are we to do?'

In his distress, the fat man wrung his hands together, and in the midst of everything else that was going on some pedant's corner of Stanley's brain recorded this: *you read of that, I don't think I've seen someone actually do it before, so that's what it looks like.*

'The only thing I can think of,' he said, 'is that we kill her together.'

'God almighty, what you say?'

'Kill her together and you can't blackmail me. But I'd still have to pay you your money, since if I didn't it would be just like you said, you'd have nothing to lose. Once you put the money back, though, you and I would be in the same boat. We'd both have everything to lose. Kill her together. You get your money. I'm free of you. We both go our separate ways. Do you see?'

Without warning, Macleavy, who'd been bent forward in the posture of a deaf man straining to hear, surged to his feet. By instinct, to avoid the attack, Stanley recoiled, the chair tumbling behind him so that he had to go scrambling and stumbling over it as he tried to escape. But Macleavy, with the long raincoat grotesque as a circus tent billowing round him, was heading out of the room.

As soon as he understood, Stanley with no sense of how the distance had been covered somehow got between Macleavy and the door. 'No! We have to wait until she's sleeping.'

'You said she was asleep.'

Stanley's mouth opened and closed. His glibness deserted him. Macleavy, though, had lost his momentum with the interruption and made no attempt to get past him.

After a moment, Stanley said, 'We have to give her longer. Come back and sit down.' And he laid his hand on Macleavy's chest and pushed him gently, like a tug turning a liner towards harbour. The big man moved slowly back to the chair.

Seated, he asked, 'Why can't we?' Voice plaintive, he gave the appearance of being in a daze.

Stanley went over to the desk. When he lifted the pot off the soapstone, his hand shook so badly he'd difficulty pouring his coffee. 'I think you should have one,' he said. Without waiting for a response, he put the hot milk from the jug into the clean mug and filled it up with coffee, strong and black out of the glass pot. As he did so, it occurred to him that he'd planned to pour Macleavy's coffee first, and then his own into which he would have seemed to pour milk out of the by then empty jug. The sequence had been carefully thought out to allay suspicion; so that both men would seem to be drinking out of the same jug and pot. And none of that planning, none of that careful preparation mattered, since while all this was going on Macleavy had been staring at the floor. Handed the mug of coffee, he took it automatically and began to drink.

Stanley picked up his tumbled chair and set it down near the desk. Sitting down again, he said, 'The thing is, she reads and dozes before she goes into her night's sleep. Give it half an hour. You wouldn't want her to wake up while—'

'God, no. I can't do it,' Macleavy said. He took another long gulp of coffee. 'I'd rather go to the police.'

'How long does a solicitor get for embezzling half a million?'

'You'll have to do it yourself.'

Stanley shook his head. 'I thought we'd been through that. It's both of us or not at all.' An interminable silence followed. He forced himself not to break it. At last, coaxingly, he began: 'You've been imagining horrors, it won't be like that. All you'll have to do is close her nostrils and cover her mouth with your hand. I'll lie on her chest. She's quite frail. She'll be dead in moments.' It was the method used on the old and sick by Burke and Hare, but he didn't think Macleavy would be interested in that. 'You'll be surprised how easy it is.'

Macleavy was staring at him in what seemed like horror, but he didn't protest. They sat in silence and Stanley began to watch the clock that he'd put on the bookcase.

After a time, Stanley asked, 'Is your car out front?'

'I put it at the side of the house.'

After a time, Macleavy said, 'Could I have another coffee?'

Stanley got up and went to the desk. He picked up the jug. 'We're out of milk. I'll get some.'

'No. Don't bother.'

Stanley didn't argue.

The minutes dragged past.

This time when Macleavy stood up, it was slowly.

Too soon, Stanley thought. *Christ, he's too soon.*

'We'll do it now. I can't wait any longer.'

Despite the sweat and the wild eyes, the impression he gave was of a ponderous inflexible purpose. He started towards the door, and Stanley was suddenly afraid if he tried to stop him, this time Macleavy would sweep him aside and go on alone.

'Right then, right then! Come on!' He forced his voice high and shrill, the hysteria only half pretence. 'You want to do it now! We'll do it now! Hurry! Come on, come on!'

He got out first into the hall and began to back up the stairs ahead of Macleavy, all the time urging him on frantically. 'You think I want to do it? Let's get it done! Come on! For Christ's sake, come on!'

And Macleavy, struggling and panting, hauling himself by both hands on the bannister, yelled out himself, 'Stop shouting! You'll waken her!'

And he overrode that, crying out, 'Together or it's off. Right! You want to? You want to? Come on then! Changed your mind?' And now he was on the landing and Macleavy was still climbing, suffering but going to make it. 'Fat bastard! Go to the police! Die, you cunt! Come—'

Almost at the top, so close that when he reached out for Stanley with both hands Macleavy almost caught hold of him, but without the support of the bannisters swayed, screwed up his eyes as if his vision had blurred, asked, 'What have you done to me?' As he fell, he caught again at the bannister rail, which bent, cracking and groaning. He held on and for a second snagged on a step, folded, feet above head, arms outstretched like a rower on the rack, until his weight broke his grip and down he went sliding and twisting to where he hit the bottom, slid across the polished floor into a table and lay still.

Now it was quiet as Stanley crept down the stairs. It seemed impossible so gross a man could fall downstairs without breaking his neck at best, bones at least. But when he came close to him, he could hear him breathing, soft distinct sucking gasps for air. Retreating, he sat down on the bottom step of the stair to contemplate the wreckage while, chin in hand, wondering what to do next.

He hadn't thought beyond this moment, though as he'd imagined it Macleavy would have been snoring in the study, on a chair or flat out on the carpet. Ten milligrammes of temazepam habitually sent Eileen to sleep. This evening to make, as it were, doubly sure, he'd given her a second tablet as well in her glass of milk. For Macleavy he'd doubled the dose again. Forty milligrammes, enough to send even Macleavy to sleep, allowing half an hour for it to work. Which left the question, what to do then? What had he imagined he would do then?

How a small man killed a very large one was a hard question to answer in a culture where for a man like him a gun wasn't easily come by. He was a criminologist who had never fired a gun, though once during a conference he'd gone on a visit with a group to a private gun club. A large revolver had been passed from the instructor back along the seated rows of spectators in the firing range. He remembered it being unexpectedly heavy and that he'd turned it round without any idea what to do with it. The man next to him, an ex-journalist who'd swapped small wars for punditry in the lecture room, flipped it open and spun the chamber deftly. At the end, as his party piece the instructor set a melon the size of a human head on a stand at the far end of the range. When he hit it, the bullet made it explode in water and pulp. He'd laughed then and said, 'I was told I could do this as long as I cleared up the mess afterwards.'

It seemed if a gun was the answer, it was a messy one. How long would it take to clean the hall afterwards? Not just soap and water, you'd have to repaint the walls. And if you shot into the body, how many bullets would it take? And where in that mountain of blubber could you be sure of finding the heart? Same objection to a knife. But not if you pushed it into an eye. Strangle with a rope? Stanley looked at his hands. Not much bigger than a child's, he wouldn't have the strength. But suppose a rope wound round that great neck with just enough slack to slip a stick in, a walking stick; then twist, tourniquet style. *Yes!* Did he have a walking stick? He'd had one once. Pulp and water, sliced eye, marks on the throat. Hardly death from natural causes. Poison. Get him over on his back, wedge open his mouth and use a funnel to pour it in. Pour what in? The bathroom cabinet was clean out of undetectable poisons.

As Stanley sat there in shock, lips moving as he talked to himself, Macleavy gathered hands and knees under him and got up. By good luck, he was facing away from where Stanley sat on the stairs. Supporting himself by a hand on the wall, he felt his way the length of the hall and went out, leaving the door open behind him.

Wakening in the morning, Stanley was sure he'd forgotten to close the front door. Half in a dream, he thought, we could have been murdered in our beds. Without a transition then he was awake, so that all his troubles flooded back and he knew he was done for. Perhaps he groaned aloud. Eileen beside him muttered something.

'What is it?' Automatically he tried to soothe her. 'You're all right.'

She made a face as if there was a bad taste in her mouth. He had a glimpse of her tongue, coated white. Her eyes flickered and opened. Unfocused, they stared up and seemed to look into him or beyond him.

She said with a kind of wonder, 'I'm alive.'

'Why wouldn't you be?'

She turned her head and, it seemed to him, could only be looking at the table beside the bed. The only things on it were a clock and the glass that had held the milk he'd brought up to her the previous evening. She sighed, her eyes closed and she was asleep.

He slid out of the bed infinitely slowly so as not to waken her. Probably all his care was needless, though, for standing he saw she had paled as if slipping under the surface into a deeper, more natural sleep. In red numerals, the clock marked the time as twenty past six. He put on slippers and dressing gown and went downstairs. He was in the kitchen washing it under the hot tap, scrubbing round and round the inside of it with his fingers, before he realised he'd picked up the glass from the bedside table.

The sun through the drawn blinds made the kitchen glow with honey-coloured light. It occurred to him like a thought from another life how much he had loved this house. Surprisingly, they were out of bread, but he was glad of something to do. After Eileen visited an alternative health practitioner, who'd hung elecrodes in her ears and sent her home with a list of allergies, he'd bought a breadmaker. He'd made gluten-free loaves for her; and then, getting interested, wholemeal and French and granary and tangy cheese and malt and egg and even cajun ones for himself, to some of which he'd add currants or nuts. The result was that often they had too much bread, and had to throw half of the last loaf out so they could eat the next one fresh; which was why it was so unusual to find the breadbin empty. He decided since he was up so early he would make a loaf and have it ready in time for Eileen's breakfast. Unhurriedly, drifting in the honey-coloured light, he gathered the ingredients from the baking cupboard and the smaller refrigerator. He beat the eggs and butter, cider vinegar and lukewarm water, then poured the mix into the base of the bread pan. On top, he put the dry ingredients, the flour and salt, the cheese and dry mustard and the rest. Finally, he poured a packet of dried yeast into the hole he'd poked with his finger into the flour. Finished, he set the pan into the bread machine, set it to normal bake with a light crust and pressed START. Methodically then he set about wiping the surfaces and tidying up. He'd used up the GF flour and, when he went to put the empty bag in the sack hung behind the door of the cupboard under the sink, it was crammed so full of kitchen rubbish the bag had to be folded before he could slide it inside. Moved by the same conscientious impulse, he unhooked the sack in order to take it out to the bin. Despite everything, as he opened the back door he felt better. A bright still morning. Birdsong. The air already warm. A large car had been pulled up close to the wall of the house and so near to the kitchen steps that he could see at first glance that Macleavy, sprawled back in the driver's seat, was almost certainly dead.

With exaggerated care, he lifted the lid of the bin and dropped in the bulging rubbish sack. Then he tried to take stock of the situation. Although the front hedge was a reasonable height, a glance over the gate by which Macleavy had come in couldn't fail to show the car to anyone passing in the street. It was true, though, that it would take a deliberate turn of the head to see it, and most people, busy with their own affairs, wouldn't bother. In front of him, the hedge between his side drive and the neighbours' wasn't high at all. Luckily, though, the gable end had been built without windows. All the same, anyone coming out of the back door couldn't miss seeing the car. On the other hand, it had been late evening before the car was parked, and as for this morning, the Jacksons were retired and neither of them was an early riser.

To get to the driver's door Stanley was forced to step on to the grass. As he did so, morning dew struck damply up through the soles of his slippers.

Through the glass, he saw the keys dangling from the ignition and had a moment of panic for fear the door was locked. But it opened and Macleavy's arm flopped out. The skin of the big hand was cold.

Necessity: get rid of the body or give up. And to dispose of it – how else? – he would have to use the car it was in. To do that, somehow he'd have to hide the body inside it. Macleavy was too big to go in a boot. Anyway too heavy for him to get out of the car and move. After a moment of dreadul blankness, he did the only thing he could think of and began to wind the seat back. When it was resting on the one behind, he began the struggle to roll Macleavy off into the footwell between the two front seats and the three in the second row. Even the arm when he tried to put it back into the car resisted him. It wouldn't bend. He opened the rear door and pushed the second row of seats back as far as they would go towards the three at the rear. The whole body was stiff and awkward. It fought him to the last. He crawled on top of it, slid into the back and hauled at it, clambered back through to the passenger seat and leaning against the dash for leverage kicked it under with his feet. When he'd done all he could, the body still reared up like the hump of a whale. The footwell was too small to contain it. In the garden hut, he found cans of fence paint and stacked them about the body to hide its shape, then covered it over with an old travelling rug.

And coming out of that frenzy of effort, forced himself to stop. He returned to the house, put on gloves and came back with a cloth with which he wiped every surface he'd touched, including the cans. From the open kitchen door, he heard a clock chiming. Eight? He ran into the house to check. Seven o'clock. It took ten minutes to dress, tiptoeing around the bedroom, easing drawers open for underwear, shirt, socks. He put on a raincoat and took a briefcase as a kind of commuter's talisman: already he had planned what he was going to do.

He joined the bypass at Fairmilehead and left it at the sign for Tranent. Already the traffic was heavy, most of it going the other way into town. At a roundabout, a van driver perched up at just the wrong height seemed to be looking in not at him but the crowded space behind him. It took an enormous effort of will not to turn and make sure everything was hidden. In Tranent he turned left at the beginning of the main street and headed down to Preston Pans. The car park at the rail station was just beginning to fill up. He found a space at the far end and had the driver's door open and was out of the car before he saw Macleavy's shoulder. The travelling rug had slipped down and left it uncovered.

The commuter train arrived in just under ten minutes. Like everyone else, he bought his ticket on the train from a hard-pressed conductor who didn't even look at his face. By eight twelve he was only one of a stream of commuters disembarking at Waverley. He walked the length of Princes Street and at the stop outside St John's Church caught a bus to Morningside.

He sat on the upper deck and looked down on the crowd of ordinary mortals on the morning pavements. At the other end, he would have a short walk home, not that he needed it to give him an appetite. By that time, the bread would be made, and he would give Eileen breakfast.

BOOK FIVE

Blind Blood

CHAPTER THIRTY

'The whole thing was most unsatisfactory.'

Broadie, Alex Hodge's lawyer, frowning from Meldrum to Shields and then round at Stanley, was not a happy man.

'Why would that be, sir?'

'For a start, those men were far too like my client.'

'I hope not. Though under the usual circumstances that would be something you'd want for your client. It's possible, of course, we were thinking too much along the usual lines, but even so we couldn't have people in the line-up who were absolutely different from Mr Hodge.' Two West Indians, say, a guy with an eye patch and a wooden leg, a dwarf and a Red Indian with his war bonnet on. 'That would have made a positive identification worthless from your point of view – and ours. As you saw, we put him with men of roughly the same age, all clean-shaven, but varying a good deal in height and hair colouring and build. I think it was a fair test of Mr Collie's reliability as a witness. I understand your disappointment at the result.'

Mr Collie had actually picked twice from the line-up, changing his mind after the first selection and asking if he could choose again. Broadie had been happy to agree to let him try, a normally unthinkable variation on the procedure, but then as Meldrum had said, what they had anyway was an untypical use of an identification parade. Detectives interviewing members of the Rex Casino and the guests they'd signed in on the murder evening had shown each of them a photograph of Hodge, one provided by himself as a good likeness. Half a dozen of the members had recognised Hodge, two of them were more or less sure they'd seen him that evening, none could give any opinion as to exactly at what time, and certainly they had no idea as to when he

might have left or whether he'd been alone when he did. One of these
members, however, had taken a cousin from Aberdeen along as a guest that
evening, and when as a matter of routine Hodge's photograph was scanned
through to Aberdeen, the cousin, Albert Collie, surprised the officers who
interviewed him with a remarkable claim. Collie's story was that he had gone
along to the casino not as a gambler but as a self-described 'student of human
nature'. In that capacity, on the look-out for telling examples of greed,
jubilation and despair, he'd had a disappointingly humdrum evening – with
one exception. 'Yes, oh, yes,' he'd said, nodding at the photograph, 'I spotted
him not long after Tom and I went into the big room on the first floor. To tell
the truth, coming across someone in that state so early probably contributed to
my disappointment with the place as a new experience. It gave me a false
expectation of what else might happen. And, fact is, the rest of the night – all
those mismatched couples and parties of noisy clowns who might as well have
been wearing paper hats and red noses – was a bit of a bore. Tom was at the
baccarat table and I was watching him and maybe that's why I noticed this
chap. He was watching the table as well – and he was sweating, I mean really
sweating. I don't know whether other people would, but with me being in the
habit of studying faces and body language – put it this way, I could read him
like a book and he was a horror story. If he'd been gambling, I could have made
sense of the state he was in. I'd still have paid attention to him in that case, but
maybe not been so intrigued. I'd have said to myself, he's losing, he's down to
his last bet and if it goes wrong he's bankrupt. But like me he was just a
spectator. So then I tried to see if he was watching someone in particular – you
know, a lover or somebody who was chucking away the family silver. But just as
I was doing that, he swung round and marched off. By that time, I was so
curious I marched after him. He got his coat and ran out of the building –
literally, I mean, down the stairs two at a time. What? No doubt about it, right
out of the building, I followed him all the way – like I said, I was fascinated.
Time? Well, I know when we went in and we weren't there more than half an
hour when I first spotted him. Alone? Oh yes, from when I saw him till he went
outside. When I got down, took me a bit longer than him, I stood in the hall
watching him through the door. There was a taxi passing and he waved it
down. I'd been hoping all the time, you see, he'd change his mind and come
back. There was something about him. And I was right, eh? After that the rest
of the night was a bit of a washout.' With an account of the interview in front
of him, Meldrum had pointed out to Broadie that an identification parade

would be compromised by Collie having been shown the photograph of Hodge. All the same, it had seemed, certainly to the lawyer, something worth doing. Given such an impressively confident witness, everyone including Meldrum had taken it for granted that confirming the identification would be a formality. Unfortunately for Hodge, even given a second chance, Collie had failed to pick him out.

When he'd first learned of Collie's statement, Broadie, a solicitor more at home with conveyancing than crime, had brightened up and begun to look less like a fish out of water. As for Hodge himself, at that point he'd been so convincingly relieved that it might have seemed he had to be either a remarkable actor or innocent. Meldrum, however, had once chaired a press conference at which he'd been deeply moved by a father's grief. Six months later he'd been in court when the same man got a life sentence for his daughter's murder. Since then, he'd had a notion there might be more remarkable actors around than there used to be, people watching a lot of television nowadays. On the other hand, it was possible, then or now, that being a psychopath helped.

Back in the office after the identity fiasco, Hodge seemed to be gutted. On the other hand, disappointment had unexpectedly energised Broadie.

'In a previous interview,' Meldrum told Hodge, 'you admitted to taking part with Brian Ashton in a number of homosexual assaults.'

'I don't think so,' Broadie said.

'Eh? We have it on tape.'

'Then I suggest you check your tape. By my recollection, Mr Hodge made the point quite explicitly that no one came to harm in these encounters. From what he told you, it would be quite inappropriate to describe them as assaults.'

'Oh, how would you describe them then?'

'It sounded to me like horseplay.'

'Did it really?' Meldrum studied the lawyer for a long moment. Broadie blinked, but didn't look away. 'Tell me, Mr Hodge, was what happened to James McCluskie horseplay?'

'Don't answer that! Broadie snapped.

Apathetically staring out of Meldrum's window at the brick wall which blocked the view, Hodge accepted the instruction.

'Is that how you'd describe a broken nose and a broken cheekbone? There were ribs too, I can't remember how many.'

Thin-lipped, Broadie said, 'Check that tape of yours again. You've been told Mr Hodge had nothing to do with that.'

'We have a witness who identifies Brian Ashton as one of the two men in drag who went off with McCluskie.'

'But not my client. He wasn't there.'

'Brian Ashton gets dressed up in drag and beats up homosexuals – all right! *takes the piss*, was that what your client called it? Whatever. It seems pretty weird to me. Middle-aged man, own business. Pulling stuff like that. Weird. I don't think many people would do that.' Meldrum squeezed his cheeks with his fingertips and sighed. 'But you're asking me to believe Ashton didn't only recruit Mr Hodge – after all he'd known him for years – but that he got someone else to join him?' And before Broadie could answer: 'Is that what you're asking me to believe, Mr Hodge?'

'I always did what Brian wanted. From the day we met at school until he died. Now it's like a bad dream,' Hodge said in a dull monotone, his gaze fixed on the blankness beyond the window. 'Sitting here, you think that stuff doesn't seem crazy to me?'

'Yes, of course, it does,' Broadie cut in. 'You were entirely under his influence. But, of course, the "stuff" you're talking about has nothing to do with what happened to the unfortunate Mr McCluskie. Nothing whatever.' He turned to Meldrum. 'You do understand that?'

Meldrum chose not to answer at once. No chance, Meldrum thought, of Shields breaking the silence; he was in passive mode, even more than usual. And Stanley with the lawyer hostile knew he was only there on sufferance. Sometimes silence was a useful tactic.

But he'd let it go on too long. With something like reluctance, he began the familiar process again.

'Forget Mr McCluskie for the moment. Let's deal with the assaults on the other homosexuals. I'd like you to give me the dates of those.'

'Why?'

'You say there was no violence involved. It would help me to verify that if you could give me the dates.'

'I can't. I don't remember.'

'We're not talking a long time ago. This is within the last year, isn't that right?'

'I don't remember.'

'It's not the kind of thing most people would forget.'

'I couldn't give you dates.'

'Days then. Which day of the week?'

'What do you mean?'

'Monday? Wednesday? Friday? Saturday? Which night did you usually meet Ashton?'

'There wasn't one.'

'Explain that to me.'

'Brian would phone me at the agency. He'd say something like, fancy an outing tonight? You know, put it in a way I'd know what he meant – not just out for a drink or whatever.'

'He rang you at the agency. So this was always during the week?'

'Or at the flat. Sometimes he'd ring the flat. I don't remember.'

'That's a convenient memory you have. You don't remember even one of those dates?'

'I call this harassment,' Broadie said.

And I call it a murder enquiry, you cunt, Meldrum thought; and smiled; and said something bland.

Not long afterwards they finished. Hodge went out into the corridor. Broadie, about to follow him, turned back.

'You've been very fair-minded. I felt I should say that. You'll appreciate I have a job to do as well. If I was expressing myself strongly, it's because for me this unfortunate business isn't just about a client in difficulties. Alex and I were at school together.'

Without waiting for an answer, having made his point, he left.

'Not just an arsehole,' Shields said, 'but an arsehole who wants to be liked.' He grinned. 'I think I mean liked.'

Mr Political Correctness strikes again, Meldrum thought. Stanley, however, for what it was worth, was also smiling.

Before anything else could be said, the phone rang. An alert sergeant had picked up on an early morning emergency call. Arthur Macleavy had been reported missing.

CHAPTER THIRTY-ONE

Not far from the centre of the city, the Macleavy house was in the middle of a short street which Meldrum had more than once heard described as the best address in Edinburgh. He'd been surprised to be given it as their destination. The impression he'd formed of the fat man was that he'd been farmed out to a rundown office with the unprofitable clients no one else in the firm wanted. Seeing the house did nothing to lessen the surprise. It sat about a third of the way along the arc of a terrace: wide frontage, three storeys, a front lawn big enough to herd sheep.

Looking at it, Shields shook his head and said, 'Bloody hell!' It seemed he'd formed the same low opinion of the fat, seedy-looking lawyer. As Stanley got out of the car to join them, he asked him, 'What do you make of that?'

'Nice house,' Stanley said.

'Bit more than that. I've got a *nice* house. Nice, bloody wee house.'

'It's impressive.'

'Remember that office of his? It doesn't figure. He must be a crook. That'll be it. One of these drug barons, eh? And that's why he's had to take off.'

'Or,' Stanley said reasonably, 'it may be inherited.'

Unplaced, Shields continued to grumble as they made the long march to the front door. 'What do you think? Over a million?'

'Yes, of course.' Stanley sounded startled.

'To buy this. Prices now. Over a million, I'll bet you.'

'Doesn't make sense,' Stanley said.

'You can say that again.'

An elderly woman in a cardigan opened the door. Surveying them, her mouth turned down dourly at the corners.

'Police—' Meldrum began.

'I hope you're not going to upset her.'

'We're here to see Mrs Macleavy.'

'She's making herself ill, and the last lot didn't help.'

But as she spoke, she was moving back. As they came in out of the sun, the long hall papered in faded green and gold created the effect of stepping into a cave. Meldrum almost stumbled over a vacuum cleaner set in the middle of the carpet. The woman made as if to move it, but then stood holding it by the handle and blocking their way.

'If she needs anything just call me. I do the cleaning, but I'm like a friend to her. She keeps asking me if I know where he's gone. She's got the idea he's met a woman. Well, I don't know what to say to her when she says that. I try to tell her, wherever he is it's not with a woman, but I can't say it too plainly for fear of hurting her feelings. I mean, if you'd seen him.' She offered to share an unwilling smile. 'I can't imagine any woman that desperate. Don't get me wrong, he's got a heart of corn. I got this job after he did my divorce, and he couldn't have been nicer. But not many women would see past his looks.'

Meldrum took the vacuum cleaner out of her grasp and set it back against the wall.

'Would you take us to Mrs Macleavy, please?'

'She's in the back sitting room.' She began to lead the way down the hall. 'It gets the sun, and she says she needs to see the sun or she'll get melancholy.' At the door of the room, she paused again. She seemed to nerve herself, then asked, 'You've not found him?'

'I've just learned he's missing,' Meldrum said impatiently.

'Is that the truth? You're not coming to tell her he's been killed?'

Stanley made an odd throat-clearing noise. Meldrum looked at him, waiting for him to speak, but got in return a look so emptied of expression he decided Stanley didn't realise he'd made a sound.

As the woman was about to open the door, Meldrum put his hand over hers on the handle and stopped her. 'What makes you think he might have been killed?'

As if afraid now of being heard from inside the room, she said in a hasty undertone, 'The car's not in the garage. When I got here this morning and she told me he wasn't in the house, it was the first place I looked. I've had a lift from him. He's a terrible driver.'

It said something, Meldrum had thought, of the impression Macleavy made that all three of them had been surprised to be told that it was Mrs Macleavy who had reported him missing. Checking one another's reaction, they agreed the fat lawyer had struck them as one of nature's bachelors. On the other hand, the unlikeliest candidate for marriage only had to persuade an electorate of one. Or, as Shields had put it, beggars can't be choosers. Himself, Meldrum would have gone for the kindlier old saying, as God made them, He matched them. As he followed the cleaning woman into the back room, then, he was half prepared for a fat woman weeping.

The room was small, the back wall recessed into a curve, the front filled by a bow window. It was like a bowl overbrimming with afternoon sunlight. Sitting with her back to the window, the woman had a halo of brightness round her head, so that it took as long as being introduced and being seated in front of her for Meldrum to realise her hair was white. Occasionally, as she spoke, her voice quavered, but there were no tears. The upright, unbending posture suggested a habit of self-discipline. The eyes were faded but sharp, the lips thin, it wasn't a face made for tears.

'The policeman who came this morning made me angry,' Macleavy's mother said. 'So sure of himself, he wouldn't listen. I had no confidence in him. Are you going to listen?'

'Yes,' Meldrum said. He made the plain statement, and didn't elaborate on it. The old woman nodded.

'Arthur went out last night. It was late in the evening. I can't give you the exact time. He comes and goes as he pleases. When I wakened this morning, I lay listening to the wireless. I naturally assumed he'd come home again the previous evening. But by half past eight, I realised something was wrong.'

'Why?'

'Arthur brings me a cup of tea and toast before he leaves for work. Every morning. Without fail. Those aren't just words. Always, every morning. He had pneumonia once. All the time he was in hospital, I couldn't sleep. Because he wasn't in the house, I couldn't sleep. He signed himself out. At your own risk, they told him. But he insisted, knowing how I would feel. Arthur's father died when he was thirteen. It's all right, Mummy, he said to me, I'll look after you. And he has all these years. How many sons would take their mother on holiday every year? For my eighty-third birthday he took me to the opera in Verona. We had a wonderful time together.' She paused and seemed to gather her thoughts. 'I got up and went to his room. His bed hadn't been slept in. I couldn't seem to make them understand.'

'If your son has disappeared, we'll do our best to find him,' Meldrum said.

'They asked such stupid questions. Had he gone off like that before? It was only one night, perhaps he'd been held up somewhere. Had I tried his office? He might be in touch today. He might come home this evening. Perhaps he'd stayed with friends. Could I give them the names of any friends? Oh, they beat around the bush, but it was obvious they meant women. Arthur brings me breakfast every morning. *Of course* he's missing.'

'I take it, though, someone has contacted his office?'

'Mrs Paterson came in at nine o'clock. I asked her to phone the police. She said about his office. If you must, I told her, but he won't be there. And he wasn't. Then she phoned the police. What's being done?'

Under normal circumstances, to find a grown man missing overnight who lived with his mother, not much would be the honest answer. With Macleavy, it was too early to tell, but it just might be different.

'Did your son have any money worries?'

'Don't be silly.'

'I'm sorry if you've already been asked. It's something we have to consider as a matter of routine if someone goes missing.'

'My son worked hard. We live simply. He had no money worries.'

'And if he had,' Stanley said. He paused as if trying to choose his words. 'Even if he had, he wouldn't have had to disappear. This house must be worth a great deal.'

'What business is that of yours?'

'I'm sorry. I put that badly. All I meant was that selling a house like this would clear off most debts.'

'What an extraordinary thing to suggest.' A vertical frown line appeared between the keen, faded eyes. 'I came to this house as a bride. I shall die in it. Arthur would never sell this house.'

'I see,' Stanley said.

'I love this house.' Something in that, perhaps the word "love", got behind her defences. If her self-discipline was breached, however, it was after her own fashion. Dry-eyed, she said in a tone so metallic it could have been mistaken for anger, 'But I would walk out of it now and never want to see it again, if only Arthur would come back safe to me.'

CHAPTER THIRTY-TWO

They were dropping Stanley for a university faculty meeting when Shields took the call about Ivor Warren.

He said smiling, 'The old guy that lives across the road from the Ashtons just phoned in and demanded to talk to you. Apparently, he's in a right old state.'

'Ivor Warren?'

'Right.'

'Hold on,' Meldrum advised Stanley. 'Just in case.'

In the back, one foot out of the car, Stanley had paused. Now he swivelled back into his seat and shut the door again as Meldrum took the phone. There wasn't much to be learned, though, from the one-sided conversation which followed.

Finished, Meldrum shook his head. 'Sergeant says Warren hung up before I got a chance to talk to him. Said he couldn't wait. He'd to get back to guarding the prisoner. But would they get the message to me urgently. Top priority, as he put it.'

'Prisoner?'

'Warren caught the boy Finlay snooping round the back of the Ashton house again.'

'And he's taken him prisoner?' Shields said. 'Fucking old loony's the one needs locking up.'

'It doesn't sound important,' Stanley said.

'It won't be. I wouldn't miss your meeting for it,' Meldrum told him.

All the same, he surprised Shields by turning away from the town centre when they came back to Holy Corner and starting instead the familiar run up Morningside Road.

' 'You're not going to see Warren?' Shields didn't try to keep the disbelief out of his voice.

'Might as well.'

'Because he caught the boy at the Ashtons? I thought you said it wasn't important.'

'I changed my mind.'

There was silence for a bit. Perhaps Shields was waiting for him to explain.

Finally Shields said, 'Likely he was just looking for a quiet place for a wank.' Silence. 'The boy, I mean.' More silence. 'And what was old Buggerlugs poking his nose round there for anyway?' Silence, brief but fraught. 'Probably wanted a wank as well.'

As he drove, Meldrum was in fact wondering what had made him decide to go and see for himself rather than have a constable respond. Because Warren had wanted him to give it top priority? Hardly. Curiosity, he told himself. After being put through the mill for being caught there the first time, what had drawn Terry Finlay back to the Ashton house? But then, not being given to self-deception, Meldrum came up at once with the obvious answer. He'd seen the photographs Toni Ashton had let the boy take of her. The photographs alone would give any healthy boy an erection. For the woman, the woman herself, a woman like that, he'd cross a desert, panting all the way. Chasing a mirage. Photographs or not, had to be a mirage. He didn't believe Toni Ashton would ever have let the boy touch her. Why the photographs then? Maybe she liked to be watched. Maybe Terry Finlay's excitement excited her, a game to pass an hour. Maybe she liked to see his excitement. If it was excitement you wanted to watch, couldn't beat a teenage boy, give him an erection, he'll fly the flag all afternoon. And talking of erections: so who was chasing the mirage, being drawn to the magnet, the boy or himself? Sometimes it didn't do to to examine your own motives too closely.

Deciding that sometimes self-deception wasn't a bad idea, by the time they got to Warren's, Meldrum had put himself in a vile mood.

As they got out of the car, he broke the long silence. 'Look at the size of that house,' he snarled.

'What?'

'If he wanted a wank, Warren's got the whole of it to wank in.'

Taken by surprise, Shields said nothing. Wonder he didn't burst out laughing in my face, Meldrum thought, and calling himself a bloody fool led the way up the path.

As they waited for the door to open, though, Shields said, 'Maybe the old fellow needs a bit of risk.' And, rallying further, expanded on the notion. 'You know, like the guys that screw in elevators?'

At this, the door seemed to implode to reveal Ivor Warren, so scarlet in the face he might have been eavesdropping. Instead, it quickly became plain the heightened colour was due to a heady mix of triumph and self-congratulation.

First, however, grievance had to be got out of his system. 'I thought you'd be here sooner. Did they tell you how urgent it was?'

'You've got a hold of the boy for trespassing,' Meldrum said, drawling it a wee bit in his irritation.

'Trespassing be damned!' Warren cried. 'Come in.'

He turned in the hall to shut the front door quietly, then, pulling a face and tapping a finger on his lips for them to be quiet, ushered them into the front room. It was surprisingly untidy; an ornament filmed with dust lying on its side where it must have been knocked over some time ago particularly caught Meldrum's eye; for an old seadog, the room wasn't shipshape at all. A glance showed it to be empty.

'You've let the boy go home?' Meldrum was oddly torn between annoyance and relief.

'Nononono,' spluttering it out as a single dismissive word. 'I put him in the main bedroom. Don't worry, that door has a lock. But I thought it would be better if I briefed you. Before you spoke to him.'

'You've locked him in?'

'Oh yes.'

'How long has he been up there?'

Warren checked his watch. 'About an hour. Came down to phone you. And you weren't there. So I was waiting for you.'

'You have got in touch with his parents?'

'You first, I thought.'

'You haven't been in touch with them.' Meldrum took a breath. 'Right. Well, let's get the boy down here at once. And then we'll see about contacting his parents.'

'Nonono, wait a moment!' Warren held up his hand as if stopping traffic. 'You don't understand.'

'I think I do. You found him trespassing at the back of the Ashton house. You brought him over here. And he's been shut up for an hour in a locked room. I'm asking you to bring him down at once. Have I missed anything?'

'He's confessed that he killed Brian Ashton.'

Meldrum was so intent on his own agenda that he was on the point of continuing to insist that the boy be brought down. It was the look of astonishment on Stanley's face, confirmed by a glance at Shields, that made him register what he'd heard. 'He did what?'

'Oh, not at once. You can see why I felt you should be in the picture before you see him.' Warren, hands clasped in the small of his back, rocked himself up on his toes, a man in command of the situation. 'I happened to be at the window, when I saw him going into the Ashtons. I knew something wasn't right. He'd gone past before, too slowly, if you know what I mean, having a good look as he went. This time he stopped altogether. After a bit, he looked round him, then up and down the street. He didn't see me, I took care to keep behind the curtain. And then he opened the gate and marched in as if he owned the place. I thought, give him a chance, maybe he'll try the front bell and come out as fast as he went in. But when he didn't, I went over and collared him.'

As he paused for dramatic effect, Meldrum said, 'Mr Warren, I'm going to stop you there.'

Warren gave him a blank stare and went on. 'I brought him—'

'I'd like you to come up with me, and show me the room where the boy is.'

'I haven't taken you through what happened.'

'It can wait.'

'Why the devil should it?'

'You say you've locked him in your bedroom.'

'So? You don't think he's going to jump out of the window, do you?'

'Do you have a bathroom off the bedroom?' Warren nodded, staring as if he thought Meldrum had taken leave of his senses. 'Do you keep medicine there? Paracetamol? Sleeping tablets?'

'Both.' The high red colour mottled with white. 'You don't – you can't imagine he'd do something—'

'He's been left on his own after confessing to murder. I think we should check.'

'Absolutely,' Warren said. Suddenly the intelligence muffled under all the mannerisms showed. Oddly, though shocked, he looked younger.

As he led the detectives upstairs, he called out twice, 'Terry! Terry!' It was as if he was trying belatedly to offer reassurance. As this occurred to Meldrum, his own primary emotion remained irritation, most of it directed at the old man, some of it at the boy. Not for a moment did he take the idea of Terry killing

Ashton seriously; though there was a fair chance the idiot of a boy might try to kill himself.

At the bedroom door, Warren put the key in the lock. As he fumbled with it, he called again, 'Terry!' There was no sound from inside the room. Shields put him aside, and without fuss coaxed the key into turning and pushed the door open.

The room was dominated by an exceptionally large double bed. Its size dwindled the boy curled up on his side, hands between knees drawn up to his chest, so that he could as easily have been nine as seventeen.

'Oh God,' Warren said.

Shields made it over first, feeling for the pulse under the boy's ear. Meldrum looked for any sign of tablets or a bottle on the bed or either side of it. There was nothing, apart from a framed photograph lying on the bed by the boy's face. As Warren picked up this photograph, Terry Finlay opened his eyes.

At the same moment, Shields straightened up, saying, 'He's fine. Nothing wrong with him.'

His voice cracking with indignation, Warren cried, waving the photograph at the boy, 'How dare you? You shouldn't have touched it.'

Terry Finlay uncoiled like a spring, sitting straight up and looking wildly around him.

'Easy,' Meldrum said. 'Take a deep breath. You've been sleeping.'

The boy stared at him, then was overwhelmed by an enormous jaw-cracking yawn.

Warren was setting up the photograph again where it must have stood on the bedside table. It showed a pretty, smiling girl sitting on a farm gate.

To Meldrum, he said, 'That's Dorothy, my wife. She never changed. We met in Lincoln in August 1941. Got married three weeks later. That's the way it was during the war. Things happened quickly because you didn't know how much time you had. She died last year.'

Listening, Meldrum understood the state of the front room. A lot of dust can accumulate over a year.

CHAPTER THIRTY-THREE

For the third time Terry Finlay was making an extraordinarily good job of sticking to his story. Extraordinarily good, of course, only if he was lying; but from the moment Warren told them the boy claimed to have killed Ashton, Meldrum had almost taken it for granted that the confession had more to do with the boy's hormones than any factual account of something that had really happened. Certainly, that had been his starting point when in Warren's dusty front room he questioned the boy for the first time. The second time had been in Terry's own home. He'd taken the boy there in hope that with his parents present he would crack. The same stubborn assumption had made him agree to leave the boy with his parents overnight and have the father bring him in for interview the following morning. That way his parents would have more time to work on him and get at the truth. Next morning, though, when they turned up with a lawyer, father and mother were exhausted and the boy, who looked the freshest of the three, hadn't changed his story. At that point, Meldrum finally reminded himself that a detective who began by being certain of the truth was a bad detective.

Terry wasn't technically a minor, and Meldrum excluded the parents from the interview room. The boy had to be brought up against the reality of the situation he was creating for himself. As another grim-faced adult, it was useful to have Stanley there also. The lawyer had checked with the father, who had accepted Stanley's presence almost eagerly. Maybe, confused by the Dr, he'd thought Stanley some kind of psychiatrist who would come up with a diagnosis in proof of his son's innocence.

In the interview room, Meldrum leaned back and took a moment. They had gone through everything again with the boy unruffled and consistent. Meldrum could see that Shields, who had begun at least as sceptically as himself and joined in pushing Terry with questions, was showing signs of accepting the boy's version. It was harder to tell with Stanley, who had spoken hardly at all. Was it possible the boy was telling the truth?

'I want you to tell us again what happened, Terry. From the beginning. Take your time, we're in no hurry.'

The boy looked at his lawyer as if for guidance.

Before the lawyer could speak, Meldrum said, 'It really is in your own interest to go over it until we get everything straight. You've confessed to a very serious crime. The most serious one there is.'

With repetition, the story was coming even more fluently. 'Toni was kind to me. But that's *all*. I could talk to her and she'd listen. There wasn't anything I couldn't tell her. Being with her was the best thing ever happened to me. She was so beautiful. I was in love with her, but she didn't know. She was just being kind. Don't let those photographs I took make you think any different. She didn't even know how I felt about her. I can see how those photographs look on their own, but if you'd been there it wasn't like that. We were laughing all the time, and it was just fun. For her it was just fun. It was more than that for me, but she didn't know. You know what I did.' This was a reference to the fact they'd found a pair of knickers hidden at the back of a drawer in his bedroom. They'd been stiff with more than one deposit of semen. 'And it was worse than that. I did it in her bedroom.' As he said this, his face flushed a deep red. Among the other oddities of the boy's behaviour, it struck Meldrum he seemed more guilt-stricken about masturbating into a stolen pair of Toni Ashton's pants than killing her husband. 'I knew she was away on holiday and it was easy for me to get in. That same afternoon she let me take those photographs of her, you see, I'd lifted her keys off the dressing table. She didn't even remember putting them down there. That's what she was like. I hid the keys away, not that I'd a plan or anything when I took them. But then she and Naomi were going on holiday, and as soon as I heard that I knew what I wanted to do. I went there the first day they left and every day after that. But it came near the end of their holiday, she was due home, and there wouldn't be many more chances. So I climbed out of my bedroom window late that night – the night it happened. I was sitting on her bed in the dark and I heard the noise of someone coming up the stairs. I was paralysed with fright. When the light went on, and I saw what seemed to be a woman I thought it was her. Just for a minute, but I nearly died of shame. I don't know if you can understand this, but when he spoke and it was a man's voice, I was terrifically relieved. And then he told me who he was.'

'Ashton was alone?'

'Oh, yes. As soon as he said, I could see it was him. I've known him since I was a kid. He knew right away exactly what I was doing there. He laughed at me.'

The same story unchanged at the fourth telling. Only at this point Stanley interrupted. 'Did he try to have sex with you?'

Meldrum's head snapped up. It was an outrageously leading question. The boy stared at Stanley, eyes blinking furiously, for what seemed a long time. At last, he said, 'Yes.'

'You didn't mention that before,' Meldrum said.

'I was too ashamed.' He looked, however, completely calm again. 'It was too horrible to talk about.'

'You're saying Brian Ashton tried to sexually assault you?'

'Yes.'

'How?'

'Sorry?'

'What did he do?'

'He grabbed me between the legs.'

'Was this before or after he laughed at you?'

'After.'

'Not instead of?'

'He laughed at me. Said he knew what I was doing there. Then he told me to get it out and let him have a look.' The words coming quickly now. Fluently, Meldrum thought, coming fluently again. 'Then he grabbed me.'

'And then what happened?'

'I pulled away.'

'And then?'

'He scrambled across the bed after me. And I picked up the knife—'

'Where from?'

'Like I told you. It was on the bedside table.' .

'Go on.'

'Then I stabbed him.'

'Where did you stab him?'

'I don't know. I just lashed out and ran.'

It was an effective story, not too elaborate, the emotions plausible, not too detailed. A story, in other words, that was hard to shake. A story, if he kept his nerve and stuck to it, that could take him all the way to court and into the dock with a prison sentence to follow. Meldrum had worked with detectives who'd have settled for that and called it a result.

Afterwards, Meldrum, Stanley and Shields sat looking at one another.

'Well,' Meldrum asked, 'do you believe him?'

'Young love,' Shields said. 'Could be. Kids do crazy things.'

'Oh, come,' Stanley said, 'in a world where even the five-year-olds can spell clitoris, can you believe in something called young love?'

'I believe the wanking all right. And the rest of it could have happened like that.'

'Jim?' Stanley appealed to Meldrum.

'I wouldn't call it young love,' Meldrum said. 'Obession, maybe. You never saw Toni Ashton, Henry.'

'I saw the photographs. Top shelf, run of the mill, I'd have said.'

'Not when you saw her.' In real life, he'd almost said, whatever that was. In the flesh, don't even think about it.

'Best-looking woman I ever saw,' Shields said. 'In real life, you know? Pity she's a lezzie.'

'A lesbian? According to Naomi Morgan, yes? But then why would a lesbian be interested in Terry Finlay? Or give him any encouragement?'

It was an easy target. Hardly able to believe his luck, Shields tumbled over himself to hit it. 'You're the psychologist. But – just thinking about it, you know – maybe she just fancied having somebody around to admire her? Would that be possible? And it wouldn't matter a toss if it's a boy or girl – either would do for telling her she was the best thing since sliced bread. Some women are like that. If they're stuck, they'll run out and buy a dog and clap it till its tongue hangs out. Just a thought, could be wrong, I wouldn't pretend to be an expert.' Shields grinned, well pleased with himself.

'Sociologist,' Stanley said. 'Not psychologist – though I have a qualification, as it happens.'

As a counter, it didn't amount to much. Shields's grin widened.

'Whatever,' Meldrum said dismissively. The peacemaker. 'The boy was convincing. Do we think he could make it up that well? And why would he?'

'You put your finger on it yourself,' Stanley said. 'An obsessive boy. That makes for a rich fantasy life. As for him telling his story well, that's a function of intelligence. I don't get the impression he's stupid.'

Meldrum nodded slowly. He was wondering why Stanley was going at it so hard, as if he'd appointed himself as Terry Finlay's counsel for the defence. Maybe because Finlay was only a boy, bright and vulnerable. If so, it was a side of Stanley he hadn't seen or suspected, and he liked him for it.

'One thing for sure,' he said, 'he's smarter than his father.'

'I don't for a moment doubt,' said Stanley, 'that may be a large part of the trouble. Anyway, don't we already have a suspect? Before we take the boy's story at face value, we shouldn't forget about Alex Hodge.'

CHAPTER THIRTY-FOUR

Billie Hunter had left the door of his tiny office open. As they talked, Meldrum was conscious of the unremitting surf of voices from the bar. Too often as well he caught a whiff of the acrid stench of piss as someone went in or out of the Gents in the corridor. Even in the middle of a weekday afternoon, it seemed, The Flying Fox kept merry and bright.

'We've been through all this.' Hunter rubbed a hand like a shovel over the scars on his bald head. A coil of grey-blue smoke rose from the cigarette he'd balanced on the edge of the paper-strewn desk at the near end of a line of burn marks. 'This is what I get for being a good citizen.'

Shields snorted. He was standing, leaning one shoulder against the wall, not fancying the precarious little stool any more than Meldrum had. 'That what you are?'

'I've contributed to a few police charities in my time. Right enough, some of them forgot to give me a flag.'

'Not sure where to stick it maybe.'

'You're mistaking me for one of your friends.'

Girls, girls, Meldrum thought. Which wasn't fair to Bobbie Shields. Or even Hunter, who sodomised the young men he brutalised. To be even fairer to Shields, who didn't usually go in for this stuff, Hunter had that effect on a lot of policemen. An effect due not simply to him being an evil bastard, but in part because, poof or not, in a brawl he'd take most of them apart, Shields not excluded.

He sighed as Shields levered himself off the wall, frowning.

'Enough,' Meldrum said. 'Tell me about the good citizen.'

Hunter eyed him warily. 'I reported what happened to McCluskie.'

'You had information about a man being beaten half to death, and you went to the police.'

'Plenty wouldn't have.'

'But you did. Now, why was that?'

'How do you mean?'

'Let me guess. I think it was because Ashton and his friend picked McCluskie up in here. And this is your patch. Right?'

Hunter took a drag on the cigarette, scattering ash across the papers on the desk. 'I was a mug. I reported it and nobody cared a fuck.'

'So you should be pleased I'm giving you a second chance,' Meldrum said.

'To do what?'

'Even the score.'

'Ashton's dead.'

'But his friend isn't.'

'Ashton was the mouthie bastard.'

Meldrum swept a corner of the desk clear.

'Careful!'

'Am I spoiling your filing system?' He rested a haunch on the desk and leaned over above Hunter. 'Let me explain. I want something on this friend of Brian Ashton's, right? This friend admits he was there when gays were attacked. But according to him it was all done by Ashton. He was just a spectator.'

'Shite.'

'Probably. But the problem's proving it. And he claims not to remember dates when any of the incidents happened. He's got one of these convenient memories.'

'You know the date when McCluskie got hammered and—'

'He says he wasn't there that night. Maybe that's shite too, eh? But with McCluskie being dead we'll never know. What I need are some names.'

'What kind of names?'

'Come on, Billie. You're not stupid.'

'McCluskie's the only one I knew about. Why don't you look back through your records?'

'We have. Nobody we've traced admits to being attacked by men in drag. Maybe because they weren't. Maybe because to admit they were would raise too many awkward questions. For the same reason, there's a good chance none of the assaults by Ashton and his friend were reported at all.'

Hunter brought up his arm, shot his cuff and checked the time. Between the watch and the rings there was enough gold to salt a small mine. 'I've got deliveries due.' He stood up. 'Like I told you, they were in here twice, maybe three times. I warned them off. They came back and McCluskie got a doing. End of story.'

Meldrum too stood up. It was a narrow room, and between them he and Shields blocked the way to the door.

'It's a small world,' Meldrum said. 'And the world you're in's even smaller. Two guys in drag start preying on gays. I think that would be talked about. And nobody in the community hears more than Billie Hunter.'

'Suddenly some hoofs getting the crap kicked out of them is a big deal to you guys?' Hunter had to look up at Meldrum, little pig eyes studying his face shrewdly. 'I don't think so. Ashton got himself murdered. Did the friend do it?'

Certainly, Hunter wasn't stupid.

'If he did,' Meldrum said, 'chances are he's going to get away with it.'

'If he did,' Hunter said, 'he should get a fucking medal.'

'And get away with McCluskie. And whoever the others were.'

'I hear you,' Hunter said. 'I'll think about it.'

'Not for too long,' Meldrum said, and moved aside.

CHAPTER THIRTY-FIVE

As the affair was reconstructed in court, the trouble had started the evening before with the wife's confession. Why he hadn't gone for her then had to be something of a mystery. His defending solicitor offered it as evidence of how hard his client had tried intitialy to restrain himself in the face of provocation. The other interpretation saw him as one of nature's slow burners, an egotist who needed a brooding interval to get over his incredulity and begin numbering his injuries until he'd got the sense of grievance fully stoked.

In any case, there seems to have been no sign of the previous evening's turmoil when he arrived at work. By mid-morning, hovering and swooping around the head of a prosperous young matron, scissors in hand, he was the complete artist craftsman.

'Can I leave that to you, Sam?' The matron smiled at him in the mirror. 'You've never let me down for a wedding yet.'

'And when's the big one going to be?'

'Lucy? It's more likely to be Peter.'

'Peter!' And this as not exactly a squeal so much as a squeal orchestrated for baritones, accompanied by a flick of the wrist, not camp but again just lightly in that general area, less a sexual orientation than a professional mannerism. 'What age is he now, for goodness' sake?'

'Nineteen. But he's running riot with the girls at Cambridge. So my spies tell me. Some of the girls Peter was at school with went to Cambridge. They tell their mums — and it comes straight to me.' She laughed. 'Poor Peter. He has no idea how much I know what's going on.'

Swoop. Snip snip. Contemplate.

'Do tell, what he's up to?'

'Boys will be boys.'

'My money would still be on Lucy in the marriage stakes. She was a pretty little thing the first time you brought her in. Now she's stunning. And a wonderful personality. My very favourite client. Present company excepted!'

'Sam!'

Look in the mirror. Snip.

About that point, Marie McConnell put in an appearance. In retrospect, since it may be assumed fifteen years of marriage had given her some insight into her husband's character, it was a risky thing to do. As she said afterwards, however, fifteen years of her life had gone into building up the business and he wasn't going to frighten her out of it. No way.

As the matron recalled it, husband and wife nodded to one another, 'perfectly civilly'. Quarter of an hour or so passed. One of the long-legged assistants who were a feature of the place finished washing a customer's hair, and Marie McConnell began work on it. She was two chairs away from her husband.

Bodge! the matron thought he was shouting as he deserted her and swooped snipsnap on his wife. Bodge? Could that be a hairdresser's word for botch? He was such a perfectionist, had he spotted his wife making a mess of the client's hair?

'Hodge? Hodge? You did it with a cunt like Hodge, ya cunt?' were his actual words.

He followed this with a punch in the face; later described by him, as he paid a substantial fine, as worth it at twice the price.

'Cursing and swearing,' as the matron explained to her daughter Lucy, 'he showed himself in his true colours.' And as an afterthought, 'And then hitting her. What my mother would have called a keelie. The mask came off and there he was, under all the manners he's learned, really just a Glasgow thug.'

All the same, she was there for her next appointment, never gave a thought to not keeping it. There was after all, no getting away from it, a kind of frisson in what in every sense might be called rough trade.

Or as she put it herself, 'Nobody understands my hair the way Sam does.'

CHAPTER THIRTY-SIX

Mr Smillie, surviving partner of Carter, Macleavy and Smillie, wasn't smiling. An indication of his mood had been the number of difficulties he raised before finally agreeing that Stanley could be present.

'I don't know what bearing this could have on your investigation. I don't see how it can have any, but obviously you have to be informed.'

'Because it concerns Mr Ashton?'

'Mr Ashton's estate. Well, not directly but this . . . development will have implications for it.'

'Is this about George Snoddy's Trust Fund?' Meldrum asked.

Smillie gaped at him. 'How do you know that?'

'Mr Snoddy told us that Macleavy was making difficulties about him getting his money out of the Trust. It crossed my mind, when a lawyer starts—'

'This kind of thing is very unusual.' He shot a glance at Stanley. 'What I'm telling you has to be a matter of strict confidence, you do understand?'

'Unless it had to be used in court, of course.'

'. . . I feel I've no choice. As I said, it will affect Brian Ashton's estate. And you are investigating his death.'

'His murder.'

'Yes.' He stared absently at Meldrum, as if searching for the thread of whatever he'd planned to say. He was probably in his middle forties, but at the moment the dark patches under the eyes made him look careworn. At a guess, he hadn't slept much the last couple of nights. Gathering himself, he said, 'Arthur Macleavy has stolen money. When he didn't turn up for work, his secretary rang his home. Then she took a call from Mr Snoddy. He became quite upset when she told him Macleavy wasn't available. That's when she got in touch with me. I've been going through his records since then.'

'How much did he steal?'

'I'd rather not say. Anyway, it's too early to be sure. That will have to be worked out with your colleagues.'

'But you can confirm for me that money has been embezzled from the Snoddy Trust?'

'If it were only . . . Yes. Others as well, you'll have gathered that. Old ladies, smaller amounts.' He launched, escaped it seemed, into an explanation. 'Trusts are very various. There are single shop-front firms in the North East which are in fact very wealthy legal practices because of the Trusts they administer. What Macleavy did to the Snoddy Trust isn't unprecedented. But perhaps the amount, from one client . . . There's insurance, of course. But the Guarantee Fund premium for next year will go up because of this for every solicitor in Scotland. And for it to happen in a well-established firm with computer systems in place! The Law Society tends to audit small firms more often and more closely. With a firm like ours, the assumption would be this simply shouldn't happen. Macleavy slipped through our net by a measure of good luck, some long-term bad practice and ingenuity. I've been totally taken aback by just how ingenious he was. If he'd been half as clever in his proper . . . When I joined this firm, the Carters were here, father and son, fine people. I thought of Macleavy as a bit of a passenger. Doesn't matter. In our defence, you have to say that if someone is willing to be downright crooked, to the extent of forging clients' signatures, it's very hard to stop him.'

'I'm grateful to you for telling us about it,' Meldrum said.

'I don't suppose it has any bearing on your murder—' Smillie was overtaken by an enormous yawn. He frowned, as if suddenly too exhausted to think straight. 'Sorry. But, a thing like this, I want everything to be absolutely above board. He wasn't typical. When it happens, usually it's someone on his own, power of attorney for an old lady and cash-flow problems, to pay his bills or his staff. You can understand the temptation. Most of those cases have an element of pathos. As for Macleavy.' He made a gesture of helplessness.

'Maybe he gambled.'

'This morning I've traced some property deals he made, one in particular seems to have gone spectacularly bad.' He shrugged. 'So, yes, I suppose you could say he gambled and lost.'

CHAPTER THIRTY-SEVEN

Marie McConnell had done her best to hide the livid bruise on her cheek with make-up, but not even a change of hairstyle could entirely hide the black eye.

'Sam was away,' she said. 'Visiting his mother in Glasgow. Every time she's supposed to be ill, he's through there. He wanted to buy her a house in Edinburgh. You should have heard her, but. "Oh my, don't ask me to do that, I couldn't bear to leave the family home and all the old neighbours." We're talking Cranhill here, you understand. Never mind the business, never mind how the important clients don't like to be fobbed off with somebody else, Mammy needs him. Of course, she's got him on a string. I knew that first time he took me to meet her. And right from the off, I never believed there was all that much wrong with the old bitch's heart. Apart from being made of stone, that is.'

'Could we slow down?' Meldrum asked. 'I'd like to get a few things clear before we go on.'

They were in the living room of Alex Hodge's flat. A big room, it was full of early evening sunlight. One of the windows was open, the curtain stirring occasionally, so they could hear traffic going by below in the street. Hodge and Marie were sitting side by side on the couch with Shields and himself facing them.

'Most important,' he said, 'we are talking about the night Brian Ashton was murdered?'

Hodge nodded, looking surprisingly morose for a man in process of being provided with an alibi. 'When I left the Rex Casino, I came straight home.'

'Only he didn't make it,' Marie said. 'I'd been out—' She broke off. 'I was coming up the stair when I heard him running up at my back. I said something to him. I can't remember—'

'You said, is the devil chasing you?'

'And you said, he might as well be.' She took his hand. He shifted uncomfortably but let it lie in her clutch. 'I was feeling pretty low, and he looked in a bit of a state. I asked him in for a drink.'

There was a silence. 'And?' Meldrum prompted.

'He stayed the night.'

'All night?'

'Till the dawn's early light.'

'Do you remember the time when you met one another coming up the stairs?'

'It was half past nine.'

The members' guest book at the Rex Casino had been signed by Hodge at eight forty-five. He claimed to have stayed about half an hour before his nerve broke and he'd fled the casino. Quarter of an hour then to get home. It fitted. If she was telling the truth, Hodge was in the clear.

'That's very exact. Are you sure?'

'I'm sure.' She looked up at Hodge. 'I was to meet someone. He'd told me he'd booked a table at the Stac Polly for a meal. For seven o'clock. When he hadn't appeared by half seven, I ate dinner on my own. Every bite, I felt like a damned fool. Would you believe, all the same, I stretched it out till nine? I kept hoping he'd come. By the time I'd paid the bill, I walked down to Princes Street before I got a taxi, I was so fed up I just wanted to get home, it wasn't any later than half nine by the time I got back.'

'Why not say this before?' Meldrum asked Hodge. 'You know the trouble you could have got into? Brian Ashton was murdered.'

'I'm not surprised,' Marie said. 'Alex told me about him. Dressing up as a woman and the rest of it. I don't think he was right in the head.'

'When did he tell you?'

'That night. He said the devil was after him, and I asked him in for a drink and he told me about Brian and what they'd been doing.'

'He told you he'd been involved too?'

'He was upset. And I was feeling pretty awful as well. So I told him about Brian standing me up.'

'*Who* standing you up?' Shields asked.

Always good, Meldrum thought, to know he was following the conversation.

Surprised himself, he asked, 'Brian Ashton?'

'Of course,' she said. 'Brian said to me, I hear Sam's away, that must be a bit lonely for you. Sam had been making such a fuss about me getting on too well with Brian that I thought, why not? I agreed to let him take me to dinner. And I waited for hours like a fool. And then Alex told me where he'd been while I was waiting for him. We just sat drinking and talking about what a bastard he was. Is it any wonder we finished up in bed?'

Answer, sourly, no. As far as Meldrum could tell, at the moment the world and someone else's wife were jumping all the time into every bed in sight, his own excepted.

'So why didn't you tell us,' Meldrum asked Hodge, 'that you'd an alibi?'

'Because Alex is a gentleman.' His hand had escaped, she took hold of it again. 'I feel safe with him. Alex will look after me.'

When he was seeing them out, Hodge followed them on to the landing. He spoke very softly. 'Would you, could you possibly, have a word with McConnell?'

'What about?'

'Warn him to stay away from us.'

'Domestic dispute,' Meldrum said. 'We try to interfere, he'd have a good complaint. If he goes over the score, get her to take him to court. She could get a restraining order so he has to stay away from her.'

'And what about me?' A hangdog figure, he peered nervously over the bannister. 'You can see his door from here. I'm frightened to go past it in case he jumps out at me. He's a madman.'

In the car, Shields started to laugh. 'Estate agent meets hairdresser. Could sell tickets for it.' He was a boxing fan. 'No pleasing some people, eh? But looks like he's off the hook.'

'Looks like it.'

'Well, if he is, we've still got Terry Finlay.' Shields began chuckling again. 'Way he was going on, Henry Stanley won't like that. But, one thing for sure, there's nobody else in the frame, is there?'

CHAPTER THIRTY-EIGHT

The Judge was a quiet bar, not one frequented by policemen, or academics come to that. Maybe that's why the two of them had picked it, Meldrum thought. Not, of course, that there was any reason he shouldn't meet Stanley for a drink. They'd done it twice already, and Meldrum, a solitary man, had looked forward to this third time more than he had admitted to himself. It didn't bother him that all they talked about was the Ashton case. If it crossed his mind at all that Stanley was using him, for his article or book or whatever it turned out to be in the end, that didn't bother him. An obsessive himself, if Stanley wanted to obsess about the case, that was fine by him. Meldrum told him about Hodge being off the hook, and listened with interest as Stanley tried to hang him back on to it. As a witness for the defence, Marie McConnell didn't impress him. On her own admission, she'd been badly treated by Brian Ashton, so wasn't it possible that she might have lied about spending the night with Hodge? But, Meldrum told him, we checked and she was in Stac Polly like she said from seven till about nine. One of the waitresses who got her hair done at the McConnells' salon had kept an eye on Marie that evening, expecting Sam McConnell to appear and when he didn't wondering if it was him or someone else who'd so obviously stood her up. Reluctantly Stanley yielded the point, but countered that the fact she'd been in the restaurant didn't prove she'd met Hodge later or slept with him. They went back and forward on it, had a few beers, and by the time they were finished Meldrum went home with a slight buzz and slept better than he'd done for weeks.

When, though, after sitting in on the morning briefing, Stanley joined them the next morning and continued to pursue the same topic, Meldrum was mildly irritated. He had more things to think about and left the argument to Shields.

'I don't get it.' Shields bit into his doughnut and took a gulp of coffee. 'How come you're so sure about Terry Finlay? Far as I'm concerned, he fits the frame better than Hodge. I don't think he could have made all that stuff up. We've got those photographs she let him take of her. And he doesn't have an alibi. Which, whether you like it or not, Hodge has.'

'Do you remember,' Stanley wondered, 'when I asked the boy if Ashton tried to have sex with him?'

'So?' Shields stuck what was left of the doughnut in his mouth.

'Well, Terry hesitated, thinking about it before he answered. If he'd really been threatened with a sexual attack, he wouldn't forget.'

Shields sprayed crumbs in his eagerness to answer that one. 'You don't suppose he might have been working out what would help him in court? Like having the victim grab him by the balls?'

Meldrum's phone rang, distracting him from Stanley's answer. As he picked it up, he was wondering again how come Shields was able to score so easily against someone as smart as Stanley. He was reminded of arguments he'd seen about religion or politics, the one who cared too much tended to lose to the guy who kept cool because he didn't give a toss. Why would Stanley care too much? As he listened, though, the question was forgotten.

Something in his responses must have alerted the others. As he finished, they were watching him expectantly.

'There's a body we should have a look at,' he told them.

'Why?' Shields asked.

'From the description.'

Before Shields could respond, Stanley asked, 'Where is it?'

'Station car park at Preston Pans.'

CHAPTER THIRTY-NINE

Right at the end of the row like that, beside the boundary fence and well away from the road, the car and its contents might have gone unnoticed for even longer if the offside back window hadn't been cracked open. It wasn't much of a gap, the kind that happens when people don't take care. Most times it wouldn't have mattered, even to a car thief, who if he were half-way competent would have had easier ways to get in. The weather had been warm, however, which meant that in the car it had got very warm. Parking her Peugot 306 beside it, Mrs Baillie, sixty-six and keeping busy, glanced across and was puzzled. Although her train into Edinburgh for an afternoon's shopping was due, she had a well-exercised faculty of curiosity. She got out and walked slowly round the Ford Galaxy. First, with a touch of disgusted unease, she identified the shimmering cloud she'd glimpsed as flies and bluebottles crowding the interior. Then as she bent closer to peer inside, her nose came close to the gap at the window and she caught the smell.

'Did he commit suicide?' Snoddy asked when they told him.

'Why should you think that?' Meldrum asked.

Templars, whatever the state of its finances, was still popular. Snoddy had led them through the busy restaurant between the lunch tables, down a narrow stair beside the toilets and out of an emergency exit into a basement garden. They'd climbed three worn steps to where on the far side of an etiolated lawn five big wooden chairs were arranged on patio slabs around a table. The midday sun poking down between the tall buildings warmed the four men as they talked.

'You tell me he was found dead in his car. It seems to be the obvious conclusion.'

'Most people would think of a road accident first.'

'Most people,' Snoddy said bitterly, 'wouldn't have had hundreds of thousands of pounds stolen from them.' Despite his loss, he was plump and sleek as ever. Even the repeated gesture of combing the mane of white hair with his fingers was hard to read as a sign of agitation when after each pass it fell back undisturbed in the same glossy waves. 'It's official now. Confirmed by Smillie. He's the lawyer.'

'We've spoken to Mr Smillie.'

'He kept telling me there was insurance. I said to him, if Peter Carter had been alive, this would never have happened. The whole thing has been an appalling breach of faith. Naturally when you told me Macleavy was dead, I assumed his conscience had got the better of him. But it was a road accident, you say?'

'His car was found this morning abandoned at a rail station. The body had been crammed down between the seats and hidden under a rug.'

'I don't understand.'

'There hasn't been a medical report yet. We can't say for sure until the cause of death is established, but it seems likely that he was murdered.'

Snoddy waved a large white hand in a gesture of dismissal. 'Who would want to do that?'

'You mean who would have a motive?'

'I suppose that's the way a policeman would put it.'

'Since Macleavy was found, we've been considering who would have had a motive for wanting to see him dead,' Meldrum said.

Snoddy looked first at him, then questioningly at Shields, and almost as an afterthought at Stanley, who he'd been told wasn't a policeman.

'Money,' Shields said. 'That's a motive.'

'The commonest motive,' Meldrum said.

'People get killed so that someone can steal their money.'

'Or,' Meldrum said, 'people can get themselves killed because they've stolen someone's money.'

'If you're suggesting I might have killed him,' Snoddy sounded genuinely astonished, 'even hinting at the remotest possibility of such a thing, I have to say I've never heard such nonsense.'

'Just as a remote possibility,' Meldrum said, 'we have to recognise that the two men involved in taking so much money from you are both dead.'

'Two men? Do you mean Brian?'

'Mr Ashton deceived you about the money you put into the business. And Mr Macleavy embezzled from you.'

'I could never have harmed Brian. To say I could have isn't just nonsense, it's obscene.'

'Purely as a matter of routine, I'd be grateful if you could let me have details both for where you were the night that Mr Ashton was killed and for —'

'No!'

'I'm sorry?'

'I won't co-operate in such a farce. Find out without my help.' Snoddy threw back his head, stuck out his chin. 'It won't bother me if you pry. Ask all the grubby questions you want, no one who knows me will take them seriously.'

With a mixture of disbelief and exasperation, Meldrum recognised the signs of a weak man digging his heels in. That it was the wrong stand at the wrong time wouldn't prevent him holding to it with the stubbornness of a mule.

'That isn't sensible, sir.'

'If it will help, I can tell you that most of the time I'm either here or at home. And I live alone.'

'Leave Macleavy aside for the moment,' Meldrum said with a touch of weariness. 'You've told us how much you thought of Mr Ashton. We're trying to find who killed him. Wasting our time really doesn't help.'

'If you want to find his murderer, find his wife. Or the man she got to do it for her. Of course, she killed him. Apart for that woman, there isn't anyone in the world who would have a bad word to say for Brian.'

At that point, it was perfectly legitimate to tell him about the attacks on homosexuals, how Ashton had been dressed when they were made, and that subsequently to the worst of them a man had died. Meldrum had no reason to feel badly about that. He was surprised, however, at the effect on him of the devastation he saw on Snoddy's face and the strange momentary expression on Stanley's, as if the little man had stood witness to an act of cruelty and been made afraid. The absurd thing was that if he had given in to the impulse to make an apology he wouldn't have known to which of the two it was owed.

'After all these years, you make me ask myself, did Brian ever really care about me?' Snoddy said at last.

CHAPTER FORTY

When Billie Hunter rang, Meldrum wasn't feeling particularly co-operative. It had been a long day.

'I've got someone wants to talk to you.'

Meldrum recognised the gravelly voice. 'Billie Hunter?'

After a pause, there came a grudging 'Right.'

'What's with the Mr Smith shite?' As Mr Smith, Hunter had pestered the desk sergeant until he'd put him through to Meldrum.

'I'm doing you a favour. So it's confidential.'

'Fine.'

'Confidential, understood?'

'If you've something to tell me, get on with it.'

'I should just hang up.'

Meldrum stared at the files and scatter of papers that hid his desk. It looked like a mess. It was a mess. There had been a time when he wouldn't have let it get that way. Knocking over a half-full cup of coffee hadn't helped. He needed to get a grip. 'One phone call doesn't make you a grass, Billie. Don't worry, anybody in here asks me, I tell them I'd a call from a Mr Smith.' There was a silence. 'Okay?'

'This is a one-shot deal. Either you see him tonight, or you can forget it.'

Meldrum looked at his watch. Fucking marvellous. It was nearly nine o'clock. What he wanted to do was go home, have a whisky and read yesterday's paper and go to bed. What it looked like he was going to have to do was listen to a sweating queer explain how he just happened to go for a walk with two nice men in dresses.

'We can do that,' he said.

'Just you. And he won't come in there.'

Meldrum sighed. 'Surprise me. So where and when?'

'Let me check with him. I'll ring you back.'

'If you make it too long, I won't be here.'

'I thought you wanted something on the Ashton thing. You were the one came to me. You were fucking keen enough then.'

As Meldrum hung up, he thought there was a fifty-fifty chance at best of Hunter ringing back. He could have handled things better, but after Marie McConnell's alibi he was less intent on pursuing Alex Hodge. It was also true Macleavy's death had distracted him. That wasn't logical, since there was no proof of a connection between Ashton's murder and Macleavy's, far less that they might have been killed by the same person. But if they had been, then it was hard to see what reason Hodge could have had for murdering Macleavy. As for Terry Finlay, a reason for him killing Macleavy looked somewhere between unlikely and impossible. On the other hand, apart from the obvious link that tied Snoddy to both of them, at the moment he could see no connection anyway between Ashton and Macleavy. Meldrum rubbed his eyes and checked his watch for the third time in ten minutes.

When the phone finally rang, it startled him out of a half-sleep.

The suggested meeting place came as a surprise. He'd expected the lounge of a quiet hotel or if it was a bar some out of the way place, not one attached to a rugby team's social club. When he got there, the place wasn't weekend full, but it wasn't quiet either. Looking around from just inside the door, he cursed Hunter who, when he'd asked him how he'd recognise the guy, had laughed and hung up. As he stood uncertainly, a man left the bar and headed straight across.

Pausing in front of Meldrum, he stuck out the hand that wasn't holding a pint, and said, 'Jim, is it? Or do you prefer James?'

A big man, maybe four inches smaller than Meldrum, which would put him at six feet, but a lot broader, with a neck like a ballet dancer's thigh. For some reason, when he'd heard where they were to meet, Meldrum had been expecting a spectator not a player. This guy, one ear crumpled, nose that looked as if it had been broken more than once, was unmistakably a player.

'Jim'll do.'

'Call me Deekers, everybody does in here. What'll you have? Best pint in town.'

Seated at the table, waiting for him to come back with the drinks, a head of

exasperation built in Meldrum, partly because of the man and the place, partly
because he was almost sure he was wasting his time, mostly because irritation
nowadays boiled too often under the rigidity of his self-control like magma
knocking on a lid of rock. If the guy didn't want to give his name, it didn't
matter. If there was anything worth using, time enough later to get his name. It
was stupid, unprofessional to bother about it now. It didn't matter.

'Never mind the Deekers stuff,' he said as the man sat down. 'What's your
name?'

It was the look on the man's face that clued him in. Once in Jenners he'd
stood beside a guy who was looking for monogrammed underpants. He'd got
the same look on his face when the assistant asked what his initials were. The
celebrity look: You don't know who I am?

'Wait a minute,' Meldrum said. 'You played rugby for Scotland.'

'A few years back,' Deekers said modestly, but the look had gone.

'I never thought you were —'

'What?'

'You know, gay.'

Which was crass. In excuse, Meldrum had only ever had a handful of heroes
in his life.

'You mean queer?' Not the celebrity look this time, but straight astonishment.

'Forget it.'

'Where do you get that idea?'

'Billie Hunter for a start.' Meldrum's irritation knocked the lid again. 'So
you had fun in the scrum. I don't give a fuck.'

Deekers leaned over the table, tapping it for emphasis with a finger the size
and colour of a beef sausage. 'I am not,' he looked round and lowered his voice,
'what you just said. Understood?'

'Is there some kind of mix-up?' Meldrum was bewildered. 'You asked Billie
Hunter if you could see me?' He got a nod. 'So what then? Is this not about
Brian Ashton?'

'Of course it is. Did Billie not say to you?'

Meldrum took a deep breath. When in doubt go for the simple question.
'How the fuck do you know Billie Hunter?' he asked.

'Model ships.'

'What?'

'I don't mean kits. Proper miniature ships. Build them and sail them.

Historically accurate above and below decks. As far as the engines are concerned, it's really precision engineering.'

'Billie Hunter builds model ships?' It felt like being told Jack the Ripper was keen on macrame.

'Oh, Billie's about the best of us. He's got a wonderful pair of hands.'

'I've heard that,' Meldrum said.

'So that's how I know him.'

Hero improbably back on pedestal.

'So how come you want to see me?'

'Bad conscience.' He enfolded the pint in one enormous fist and seemed not so much to swallow as inhale half of it. Looking into Meldrum's eyes, he held them in an unwaveringly solemn gaze. 'I've always been very clear on the line between right and wrong. This thing that's been on my mind. I just haven't been able to keep from worrying about it. I tried to tell myself it wouldn't be any use to you – but I knew fine that was garbage. Then Billie Hunter mentioned that he knew you.'

'Oh yes,' Meldrum said drily.

'The whole thing was like a sign. Lovely day. The boats on the water. And out of nowhere they started talking about Brian Ashton – all that stuff in the papers. Not surprising really, after all, a few of us had known him. And then, just for something to say, I suppose, Billie Hunter said he'd met you a few times. So I got hold of him afterwards and said I needed to talk to you, but it had to be discreet. Could he arrange a meeting? To be honest, I didn't put a lot of stock in him being able to do that. But, I'd told myself, no more excuses, at least give it a try. If he'd said he couldn't, I don't know what I'd have done. I'd like to think I'd have found another way. But when I asked him, he said, no problem. In fact, he seemed pretty pleased with the idea.'

While they'd been talking, different people had nodded in passing or called over a greeting. 'This is discreet?' Meldrum asked, as it happened again.

Deekers nodded seriously. 'There isn't a place in Edinburgh I could go and be sure of not being recognised. Nobody thinks twice about seeing me here. Just having a quiet drink with a friend.'

'Right,' Meldrum said slowly. Give him that. He wondered if his underpants were monogrammed, but after the Billie Hunter misunderstanding it didn't seem a good idea to ask. 'So what's been worrying you?'

'I don't suppose you've heard of a man called John Markham.'

Suddenly Meldrum was properly awake, the adrenaline flowing.

'Runs an investment company. That the one?'

Deekers looked surprised, then he said, 'I saw Brian Ashton at John Markham's the night he was killed.'

The breath went out of Meldrum as if he'd been poked in the solar plexus with a stick. He willed himself to stay calm.

'Go on.'

'You're going to ask me why I didn't go to the police.' He chewed on his lip. 'I was at one of Markham's parties at the time. And they're kind of . . . unusual. I was there with two girls. A bit young. Not illegal. Near enough. They were sixteen. You probably know I'm married. And I've got kids.'

Hero knocked off pedestal. Too bad, Meldrum thought, but he was too old for heroes.

'When you say you were at Markham's, where was that?'

'He's got an estate down the coast.'

'And you saw Ashton there? Did he have someone with him?'

Deekers nodded.

'A man?'

'Oh yes.'

'Can you describe this man?' Meldrum asked, trying to keep the excitement out of his voice.

'It's kind of hard to explain. We're talking about a cross between a mansion and a castle, you know the style? I'd been upstairs with these two girls. I came down for – something.' Meldrum had heard that kind of hesitation before. People met a policeman socially, relaxed to the point of forgetting his job, then stumbled over a near admission as they remembered. Maybe the big man had moved on from steroids in the pharmacopoeia. 'When I got to the landing, I heard voices. Johnnie Markham talking to somebody. There was a man standing with his back to the fire. As I looked down into the hall, Johnnie was just going back into the old library. No sooner was he in than this woman came out of it – out of the library, right? She joined the man and the two of them went outside. Out to a car, I suppose, leaving the party.'

'This man, would you recognise him again?'

'Doubt it. Didn't pay any attention to him. Too busy trying to see the woman's face. Always had a thing for redheads. Later I asked Johnnie Markham, who's this terrific woman he's hiding away. And he laughed and said, Brian Ashton.'

'Anything else?'

'I told him, you're having me on, and he laughed. I got what I'd come down for, and went back upstairs. Almost slept in the next morning, I'd a London plane to catch. It was three days before I heard.' He picked up the glasses. 'Again?'

'What?'

But he had taken consent for granted and was heading to the bar.

When he came back, Meldrum asked, 'It was three days before you heard about Ashton being murdered?'

'That's right. First thing I did was phone John Markham. Try to phone him. He was always out of the office or in a meeting and she'd get him to ring me back. But he didn't, not that day. The next night he rang me at home. When I told him what it was about, he laughed.'

Meldrum waited, asked, 'What was funny?'

'Nothing as far as I was concerned. He told me he'd just been joking.'

'But you didn't believe him?'

'As far as he was concerned I did. And maybe I would have but—' Deekers did his vanishing act with the pint again. 'After he said, forget it, and I said, glad to, he said something like, pretty girls those two, meaning the two girls I'd been with, and then he asked how my wife was and how the boys were doing at school. I got it into my head, thinking about it later, he'd been warning me. Forget it or else. And I didn't like that.'

CHAPTER FORTY-ONE

'It's a surprise seeing you back here,' John Markham said. He happened to be looking at Henry Stanley as he came in, but of course he was speaking to all three of them.

'We've had some new information,' Meldrum said.

'Really? And you think I can help?' He smiled at the woman, who was laying brochures on one of the tables by the window. Her legs were just as improbably long as Meldrum remembered. 'Val, we'll use my office. Be a sweetie and hold my calls, would you? Unless it's McLaren – or anything else you feel shouldn't wait.'

He led the way out of the reception room. As he followed, Meldrum checked the position of the big fire, set in a hearth in one corner, then glanced up the broad stairway to the landing above. A man standing up there would be able to hear people talking below in the hall; his view, however, would be restricted.

'One of these rooms will be the library, I suppose.'

Markham looked round sharply. 'Yes. The old library, that is. I use it for meetings. How did that come up? I suppose Val . . . ?'

Meldrum smiled and left it at that.

If Markham had been disconcerted even slightly, there was no sign of it as he settled himself behind his desk and waved them to seats in front of it. The desk was outsize, but then it was a big room. Tall glass-fronted bookcases still lined the walls. Behind the meshed glass, Meldrum's impression was of leather bindings, runs of series and volumes. He'd seen the same kind of library in other large country houses: Scott and Dickens, books on fishing, county history, law books sometimes or medical, statistical accounts. Here, they seemed like decoration, left in place to create an effect. Used for meetings, Markham had said, and there was a table with a dozen upright chairs round it under the window. Meldrum, however, found himself shifting his weight uneasily in a leather armchair, with Stanley in a second and Shields's thighs spread apart in a third. Markham, eschewing the fourth, instead had chosen his seat behind the desk, facing and above them. As a man who had served his time as a carpenter, Meldrum yielded an involuntary moment of distraction in appreciation of that desk, its top a gleaming spread of burr walnut, the channels of life shaped in brown and gold. Behind a desk like that, in a room like this, arrogance might come easily to a man.

'A surprise,' Markham said. 'All three of you again, too. I do hope you haven't come all this way for nothing.'

'Let me tell you what brings us, sir,' Meldrum said, giving the 'sir' a little roll at the end, the merest shade of emphasis. 'We've been approached with some new evidence. A little late in coming forward, but we're grateful to have it. I wonder, do you know a man called D. K. McGroarty?'

'Deekers? Everybody knows Deekers!'

Not a blink or twitch out of him, Meldrum thought, so it's not going to be easy.

'According to him, he was at a kind of a party – would that be the right word? – held in this house, on the sixth. That's the sixth of this month. Would that be correct?'

'What's this about? Has Deekers been getting up to mischief? Is he in some kind of trouble? Enormously likable, of course, but a bit of a Peter Pan. Surprising number of the great sportsmen are like that.'

'Could we verify the party first, sir? That there was one, and on that date. The sixth, as I said. That's of this month. Could you confirm that for us? Or would you have to check?'

'In a diary, you mean? Of course, you'll need one in your line of work. Yours too, I expect, Dr Stanley.' He leaned back and smiled from one to the other. 'I'm one of those boring people blessed with more or less total recall. I keep everything in my head. Yes, then, to both your questions. And yes to the third question, too. I'd call it a party.'

'And Mr McGroarty was at this party?'

'Absolutely. Came early, left late.'

'With a memory like that,' Meldrum smiled appreciatively, 'you'll remember telling him that the redheaded woman he asked you about was Brian Ashton.'

Markham gave a little grunt, then he began to laugh. 'I did, didn't I! Is that what this is about? So much for my wonderful memory. I'm suitably downcast, I'd forgotten all about it.'

'Even though Mr McGroarty phoned you after the murder to ask about it?'

'If he did, I don't remember. We're handling a major investment programme just now. Perhaps my memory is shutting itself down for everything but business.'

'But you admit you did say to him about Ashton being there?'

'Sorry. You *have* had your journey for nothing. I was joking, of course.'

The unembroidered lie and stick to it worked more times than not. But this one was too absurd. Meldrum glanced across at the other two. He couldn't read Stanley's expression, but obviously Shields, frowning in disbelief, felt the same way. Then why didn't he join in the questioning, for God's sake? How did I let things get to this stage with him, Meldrum thought, it can't go on. Hard cop soft cop, fine; but missing cop?

'It's important to get this clear,' he said. 'You're claiming now that it wasn't Brian Ashton?'

'God, no. If it had been, you'd have had me on your doorstep the moment I heard about the murder.' Markham came out from behind his desk and took the remaining armchair, pulling it round to complete the circle and leaning forward confidentially as he began. A wide-shouldered man, in black casual gear so that the pale, big-boned face stood out like the blade of an axe. Above it, hair so black it shone; a single streak of white running back from the brow. 'What happened was, early on in the evening someone came and told me we'd a couple of gatecrashers.'

'Who told you this?'

Without missing a beat, 'Roddie Amott,' Markham said. 'I rounded them up, scrawny little chap and a rather brassy woman. God knows how they got wind of the party. Never seen them before, and hope never to see them again. Anyway, Deekers saw me throwing them out, asked me who the woman was. And I told him Brian Ashton. Not much of a joke, but it seemed funny at the time.'

'And you just happened to make this strange joke on the very evening Ashton dressed as a woman and got himself killed?'

'Isn't it horrifying? It can only be coincidence. I mean, I'm not a believer in extrasensory perception. Though, I suppose, with Koestler's money funding the Department at Edinburgh University to study the paranormal, if such phenomena happen anywhere they might choose to happen here. Better chance of getting a sympathetic reception, as it were. But I'd loathe the notion I might have picked up some kind of thought transference from a murderer. I imagine that's the kind of thing you might know about, Dr Stanley.'

'I have a colleague who dabbles,' Stanley said, 'For myself I take a realistic approach. In most situations, I find people try to do what's in their best interests.'

'If we leave the supernatural out of it,' Meldrum said drily, 'even the notion of coincidence doesn't explain why that so-called joke in particular. Or why you made it to Mr McGroarty.'

'Did I say this gatecrashing woman had red hair? Like Toni Ashton. Maybe that put it into my head. But of course the real reason was that a month or two back Deekers and three of his beefy friends created a mini-riot in Templars. One of them complained about the food, they used that as an excuse to abuse the waiter, and went on to smash the place up. Sorry, should have explained, Templars is the restaurant Brian Ashton owned.'

'You told McGroarty this woman was Brian Ashton because of some brawl in a restaurant?'

'Deekers went there looking for trouble. Ashton had been screwing Mrs Deekers. Not to speak ill of the dead, he was a bit of a bastard, old Brian. Which is why he didn't go to the police about his restaurant being damaged. Anyway, thus my stupid joke.' He smiled. 'Remember, it was a party after all. I may have had too much to drink.'

Off balance, Meldrum probed for an opening with the first thing that came to mind. 'So why didn't you tell Mr McGroarty you'd been joking when he rang you after the murder?'

On his form so far, not a hard question to answer, and indeed after a moment Markham said casually, 'Stupid of me. Too embarrassed, I suppose.'

But there had been that hesitation, brief but vivid as a stammer in a flow of fluent speech, and with it Meldrum knew that he had been lying. He couldn't tell if the other two realised, but what mattered was that Markham had gone quite still.

Markham understood what he'd done.

'Oh hell,' Markham said. 'There was another reason for me telling that wretched joke. Of course there was. Things have gone quite far enough. Come with me and I'll explain.'

As they went up the impressively wide staircase, sunlight from above flooded down on them. Looking up, Meldrum saw the arch of a cupola and the sky beyond. They followed Markham, turning left on the landing and coming into a long, wide passage with high windows giving a view across the countryside. Footsteps echoed on the uncarpeted wooden floor. There was a sudden sense of constriction as they moved into a narrow, unlit, windowless corridor. Markham spoke for the first time since they'd left the library. 'Stair at the end's been walled off. We'll use this.' He opened a door and Meldrum, expecting a room, was surprised by a small lift. The four of them crowded in and it carried them up.

The rundown air of the floor below didn't prepare them for what they met when the lift doors opened. Walls papered in heavy purple; thick carpeting underfoot. A lot of money had been spent up here. They went from one corridor into another and the walls of both were lined with paintings. The smell of money. As if he had read Meldrum's thoughts, Markham glanced back and said with a smile, 'Paintings as investments.'

'They're investments?' Shields asked. Looking at four single-colour canvases hung in a row, he sounded sceptical.

'Like golf courses or factories or marinas.'

The smell of money. Maybe that's why they called it stinking rich. While this thought was occurring to Meldrum, Markham stopped by a door, knocking and opening it more or less simultaneously. As he went in, however, he stopped so abruptly that Meldrum bumped him a half-step forward. Over his head, Meldrum looked into a pleasantly decorated sitting room. Through a shaft of sunlight, a wisp of pale smoke spiralled from an ashtray lying on the window seat. With an exclamation of distaste, Markham went over and stubbed out the cigarette, rubbing it down among the remnants of at least half a dozen others.

'Sorry about this,' he said. 'I assumed they'd be here.'

Without another word, he backed them all outside, shut the door and started to return the way they'd come. He moved quickly, as if in no doubt of where he was leading. Just as Meldrum had decided they were going to take the lift down again, and was wondering what to make of this foray, Markham turned the corner into the first corridor, opened the first door, said, 'There you are,' and went in.

A big room this one, with a bar complete with high stools and fitted out with glass shelves of bottles and even a range of optics. On stools side by side, Toni Ashton and her friend Naomi were laughing together as they swung round towards the door.

'You'll burn the place down,' Markham said. 'You walked off and left a cigarette burning. I had to put it out.'

However incongruous, his irritation appeared genuine. It was extraordinary, then, to watch how easily Toni Ashton seduced him out of that mood. Leaning back against the bar, she beckoned him over. She made no acknowledgement of the other men, as fixed in their attention on her as Markham himself. Smiling, she drew his head down with her hand on the back of his neck and kissed him.

'And there you are,' she said. 'Making me say sorry. Though it was Naomi, couldn't you guess?'

'Bloody wasn't!' Naomi Morgan put her glass down too hard, slopping drink over the edge. She was edgy, and more than a little drunk. 'Clever of you tracking us down.' For a moment, Meldrum thought she was talking to him, then realised it was to Markham. He and the women seemed absorbed in each other to the exclusion of the onlookers. 'We came here to get something to drink. Time on our own, to have a laugh together. What's wrong with that? Stuck up here, can't show her face downstairs, would you grudge Toni a little fun?'

But Meldrum could contain himself no longer. 'You've been here all the time? Since your husband was killed?'

'All the time,' Toni Ashton said. 'Despite what Naomi says, it's not dull at all. All these rooms. Being so high up, you can look over the trees to the water. Don't you think it's rather wonderful, this place?' She smiled and leaned back against the bar. It was as if, Meldrum felt, she saw into his mind: the hallucinatory moment's fusion of touch and sight by which he reimagined her drawing Markham down to meet her lips. 'I'm sorry,' she said. 'I know what I did was wrong. But I couldn't bear the reporters. And I couldn't help you with Brian's death. It's nothing to do with me. I know nothing about it. So I ran away.'

'Why here?' Meldrum asked, though he knew the answer. The answer had been acted out in front of him. Still he needed the evidence of words, her own words.

'Where else would I go?' Toni Ashton asked. 'Johnnie and I are in love. You remember you asked me, did Brian leave or did I throw him out? Neither of those. When he found out about us, he was crazy with anger. But he did nothing, and that's why he left. He couldn't bear being in the same house, when I knew he was afraid. If it had been anyone but Johnnie, he'd have killed him — or killed me. But because it was Johnnie he didn't have the guts.' She took Markham's hand. 'Where else would I go?'

Markham, Brian Ashton's last-straw lover of his wife.

It was Henry Stanley who broke the silence.

'You're a remarkable woman,' he said. 'It's been a pleasure to meet you at last, Mrs Ashton.'

On the way back to the city, Shields didn't say much, taking his cue from Meldrum who was struggling to come to terms with what had happened. He'd hit a brick wall and could see no way round it. It was Stanley who filled the silence more or less unaided with the flow of comment and speculation at which he was so good. 'I wouldn't have missed it for anything,' he kept saying. He seemed to be in high spirits, perhaps because, for whatever reason, he hadn't been at all sure whether he should come with them that morning.

CHAPTER FORTY-TWO

Because she was young and, if not pretty, good-looking in the strong-featured way Meldrum had a weakness for, it was always a pleasure to see Mary Preston. In consequence, because the course of his life had taught him not to show weakness, when she was at fault he had a tendency to be harder on her than the other DCs. That meant in turn, because he was a decent man, there were occasions when he would try to make it up to her; but not too much, of course, since there was a danger that a decent impulse to redress the balance might be confused by her or someone else with that other business of having a weakness. It was complicated. Certainly, Mary Preston found it complicated; or as she put it to a friend, you never know what kind of mood he'll be in. As a result, it was on balance her preference to deal with almost anyone else in the building.

It was that tangle of attitudes which made it difficult for Meldrum to put a certain question to her when she appeared in his office the morning after the visit to Markham's estate.

'What have you got there?' he asked her instead.

'The Rex Casino list.'

'We've got the list.'

'No, sir. Not the members' guest list. I thought it would be worth getting the complete membership list.'

'How did you manage that?'

'It didn't come from the owners in London, sir.'

'No?'

'The source was local.'

'Local,' Meldrum repeated, his tone neutral.

'Goodwill, sir. With it being a murder case.'

'This particular murder case?'

'Turns out Brian Ashton had some good friends. You know, a man's man.'

'Like Lord Lucan.'

'Yes, sir.'

'Leave it and I'll take a look.'

'Yes,' she said, and turned to leave.

She was at the door when he said, 'I'm impressed.'

'Thanks.'

'You've looked through it?'

'I ticked any name I thought you might be interested in, sir.'

He turned the pages. Ashton was marked. Hodge. Macleavy. He was conscious of her watching him. When he came on the next name, he stopped. He looked up at her, then finished glancing through the list.

'A lot of people gamble.'

'Yes, sir.'

'Can I ask you something?'

'Sir?'

He mentioned the evening he was thinking of, and very straightforwardly she said, yes, she remembered it. When Meldrum went into the pub, he'd found the four of them sitting at a table. Had all four of them arrived together? No, Cormack and Paterson had come in and seen the two of them sitting in the corner and so they'd come over and joined them – and then Meldrum had come in.

'Were you having an affair?'

She looked at him for a long moment. 'No. But I think – I'm sure that's what he wanted. That wasn't the first time he'd asked me to have a drink with him. We'd go to that place thinking no one ever went there. Then that night Cormack and Paterson came in. And not long after, you did. I think he took fright. I don't think he'll ask me again.'

'What makes you so sure he—'

And because he hesitated, she found the words for him. 'Wanted to sleep with me? Just say I knew. Maybe he and his wife didn't get on. I don't know. He never talked about her. My impression was—' It was her turn to seek the right words. 'You know, I probably would have gone to bed with him. He knows so much, he can make you laugh. I was flattered a man as clever as that would want me. And all right, I knew it wasn't for my brains. But, you see, it wasn't just about being flattered. I don't think he's very happy. There's something about him that makes you want to look after him. If he'd have the courage, I believe a lot of women would feel like that.'

He sorted the list back to the first page, smoothed it flat with his hand, then opened a drawer and put it away.

'Nothing wrong with your courage,' he said. 'If you feel you have to make a complaint, I'd understand. All I can say is, there was a good reason for asking. But I'm sorry I had to. I apologise.'

With a sour little twist of the lips, she said, 'Don't worry. You learn that you don't have any private life in this job.'

'Don't learn that,' Meldrum said. 'It's better to get out than learn that.'

CHAPTER FORTY-THREE

'Because it's important.'
'I can't just let you take him out of the school. If you want to question him, his parents should be here.'

'I'm taking him home.'

'Will his mother be there? If it's serious, shouldn't his father be there?'

'We've contacted both of them. They're waiting for us.'

'I think I should phone to Terry's home.'

'You do that.'

A woman headteacher, of course. In Meldrum's experience, they were the awkward ones. More often than not, if it was a man, he'd take it on the nod, take it on authority, especially if he'd ever been in the army. He'd cover his back, make sure the paperwork was in order, and be glad to be shot of the problem. Women divided more sharply, into the flutterers and the carers. The carers, if you were in a hurry and a cold fury, as Meldrum was that afternoon, could be a pain in the arse.

In the car, Shields sat in the back with the boy, Stanley in front beside Meldrum as he drove. At one point the boy muttered something. As Shields started to answer, Meldrum cut across him, snarling over his shoulder, 'Anything he wants to ask can wait.' For the rest of the journey, he was aware of Stanley casting the occasional sidelong glance at him, but nobody spoke.

David Finlay made a show of anger at being called from work, but behind the bluster it was clear he was in a state of panic. He kept looking from his son, pale and still on the couch, to Meldrum who stood looking down on them all, having refused the offer of a seat. By the look on his face, Finlay seemed to be settling for the worst reason he could imagine for this abrupt descent.

Almost as soon as they were in the front room, he cried, 'Is Terry under arrest? Are you going to charge him?'

When they'd come in, Shields had sat bulkily at the boy's side on the couch. The mother had made him move, getting him to shift to a chair. Then she'd taken his place, fierce and upright beside her son. Now, at this outburst, she directed at her husband a look of despairing anger. Plainly, if in silence, it was her turn to call him a fool.

'The charge would be murder,' Meldrum said. He let the word crush all three of them, then went on, 'Or wasting police time.'

'What—' the father began, and stopped. No one paid him any attention.

Meldrum stood over the boy and ordered him, 'Look at me!' And when the mother opened her mouth to protest, told her, 'I want to finish this. Is that not what you want?' And again, 'Look at me! You should be in jail. Not sitting with your mummy. You think you can confess to murder and go on with your life? Are you that stupid? No, you're not stupid. That story of how you killed Brian Ashton, it's a good story.' He raised his voice. 'You pleased with yourself? Think you're smart, do you think you're smart? You think I'm the one that's stupid?'

'Don't shout at him,' the mother said.

It was as if she hadn't spoken, but now his voice was soft. 'Tell that story to a lot of policemen, they'd say thank you. Stand you up in court with that story, you're dead meat. Try changing your mind then, the jury'll decide you're lying to save your skin. I don't like jails, they smell of piss. Thank Christ, I've never spent the night in one. Jails frighten me, and I'm a lot bigger than you. And you've ruined the rest of your life. How did you kill Macleavy?'

'What?' The boy's ashen stubborn silence was broken.

'If you killed Ashton, you must have killed Macleavy. We know the same person killed them both. You remember everything with Ashton so well. How did you kill Macleavy?'

'I didn't. I don't know anything about him.'

'Can't you see he's telling the truth?' the mother cried.

'Truth,' Meldrum said contemptuously. 'We know the truth. The man who was with Brian Ashton that night killed him. And I know who that was. But you're still hanging around, wasting my time, trying to confuse things. Do you want a murderer to get away with it, because of you and your stupid lies? It stops now, understand?'

But the boy hung on, refusing to give up. 'I'm not lying.' It was frustrating.

What next? Hormones, Meldrum thought. He bent down suddenly, and spoke softly into the boy's ear. 'I know who did it. And it's nothing to do with Mrs Ashton.'

'Is that true?'

'That's what you thought?' Meldrum asked, looking down on him again, shaking his head in mocking amazement. 'Even though she has an alibi. Even though she was on her way back from America. That's what stuck me, I couldn't see why you'd confess. But of course you thought she'd got her lover to kill him. I should have worked that out before, but I'm not clever, not like you, eh? Well, you can put that idea out of your head. It wasn't a lover.'

Suddenly almost in tears, the boy cried, 'I don't believe you.'

'You're a very romantic boy, Terry. A knight in shining armour saving the lady. Even if it's not you she rides off into the sunset with – or should that be on?'

'Bastard, dirty bastard.'

'Time to shut the story-book, boy. You've been telling a pack of lies, right?'

And still the boy wouldn't give in. He shook his head and kept shaking it, lips clamped together.

It was frustrating, and Meldrum was sick of it.

'Who did you think the lover was, Terry? Your father?'

That broke him. At the mere idea, revulsion and loathing, like pus from a slashed wound, gushed out of him. After that, the tears came and the admission Meldrum needed.

Finished, they left mother and son sitting apart on the couch – when she had tried to comfort him, he'd pushed her away – and the father slumped in his chair staring at the floor.

Stanley broke the silence in the car.

'That was cruel,' he said. 'I'm finding out how cruel you can be.'

In different ways that made each of them uncomfortable, yet they finished up drinking in The Canny Man's and all three were still there a couple of hours later.

At which point, Shields was opening a buttered roll and carefully tessellating it with a packet of salt and vinegar crisps. Fuck, Meldrum thought watching him, no wonder we're dying off.

'I like this place,' Shields said, folding the roll over and pressing it flat. 'Cousin and me landed in a real dump in Gorgie at the weekend. Know what the landlord there was telling us?' He tore a chunk off the roll and popped it into his mouth. 'Young ones are taking the blues out of the lavatories. You know those wee blocks they use for disinfectant? Apparently the piss releases whatever's in them. So they sniff them and get a high. Friday, Saturday night he says he finds them all over the floor – and out in the street. He's had to start using bleach instead. Absolutely fucking disgusting, eh? Are you two not eating? Bad for you boozing on an empty stomach.'

As it happened, neither Meldrum nor Stanley was hungry; or, it seemed, much inclined for conversation.

Fortunately, this was a gap Shields was happy to fill. A few pints in him, taking their silence for approval, he reverted to the easygoing, clubbable guy he basically was.

Like a lot of men after a few beers, he reminisced about his time in the forces. 'We'd get up in the morning and go over to the mess wearing boots or shoes and the corporal would say, anyone who can't tap-dance is a poof. And we'd all tap-dance. Every morning! It was a right laugh.' Five minutes later, another trip down memory lane. 'Sixteen of us in a line in the cinema and this couple came and sat – in an empty cinema in the afternoon – right in the row in front of us. She said, I think I've seen this. Well, that was one of our catchphrases – as soon as we heard it, we said, all together in chorus, well, why don't you fuck off then? She turned round – you should have seen the look on her face!'

At some point, he told Stanley the police had a nickname for him. 'We call you Knife.'

Instead of being offended, the little man began to laugh. Once he'd started, he seemed to find it hard to stop.

'You think that's funny, hear this one.' Shields's big round face shone with good nature. 'This Englishman, Scotsman and Irishman apply to join the SAS. All three of them pass the theory exam. You'll maybe find that hard to believe with the Irishman. For the practical, their wives are invited to come to the camp and each guy in turn is told, "Go in next door and kill your wife, here's a gun." The Englishman says, "No, I can't. She's the mother of my children." The Scotsman says, "I can't. I love that lassie. She's my wee darling." The Irish guy takes the gun, goes out. After a minute, they hear three shots. And then there's a hell of a racket, shouting and screaming. The Irish guy staggers out, covered in scratches, his face is bleeding. "You didn't tell me they were blanks. I'd to strangle her."

He looked expectantly from one to the other. His grin faded.

'Is that a Rotary joke?' Meldrum asked with a poisonous smile.

Shields stared at him.

'Ah, fuck you too,' he said, and lurched to his feet. 'I'm off.' He paused. 'You told the Finlays you knew who killed Ashton. Do you?' Getting no answer, he nodded wisely a couple of times, said, 'Knew you didn't!' and was gone.

'Arsehole,' Meldrum said, reaching across and pouring what was left of the sergeant's beer into his own glass.

'You two are a puzzle,' Stanley said. 'Half the time, you ignore him. Most of the time, he seems to be simmering in a stew of suppressed irritation. Why do you stay together? It's like a penance. I wonder what he's doing penance for? Adultery at a guess. Do you know?'

Meldrum, who did, evaded the question. 'What about me?'

'Oh, I know what you're doing penance for.'

'Do you?'

'You told me yourself.'

'Oh?'

'What happened with the Chaney boy's killer.'

But if he'd been looking for a response, guilt or anger or trepidation, he would have been disappointed.

'Among other things,' Meldrum said, without a flicker of emotion.

Stanley went to the bar. He came back carrying a small tray with two whiskies, one each, and a pint of Belhaven for Meldrum. As he busied himself setting them out, he asked, 'Do you know who killed Ashton?'

'Proving it's a different thing.'

'That's true.'

Meldrum picked up the whisky, changed his mind and drank from the pint instead. He said, 'I'm going back to talk to John Markham tomorrow.'

'Why would you do that?' Stanley smiled and answered his own question. 'Are you hoping for another look at Toni Ashton?'

'There could be worse reasons,' Meldrum said equably.

'But that's not the one?'

'No.' He drank again, taking his time. 'I've been thinking about the Rex Casino.'

Stanley frowned. 'The casino?'

'Among other things. Too many coincidences. We'll see what he says this time. Do you want to come?'

'I have classes tomorrow.'

'Suit yourself.'

'You know,' Stanley said, 'I can't tell you how sick I am of classes. And Toni Ashton is a woman in a million. I'll come with you. I wouldn't miss it for anything.'

By the time they moved on to the lounge of a quiet hotel, easy chairs and low tables, a good place for talking and listening, Stanley gave the impression of being drunker than Meldrum had ever expected to see him.

He began by being sententious after his usual style. 'A Prime Minister even in a democracy is a figure with undertones of menace. In the last analysis, his authority depends upon police, army, prisons. It stems from the loneliness of a thug in a cell getting his balls squeezed by a thug in a uniform. If you don't understand that, you don't understand anything about power.' He yawned and licked his lips. 'I'm like you. I'm afraid of jails.'

At a later stage, he confided, 'When I was at university, I felt my life had changed. I was leaving the old me behind. But then one lunchtime I got into an argument. I picked up a chair, new life, you see. Anyway, the argument blew over. But outside in the street, the same chap said to me, jump on my back! And like a fool I did. He must have run half a mile with me like that. I was sick with shame. When he put me down he said, you threatened me with a chair. He was very big, but religious, so he couldn't hit me. Running down the hill like that got it out of his system, I suppose. But I was just me, same old me.'

Meldrum had read somewhere that a baby's neck had to be flexible for it to get through the birth canal. That was why its neck wasn't strong enough once born to take the weight of the head. Unsupported, the head wobbled dangerously. Watching Stanley's head tremble, Meldrum was reminded of that.

In the end, he was maudlin. 'You know what I'd like, Jim? You and I give up our jobs. Set up together. Private detectives. People would come to us to solve crimes. Tell you a secret, I don't like my job any more. And you've hit a brick wall. Invisible line's been drawn across your career. Word from the top, so far and no further for Jim Meldrum. You and I could do a lot of good. We could help people. Like – what you say to that boy? – knights in shining armour. We could do it.'

'Yes, Henry, I'd like that,' Meldrum said.

I owe him that much, he thought.

CAT IN THE LIGHT

*I*n the strip of marled tile at the top of the side column on the mantelshelf, I make out a face with a pointed white beard and wide moustaches, a brow, a suggestion of white hair, nose, deep-set eyes: the effect noble and judgemental. I've seen that face before as a cloud shape that held for minutes one summer afternoon when I was a child. A face by Michelangelo, omniscient and omnipotent, but not necessarily kind. It is so familiar, familiar from a lifetime ago, and here it is again. I'm haunted by a patriarch. Frame that face in a wig and it belongs on the bench. A hanging judge. An anachronism, yet I see in those eyes the knowledge that I am not one of those made to survive the humiliations and brutalities of a prison. Sentenced to death then. And so the Hanging Judge still. Birth and death, meeting one man instead of another, a mating sought drunk or sober, and what may follow, an unwanted birth an unwanted death. What has any of it been but accident, and my birth or his death no more unfortunate an accident than any other.

He lay listening to his breath, which was mingled with that of his wife asleep beside him. She groaned, and he thought she'd wakened and spoke her name softly. As she sighed and slept, he thought of the act of taking breath; the act which, illness apart, went on unnoticed birth to death, a wonder, like the steady motor of the heart a mundane miracle. For years, among his other selves other lives, there had been a secret life; and the women he had met in it after a time and then for a long while had held no surprises and few pleasures. It would have cost him almost nothing to give them up, for along the way somewhere he had lost what in the beginning had been a purer impulse, more tense, fearful, expectant, *alive*. Like the fetishist, the masochist, the sadist, his search had begun as an addiction and ended in the fear that if he stopped what would be left was sterility: next stop death. And so the continuing of those acts, however perverse, was, in its own way, an expression of the life instinct; or so at least, a man with a theory for everything, he had persuaded himself. Now all he longed to do was to control his thoughts, so that he avoided the anxiety of planning for the future or the futility of going over what was past and could not be undone or altered in the slightest detail. Instead, he took this unalterable past and shrank it to the last breath he had taken, and thought of how he had drawn it in slowly from the bottom of his lungs to the crammed top, held it an instant and at last released it without pause or ripple evenly until it was done; and thinking of this, unthinkingly, necessarily, he took his next breath and could not part past from present or either from the uncertain future.

'Are you awake?'

'Yes.'

'I couldn't tell if you were asleep or awake,' she said.

He boiled an egg and made toast and marmalade and a pot of tea and took it up to her on a tray.

'I'm so useless,' she said.

She said, 'I don't know why you're so good to me.'

She said, 'Promise you'll never leave me.'

'I promise,' he said.

He took a cup of coffee at the kitchen table. He'd no appetite for anything else. When the bell rang, he opened the front door and walked back up the hall to his study. Drunk, he'd written a couple of sentences and left the computer on all night. He highlighted everything without reading it, hit the delete button and it vanished. No more of that.

To Meldrum watching him from the doorway, he seemed diminished.

'I'm not too early for you?' Meldrum wondered.

When they went out to the car, Stanley paused as he bent to get in and asked, 'Where's Shields?' It sounded as if the sergeant not being there came as an unpleasant surprise.

'He had something to do. We'll pick him up on the way.'

Meldrum expected to be asked where Shields would be, but Stanley nodded and let it go. They came down through Morningside without a word, and were at Tollcross before Stanley began without preamble, 'I couldn't get to sleep last night, not right away. I almost got up again, but I was afraid of waking Eileen – she has too many bad nights – so I just lay. I got to thinking, for every period there's a murder, you could pick out a murder which would be representative. Of the society of its time, I mean. Take Crippen. Even today we have our Crippens committing cramped and domestic homicide, but their crimes don't relate to the nature of our society as Crippen's related to the repressions and hypocrisies of his. Do you understand what I mean?'

'I'll try.'

Stanley glanced at him sharply, but Meldrum was concentrating on getting to the other side of Princes Street. The traffic lights were with them as they'd been all the way, which was lucky.

'In the same fashion,' Stanley began again, 'you can learn something of the nature of American society from the death of Starr Faithful in 1931. Yes? And the best indicator perhaps of the moral anarchy in today's Russia might be the fact that at present Rostov is the world capital for mass murderers.'

'We're here,' Meldrum said.

Looking out as they reversed into a gap, Stanley asked, 'Where?'

'The Rex Casino. But you know it, don't you?'

'I wasn't sure. In Edinburgh, you never expect to get parked right outside where you want.'

Meldrum opened his door. 'Coming?'

'If it's just to collect Shields, I might as well stay in the car.'

'No,' Meldrum said. 'Better come. Just in case it takes longer.'

In the foyer, a polisher was being pushed across the parquet floor. The stairs were being swept, the long rail wiped. As they climbed, they could hear the sound of vacuum cleaners. The cleaners were busy, but for all their efforts, the main gambling room upstairs still seemed shoddy in the sifted morning light. A man and woman stood talking near one of the blackjack tables.

'There they are,' Meldrum said.

It was Shields who introduced the woman. 'Dr Stanley. Tracey Franks.'

Meldrum explained to her, 'Dr Stanley wasn't with us when we were here before.'

'I remember,' she said.

'You sound as if you're an Australian,' Stanley said.

'No hiding that.'

'You work here, I take it.'

'Beats hairdressing.'

Tracey Franks looked as improbably the outdoor girl as the first time Meldrum had seen her. This morning, however, cheerfulness repressed, she seemed constrained and even uneasy.

'Miss Franks was dealing at the table where Brian Ashton gambled, the night he was killed. Despite the way he was dressed that evening, she recognised him.'

'I read the transcript of your interview,' Stanley said to her. 'I'm privileged with this case, you see. I know everything that's going on.'

'She was the only one of the staff who did recognise him,' Meldrum said.

'You must have a remarkable memory,' Stanley told her.

'Oh, well, I'd seen him plenty of times before. He was a member,' she said. 'Like you.'

'I had a feeling I'd seen you before. Unlike you, though, I have a poor memory for faces.' Turning to Meldrum, he explained casually, 'I got a membership for a project I was involved in. The university only paid half, which I thought was a bit mean. I had to argue it out with the taxman.'

'You didn't happen to be here the night Brian Ashton was killed?'

Smiling, he turned to the girl. 'Was I?'

'Yes, you were.'

'That remarkable memory.' He sounded genuinely appreciative. He had a weakness for feats of intellect. To Meldrum he said, 'I've been a bit naughty, I suppose. I got permission to shadow you so that I could make a study of the Ashton murder. And then to my astonishment we learn that he'd been in the casino that night. I was embarrassed to admit I'd been here as well. Not a particularly academic pursuit, gambling. And, I told myself, I wasn't here for long. I hadn't seen anything. It simply didn't seem worth mentioning.'

'Oh, it was worth mentioning.'

'You don't have to tell me how stupid it was.' Turning to Tracey Franks, he said, 'Luckily, I can't have been anywhere near Ashton.'

There was a pause which went on a shade too long.

As the girl hesitated, Meldrum said, 'After ten, we should be on our way. Thanks for your time, Miss Franks.'

'Nice to have met you,' Stanley said. 'When did you say you were going home?'

'Not sure.'

'Wake up one morning and just go, eh? I read the transcript.' Stanley smiled at her. 'You see, my memory's not so bad.'

As they were going down the stairs, he realised Meldrum wasn't with them.

Seeing him look back, Shields said, 'He'll be a minute. He's something to do.'

It was quarter of an hour before Meldrum joined them and they moved off.

Roads were closed that morning. Diverted from the direct route, as they were held up in a line of cars, Shields called from the back seat, 'Look – up there! It's the opening of the Parliament.'

Glimpsed on the spine of the hill, children in procession were marching under bright banners in the sunshine. Threaded above traffic noise, the music that led them had a familiar sound, like an old song.

'After three hundred years,' Stanley said. 'History's something we catch sight of framed at the end of a street, while we're going about the daily business of our lives. Do you know what I mean?'

Meldrum grunted.

After a few minutes, Stanley asked, 'Is he expecting us?'

'Not much point if he wasn't.'

'I phoned this morning,' Shields said, leaning forward. 'Got him right away. Pity, I was looking forward to talking to that secretary woman.'

Getting no answer, he settled back.

They'd left Edinburgh behind before anyone spoke again.

'Tracey. The names they have now. Sounds like a pop star. Obviously clever, though. She should get a proper job and make something of herself. If she heard me saying that – I know – she'd laugh at me. Of course, I've never been adventurous. Not like these young Australians. They never stay in one place for very long.'

'This one might,' Meldrum said. 'She tells me she's got herself a boyfriend.'

'Then they'll both get itchy feet.' He dropped his voice, so quiet now that Meldrum could hardly hear him. 'I think you need Markham. And he has his big house, that fine estate. And the beautiful Mrs Ashton. I can't see why in the world he would change his story . . . Lie, I mean.'

Now they were crossing the flat East Lothian plain, and soon they were turning towards the Forth. They passed the ruins of a castle in a field, faced the water and turned from it as the road turned and at the end of the next mile came on the grey length of the estate wall.

As he'd done before, at the end of the long drive Meldrum parked in front of the house. Climbing out, he looked up at the bulk of grey stone looming above them.

Behind him, he heard Stanley's voice. 'It is magnificent, isn't it? Markham's a lucky man.'

'Better off than better folk,' Shields growled.

Stanley laughed and took the lead across the gravel to the flight of worn steps that went up to the front door. Before the bell was rung, Markham's voice greeted them and there was the sound of the lock being released.

As they entered, Markham came out of the reception area.

'I was keeping watch for you,' he said.

'What's happened to your secretary?' Shields asked.

'I've declared a holiday of sorts today. Didn't you notice the lack of cars? Not very observant of you. I daresay you'd other things to think about.'

Meldrum had sensed something different about the hall. Now he realised: there was no fire. The logs piled in the great hearth were black and without the flames obviously fake.

'It's warmer out here than in the library,' Markham said. 'Come to that, same with all the north-facing rooms this morning.'

'I noticed,' Shields said. 'The cars not being there. I noticed when we drove in.'

'Never mind. It will leave plenty of room for the removal vans.'

'You're moving?' Stanley asked.

'Let's go upstairs to talk. We'll be more comfortable.'

He took Stanley by the elbow and began to climb the stairs. As they followed, Shields tapped Meldrum on the arm, indicating his puzzlement. Meldrum shrugged.

'The pictures go today,' Markham said, raising his voice so that it echoed in the open stairwell. 'The ones upstairs at least. The owner is having them shipped to the States.'

'The owner?' Meldrum asked.

'Of the estate. This splendid house. The pictures upstairs. And so forth.'

He was moving quickly now, Stanley having almost to trot to keep up as they went through the long gallery. As he paced along, Markham gestured towards the lighter patches which came at intervals on the wall on their right opposite the line of high windows. 'Portraits of the ancestors,' he said.

'Of this owner of yours?' Meldrum asked.

Markham stopped. He was laughing. 'I can't imagine what a row of Mike Hamas's ancestors would look like. Hamas bought this place from a family who'd owned it for four hundred years. Long enough to have the house extended and burnt down and rebuilt half a dozen times. I saw the portrait gallery here just before they moved out. Decayed gentry, broken by bad investments and a habit of living beyond their means. A son dying too soon after his father, two sets of death duties finished them off. By the time I saw the paintings here, most of them were copies. The Raeburns in particular were badly done. I despised the pictures, but I fell in love with the house.' He nodded at the window beside them. 'I'll miss that view as much as anything I've lost in my life.'

'Lost?' Henry Stanley said. He was still catching his breath from the pace that had been set. 'Not just the paintings. You mean you're moving from here?'

'I don't know when the estate will go on the market,' Markham said, setting off again. 'But as far as Mr Hamas is concerned, Markham and Partners have a week to get out of here.'

They were in the lift before Stanley asked, 'Where does he want you to go?'

Markham waited until he'd opened the gates and they were stepping out before he answered. 'To hell, I gather.'

Unlike the empty walls of the gallery below, this corridor was crowded with paintings, some of them enormous, some stark, not a few resembling fabric samples. Waving a finger at them, Markham said, 'Bad examples of past fashions. But try telling that to Hamas. He thinks they're an investment.'

'Bad investments?' Stanley asked. 'Is that why he's fallen out with you?'

'Rash,' Markham said. 'I admire your courage. Or are you like me, and feel you've nothing to lose?'

When he spoke, Stanley's voice was level and calm. Too calm, Meldrum thought. Does Markham see that too?

'If I had a woman like Toni Ashton, I'd still feel I'd something to lose.'

'Good point,' Markham said.

Following him along the corridor, Meldrum wasn't surprised when Markham stopped and opened the door of the room they'd been in last time, the one with the bar. He did no more than glance in, however, and turned back with a smile for Stanley. 'Oh dear. No one there.'

He closed the door and walked on, saying, 'Most of our investments were rather successful, as a matter of fact. But Mr Hamas is an intensely private man. Not that we have anything to hide here. But when he heard the police were poking around, he didn't like it. And if you're very rich and you don't like something, you walk away.' Turning the corner into a second corridor, Markham went almost to the end of it before stopping at a door. About to open it, he paused and said, 'How would you know you were as rich as that, if you couldn't ruin lives?'

Meldrum, following on after Stanley and Markham, expected to find himself in some kind of sitting room. As he went in, he was distracted, trying to decide if he should let the situation develop or take a grip at once, ask his questions and seek a conclusion. He was startled to find himself in a bedroom. Beside him, he heard Shields draw in his breath sharply.

It was a bright room. Sunlight came from his right through french windows.

Beyond them Meldrum saw the stone balustrade of a balcony. Disoriented, he took that in, then his eyes went back to the bed. He made out the shape of a body under the blankets, but the sheet was drawn up to cover the face. The body lay absolutely still. All that showed of it was one hand poked out and lying on the pillow. The nails painted red. A woman's hand.

'My God,' Stanley whispered. 'You've killed her.'

As sometimes happened, it was Shields who reacted first. Pushing Markham aside, he went to the bed and folded the sheet down. For a moment his bulk bending over the woman prevented them from seeing her.

'She's breathing,' he said.

As he straightened, they saw the woman's face. As if conscious of their gaze, Naomi Morgan moaned softly and, still sleeping, laid an arm across her eyes to shut out the light.

'Sedated,' Markham said. 'I watched her take the tablets and then removed the bottle. Just in case. She was badly upset.'

'I thought it was—' Stanley began.

'I'm afraid not,' Markham said.

Silver-backed hairbrushes on the dressing table and a dozen other signs indicated this was a man's bedroom. 'Is this your room?' Meldrum asked. 'Where is Mrs Ashton?'

'As Dr Stanley can tell you,' Markham said, 'this whole floor is – was, I should say – used by Mike Hamas. This is his bedroom.'

Shields hadn't moved from beside the bed. Looking down at Naomi Morgan, he said, 'She didn't fancy men. What's she doing here?'

'Policemen are great moralists. You always suspect the worst,' Markham said. 'I assure you she wasn't raped. She wasn't forced. She's sleeping there because it's as near as she can get to Toni Ashton. I do hope she hasn't chosen Hamas's side by mistake.'

At that point, Meldrum understood. To his surprise, the clever Henry Stanley clearly didn't.

'What the hell has Hamas got to do with it? It was you and her. We saw how you were together.'

'Poor little Naomi and I?'

'You and *Mrs Ashton.*' On the edge of losing self-control, Stanley spat the words out. 'Don't play games with me.'

'Like charades?' Markham said. 'We must have done it terribly well.'

'You were all over one another.'

'Do you remember Roddie Amott?' Markham asked. From Stanley, with the merest exaggeration of the air of a man remembering his manners, he turned to Meldrum. 'Sorry. You don't know about this. I explained it all to Dr Stanley on an earlier occasion. It was Mike Hamas who beat up the Chinaman at the casino. Roddie covered up for him. Don't you want to ask me why?'

'I don't have to.'

Markham raised his eyebrows. 'I think you must have to.'

'It's not difficult,' Meldrum said. 'Listening to you this morning, it sounds as if without Hamas you don't have a business. So when he wants to beat someone half to death, Amott covers up for him. And when he wants to screw Ashton's wife, you play at being her lover.'

'That's rather bright of you,' Markham said.

'I think you're lying,' Stanley said. 'I don't know why you're lying. Toni Ashton and you are lovers. She's here somewhere, isn't she?'

What I'm seeing now, Meldrum thought, looking at him, must have been there all the time. Behind the posing and the vanity, a man struggling every moment to hold himself together. How long has he been waiting for the thing to come along that would destroy him?

'You still don't get it, do you?' Markham said with a kind of surprised contempt. 'You should climb in beside her.' Smiling, he pointed at the bed. 'She didn't get it either. When Hamas brought Toni out to LA for a holiday – that's where she was when Ashton was killed – he brought poor little Naomi out as well. Her idea was that Toni and she were using Hamas. And I thought if Hamas was besotted enough with Toni, it would hold him here despite everything. So you could say I didn't get it either. Nobody uses Toni. Toni uses everybody. She contacted Hamas and told him about you people sniffing round here, asking about the parties, questioning Amott. The first I knew of it was when one of his people phoned to tell me we'd a week to get out of here. By that time, Toni was on her way to the airport.'

'I don't think you're telling the truth,' Stanley said. 'I'm pretty certain she's here.'

He spoke so reasonably no one tried to stop him as he went out. When the three of them did follow, he was going down the corridor quietly and methodically opening each door, looking inside and going on to the next.

'What do you want me to do?' Shields asked.

'Seeing's believing,' Meldrum said. 'Let him see.'

All the same, seized by the spirit of the chase, Shields hurried on a pace or two ahead.

Markham matched his pace to Meldrum's. Making conversation, as if out for a stroll, he said, 'I've known a lot of beautiful women, a few times in the biblical sense. But I never met anyone like Toni Ashton. This country was too small to hold her. I could imagine her storming Hollywood. Either that or Hamas would pass her on to one of his Mafia friends.'

They turned into the corridor with the lift. Shields was further ahead now. Beyond him, they could see Stanley opening doors.

Adopting the same casual tone, Meldrum asked, 'It was Stanley you saw that night with Ashton, wasn't it?'

'Of course. Hasn't that been what this is all about?'

'You should have told us at once.'

'As long as I'm willing to testify, are you going to make trouble for me over when I told you?'

There was no answer to that.

One corridor on the top floor led to the next, corridor after corridor, until they began to seem endless, their succession bewildering, the sameness of their effect like wandering in a maze. Imperceptibly, Stanley had been moving faster. In the longest corridor yet, abruptly with no transition he was running. Now the doors were being thrown back. As each door on the left-hand wall was flung open, spilled sunlight fell in stripes across the corridor. He fled from one wall to the other, like a trapped bird beating its wings, frantic to escape. It was a horrible frenzy which ended as Shields caught him as he turned from the last door and enfolded him in his arms.

'Poor wee bugger.' Clutching the little man, who had gone still, he turned in a fury on Meldrum. 'That's enough, that's enough of that.'

Arrested for the murder of Brian Ashton and cautioned, however, Stanley was subdued but in some kind of control of himself again. Strictly speaking, he should have gone into the back of the car with Shields. Meldrum, though, who'd been more shaken by what had happened than he was willing to show, made no objection as the bedraggled figure climbed in beside him.

As he wound the route back, he kept glancing over at his passenger.

At last he asked, 'Are you all right?'

'I was thinking, Jim.'

'Yes.'

'None of it makes any sense. It's like those boys you told me about attacking the firemen. Stupidity after meaningless stupidity. Ashton's death was an accident. Just a stupid accident. It has no meaning.'

Meldrum felt as if he'd climbed a mountain. Into his bones, he was tired. It was a relief to see the A1 just ahead. All he wanted now was to get back to Edinburgh.

'Jim?'

'Yes?'

'It would be hard to find two more worthless human beings than Ashton and Macleavy.'

Meldrum said nothing.

'Don't you agree?'

'It doesn't matter what I think.'

'To me it does. I can't see how you wouldn't agree.'

Holding the car on the hill, distracted as he watched for a gap in the traffic, Meldrum said what he believed. 'You met Macleavy's mother. He wasn't worthless to her.'

Spotting a brief opening, he let in the clutch and at the same moment Stanley reached over and wrenched the wheel. As Meldrum fought for control, the car spun across the southbound lane on to the other side. Facing the wrong way, they slid towards a lorry. Pumping the brake, Meldrum watched the driver's face, mouth stretched as if screaming or cursing, and then he was too close to see it. He hit the brake hard and swung right.

Later he'd work out how lucky they were. The car missed a tree by a foot and went accurately as if it had been aimed through an open gate. From there, for about fifty yards it bumped across a field and smacked into the tractor whose driver had left the gate open. At the moment of impact, Stanley hurled forward together with his seat. Then Meldrum felt a stunning blow on his ear. Everything went quiet. Meldrum looked at Stanley. He'd come to rest short of the windscreen. He touched himself under the ear and looked at the blood on his fingers. Apart from that, when they checked neither of them had any injury at all.

Shields, as he often did, had left his seat belt unfastened. The impact had hurled him forward into the back of the front passenger seat. One flailing fist had struck Meldrum on the side of the head.

Now in the long stillness, he was on his knees, head on his shoulder, with open mouth and eyes shut as if in prayer.

BOOK SIX

Sleep until Night

CHAPTER FORTY-FOUR

'Ach,' the woman said, 'when I passed my driving test, I was on forty and forty.'

She was about twenty-five, with thick blonde hair cut short. If it hadn't been for her soft squashed nose — perhaps it had been broken and badly set — she would have been pretty in a conventional way. Meldrum and she had the waiting area for that ward, four chairs in a hospital corridor, to themselves.

'I'm glad I didn't meet you coming the other way,' he said.

She'd been describing how after her abortion she'd been on twenty dihydrocodeine a day — 'a painkiller but it gives you a buzz too' — and ten diazepam at night to send her to sleep. Meldrum had noticed before how hospitals had the effect of making people confide in strangers. Maybe it had something to do with transience or a fear of what would happen next. When the nurse came, though, it turned out that like him she was there to visit someone. Just then she'd got round to asking him what he did to earn a crust, and he'd told her he was a joiner. As she was getting up, she said, you'll have a good set of tools then; and went off grinning.

While he was thinking about that, Netta Shields came out of the ward with the two boys trailing along behind her. She stared at him for a moment as if not sure of who he was, then stopped. The older boy, who was about ten, mooched on along the corridor with the five-year-old at his heels.

'I saw you were there with the family,' he said, 'so I decided to wait till you came out. How is he?'

'You know Bobbie. Never complains. Are you all right though? You must have got a shake. Should you not be in your bed?'

'I'll get something to eat, then I'll go home.'

'He'll be pleased you came to see him.'

Meldrum doubted it, but smiled and nodded. 'I was driving,' he said, 'but there wasn't much I could do. I expect Bobbie told you what happened.'

She shook her head, and he was disconcerted to see her eyes fill with tears. 'We hardly got a chance to talk about it. He said he was pleased the boys were there, and like a fool I told him James hadn't been at school. And that started him off. It's always the same. The slightest thing turns into an interrogation.' And Meldrum had to hide his amusement. Interrogation? The silent Shields? 'And you're guilty till proved innocent. I keep things from him. But it's worse if he finds out. All the time, he's on a short fuse.'

Struggling to find something to say, the best he could come up with was, 'It's not an easy job.'

'I'm sorry,' she said. 'I'm letting Bobbie down.'

'No, no.'

'It was just seeing him lying there. I got a fright when they phoned me. And then he starts all that—' She stopped herself. 'I know it's the job. I know you think a lot of him. And he's a good man. He's been a good man to me. And he's a good father. But, oh dear, he's awful hard on everybody. I mean himself as well.'

As he'd expected, when Shields saw him coming down the ward, he looked more surprised than pleased.

'I hope you haven't brought me anything to do. I'm in here for a rest,' he said.

'No. I managed without you.'

'Right.'

When Meldrum sat down, Shields, whose neck was held in a collar, had to look at him from the corner of his eye. Meldrum shifted his chair.

'So how are you?'

'They wouldn't let me move my head till they did the X-rays. Now they've decided it's torn muscles, maybe a hairline crack. You'll have to do without me for a couple of weeks.'

'I didn't think I'd get rid of you that easily.'

'No.'

'Sorry I didn't bring anything. I came straight from work. I'm on my way home. I'm going to take your wife's advice and have an early night.'

'How about the wee man?'

'We both got looked over by a doctor. Clean bill of health, more or less. Then I charge him with murder. Weird bloody world.'

'You think he'll try it again?'

In the narrow holding cell, he'd asked Stanley the same question. Do anything silly, that was the euphemism he'd used. I was always quite clear about that, Stanley had said. If it came to it, I'd commit suicide rather than go to prison. But today when I tried, I broke a promise. I promised Eileen I'd come back to her. Macleavy told me I was the kind of man who couldn't bear prison. And then Stanley had managed a kind of smile. We'll have to find out, he'd said.

'He'll be on special watch,' Meldrum said. 'But I don't think he'll try again.'

'How long do you think he'll get?'

'Macleavy was covered in bruises. But it was his heart giving out that killed him. And Ashton was in drag. If Henry gets a good lawyer, he should do all right.'

'Fucking lawyers,' Shields said, but not as if his heart was particularly in it.

On his way out of the hospital, Meldrum stopped off for a piss. As he faced the wall, shallow-breathing, the question occurred to him, it was as good a place as any to ask it, what was he going to do with his life? He thought about that last drunken evening when Henry Stanley had suggested setting up in business together. Apart from Henry being a murderer, the other flaw in the idea was that being a private detective wasn't about murder cases and being a white knight. It was about chasing small debtors and errant husbands. So what did he want to do with his life? Stanley had loosened him from his vocation, that was the truth of it. What happened next?

As he came out again into the waiting area, the woman he'd talked to earlier emerged from the other lavatory.

'Hey!' she said. 'Let me see your hands.'

He held them up palm out. 'I surrender.'

'Like I thought. You haven't worked with your hands for a long time. So if you're not a carpenter, what are you? I could guess.'

'Don't,' he said.

They started to walk back towards the reception area and the exit.

'I hate this place.' Her shoulder brushed his arm as she moved aside for a wheelchair. 'Too many sick folk. They make me feel like kicking my height or standing on my hands. I'm always glad to get out of here. Fancy a coffee?'

The reception area was crowded. They wound their way through towards the door.

'Why not?'

'What are you laughing about?' she asked sharply. She had a small white sore at the corner of her mouth.

Difficult to explain, he thought. Not at you. I was thinking about a woman called Toni Ashton. And wondering how rich a guy called Mike Hamas is. I was laughing at myself.

'Sorry,' he said. 'Sure, that sounds good. I could murder a coffee.'

When they came out, the sun was still shining and the air was warm. It looked as if the good weather might hold for a while yet, if they were lucky.

'Your place or mine?' she asked.